Eyes Without a Face

a Face

The Forbes Trilogy: Part One

Paul Taylor

ISBN: 978-1-4834-5369-9 (sc)
ISBN: 978-1-4834-5371-2 (hc)
ISBN: 978-1-4834-5370-5 (e)

Library of Congress Control Number: 2016909792

Lulu Publishing Services rev. date: 06/28/2016

Contents

Part 2 Artists 237

Author's Note

THE FRENCH REVOLUTION IS HISTORICALLY UNDER-
stood to have transformed the political face of France over a
ten year period from 1789 to 1799.

A merciless period of radical, social and political upheaval
in European history saw the monarchy that had ruled for centuries, collapse in just three short years.

Society underwent an epic transformation, as feudal, aristo-
cratic, and religious privileges evaporated under the sustained
attack from liberal political groups inspired by the mandate from
the masses on the streets.

But, in truth, the revolutionary period continued with further
sporadic outbursts of violence for another fifty odd years.

In 1848, a wave of revolutions throughout France ended
the Orleans monarchy, and led to the creation of the Second
Republic.

A particularly bloody period in the middle of the year became known as *'The June Days'* which centred upon the Paris
Guard crushing an unsuccessful rebellion of Parisian workers
protesting against a conservative turn in the First Republic's
course.

When, on the second of December 1848, Louis Napoleon
was elected President of the Second Republic, largely with the

support of the peasant vote, he immediately signed a number of arrest warrants, and embarked upon a policy of revenge against the then officers in charge of the 8th battalion of the Paris Guard.

The arrests were swift, because the officers in charge were either still in command, or were so well known within French society as to believe they were above recrimination.

Once incarcerated however, Louis Napoleon faced a struggle between his military advisors and his political backers. And so it continued, until after some ten years of imprisonment, the façade of the show trials began.

Expensive, and therefore oddly out of place in the new republic, the sentences, and repercussions of the trials were far reaching in their verdicts.

Madame Guillotine was the destination for the officers, whilst exile from France was the sacrifice facing their families. This judgement included loss of title, land and property. It was hoped that with this one final decision all traces of the French gentry would be gone for good.

Within the year, a number of grand chateaux's became state property, and were turned into schools and hospitals. But after a decade of little to no maintenance, the properties, already in a sorry state, began disintegrate.

The properties were in such a poor state of repair, that all kudos for the use of the buildings was lost on new land-lords and potential residents.

The smaller establishments fared even worse. Devoid of any upkeep for the past ten years, they soon became no more than derelict shells. Once the ornate beams had been turned into firewood, and the lavish façades dismantled, and re-born as stables, or ramshackle woodsheds, they bore no resemblance to their former glory. The lavish ballrooms reduced to no more than husks, glittering chandeliers, decorative mirrors, majestic paintings, and elaborate sculptures, all gone to new owners and incarnations.

The cruel winters had rotted the exposed beams and dislodged the stones, which had been too difficult for the peasants to remove.

The decay of the once affluent estates continued over decades to come, until their splendour was completely obliterated, and the once much cherished possessions of the French aristocracy were no more. Tattered, rotted, destroyed, or buried deep in unknown tombs.

Prologue

1860

YVETTE, CAREFULLY FOLDED THE LINEN DRAPES around the oil-skin wrapped package, and tied it with a braid made from the finest horse-hair, momentarily she stopped to admire her handy-work, "Yes, she would be proud."

Behind her someone coughed, "We don't have the time to reminisce."

"Oh, Monsieur Aspasie," Yvette, glanced at the Butler, "the Mistress always thought the drapes to be the most delightful," as she waited for a response, Yvette studied Aspasie's face, it was taught with stress, she thought better than to add to his plight, so carried-on the conversation in her head, '*and she always liked the gay golden flowers,*' as she daydreamed, she lay the package in the bottom of a trunk. '*She also loved the way the flowers blossomed over the dark crimson background.*'

Satisfied that the package would remain unharmed until her Mistress was in a position to recover it, Yvette stood back to allow the stern faced, Aspasie to place more equally lovingly wrapped items into the trunk.

Another man entered the Mistress's boudoir, he was short, and stout, his face ruddy from working in the fields, not the sort of man the Mistress would normally allow in the chateau, let alone her private chambers.

Yvette twirled around, looking at the once splendid room, which now looked shamed by its nakedness. She wanted to cover all the cracks in the bare walls which were exposed for this intruder to see, but instead she stood stone still, frozen by her shame.

"We must hurry," the small man said, his jowls wobbled as he spoke. Together the men opened a second trunk.

"Quickly," he gestured. Yvette noticed his fingernails were broken and dirty, the Mistress would not have approved.

Yvette continued to wrap the items once loved by her Mistress. She was determined that when her Mistress was allowed to return home, she should once again be surrounded by the delights of the house. When that day came, Yvette intended that all her beloved possessions would be in pristine condition.

An adoring maid, with an acute sense of loyalty to her beloved Mistress, Yvette went about packing the next trunk with pride. She incurred a number of 'tuts' and hurry-up calls from the little farm worker, but she refused to skimp on her task.

After everything that had happened to the family over these past years, she still had a strong sense of duty. Humming a tune that she and her Mistress loved, she gently cosseted more bundles into the third of the three flat-bottomed grey Trianon canvas trunks that housed the most treasured items from the Mistress's boudoir.

Yvette wrapped a lustrous porcelain figurine of a pretty girl with a flower basket, in a linen face cloth. Carefully she nestled it on top of more crimson-red drapes. Carefully she lifted the next piece of porcelain, remembering how her heart always skipped a beat when she would dust the fragile limbs that were poised so delicately.

Humming contently, she took another cloth and wrapped the figure securely. As attentive as putting a real child into a cot Yvette laid the bundle next to 'The Flower girl' on the dark-red drapes. "Just one more piece in here, we don't want to crush them." Carefully Yvette allowed every item enough space to breath.

Her task complete, she closed the lid of the trunk, and slid the catch to lock. Even now, with sadness at the forefront of her heart, she remembered the day the three trunks had been purchased.

As the two men took the trunks away, Yvette daydreamed of that day last summer, when she accompanied her Mistress, south to Paris. It was her first and only time in the city of lights; it had been the happiest day of her life.

Yvette now watched, with tears in her eyes as the last of the trunks was taken from the bedroom, perhaps it was true; perhaps the Mistress would never return.

"Come on little daydreamer," the stout farmer shouted over his shoulder. Yvette followed them down the narrow back stairs; through the kitchens, and down into the cellar.

The two men, damp and sweaty from their exertions, neatly stacked the three trunks against the back wall of a small alcove. Yvette, realized that most of the wine racks had been emptied, a few bottles lay broken on the ground, and the over-ripe aroma of blackberries drifted heavy in the air. The area that housed the three trunks was where the evening's wine was usually pre-pared, but not tonight, maybe never again. Yvette began to sob.

"Stop it," Yvette said sharply, "Mustn't think like that."

"Like what?" the farmer asked, a bead of sweat poised on his upper lip.

"Like the Mistress is never coming home."

In response he drew his dirty thumb across his throat, and made a whooshing sound. His laughter was coarse. Aspasie made eye contact, and he stopped laughing abruptly.

Alone, Yvette watched the men place the smooth squared stones across the face of the alcove. Within the hour it was completely bricked up.

"It will be safe now, until she returns." Aspasie said.

Yvette pressed her hand against the new wall, "Are you sure?"

"Yes, of course. Now, quickly we need to leave," the farmer ushered her away, his broken fingernail catching on her woollen shawl.

"After you," Aspasie stepped aside to allow the little man to leave the cellar.

As he passed, Aspasie plunged a dagger into the man's chest.

The farmer staggered back, falling against the wall. Aspasie followed him, keeping the pressure on the blade. The farmer reached up, and clasped his filthy hands around Aspasie's throat. But the taller man twisted the blade, forcing him down to the ground. Behind them Yvette screamed.

"Shut-up, if I don't silence him, he will come back and take the family silver, and sell all those little statues at the market."

A gurgling sound came from the farmer's throat. His hands slid to his side.

Aspasie, pulled out the dagger, and wiped it on the farmer's shirt.

He held out his hand to Yvette. "Come on, it must be like we were never here."

Yvette stood trembling, looking down at the fat corpse.

"Yvette!" he shouted. Shaken from her trance, Yvette stepped over the body and ran to Aspasie.

They emerged from the kitchen door. It was early morning. An innocent bird was singing in the trees, as the dew still adorned the grass, Yvette and Aspasie left the chateau, and headed south toward the city.

2008

THE LEAD STORY ON EVERY TV NEWS CHANNEL ON the 21st of July was the joyous report that former Bosnian Serb president, Radovan Karadzic, had been captured, after more than a decade in hiding.

CNN had decided to go with a live feed from Kalemegdan Park, Belgrade. They had scooped some major stakeholder interviewees, and their most enigmatic war correspondent, Kaylee Dean was on the streets looking good.

Over video footage of large crowds celebrating in the streets, the pretty CNN reporter commented, "News of Karadzic's arrest was greeted with jubilation on the streets of Belgrade and Sarajevo. The Bosnian capital had received very heavy shelling and many casualties during the war."

The scene switched to a close up of Kaylee, her pretty face stern enough to show the seriousness of the war, yet her smiling-eyes were large enough to convey empathy with the crowds. Behind her, happy faces smiled at the camera, hands waving in jubilation. In the bottom corner of the screen a video of the former Bosnian leader, bedecked in black-tie, taken during his reign, dissolved into, and replaced with shots of a dishevelled man, being taken away by the police.

Kaylee Dean continued, "Karadzic, 63, stands accused of war-crimes, including genocide, the ethnic cleansing of Bosnian Muslims, and Croats, crimes against humanity, and violating the customs of the war that followed Bosnia-Herzegovina's secession from Yugoslavia."

The screen changed to library footage from the war, where emaciated half-naked prisoners, gently touched the barbed-wire strands of their compounds.

Kaylee sustained the voice over. "Last seen in public in 1996, Karadzic was the Bosnian Serb political leader during the 1992–1995 war. The conflict included the Srebrenica massacre of thousands of Bosnian Muslims, during the forty-four month siege of Sarajevo."

The newscast picture changed again, now showing an interview in an elaborately decorated room with a thin man wearing metal-framed glasses. The name, 'Serge Brammertz' was in a red tag at the bottom of the screen.

The male interviewer introduced Mr. Brammertz as, "The chief prosecutor of the International Criminal Tribunal, for the former Yugoslavia."

The thin man lent forward as if on cue, "I was able to offer my congratulations to the NATO Stabilization Force officers responsible for taking Karadzic into custody," he continued, "It is an important day for the victims, and the families of the victims. It is an important day for justice," his voice got stronger, filled with national pride. "It clearly demonstrates that nobody is beyond the reach of the law, and sooner or later all fugitives will be brought to justice."

The picture went blank; then the action cut back to Kaylee, still in front of the exuberant crowd, she was now joined by a NATO officer, the soldier looked extremely uncomfortable. The officer's name appeared at the bottom of the screen. 'Captain Giancarlo Minardi'.

She swept back a loose strand of blonde hair, and opened the interview.

"With me is Group Captain Minardi, of NATO." The smile faded to solemn as she began asking her serious questions. "We understand you were the arresting officer, did he put up much of a fight?"

"Yes." Minardi offered no detail.

Awkwardly she covered the silence, "Where will Karadzic be taken now?"

"Authorities will determine when Karadzic will be transferred to the tribunal at The Hague." His Italian accent appeared to be on the brink of emotion.

Kaylee willed the handsome Italian officer, with the bright-blue beret; adjusted to the jauntiest of angles, to give a little more detail, but the man remained stubbornly silent. Kaylee turned back toward the camera, her face showing the signs of the frustration she felt at the poor commentary, from the tall, handsome, camera friendly officer. "Okay, we can go live now to the Sarajevo Houses of Parliament, for comments from Zlatko Lagumdzija, the former Bosnian prime minister, who was wounded during the siege." The smile stayed in place until the red light on the camera was extinguished.

The public saw the sad-eyed former prime minister, reclining in an armchair, the pained expression on his face was as if the wound were still giving him trouble. "Today, I can tell you that I feel kind of good. I wish I could shake the hand of the NATO troops that brought the monster to justice." He nodded his head. "The arrest could offer a chance for new thinking here in Bosnia, to help us whilst we are still grappling with the scars of war," he made eye contact with the camera. "Today it looks like a new wind is moving from Belgrade." The words, and sincere look, were intended to win votes at the forthcoming election.

The director of the CNN broadcast decided that the players were not adding to the viewing figures, and decided to pull the plug on the live broadcast.

As viewers around the world were introduced to the next news item, a disappointed Kaylee Dean turned to Minardi, "Hey, you could have been it bit more forthcoming, you're supposed to be a hero; I'd have made you look the part."

Minardi turned back from the monitor, "Scars of War? Wind moving from Belgrade? Christ who do these people think they are." He took off his blue beret, and gingerly prodded at a large lump on his head.

Suddenly Kaylee was brought down to earth. "Tough day, Captain?"

Minardi nodded, then gave a measured response, "Serbia's government has been under increasing pressure to arrest those accused of the war crimes." He pointed his finger at the reporter's chest. "Suspects, believed to be hiding in Serbia, rather than Bosnia. If that prick!" he gestured to the monitor, "had done as we had asked; Karadzic would have been captured, and brought to justice in Vienna, a little over three years ago."

Kaylee Dean silently willed the cameraman to switch the camera back on, this was the stuff Pulitzer's were made of, but, in the interim, she just nodded and allowed the NATO officer to sound off.

"But you got him, you must be pleased?" it sounded a lame question, even to her.

Minardi's Italian temper flared, "Pleased?" I lost two men down in those tunnels. Two men killed in a bloody pointless fire-fight. No my friend I'm not pleased."

She knew it was the wrong thing to say, but being a reporter prompted her to say it anyway, "I understood four of you went into the tunnels, what happened to the fourth soldier?"

Minardi's lips went tight, he wondered how she gotten hold of that information. Hopefully the identity of the fourth man, and the fact that he was British SAS would remain undiscovered. Minardi nodded, "Yes, four men. Two are dead, the other trooper, a friend of mine, is now in hospital," he replaced his beret, turned and walked away, interview over. He could not bring himself to tell the supercilious reporter about the atrocities he had seen in the catacombs beneath the Belgrade Fortress, and the fact that their actions had not been authorised by NATO. As he walked away he knew it could have been worse, no uniforms, no authority; yes it could have been much worse.

The *trooper* that had been hospitalized could have been killed along with the others, and if he had, then, Minardi would have died too. The *trooper* had been injured whilst saving Minardi's life. As the Italian pushed through the cheering crowds, the sound of his men being killed and his friend screaming in terror was all he could hear.

Many miles away, the CNN director decided that the fiasco he had just witnessed would be the last time that war-correspondent; Kaylee Dean ever worked for CNN.

2010

IT HAD LAIN UNDISTURBED FOR ONE HUNDRED AND fifty years, wrapped in an oil-skin pouch, tied with braid made from the finest horse hair, sandwiched between two, early 19th century, beautifully printed linen drapes.

PART ONE

Paintings.

Chapter 1

LANDSCAPE WITH AN OBELISK (FLINCK 1638)

Paris, France.
Wednesday, May 19. 2010.

ALL CITIES THAT HAVE MATURED BY RIVERS INEVITABLY change by the bond formed between the stationary and the constantly flowing nature they share. The river is a mirror in which the city finds its cultural reflection. For centuries, poets, artists, scholars, storytellers, designers, lovers, suicides, and eventually tourists, all understand this potent attraction.

Across the mighty boulevard of trade and transportation that is the River Seine, the Eiffel Tower stands in silent solitude. An obelisk dressed in a million shimmering lights. The iron-lady still looks splendid, and remains every inch the proud symbol of modern-day Paris after all these years. With regal dignity she looks over her city with the eye of a proud monarch.

Her mighty searchlight atop the tower scans the landscape below, surveying the 'City of Lights' like a trusted guardian.

Just before midnight, on this night, (as with every other); the powerful searchlight cut a swathe of light across the Seine, momentarily illuminating the splendour of the Palais de Chaillot on the Trocadero.

In the wake of its sweep of brilliant light came complete darkness. The black night closed in around the buildings and statues like a velvet glove; shrouding the pavements in inky obscurity.

As the first moment of black darkness descended over the Trocadero, blanking out the Paris Museum of Modern Art, the Holmatro CU007 mini-cutter exerted a pressure of 24.5kN/ton on the high-tensile steel padlock on the rear delivery gate. Within two seconds the lock sheared, and fell to the floor, with a light metallic thud.

The intruder closed the gate behind him, hanging the broken lock on the latch. He entered the grounds, keeping close to the wall as he made his way across the tiny courtyard, just another shadow among shadows.

At the window he took his Drake suction pad from his backpack and affixed it to the glass. For a moment it whispered as it sucked the crushed glass into the hollow handle. Carefully, he reached through the hole and popped the lock. The window slid open. No alarm sounded.

In one athletic jump, he was in. He slid the window closed. Settling the night-vision goggles in place, he followed the droplets of luminous paint that he had sprayed on the ground earlier in the day.

On rubber-soled shoes, the figure moved silently and quickly through the Grand Hall, passing, without a second glance, the giant Jean Michael Baquiat canvases, resplendent in the eerie green phosphorus glow.

His reactions, when he heard the sound were lightning fast.

Even though there were supposed to be no guard movements during this and the next hour, the noise barely made his heartbeat rise. He stopped, as still as the stone statues around him. He waited, the seconds dripped past. There it was again-, the click of a heel on the stone floor. When the sound clicked again, the intruder was able to locate the direction, he dropped to the floor, wriggling like a snake behind one of the heavy, chintz-covered visitor couches. A moment later the sway of a flashlight beam cut through the gallery. In the shadow of the couch the indistinguishable shape waited motionless for the threat to pass. Tomorrow words needed to be spoken about this deviation from the plan, but those thoughts were for tomorrow. Right now he needed to remain calm. The metronomic footsteps retreated and quiet descended again. He'd lost maybe four minutes.

The figure raised his head and scanned the gallery through his night-vision goggles. He poked his head around the base of the couch, and slithered out from his shelter.

The night-vision goggles picked up stains on the couch that had gone un-noticed by the thousands of art-lovers who sat on the seat every day to admire and absorb the latest work of art to be exhibited.

The figure crossed the gallery, and entered the arena close to the Palace of Tokyo.

For the next hour, the lone thief meticulously split the backing canvas from the frames of five, previously identified paintings. With the skill of a surgeon he extracted the paintings, before carefully rolling and sliding them into his black carbon-fibre tube. Without fuss the intruder left the building by the same route he had entered. He paused only briefly to pick-up the mini-cutter, and replace the broken padlock on the closed gate.

The figure arrived at the rendezvous point. Here, there was to be but a short heart thumping wait on the curb. Here was his chance of exposure, now was the risk.

To blend in, he removed his mask. He knew that the risk was that he would be visible, and vulnerable to any passing motorist with even half a memory for the event. But it was a necessary risk, after all everyone remembers a man wearing a mask, no one recalls a pedestrian walking the streets at 1:16 in the morning!

The stolen, blue Citroën C5 estate stopped only momentarily to allow the lone thief to ease his black neoprene suited body into the back seat. Cosseted in the warmth of the interior the thief relaxed. The car smoothly accelerated away, and soon joined the other innocent vehicles driving along the Avenue Kleber. Relief flooded through the thief, who was now certain that nobody had noticed anything untoward on the street.

This brazen overnight heist at the Paris Museum of Modern Art had netted the perpetrator five major works of art, by Picasso, Matisse, Braque, Modigliani, and Leger. The haul was valued at hundreds of millions of euros. He patted the black carbon-fibre tube. It was time to report in.

Thursday, May 20.

IN AN ATTEMPT TO KEEP THE THEFT UNDER WRAPS, the gendarmes had completely cordoned off the museum by nine o'clock Thursday morning. However, thanks to the spectacle of all the police activity, and the brightly coloured tape emblazoned with, 'Police Nationale - Zone Interdite', the museum soon became another neck-twisting attraction for all the customers denied access to one of the French capital's most tourist-frequented neighbourhoods. By 9:15 the rumours were spreading and the crowds were growing.

By midday, one of the lecture theatres inside the museum had been hastily configured into a media centre. At 13:00 the world's press waited with anticipation. A buzz of excitement ran around the room as a slight man with greying hair and piercing blue eyes, dressed in a sober charcoal grey suit, took his seat easily behind an engraved brass name-plate. As Daniel Girard, the museum's chief of security reached out with his well-manicured hand to adjust the microphone, the members of the press grew quiet. Behind Girard, a screen came to life, showing an aerial shot of the museum.

"Good afternoon, ladies and gentlemen," he said. Girard spoke French, with a heavy Parisian accent. The reporters mumbled an excited response.

Without any other pre-amble the slight man launched into his report. The screen behind him showed CCTV footage of a single masked intruder leaving the museum. "As you can see from the footage, I am here to report that last night; we were victims of an audacious theft from the museum." He fell silent and let the tape tell the story.

The black-clad figure rounded the corner, and disappeared. The screen changed to an internal shot of the intruder as he crossed the main gallery floor. Then the screen showed the same two pieces of footage again.

"Is that the only footage?" someone called out.

"Yes."

Before he could continue, Girard was interrupted, "What about the internal security system?"

Girard cleared his throat. "The entire internal security system was disabled. All we have is the CCTV footage that you see now." Girard changed the picture to two stills of the thief. Girard shone his laser-beam onto the screen, highlighting the grainy silhouette of the thief. "Here and here."

"What did he take?" a reporter shouted out.

"How were the security systems disabled?" another asked. Colleagues waited for a response.

Girard, simply ignored the questions, and continued with his well-prepared script. "Investigators are trying to determine if he was working alone," Girard paused. He smiled without mirth.

"You say that the internal system was disabled, but what about the security guards?" another reporter asked.

"Three guards were on duty overnight, but they saw nothing."

The first reporter's voice grew more insistent, taking on a mocking tone. Loudly, to be heard over the muffled backdrop of chatter in the room, he shouted, "What did the thief take?"

Girard ignored the question again, "I can promise you-"

"Five paintings!"

The reporters all turned to see the source of the comment. The words were spoken from the back of the room, and they were spoken in English.

The voice was confident, but what the reporters saw shocked them.

The man striding down the aisle, was unmistakably English; no one with an iota of European sartorial elegance would have been caught dead wearing such an outfit.

William Forbes strode with an air of drama down the

make-shift aisle separating the two banks of reporters. Tall, with a once athletic build, his was a look that confused most onlookers. None of the reporters could accurately state his age, but guessed he was either late thirties, or early forties. He had a face so bland it was devoid of expression and emotion. The puffy features erased the definition that would allow the face to be thought of as handsome, which meant that lately he'd either been enjoying a lot of comfort food, or been pumped full of drugs. His mousy hair was over long, and thinning, but he carried it all off with the confidence of an Eaton education and a former commission in the British army.

As he walked to the desk, Forbes felt an energy course through his body. *It feels good to be working again*, he thought. Once more he had meaning to his life. With clear instruction, purpose and objective, the ability to use his own initiative; flex his muscles and use his many skills.

His highland-green, blue checked tweed suit, worn over a mustard yellow waistcoat looked so out of place among the fashion conscious gathered in the room that some reporters actually winced at his appearance.

"It is Toad of Toad-Hall," one whispered.

Without a hint of self-consciousness he stood in front of the desk, and addressed the reporters. Suddenly their senses were torn. Visually the man looked absurd, but his oratory was exceptional, and his message compelling.

His voice carried an honesty that had motivated troops during his time in Bosnia. Forbes, in fact had seen action on various battlefields throughout the world. As he spoke, it was easy to see how he had motivated his men, and become a proven leader. His forte had always been in enabling his men to perform to the highest standards on dangerous missions. It was easy to see how that skill could be transferable to civilian life, and used to lead investigations such as this, "I shall be leading this investigation..."

"Wait one moment," Girard attempted to halt him, but was silenced with one withering look.

William Forbes had always been an excellent leader. He carried many skills, both physical and mental that stood him in good stead from the rubble strewn streets of Kosovo to the ruthless auction-houses of London and New York. It was just a shame that he had no dress-sense.

Forbes continued, "The prosecutor's office initially estimates the total worth of the five paintings as €500 million euros."

The reporters gasped in amazement. Girard pushed back his chair, and tried to gain order in the room, he plucked the microphone from its cradle and tried speaking over Forbes. The look of hatred on his face hinted this was not the first time the two of them had crossed paths.

"Non, c'est impossible. We estimate the value at just under €100 million." His index finger wagged in denial, his credibility evaporating rapidly.

Forbes ignored the interruption, and with a flourish of a magician pulling a rabbit from a hat, extracted a neatly folded sheet of paper from his pocket. He shook it open, "Le pigeon aux petits-pois – The Pigeon with the Peas, an ochre and brown cubist oil painting by Pablo Picasso, 1911."

"Non, non, non," Girard screamed behind him, "Don't tell them."

But of course it was too late. The reporters, scribbled down every detail. Some were oblivious to the works, and their values, other grimaced at the choice of the word Pigeon, over the much more aesthetically pleasing art term choice of Dove.

Forbes continued, "The Picasso is valued by the Art Loss Register as €230 million."

Girard leaned over the table, reaching out he grabbed the back of the Englishman's jacket.

"Do you think it is wise to reveal this much detail?" the contemptuous tone crossed the language barrier with ease.

Forbes shifted his weight, detaching the hand from his jacket. He shuffled forward in a petulant attempt to move out of range of the well-manicured digits.

"La Pastoral, Pastoral, an oil painting of nudes on a hillside by Henri Matisse; valued at €75 million."

The reporters watched with devilish anticipation as Girard came running around the desk to confront Forbes. The difference in their stature took on a comical appearance.

"Stop this immediately," said Girard, his fists clenched at his sides, his face tilted up at an awkward angle, and a deep shade of red. The microphone gave off a shrill scream of feedback.

Forbes lowered his sheet, and looked down at the slight chief of security with a look full of pure contempt. Forbes shot out a hand, and turned off the microphone, the room went silent. "I'm in charge of this investigation, so get back in your box … Girard."

The slight man looked like he would explode. He stuttered for a reply, but Forbes whispered in his ear, "The sooner the titles are common knowledge the sooner we close the outlet for the works to be sold on."

Girard swallowed hard, and nodded in submissive agreement.

Forbes took one step to the left, and continued with his address.

"Other paintings stolen were, 'L'olivier pres de l'Estaque', Olive Tree near Estaque, by George Braque. 'La femme a l'evntail'. 'Woman with a fan', by Amedeo Modigliani, and 'Naturemort aux chandeliers'. 'Still-life with Chandeliers', by Fernand Leger," with a flourish, William Forbes, investigator with the Art Loss Register of London finished his press conference by returning the sheet to his pocket, "The theft appears to be one of the biggest art heists ever, considering the estimated value of the works, the prominence of the artists, the high profile of this museum, and the apparent failure of the security systems; we will of course be checking why they failed," he paused for effect, noticing how Girard seemed to be visibly shrinking in front of him, as every word about the museum's security failures was recalled and written down by the reporters.

"So if you'll excuse me gentlemen, I have some criminals to catch."

Girard looked up at him with a hint of devilment in his eyes; he spoke quietly, so no one else would hear. "Your suit is so loud it has given me a headache. Do you have any pills I could take?"

Forbes felt his world collapse, the room began to spin; it was as if Girard had thrust a knife into his gut. "No!" Forbes brushed him aside and exited the room without a backward glance.

As the door shut, Girard smiled at the visible effect his comment had had on the pompous Englishman.

Outside, Forbes allowed himself a deep breath of Parisian air. He held on to the wall for support as he stumbled down the steps. Resisting the urge to go for his pills he lifted the 'Police Nationale - Zone Interdite' tape, which surrounded the museum, and headed for the car. He needed time and privacy to reflect upon the scene he had just created. Safe in the knowledge that the investigators at the museum would collate all the information about the theft, Forbes wanted to focus on the future. The paintings were gone. A single thief had taken them.

Forbes needed to understand where they could be now, and who was responsible. He jumped into the back seat of the late model Peugeot, and allowed the driver the luxury of spinning the wheels as they pulled away from the museum; much to the delight of the massed crowd of on-lookers.

News of the theft hit all the TV news channels at the next hour's broadcasts. Within the hour, Interpol had responded to eight hundred calls on the theft. Before rush-hour on the Périphérique, Police and Customs officers began co-ordinated searches at all international borders, airports and seaports for the stolen masterpieces. Forbes was pleased with their response times; they were within six minutes of his estimation, and just five hours too late.

Just after official closing time, the museum security guards completed fixing the laminated signs on all the doors, apologising for the closure, due to technical reasons. But, by now the crowds that had gathered had lost interest and dispersed. On the heavily cordoned-off balcony behind the museum; police officers in blue latex gloves and white cotton face-masks examined the neatly broken window, and severed lock. They dropped the broken padlock into a plastic bag, and rushed it back to HQ.

Inside, similarly attired officers painstakingly took tiny fibres from the edges of the frames. Other officers reviewed the CCTV from the day. Because the paintings appeared to have been carefully removed from the disassembled frames and not sliced or ripped out, the team soon came to the conclusion that this was a very carefully planned and executed crime.

Chapter Two

Sunflowers (Vincent Van-Gogh 1888)

Paris, France.
Friday, May 21.

WITHOUT A BREAKTHROUGH, OR EVEN A FOLLOW-UP press conference, the morning newspapers were forced to lead with a tame re-worked headline …

'A security guard at the museum said the paintings were discovered missing by a night watchman just before seven a.m. Thursday morning.'

The security guard in question was, at this time unable to be named because of security reasons. But he was still paid handsomely for the useless information that the reporters, and public at large were desperate for.

Television stations went one better, they interviewed the Mayor of Paris, Bertrand Delanoe, and the museum's director, Pierre Cornette de Saint-Cyr Paris. In the mayor's statement, he said that he was 'Saddened and shocked by this theft, this intolerable attack on Paris's universal cultural heritage'.

In front of the museum, police cordon tape flapping

everywhere, the director in chief of the Museum of Modern Art was bullish in his condemnation of the thieves.

"Fools," his arms flailed, and he gave the famous Gallic shrug. Microphones were pushed in front of his face.

de Saint-Cyr Paris pulled himself up to his full height, which was only slightly more than his girth, he looked directly into the cameras, "You cannot do anything with these paintings. All the countries in the world are aware of their importance. No collector is stupid enough to risk his liberty to buy these paintings,"

"Why is that, Monsieur Director?"

He held up his thumb, to indicate 'one', "No collector would be vain enough to buy a painting that he cannot show off to his peers," de Saint-Cyr Paris held up his index finger, "and two," he shook his head vigorously, "Risks sending him to prison for a long time. In essence, you will find that these five masterpieces are worthless, they are un-sellable. So, thieves, sirs, you are imbeciles, I implore you, return them immediately."

❦

HEAD OF THE ART LOSS REGISTER'S LONDON OFFICE, Michael Carrington, had the persona of everyone's favourite uncle. Big, cuddly, with a friendly face, and unassuming curly hair, Carrington was an expert in almost every field of the arts. He was also a ruthless negotiator, and a stickler for process. His appointment to the role at the ALR had been a labour of love for the self-confessed art lover.

He had travelled to Paris, to personally re-enforce the urgency of recovering the paintings, to his man in the field, William Forbes. When he discovered Forbes had not left his hotel room that morning, he was furious. His finger poked the speed dial, and his blood pressure rose as he waited for an answer.

"Forbes." The sleepy voice was quiet and slow.

"Bill, where the hell are you? I've got the police, Interpol, and the world and his art-loving dog waiting for you to start investigating."

"Morning Michael, I needed some time to think things through ..."

"Are you alright, Bill?" Carrington was quite aware of the fragile state Forbes had been in when he took him on at the ALR. He knew that the ex-SAS man, tough as old boots and had a nasty turn in Belgrade, when capturing Radovan Karadzic. Whatever had gone on in those catacombs had left Forbes unable to cope with everyday life. PTSD, post-traumatic stress disorder they called it now, shell shocked was the term he had known it by since the First World War.

Forbes felt the question was a warning shot, "No, everything is fine, but with so many idiots shooting their mouths off, I needed time on my own to go through the details of the theft."

"Okay, shall we meet for lunch?" Carrington asked gently, afraid to probe any deeper.

"Sure, where are you?" Forbes responded, afraid Carrington had seen through is flimsy cover story.

"Hotel du Louvre, meet me here at midday." That should give him time to get his act together, thought Carrington, checking his Rolex.

"Fine, I look forward to it," Forbes glanced at his Tudor Heritage wristwatch, and then glanced at his un-shaven face in the mirror. That should give me enough time to get my act together.

CARRINGTON WELCOMED FORBES INTO HIS SUITE. "Good to see you Bill, how have you been?" the words cut through Forbes like a knife, paranoia swept over his body like an aggressive wave crashing on a beach. He wondered whether Carrington was going to relieve him of the investigation.

"I'm fine Michael, really."

Carrington gave him one of his famous open smiles. It was meant to re-assure. It didn't work, "That's good to hear. Now, how's the investigation going?"

Forbes, thought the worst, believing that somehow he'd got to hear about Girard's reference to the 'Pills' at the press conference, he was lost for words.

Carrington sat on the Louis XV chair, facing the flat screen TV, "I was appalled by the media circus on TV this morning."

Forbes lent against the wall, "Yes, it was rather amateurish."

"Thought I'd come over, offer some support. I'm going to insist that these so called experts be banned from giving interviews."

"That would be helpful, the Mayor was very counterproductive."

In disgust, Carrington pointed the remote at the TV. The screen went black.

Carefully he placed the remote on the ornate table, and settled back in his chair.

"You really upset Girard at the press conference."

Forbes shrugged his shoulders, he knew what was coming. Carrington held up his hand, "Upset that little snake at your peril, but look at the damage he did by suggesting the TV people interview those idiots. He'll try to scupper you, Bill, so be on your guard."

"Do you want me to say sorry?"

"Good God no! Upset him as much as you like, but make sure he doesn't allow his so called experts to threaten the investigation; and ruin your chances of recovering the paintings."

"Maybe you could get him off the case completely?"

Carrington let out a huge belly laugh, "That really would be a cruel stroke.

You've already got the investigation into the biggest ever art theft. Don't forget I sacked him from the ALR. You got his job. I think he hates me just as much as you."

"I don't think that's possible, still if you could keep him side-lined."

"I'll try. Let's face it Bill, this is the biggest heist since the 1990 Isabella Stewart Gardener Museum heist in Boston."

Forbes nodded, "Yes, and they only got a Vermeer, several Rembrandts, and an inferior Degas."

"An inferior Degas," Carrington nodded in agreement, then he grew serious, "and none of those paintings were ever recovered, Christ we don't ever recover more than 10% of whatever they pinch!"

"True, but it adds to the theory of 'Theft to order' for some wealthy collector. Once it goes into his collection it's never seen again," Forbes offered.

"You'll get a lot of people buying into that theory for his theft too, especially with the cost associated with the five paintings."

"But then again, the FBI maintained a local criminal gang, undertook the Isabella Stewart robbery, and used the paintings as collateral for a loan, to expand their drug business," Forbes said.

"There would have to be a lot of people involved in this heist, if a Picasso, £250 million pound note is going to be used to buy some drugs."

"There are other explanations that could take it beyond art."

"Terrorists?"

"It's beyond my remit if this involves a nuclear-arms trans-action, or Dictator Deposition, or buying a small island in the Caribbean? You name it, if it isn't contained in the art world; I'm out of my depth."

Carrington looked soberly at Forbes, "That used to be your forte."

"I didn't think you'd want me to get dirty."

"I want you to recover the paintings not blow up an Embassy."

"I doubt I could do that on my own."

"Do you think you can bring the Pigeon home, Bill?"

"Yes. For criminals dealing in drugs, a rolled-up Picasso is a clever way of carrying a large amount of 'currency' across International borders, even if they trade at only a tenth of the actual value, but somebody has to want to buy it."

"Do you think that's what this is? Drugs?"

"Hell no, the paintings are much too recognised. These masterpieces were specifically chosen. If they'd wanted some-thing just for the value, they would have taken something that had little value. Something to trade, these paintings can't be traded. You can't sell these."

"Then it's art theft for art sake."

Forbes nodded, "Someone wanted them."

"A syndicate?"

"No, one weak link would bring them all down, no this is one customer. One plan, one theft. One thief."

"A specialist."

"Very. He did the theft, and he took care of the security system."

"And the customer?"

"Someone who'd appreciate the art."

"Who'd have the nerve to set it up? Stealing five of the world's most recognisable paintings, knowing he could never show them to anyone else. What kind of man does that?"

"Someone wealthy."

"Wealthy," Carrington laughed, "He'd have to be rolling in it. There can't be more than a handful of men in the world that could afford such a luxury."

"That's what I wanted time to think about. I've made a list of 'evil rich' art connoisseurs." Forbes's eyebrow rose theatrically.

"You have thoughts on who's behind this?"

Forbes nodded, "I do."

"Come on Bill if it were that simple, whoever planned the theft, would know he'd be under the spotlight."

"But he's rich enough not to have to explain where the purchase price came from, and he's big enough not to have any loose ends afterward."

"It must be very exclusive, this 'evil rich' list you've compiled." Carrington leaned back, his body language said, 'Okay, I'm open to ideas'.

"It would be an informed guess, but it is a very exclusive list," Forbes said, his palms open and wide, a hopeful yet desperate gesture.

"Come on Bill, make an old man happy, who'd you put your

money on?" an easy smile curled his lips, like a father encouraging a child.

"I think its LeCoyte Chellen, Multi-billionaire. Dutch national, well dual nationality actually, made his fortune in the states, and then exploited the Middle East when the Sheiks were just discovering what their black sticky oil could really buy."

"He heads the Chellen Corporation, international telecommunications company. Well they're certainly diverse enough, and he's certainly rich enough to channel funds, and powerful enough. Well connected too, Chellen has galleries all over the world, loves his art. Good choice. Who else?"

"Kerim Beynachinski."

"Ah, yes, Comrade Beynachinski. Moscow born and bred, there was always a whiff of Nazi plunder about him. Icons and artefacts in the 60's which turned into old masters when the decadent western flower power people finally came back down to earth; and now the provider of art for every oligarch in Russia."

"The 'go-to' man for everything in oil that doesn't come from the ground."

Carrington held up a finger, "I ran into him in Saint Petersburg, a year or so back, very focused gentleman. I never relished going toe to toe with him at the auctions," Carrington tapped the finger against his lips, "You're right Bill, I could see him looking at the Picasso in his private gallery in Murmansk," Carrington raised his eyebrows, inviting Forbes to continue.

"Chandhok Nahmad."

Carrington clapped his hands, "Very nasty piece of work, rumoured to have actually committed murder during his gangster days, quietened down a lot since then mind you. Still he kept the ALR employed for nearly a decade in tracking down the forgeries he slipped into the European market."

"They're my top three; they tick all the boxes, rich, ruthless, and capable, with the desire to own the five masterpieces without feeling the need to show anyone else. Any of the others, ambitious enough, wouldn't have the nerve, because it would mean having to tread on the big three's toes to execute such a theft in Europe, and risk exposure from the thief they hired."

"Who else would you be looking at?"

"I can only think of a small number of Chinese and Arabs that would have the nerve to approach a gallery owner or an informed chancer at one of the big auction-houses ..."

"Why involve anyone else at all?"

Forbes pondered on his reply, when it came it was delivered with the passion of an art-lover. After all, Forbes did have a degree in Art History, and he had worked, in-between his military adventures, for Bonhams, the privately owned British auction-house, one of the world's oldest and largest auctioneers of fine art and antiques. "Art is such a personal preference. Whoever performed the theft, was an expert in his field, it wasn't his debut. So, he was approached for his talents. That means someone had to tell the customer where this master thief could be found. That sways me to galleries and auction-houses, the discerning customer would have definitely visited many of those over the years, and no doubt had been approached by black-market chancers, to test the water on black-market purchases. Then again, the thief didn't specify which paintings were taken, that was the customer. The Chinese or Arabs don't go for paintings for themselves. They like to show off their wealth, their appreciation for art, usually by showing it to their western allies."

"Good reasoning, Bill."

Forbes stood straighter, the professional re-surfacing, "Beyond those, maybe a hundred millionaires or so would be interested in one of the pieces, but not all five."

"So, less than two hundred suspects in the entire world, that's pretty good odds for an old soldier like you."

"I think you're right, I may have to get my hands dirty on this one."

"Whatever it takes, Bill. Find them. Find out who's behind this, and get the paintings back." He reached forward and picked up the TV remote.

"Yes sir," Forbes knew the conversation was over. He left the suite, hopeful that he'd impressed his boss enough to be-lay any fears of his mental capacity to get the paintings back. The physical capability had never been in doubt. As he left the hotel he made a phone call, he walked as he waited for the connection. Forbes felt less than confident, that with Girard still involved in the investigation the all-important break would be coming anytime soon.

The call was answered.

"Hi there Gianni, been to any good operas lately?"

THE DAY AT THE OFFICE HAD DRAGGED, BUT NOW JEAN-Baptiste Giboez was heading home for the week-end. Time took on a different meaning now that the office was behind him. He turned off the motorway to enjoy his favourite country road home, where the constant sunshine throughout the day had persuaded the sunflowers in the fields to turn their faces to catch the fading light.

Window open, radio playing, Jean-Baptiste, black curly hair blowing in the breeze, took in the aroma and warmth of the countryside, the sounds of birds squabbling over the seeds which had spilt upon the ground. No doubt about it this was a good day to be alive.

In the distance he saw a figure stumbling along the verge. At the sound of the approaching engine, the figure turned. Jean-Baptiste recognised the figure as that of a man, and that he had been injured. As he drew closer he could see the man's face was covered in blood. The man swayed, hands waving in a gesture for help.

Drunk, or stoned, car accident, or mugging, this man clearly needed help.

But, as it was the week-end Jean Baptiste drove past the stricken man.

Instantly filled with remorse, he applied the brakes and brought the car to a halt. He glanced in the mirror. The man was holding his hands to his head. Jean-Baptiste could clearly see the hands too were caked in blood.

"Accident," he reasoned. Jean-Baptiste got out of the car. Instinctively he started pressing the keys for the emergency services. He knew he was not equipped to deal with such an injury, and what if there were more victims. He scanned the sunflower covered fields to see if he could see a crashed car.

The man collapsed onto the road, Jean-Baptiste ran to his side. The man lay on his back, his head covered in blood. Jean-Baptiste's hands shook, his fingers trembled as he began punching the buttons on the mobile. The office seemed a long way away now. Time had stopped altogether, and the only sound he heard was of his own heart thumping in his chest. Now, they were the only two people in the world. He'd never seen an accident victim before, never felt the need to 'rubber neck' at the sight of a traffic collision. His eyes moistened, he knelt down by the head of the stricken victim.

The man groaned, it was just a weak, pathetic sound, Jean-Baptiste lent closer, "Don't worry friend, I will call for help." He could see that the blood was coming from a long cut on the skull just above the hair line.

The man's eyes opened and one hand shot up, slamming a powerful fist onto Jean-Baptiste's chin. His curly hair flicked out from the impact. He dropped his mobile. The man was suddenly on his feet, swinging another vicious blow into Jean-Baptiste's cheek. The bloody man closed in, gripping Jean-Baptist's dark curly haired head between his powerful hands. The man flexed his shoulders and twisted; and Jean-Baptiste's neck snapped. The blood stained hands released the corpse.

A blood stained hand picked up the discarded mobile. He looked at the screen, and praised his luck. The driver had not completed the sequence. He had been one digit short. He cancelled the call, and put the mobile in his pocket. He caught hold of the body beneath the shoulder blades and dragged the corpse into the sunflower field.

Back at the car he pulled a spare sim card from the lining of his lapel, he exchanged it with the driver's sim card. He snapped the plastic case back on the mobile. He slipped into the driver's seat. He punched the buttons, wedging the mobile between shoulder and ear, he waited for his call to connect.

"Yes?" The voice was dull, and noncommittal, altered by the de-coder.

"I was compromised at the rendezvous point." The words hurt as much as the gash on his head. He'd been taken by surprise, the attack had been vicious, but not as vicious as the revenge he now planned.

"And the merchandise?" The voice asked, hopefully, but instantly knowing the answer.

"I do not have it. But I plan to get it back …soon."

After a moment, to allow the news to sink in the voice responded. "Well, I better let you get on with it. Keep me updated, I'll keep my ear to the ground."

He adjusted the seat to accommodate his powerful athletic frame, and drove away.

Not having eaten since Wednesday, he was desperately hungry; but he knew he'd have to clean himself up before presenting himself at the nearest service station for a meal.

Chapter Three

THE SCREAM (EDWARD MUNCH 1893)

Cumbria, England.
Monday, May 24.

KAYLEE DEAN WAS NOT THE TYPE OF REPORTER TO let a little bad weather get in the way of a good story, but this was May for God sake, supposedly summer.

Other crews, less determined than she, had already given up on the chance of an early morning interview. But Kaylee had stuck it out. She would show them, she would soon be back in the big time.

Kaylee stood resoundingly up to her ankles in mud, in a field in Cumbria. Her determined attitude was beginning to wear her own crew down. They were already making hushed comments that they too should abandon the location.

Her chin rubbed against the damp scarf, which was pulled tight in an attempt to stave off the biting cold wind; did this place ever get warm? She stamped her feet, hoping to revive the circulation, but nothing shut out the cold that was seeping into her body, *'Give me Kosovo any day,'* she thought.

Suddenly her ear-piece came to life. "We're going live.

Complete the background story then cut into local news. The finder will be with you in five minutes."

Max the cameraman, stumbled out of the car. "Yo, are we good to go?" He hoisted the camera on his shoulder.

Kaylee brushed back a damp strand of hair, and turned on her most charming smile. In her ear the producer chanted, "On air in 5, 4, 3 …"

"Good Morning. A Roman helmet unearthed in this very Cumbrian field by a metal detector enthusiast will soon be going up for auction at Christie's in London. I will be speaking with the man who found the relic, estimated value four hundred thousand pounds, after the news where you are." The smile stayed in place until the camera had switched off.

They watched, as an old, battered Land Rover Discovery pulled up.

"Tin-man's here," Max shouted. Kaylee tried to move, but the cloying mud, agitated by her constant stamping had rooted her to the spot.

She observed a large man with a bulbous red nose, and bullet-proof thick glasses approach her.

"Miss Dean?" he waved, "I'm Lawrence Dunn. I found the helmet." He looked pleased with himself, but his smile repelled her, he looked to her like a child molester, or a train-spotter. As she welcomed him to her soggy hell, she couldn't make her mind up which activity offended her more.

Enthusiastically she said, "We've got a couple of minutes to prepare. How would you like me to introduce you?"

"Oh I don't want anyone to know my name," Dunn replied, his breath smelt of garlic. His eyes roamed over her body.

"Then how am I going to announce you?" her smile began to fade.

"Oh I don't want to be on the telly," he leered.

"Then why are you here?" Probably just to ogle me, she thought.

"I thought you wanted to know where I found the helmet; and I wondered about an autograph."

The journey back to Manchester was fraught with tension, finally Kaylee exploded, "What a complete dick. I don't want anyone to know who I am," she snorted. "Where did you find the helmet?'" she said in a childish simper, "Over there, he said pointing at that sodding field. Christ we could have done the interview at the service station. I'm bloody freezing."

Max the cameraman laughed, in a supportive manner, "Never mind, Kaylee, by the time it goes up for auction, everyone will have forgotten about it. Once it's sold, no one will ever mention Crosby Garrett again … do you think they'll want you to do coverage of the auction?"

"Sod that, I want nothing to do with that stupid helmet, or that sick pervert ever again," Kaylee put her hands against her cheeks and screamed, stamping her frozen feet in the foot-well. "Turn that bloody heater up."

Marseille, France.
Tuesday, May 25.

THE STATUS OF MARSEILLE AS THE COSMOPOLITAN centre of southern France owes much of its success to its sea trade.

Marseille Port is France's second largest container port. It is the oldest and busiest sea port in France, receiving thousands of commercial and private ships each year. Containers, carrying every type of produce are transhipped in and out with the meticulousness of a traffic-warden with O.C.D. In the last year, Marseille box shipments rose to 741,548 twenty-foot units.

The man in charge of stock-control, smoothly moved the joystick to the right. He watched the screen with intense concentration, as the camera followed the movement of his hand.

The two men behind him watched his movements with hardly contained boredom. Arms folded, jaws tight with frustration.

"Every container is booked in using the very latest in Container Security Radio Frequency Identification Discs …and scanners." He stroked a dial, and the camera began to zoom in.

The two men exchanged a knowing glance.

"So, please can you tell me where that box came from?" He pointed to the screen, turning to view their reactions.

The two men were instantly galvanized into action, leaning over the stock-controller's shoulder to view the screen. The name badges on their Hi-Viz jackets read 'Charles' and 'Mac' they now looked at the recalcitrant container, and then each other in total amazement.

"Well?" asked the stock-controller sarcastically, "What are you waiting for?"

CHARLES AND MAC JUMPED OUT OF THEIR OLD
Peugeot van, and approached the lonely container.

Charles slapped his hands against his thighs. "I swear to
god this was not here when I finished my shift yesterday."

"Of course not, I blame the fairies," replied Mac.

"Blame who you want, I didn't put it here."

"Let's see where it came from, what's the seal number?"

"There's no seal," Charles said as they approached the
doors.

"Naughty fairies," Mac grasped the lever that opened the
doors. Both men pulled on the locking bars, so that the doors
swung open.

The doors creaked on rusted hinges to reveal the illicit
cargo.

Containers have been used to transport stolen cars from
Europe to Asia for many years. The most popular 'stolen to
order' models are 4x4 Range Rovers, Bentleys, Aston Martins
and Ferraris. But the car they found inside the container was
just a normal family estate. It was a car that both men could
easily have afforded, but neither would have wanted, because
the car was now just a burnt out hulk.

As Charles entered the container he noticed the walls were
blackened from the particles of paint emitted by the car as it
had burned. "Hey, Mac, they torched it in here," he said. He ran
a finger down the container wall, smearing the blackness. His
finger came away tarnished in filth. "Yuk." He shuffled down
the container, trying hard not to touch the car or the blackened
walls again. "The police will love this."

The roof of the vehicle was not completely burned, and a dull sheen of blue paint shone through the grime. "It was blue."

Carefully, Mac went down the other side, looking back at the inside of the container doors, they too were blackened. "Yes, but they closed the doors too early, cut off the oxygen, stopped it being burnt to a crisp."

Mac arrived at the passenger window, his boots crunched on tiny pebbles of broken safety glass. He dipped his head inside and shone his flashlight into the burnt-out interior.

At the same time, Charles reached for the driver's door handle and opened the door of the blue Citroën estate.

Mac's scream was loud and piercing, shrill and much too high-pitched to be coming from his workman's throat.

Charles jerked back in shock, slamming into the blackened container wall.

"Jesus fucking Christ, there's a body in there," Mac pulled his head out of the car and stumbled back along the container wall, bouncing off the side of the car, smearing his jacket with back soot.

The shockwaves travelled through the chassis and down Charles's body as he began jerking backward, trapped between container wall and open car door.

The tremor continued through his arm and hand as he desperately shook it to release the door handle, but he could not release himself.

Panic grabbed him, and the car started to rock. The movement was just enough to dislodge the charred head from the incinerated shoulders of the corpse. As the head fell, wisps of burned flesh detached and floated in the air.

As the burned head hit the container floor, it burst open. The skull collapsed, resulting in a small ash cloud rising.

Charles watched the head disintegrate in front of his eyes, his own scream, was low, and reverberated around the container.

∿℘◯

Friday, May 28.

EAGER TO START HIS VACATION, THE TRACKING-DOWN of the stolen paintings from Paris was the last thing on the mind of, Jerome Dollet, detective with the Marseille police department.

He skimmed through the preliminary forensic report on the 'Marseille Container Murder', he was certain this was just another example of the drug barons flexing their territorial muscle.

The report concluded that the body had died of multiple blows to the head with a blunt instrument. He was already dead when the car was set alight. The body, burned beyond recognition contained traces of accelerant, including 'Napalm', and the explosive 'Cyanogen'.

"Wow, explosives, bang, bang they wanted you dead, my friend." Dollet, *Googled* 'Napalm', the page highlighted the effect of the inflammable liquid on the skin. "It sticks, so once attached; it allows no chance for removing the burning substance from a victim …. Oh very nasty," he said dismissively.

The evidence of an accelerant and explosive defiantly warranted the report being sent to Interpol. But, not wanting to be held back in the office on a Friday, he decided not to forward the report to Interpol HQ in Lyon, as asked on the 'anything out-of-the ordinary' report. Instead he stamped it, with an 'Ongoing' stamp, and threw it in his out-tray.

He lent back in his chair, let out a long breath and a slow whistle, already feeling the Caribbean sun on his body. Dollet relaxed, safe in the knowledge that the report would not reach the Inspector's office until Monday, and by then he would be on his vacation. Job done.

The report would remain with the Inspectors until forensics had identified the body. If that happened in the next two weeks, then another officer would take on the case. Not his problem, he hummed a reggae tune, and tapped his fingers on the desk. "No Woman, no cry."

If only he had *Googled* 'Cyanogen' instead of 'Napalm', he would have discovered that the explosive was first synthesized by Joseph Louis Gay-Lussac in 1815. The repot he would have read, goes on to say, 'The explosive attained importance through the growth of the fertilizer industry in the late nineteenth century. It was also used as a stabilizer in the production of nitrocellulose. Like all inorganic explosives, cyanogen is very toxic, because as it undergoes reduction it becomes cyanide, which binds more strongly than oxygen, thus interrupting the mitochondrial electron transfer chain. Cyanogen gas is an irritant to the eyes and respiratory system. Inhalation can cause nausea, vomiting, loss of consciousness, convulsions, blindness and death.

Cyanogen produces the second hottest known natural flame, with a temperature of over 4525°C when it burns with oxygen. In a refined form it was used by the nineteenth century Dutch artists to melt fossils to produce oils, for painting. More recently it has been used to replicate, oil colours in an attempt to reproduce particular colours used by the Dutch Masters. In summary it is used as a tool in art forgery'.

Over the following days, the dental information was recovered from what was left of the skull. The details were sent away, and matched with records already on file.

~✍◯

Wednesday, June 9.

THE HEADQUARTERS OF THE DIRECTION RÉGIONALE de Police Judiciaire de Paris, is often, simply referred to as just '36' because of its address, 36, quai des Orfèvrs, Paris. Its 2,200 officers investigate about 15,000 crimes a year, but none so far had come close to the attention it had been getting over the past two weeks in response to the missing five masterpieces.

Bill Forbes tossed the padlock in his hand. "Well done!"

The long awaited breakthrough had come from the examination of the severed padlock. A number of different cutters had been used on similar padlocks to replicate the sheer pattern on the steel lock. Finally the unique damage was replicated.

The Holmatro CU007 mini-cutter was the first identified culprit of the theft. When Forbes had arrived at the '36' about an hour ago, he instructed the investigators to contact suppliers and stockists of the cutter.

"Start in Paris, and work out, we'll go all over Europe if we have to."

Sales records were forwarded, and thefts were analysed. Early in the afternoon they came up with the second breakthrough.

A Holmatro CU007 mini-cutter had been purchased in Paris, with a MasterCard that had been reported stolen at the Notre Dame cathedral in Paris, just two days before the theft.

In the state-of-the-art Paris surveillance centre, known as the 'Vidéoprotection' department, looking at twenty screens showing footage of CCTV views; a greasy-haired girl named Yasmine Khan, with nose stud, and veiled tattoos under her sheer blouse, sat alone. Her colleagues, who all sat at similar desks, watching the 50,000 cameras keep Paris safe, thought her too weird to associate with. But it was she that looked the most startled when a Highland-green and blue check tweed suited, William Forbes came to sit with her. "Hello, I'm told you can help me." He began, his mustard coloured waistcoat was dazzling.

"Of course, what do you need?" she answered honestly.

"Can we view CCTV from Notre Dame from May 17?"

"Of course, what time?" Her fingers danced over her keyboard.

Forbes smiled, "11:15, please."

Camera A4/679 reported for duty. Yasmine fast forwarded to 11:12.

"Okay let's take a look." Together they watched the scene unfold.

With growing excitement Yasmine realised she was watching an actual theft. The victim was busy taking photographs of the famous old cathedral. The thief came purposefully from behind. The touch was brief and light. Yasmine paused the footage; and executed a screen shot. The printer buzzed beside her. She handed Forbes the photograph.

"Thank you, you've been most helpful. Can you send the picture through to '36'?"

"Sure, not a problem. We will have to wait until they run it through their database."

"How long could it take?" Forbes asked.

"Couple of hours. Probably best to come back tomorrow morning." She wondered what the strange man had planned for the evening.

"You've been very helpful, thank you." And with that Forbes was gone. Idly he wondered what she would have said if he'd asked her out, but for a man with as much baggage as he had, he decided to go back to his hotel and take his pills, alone.

Thursday, June 10.

YASMINE, WITH FRESHLY WASHED HAIR, MINUS THE nose stud, sat waiting for Forbes to arrive. When he entered she gave an excited wave.

"Any news?"

"Yes, but not good I'm afraid. '36', identified the man in the photo. His name is Tommaso Buscetti, he's Italian. Because he is a foreign national, they forwarded the information to Interpol."

"And?"

"Interpol report that Tommaso Buscetti is dead. Murdered."

"Shit."

"I have the report."

"Good girl, how did you get it? I thought Interpol didn't like to give out their reports." Forbes asked, genuinely impressed.

"I decided to contact Marseille myself-"

"Marseille?"

"It's where they found the body."

Forbes let the information sink in. Buscetti was killed in Marseille.

"I spoke to the pathologist; she confirmed Buscetti's dental records had recently been used to verify his identity." She handed a thin file to him.

Forbes began to read, "Marseille Forensic Department." He looked at her triumphantly. "He was found on Tuesday, the twenty-fifth."

"I'm surprised Interpol were not informed immediately, what with the car and body being burned using explosives."

"What car? Does it say?"

"A Citroën C5 estate. The chassis number is in the report."

Forbes's mind began to work over time, "Could you-"

"I already traced the car. It was stolen in Paris, Wednesday the nineteenth."

"Check the CCTV from Avenue Kleber, Wednesday midnight, until Thursday, say 1:20 in the morning. Run the footage from the Trocadero to the Arc du Triumph, for the following couple of hours. I'll bet the thief got picked up between 1:15 and 1:18."

"They may have changed the registration plates."

"It doesn't matter, if we see a blue C5 estate, we will have them."

Working through her lunch break, Yasmine trawled through the CCTV footage from Avenue Kleber. For the three minutes

39

of Forbes's estimated time, sixteen cars passed under the lens. One was a dark blue Citroën C5 estate.

"Here he is." She paused the footage.

Forbes looked at the screen; the Citroën was still getting to the centre of the road. "The thief knew exactly where the CCTV picked up the picture, what a very well-informed thief he was. Well done, Yasmine. Now, can you follow the car, see where it goes?" It was then Forbes lent forward and kissed her. "You have been amazing, very helpful. Thank you. Here's my number," Forbes passed her his business card. "Let me know when he goes out of range." Waving the report he almost danced out of the office.

Yasmine smiled as she felt the kiss tingle on her cheek.

Back at '36', Forbes ordered a pizza, and settled down to work through the night if he needed. The paintings had been stolen three weeks ago. The French police had come up with nothing. No ransom demands, no movement on the black-market, nothing. This was his only lead. The car, and now a dead body in Marseille, someone was cleaning up the loose ends.

Because he had nothing else to go on, Forbes ran a report on Tommaso Buscetti's known associates. Nothing came up in France, so he decided to make another call to his opera loving friend, Gianni.

Professionally, Gianni was known as Giancarlo Minardi, former NATO group captain, now working for the Guardia di Finanza (a police department with responsibility for fraud). Forbes persuaded his friend to utilise some time on the Italian national police crime computer.

When Minardi called him back an hour later, Forbes knew it was time well spent.

Chapter Four

The Concert (Vermeer 1660)

Verona, Italy.
Friday, June 11.

WATCHING THE OPERA, AIDA, FORBES FELT THE PRES-
sures of the investigation lifting from his shoulders.

An elderly German woman sat to his right, fortunately her
habit of conducting the orchestra with her left hand had not
distracted him too much.

To his left sat his good friend Giancarlo Minardi. One time
group captain with N.A.T.O in Bosnia, Minardi owed his life to
the ex-SAS man.

In July 2008, they had together undertaken an unauthorized
assignment to capture Radovan Karadzic in Belgrade. The
mission had been a success, but the consequences had been
very difficult to come to terms with.

The night's performance was heavy with drama, culminating with the performers re-enacting the march into the temple.
As the trumpets serenaded the audience, Forbes could not
resist revealing to Minardi the small trivial piece of evidence
that had led him to the opera in Verona, tonight.

"We found out which type of cutter had been used to break the lock. Then we found out that a cutter had been bought with a stolen credit card. We checked on CCTV and saw the thief taking the victim's wallet. Ran his picture through the computer and came up with Buscetti. Interpol confirmed Buscetti had been killed in Marseille, hit over the head then burned to death in the vehicle used to take the thief away from the museum. I got CCTV of the car, right place, and right time. Then you very kindly come up with Buscetti's best buddy."

"But all this took you three weeks, the paintings are long gone my friend."

"I'll find them, but your help was invaluable."

"I can only give you these twenty-four hours, Bill, and then I must forward my findings to the Carabinieri, and Interpol."

"I have no problem with that, I just need a head start before the police come crashing in and tie everything up in red-tape." Forbes was getting angry.

"How are you coping my friend?" Minardi tried to calm him.

"Things are good … better than they were."

"I'm pleased to hear that," Minardi shook Forbes's shoulder, "I was worried about you."

"It's nearly two years, I never felt better."

"Tough guy, ex-SAS. But you're still taking the pills, right?"

"Only when I have to."

"Good, things are looking good … You're not going to tell me what happened down there in the catacombs are you?"

"No, I don't want to spoil the night." Forbes took a deep breath of night air, as he looked around the magnificent venue.

Think of a rather less battered version of the Coliseum in Rome and you have an accurate picture of the Arena di Verona.

Built in 30AD just outside the city walls, the Arena was conceived as a stadium for games and circuses.

Original white and pink limestone cladding disappeared sometime after the earthquake of 1117. But it was the Renaissance that became the salvation of the Arena. With the revival of interest in Classical antiquity, the stadium was pressed back into use as a theatre.

The birth of the Verona opera started in 1913, when musical entertainments were once again staged at the amphitheatre.

Despite its lack of roof, the Arena delivers near perfect acoustics to every seat in the house.

Gianni Minardi watched tonight's performance of Aida, with the true passion of an Italian. He applauded wildly, as the performers took one last low bow.

"What did the Roman's give us? Good acoustics it would seem."

Forbes too was clapping, transformed into the Egyptian world of Aida. He had been carried along by the story of love and loss, with all the pomp and circumstance the performers and music could muster.

"Magnificent. You were right to wait until the end of the performance to update me on your findings." Forbes appreciated all forms of art. He'd graduated from Eaton in 1989 with a degree in art history, before joining an archaeological dig in northern Iraq.

He'd always craved adventure too, and so it was no surprise that he joined the Royal Scots Dragoon Guards, his father's regiment, in 1974. Here he saw action in Bosnia as part of the SFOR. Then at the end of his tour, at the age of 27 he was seconded into the SAS, staying with the Hereford crew until he was 30, when he began working for Bonhams.

He stayed with the privately owned auction-house for six years, before signing up with the SAS(R) reserves stationed in Yemen, hunting Somali pirates, and then supported the NATO contingent tasked with assisting local forces in hunting down Bosnian war criminals.

All that had come to a crashing halt in 2008, when PTSD forced him out of the military and into rehab for almost 12 months. Then a year ago he'd landed the exciting job of investigator with the Art Loss Register. Since then he'd hidden his debilitating illness from anyone that got too close.

But tonight he was about to go back into action, and get dirty.

As the applause finally began to die down, Minardi checked his watch, "It is time, let's go."

As they walked through the thinning crowds, Minardi updated Forbes. "His name is Giovanni Mosca, born in Napoli, but commits crime all over Italy. He's never homesick."

"What are these crimes?"

"Patience, I'm coming to the good bit."

"Go on."

"He works as a security guard in the museum here in Verona. How he got the job I'll never know, he's been convicted of selling stolen good."

"What goods?"

"Paintings."

"Bingo."

"Whatever, he was on vacation the last two weeks in May."

"This just keeps getting better."

"We are going to see him now, his shift started half an hour ago."

Forbes put a restraining hand on Minardi's arm, "Okay hold it right there. This is not your fight. I'm going in alone." The look in his eyes told Minardi it was not worth even trying to argue.

"Okay, the museum is called 'The Castle' it's beyond Scaliger Bridge."

"I know it."

"You only have tonight. I release my findings at nine in the morning. Oh and, Bill, this meeting never took place."

"Release away, I only need tonight, to establish if he's our man, then I will need as much help as I can muster." The smile was supposed to reassure Minardi that all was under control. It didn't. They shook hands and went their separate ways.

FORBES CROSSED THE BRIDGE, AND ENTERED THE castle by the small wooden drawbridge.

Once within the courtyard, floodlights illuminated his route to the other side of the well-trimmed lawn. As instructed, he arrived at the museum's security entrance. He put on his surgical gloves and pressed the intercom. After a moment the door buzzed loudly. He pressed against it, and entered the museum. As the door shut, he felt the press of stone walls close around him.

No matter what wonderful contents are on display, an empty building at night still feels eerily empty. Only the emergency lighting illuminated the corridor. Forbes listened to his own footsteps echo off the stone-flagged floor. There was no chance of sneaking up on anyone in here.

In the first of the 29 rooms open to the public, he was immediately struck by the austere elegance of the architecture, majestic, yet not without a hint of frivolity. The castle dated back to 1356. Built on the orders of Cangrande II della Scala, to serve the dual purpose residential palace and stronghold. It still had a feeling of strength in its structure. Forbes let his fingers trail along the stone wall. So where was this man Mosca?

He breathed in the fabric of history, during the years the castle has been used as an ammunition depot, a military collage and barracks, such is its vastness. In 1925 it became home to the Verona Civic Museum.

Forbes followed the signs to the main reception.

In the modernised reception area, a light shone from beyond a frosted glass door, it painted a weird shape on the glass. Forbes knocked. No answer. The emptiness was overbearing. The silence seemed to mock him.

"Senior Mosca?" No response. No radio music, no smell of cigarettes. Nothing. It was as if Forbes were standing in a crypt.

"Hello! Senior Mosca." Louder this time, surely it would provoke a response. After all someone had buzzed him in.

His patience began to wear thin, and frustration crept into his attitude. Was it time to take yet another little pill?

Taking control of his actions, Forbes opened the door. The table-lamp lay on its side, shining up onto the leg of the table, a broken PC monitor smashed on the floor, a plastic in-tray lay close by, split in two. Papers were strewn over the floor.

The office had been ransacked, Forbes's mind screamed

at him to get out and call the police. He stepped into the office, his hand still on the door-knob.

Looking over the desk slumped against the back wall, he saw the beaten and bloodied corpse of Giovanni Mosca, arm thrown carelessly to his side.

It appeared this had been the right route to follow in his search for the paintings, and the corpse told him that he was not alone in his search.

Someone had buzzed him in.

Forbes closed the door behind him. The office was too small for the murderer to be hiding in, and it wasn't as if Mosca was going to get up and fight him.

Forbes felt his head go light, the room began to spin. He grasped hold of the desk to stop himself from falling. "Get a grip man," he chided himself.

He began sounding off the names of everything he could see, he desperately needed to focus. "Papers, chair, filing cabinet, computer."

The world stopped spinning. Forbes stumbled around the desk. Crouching by the body, he recognised that death had been recent, very recent. The blood was still fluid, the bruised and pulped face was still warm.

Someone had buzzed him in.

Forbes tried to find the epicentre of the fight. He kicked aside the in-tray, and nudged the computer with his toe, the disc tray remained closed.

The drawers were closed on the filing cabinet. The struggle and search, he concluded, had been centred on the desk.

His memories kicked in. Mogadishu, Somalia. Christmas, 2006. Forbes giggled to himself, "Damn your eidetic memory."

He remembered the sound of wild-dogs barking on a rubble-strewn African street; it felt so real it made him look over his shoulder. It was a memory he'd never needed to forget, not until the Belgrade catacombs. After that memory everything had changed.

Forbes felt the African heat on his body. He recognised the change in his body odour, he smelt of Africa again. Although he was looking through a ransacked office in Verona, he imagined he was back in Mogadishu.

The hot sweaty night had been a race against time. Then the task had been to find a mobile phone, which a Somali pirate had programmed as a detonator.

A yacht in the harbour would be blown-up unless he found the phone. Now, Forbes felt the same imperative, but unlike Mogadishu he did not know what he was looking for, or why it was a race against time…

Someone buzzed him in.

"Someone buzzed me in," Forbes came back to reality with a shock. The cabinet was untouched, the drawers closed. The killer had not completed his search. Whatever he was looking for in the office was still here. Forbes had interrupted the search when he arrived.

The fight had centred on the desk, the room began spinning again. Forbes scanned the floor, what was so important in here? From the back of his mind he heard the swish of the machete. Suddenly, the Somali pirate was here in the room with him, Forbes faced him. The pirate charged forward.

The two timelines had collided. He felt the hot breath of the pirate on his cheek. The pirate swung the machete, in his mind it cleaved into his skull.

Forbes dropped to the floor to avoid the blow. His hand crunched down on broken glass, the pain brought him back to the here and now.

With a gasp he was back in the office in Verona. Mosca lay where he always had. The 'thrown-out arm' was pointing to this very spot. Forbes felt the glass cut through the thin glove and into his palm, he ripped off the gloves.

He looked down and saw an abstract shape turn into a photo-frame.

A shiver brought him back to reality. He remembered that the pirate had missed with the machete; but Forbes had not missed with his Glock.

Forbes picked up the photograph. The memory of Mogadishu was all but gone. The fetid smell of death was explained by the corpse beside him. The months he'd spent in rehab, recovering from Post-Traumatic Stress Disorder were forgotten now. Surely this was the evidence he needed, Mosca was actually pointing at it. Forbes turned the frame over to look at the picture.

Five individuals stood on board a yacht. Wide smiles and expensive sunglasses greeted him. Two men in mock tough-guy poses, at each end of the group. White tee-shirts barely containing the bulging steroid fuelled muscles of Giovanni Mosca and Tommaso Buscetti. In the centre of the picture stood LeCoyte Chellen, his arm encircling the waist of a copper haired beauty. Forbes studied her face. Her hair. He looked closely, there was something in her hair, suddenly he desired to understand what it was, and who she was.

Forbes turned the frame over and prised open the clips.

He slid the photo from the frame and looked at the back of the picture.

In the top left-hand corner, printed in pencil was the legend, **Monaco 2008**. To the centre left of the lower half, were the words **Sotheby contact**. On the corresponding right side were a series of capital letters, Forbes read them out aloud. "**S.E.N.G.A.M.**"

Forbes turned the photo over again, and looked at the group of five. Here was the evidence he wanted. Five people, together. Two men already linked with the Paris art theft, now dead, were linked to the man, Forbes believed was capable of masterminding the theft; ruthless enough to have the loose-ends taken care of, and self-righteous enough to have the five masterpieces locked away for his eyes only. Forbes now also knew that Chellen had a contact in Sotheby's.

Forbes said a quick silent prayer over Mosca's body. Placing the photograph in his pocket he left the office, needing all the time he had left, before the police got involved, to explore the link with Sotheby's and the mysterious SENGAM.

GINGERLY, THE MAN RUBBED HIS INDEX FINGER OVER the puckered scabbing scar that had formed just above his hairline. In the three weeks since receiving the wound, he'd had neither the time nor inclination to get it stitched.

After killing Mosca, his plan had been to take the photograph and leave Verona without delay. But fate had conspired against him. The intercom had rung, and Mosca had buzzed someone in at the precise moment his attack had begun.

Now he waited in his car behind the bushes, like a voyeur. He'd watched Mosca's visitor as he stood by the glass-door, 'Arrogant pig. Pompous Englishman.' he'd thought to himself.

Now through hooded eyes he watched the man come across the bridge. He pulled his finger away from the scab on his scalp, and picked up his night-vision camera. In silence he clicked away, getting a nice side view, and an adequate front shot. Then the man seemed to throw his head back in a strange jerky motion, almost like he was taking an aspirin. The camera snapped again and again until the man was out of sight. The man with the scar, reasoned that the Englishman had the photograph in his pocket. Even if he didn't, there would be no time to go back and look for it. The police would be here within minutes. With a grim determination to discover the identity of the visitor, he drove away. The chain reaction of events was underway.

Chapter Five

Le Pigeon aux petits-pois (Picasso 1911)

London, England.
Monday, June 14.

KAYLEE DEAN WORE HER MOST EXPENSIVE MAKE-UP, this was after all London. Christie's auction-house South-Kensington, to be exact. After a quick flutter of her eyelashes, the doorman had allowed her to sit at the back of the saleroom.

The idea was, Kaylee would get an interview with whoever shelled out the cash; hopefully it would make half a million.

"And now we come to lot 348, the Crosby Garret Helmet. Recently found in Cumbria, the helmet is one of only three examples ever to be found. It dates from the 1st century AD ..." Kaylee had already lost interest when the bidding started. She busied herself texting a friend, until ...

"At one million with you sir." The distinguished gentleman at the podium, in a pin-stripe suit and mauve tie, horrid combination, was looking at ...Kaylee stretched over to see who was bidding, but all she could see was an animated Asian girl in a

52

pink Chanel suit, on the phone. The girl stood with a group of five, equally well-dressed others, all with desk phones in their hands, clamped to their ears.

The girl nodded her head. Mr. Mauve-tie looked around the packed room. To his left a paddle lifted above the expensively coiffured hair-cuts.

"At one, one." He looked back to the bank of power dressers behind the gleaming wooden barrier. The Asian girl shook her head. Mauve-tie went back to the room, focusing on where the paddle had been raised. "At one million, one hundred thousand."

A Nazi salute went up from a male model lookalike behind the barrier. Asian girl turned to look at him. He gave her a slight smile. Chemistry?

"One million, two hundred thousand, telephone bid."

The paddle rose again. Kaylee looked to see who was bidding. The saleroom was packed, and from her position, she could see nothing but the backs of heads.

Max the cameraman, squeezed in besides her, "Good job you got your best face on, this is going to be epic, twice the estimate for a sodding old piece of tin."

"Are we selling it?" Mauve-tie asked Male-model. The hand came out again, accompanied by a slight nod of the head.

Kaylee called the doorman over, "Can we film? I'm Kaylee Dean, BBC." She fluttered the eyelashes expectedly, and twisted in her seat to reveal her black nylon clad thighs.

"I'm afraid not Madame, only in the lounge." He gestured out of the door.

"Okay, we'll get the winner out there then." The disarming smile sent him away. The man nodded, and retreated to his original position. Kaylee quickly lent over to Max, "Start filming," she whispered. Time spiralled.

The paddle rose. The audience gasped. "At two million pounds." Mauve-tie's wide eyes went back to the barrier. Male-model was now looking very shaky; he held the phone tight to his ear. Almost in slow motion, the arm came out, the hand formed a blade, and the bid was registered.

"Two point one." The crowd gasped. All eyes turned back to where the paddle was rising. Everyone waited with anticipation.

"It's with you Madame," he looked around the room, and focused on an innocent, "Do jump in sir, don't wait." The crowd laughed as a man on the front row shook his head rapidly.

Then slowly, as if forced through treacle, Madame responded, and the paddle came up again. The crowd applauded.

"Two million two hundred thousand pounds; in the room." The room thudded with a hundred heartbeats. Mauve-tie's wide eyes went back to the barrier.

Male-model shook his head.

"Are we all done?" He looked around the room, it was as still as a painting, hung on the nail of expectation. Everyone held a collective breath. A lot of people near to the paddle were looking at the bidder. Kaylee felt like she was about to dive off a high board. She held her breath.

"Two million two hundred thousand ladies and gentlemen." He opened his hand, gesturing to the paddle bidder. "With you. Are we selling? As he raised his gable, Male-model's salute rose again. The crowd screamed no pretence at being civilized anymore. Mauve-tie watched the agitated Male-model's gestures. "Fair enough, Two million two hundred and fifty thousand pounds."

Male-model pulled the phone away from his ear. He wiped his face.

Mauve-tie lent on the podium and looked back at the paddle bidder. "Madame?"

The whole crowd was breathing heavily, like a sprinter who'd just broken the tape. Eyes darted around the room.

"At two million two hundred and fifty thousand pounds; selling to the telephone bidder, fair warning."

The paddle rose, and the crowd let out a primeval scream.

An animated Mauve-tie auctioneer shifted his weight nervously on the podium. He brushed back a stray lock of hair. He announced the bid. He looked back at the telephone bidders at the barrier. Male-model shook his head.

The auctioneer went through the ritual again. Male-model shook his head again. "And selling to your client at two million, three hundred thousand pounds. We've come a long way ... Thank you so much ... fair warning. It's yours; sold." The gable came down, and the crowd erupted.

The members, seated by the paddle bidder were on their feet, hands thrust forward to shake the winning hand.

"Come on," Kaylee nudged Max. It was then that the doorman brought his hand down on Max's shoulder.

"Outside, now!"

Kaylee turned on her most charming smile, "A Roman helmet unearthed in a Cumbrian field in May by a metal detector fan, was sold today for two point three million pounds, here at Christie's saleroom in South Kensington. The figure was almost eight times the estimated value."

Max panned the camera over the exuberant crowd spilling out of the saleroom. With total professionalism Kaylee continued … "The Crosby Garrett Helmet, named after the local village where it was found, was today bought by an anonymous bidder. It will have made its un-named finder and the landowner very wealthy, and because the find was reported under the Portable Antiquities Scheme, it did not have to be declared treasure under the 1996 Treasure Act; because single items of non-precious metal are not covered by that act. The finder and landowner were thus free to dispose of the helmet as they saw fit, and in so much the colossal price has caused a huge disappointment for the Carlisle museum which has spent the last few months frantically trying to raise funds to ensure this exceptional artefact remained in the UK for public display."

Back in the studio, an editor superimposed the artefact on to the screen; the result was stunning. The gleaming bronze helmet gently rotated.

In her ear, the message from the producer, "Beautiful Kaylee, beautiful." Her charming smile remained painted and constant, "It is unclear what will now happen to the wonderful bronze discovery, the buyer may plan to keep it here in a private collection, or they may apply to take it overseas. Such a request however might cause the government to step in and impose an export bar."

"Exceptional work Kaylee," the voice in her ear encouraged.

"I'm joined now by one of the thwarted bidders for the famous bronze helmet, Mr Giles Braithwaite from the Tullie House museum, Carlisle." Kaylee positioned herself to interview to new arrival, "Mr Braithwaite, if a request were made to export this unique artefact from British soil, what steps could be taken to prevent the buyer from depraving the British public of this wonderful find?"

Braithwaite cleared his throat, "A restraining order could be invoked by the Government. This would allow time for various UK institutes to support our own bid and agree a price with the new owner to retain the helmet here."

"I understand Tullie House museum had been fundraising in the build-up to the auction, hoping to buy the helmet, and keep the artefact in the UK?"

"Yes, we had secured a quarter of a million pounds from the National Heritage Fund, at the British Museum, a further fifty-thousand award from the Art Fund, private donations took our was chest up to half a million. We thought that was enough. But once the bidding went beyond that; we were resigned to the outcome."

"I understand only two bidders were involved beyond the estimated value. Tell me what would make this item so desirable?"

"The helmet, one of only three such items ever found, is almost 2,000 years old. Described by experts as an extraordinary example of Roman metalwork at its zenith, an immensely interesting and outstandingly important find ... Its face-mask is both extremely finely wrought and chillingly striking, but it is as an ensemble that the helmet is so exceptional and, in its specifics, unparalleled. It is a find of the greatest national and, indeed, international significance."

"Thank you." Kaylee smiled at the camera again. This story would run, she would make sure of that, now all she needed to do was track down the winner.

SENGA MUNREAUX, PRONOUNCED MONROE (LIKE Marilyn) touched her décolletage, to her surprise she discovered she was sweating, *'wait'*, she thought, *'men sweat, women perspire'*, she laughed, *'and ladies merely glow'*. Well she certainly didn't feel like she was glowing at this moment.

"Two million, three hundred thousand pounds for an ancient Roman helmet, what was I thinking of?" she asked herself.

Senga didn't have that kind of money to throw around, and yet here she stood the proud owner of the Crosby Garrett Helmet.

The administrator, Julian Pritchard, finished the contract papers with a flurry of fingers on his keyboard, "That's all in order Miss Moonricks. Full payment due by the fifth of July."

"It's Moon rue, M.U.N.R.E.A.U.X." Senga corrected him about the pronunciation. "Thank you," her soft Scottish accent warmed the room, but her cold mind was firmly fixed on how she was going to pay for the monstrosity. She had three weeks to hand over the entire sum. It was certainly a very challenging time-frame that she had just signed-up to. But it was necessary. She had to have the helmet; it was all part of her plan to get her life back.

Senga knew the next three weeks were going to be very stressful. Life beyond that, she hoped would get back to normal really quickly, but in the interim it would be a fine balance between waiting for some British institution to step forward with an elaborate plan to keep the artefact in the UK and thus recompense her with most of her outlay, and allow her 'rights' to show the helmet at her convenience, and staying out of the way of her creditors.

She needed cash to pay off her new debt. How much, was

up to how much the British museum were prepared to offer her. Worse case meant embarking on a scheme which was her most adventurous yet. With a sense of foreboding, she took the paperwork, still warm from the printer.

A cold wind blew from the East on Old Brompton road; Senga pulled her silk scarf close to her throat. England on a cold June day wasn't the place to be right now. *'Sod global warming'*. Right now she needed space, and sun, and the means to get her money, and that meant ...Noah.

❧◯

St Tropez, France,
Tuesday, June 15.

IT WAS A ROOM WITH A RICH HISTORY OF DEATH.

From March to November, from dawn 'till dusk, sunlight poured in through the meticulously clean windows. It was the window area which dominated the small square attic room, and allowed the light to pour in. It was the light that poured in, which made the work completed in the room, such a joy to behold.

As well as its history of death, it was also a room where people came to life.

From great sea-battles, to peaceful country-scenes, lithe and graceful characters were born, died, and captured in time. Their lives documenting a history for future generations to admire. Viewers of the work soon became one with the paintings that were produced in this room.

You could almost hear the bugle; smell the dust kicked up by the horses' hooves. Feel disgust at the decay of the bodies on the battlefields, and feel repulsed at the garbage rotting on the slimy streets of Dickensian London.

With eyes that always appeared to be smiling, Noah Coleman viewed the two identical canvases, placed on his battered old suitcase, precariously balanced between two scruffy dinning-chairs in the centre of the room. The paintings glowed as the sunlight poured over them.

He'd already dragged a paint-stained table away from the viewing area, it was full of squeezed-up tubes of paint, so he covered it with an equally paint-stained sheet. It now stood close to an easel in the corner of the room.

Beyond these eclectic mix of objects, the room was devoid of all other pieces of furniture. The room had a special purpose.

No carpets, only a plain wooden floor of sun bleached once varnished floorboards.

Noah Coleman had a keen eye for detail, and now he watched in fascination as the sunlight caught the particles of dust that had tumbled from the sheet as he'd shaken it. The particles tumbled and twirled as if they were leaves, shaken free by strong wind. He watched the particles fall to the floor.

In the tramline gaps between the floorboards, fallen droplets of oil formed a veritable kaleidoscope of colour, a fragment of magenta here, a blob of ochre there. He glimpsed a blue; it was the same Wedgewood blue as seen on the lower sleeve of the 1885 Pastel portrait of the *'Lady at the Spinning Wheel'*

Further up the gap, he saw the vivid salmon pink which he recognised from a schooner's sail in Richard Mark's magnificent *'Shipping off Portsmouth'*

"Nothing too famous," said Noah. That was his philosophy. It was a good and profitable philosophy to have too. Good for a forger. It was that discipline over the years that had kept him off the radar, kept good shirts on his broad shoulders and good wine in his adequate cellar.

Noah Coleman had been fifty-years old for more years than he cared to remember. He'd once been an athletic man with an ambitious face, and the fathomless mind of a rogue.

This was the room in which Noah produced his finest work. Stripped of furniture, devoid of luxury, in itself it was bland, but it produced works of untold beauty. The walls had long ago given up the strain, and cracked in a mosaic of plaster flakes, and yet it brought endless pleasure to those that put their faith in a misplaced perception of knowing about art.

The sunlight hit the canvases again, a new day was about to be born. Noah flexed his long fingers, zipped up his leather jacket, he was about to go to work.

ST TROPEZ, A SMALL FISHING VILLAGE IN THE SOUTH of France, was transformed into the people-watching capital of the World, in the 1960's. Adored by the people who go there to be seen, and the tourists who flock there for a glimpse of the rich and famous.

Tourists strolled past the harbour-front café, glancing at, but not recognising the couple that sat at the front table. The couple weren't famous, but still the tourists looked, mainly it was because of the couple's je ne c'est quoi.

In their minds, the tourists would dream up a theories about who the couple were, film stars? No, were they film producers?

Possibly, no one could have guessed their real profession, or their reason for being there.

If only they'd known the woman had just bought the Crosby Garett Roman helmet for two point three million pounds, and the man sitting with her was one of the best forgers in the world. If only they'd known.

Senga Munreaux pronounced Monroe (like Marilyn) was a complicated person. Even her name was a puzzle.

Born in Hamilton, Scotland 1972, she studied at Glasgow School of Art. Graduating with an honours degree in Graphic design, she believed her career lay in advertising. But, a chance romantic encounter in Chamonix in 2005 led to a far more interesting vocation with Sotheby's auction-house New Bond Street, London, and later the Met, in New York.

She was attractive, by anybody's standards; high cheekbones, punctuated with vulnerable little freckles, cute button nose and the clearest pale green eyes ever to be seen on the Cote D'Azure. When she fluttered her eyelashes, the suggestion of a calm summer's day came ambling to mind. Combine those looks with a mane of copper-coloured hair, which she wore long and natural, with only an antique ivory Toucan-billed hair-grip, to keep the long tresses out of her face, and Senga Munreaux was guaranteed to be noticed wherever she sat.

With the precision of a surgeon she placed her white china coffee-cup exactly in the centre of the saucer. Job done, she glanced over at the man sitting opposite.

Noah Coleman, pronounced Coleman was by contrast a very simple person, with simple needs, pleasures and desires. He loved fine wines, fast cars, expensive women, and the thrill of a gamble. So much so, that he had been making and losing vast fortunes since before Senga Munreaux was born.

Today he wore his black Gucci leather jacket, purchased as the result of an outsider winning at Longchamp. He wore it over a torn white cotton tee-shirt, the result of a small silver ball dancing over the number 16 gate of a roulette wheel. With the true patience of a gambler, he now waited for her to speak. Instinctively he knew she was growing inpatient.

"Well, am I to leave here empty handed then?" Senga's Scottish accent tumbled out.

Noah didn't reply immediately, he took a drink from his wine glass, fished out a crumpled fifty euro note, slipping it beneath the ashtray that sat between them. "Come on then." His accent was harder to pin down.

As Senga stood up to leave, Noah pointed to her handbag. "Loop it over your shoulder; keep it on your hip. Hand over the top."

Senga frowned, "Why?"

"Pickpockets," he explained, his brow furrowed as he glanced around at the crowds; they swelled around them.

Senga looked at the tourists around them; she saw no danger in their faces.

"Seriously, pickpockets they're everywhere," he cautioned.

"I really don't know how you stand it here," Senga said ironically, thinking back to the miserable weather in London. "But you keep your cash in your pockets."

"Well if it weren't for the pickpockets, I wouldn't have a sex life at all."

Senga smiled openly, acknowledging his joke, "Very funny.

But really why do you stay here? You could make so much more in New York, or Moscow."

Noah linked arms with her and they began to walk. He pointed to the buildings. "Art and St Tropez are intrinsically linked ... Paul Signac discovered it, and inspired the likes of Maitisse and Marquet. Then the next generation fell in love with the light. David Hockney, Massimo Campigli ..." Noah glanced at his companion and could instantly see she'd lost all interest in his explanation. He raised his brow, and abruptly changed the topic. "My place is just up ahead."

He brought her to a halt outside a nineteenth century terraced façade. As Noah pulled the key from his pocket the front door opened, and a large sweaty man in a grey raincoat pushed passed them muttering some kind of an apology.

Senga looked at Noah, but before he could say anything a buxom, very attractive Afro-Caribbean girl appeared at the door. Her dark eyes and infectious smile lit up when she saw Noah. "Sharky!" She embraced and kissed him passionately on the lips. "Don't pay to worry to that 'needle dick' he weren't here no longer than a handshake." Her accent melted Jamaican and TV show American over a sensual French chocolate bar of English.

"Hello Daisy, been busy?" Noah asked.

The black girl gave Senga a 'once-over' look, instantly appraising her as a love rival. Recognising her beauty, she turned back to Noah. "Busy? No. I told you he was only here for a couple of minutes." She smoothed her voluptuous hair, and extenuated her ample bust. "Now unfortunately I have to go and cook some good *garlicy* food for those nice tourists who have too much money, and like cheap wine served in expensive bottles."

"You have a good night."

"Are you two going to be here when I get home? I'll bring oysters, so I can play too." She looked at Senga from beneath her eyelids.

"No Daisy, you've got it wrong this is a business colleague," said Noah hurriedly.

"But of course, and I know what kind of business." Her smile was inviting, her laughter infectious.

"This is work, art work." Noah's brow furrowed, revealing two vertical creases. "Now do me a favour, bring home a fillet, and a St Emillion," he gave her a fifty euro note. Daisy took it in her long slender red nailed fingers.

"Just for the two of us, oui?" she pouted.

Noah nodded. The girl squeezed past and tottered down the cobbled street on outrageously thin healed bright red stilettoes.

Senga looked up at Noah, "Sharky?"

They entered the house. "Yes, it's her name for me. You know, Noah. Noah's Ark – Shark."

"You live with her?" It came out too quickly.

"We have an arrangement." Noah began climbing the stairs.

"By the hour I bet." Senga watched the black girl as she walked away, she couldn't have been much older than thirty. She moved with sexually assured confidence that was guaranteed to be appreciated by anyone watching.

"She's been on more hotel pillows than chocolates, but I love her."

On the fourth floor, Noah opened the door. Its rusty hinges whined like an air-raid siren. Senga followed him into the room.

Sunlight flooded the attic, illuminating two identical paintings which sat side by side on a battered old suitcase.

Senga made directly for them, "Incredible. Really Noah, this is fantastic, which one is mine?"

"You tell me. Which one did you pay nearly half a million for?" he teased, challenging her to identify the fake.

Senga exhaled. Lovingly she ran her experienced fingers over the two canvases. She sensed history in both pieces. "Well one isn't still wet?"

Noah offered her a small tortoise-shell Loupe, "To help you with the detail."

"No thanks, I'm on top of this. Don't forget I own it." But it took a full minute, in which time her admiration for Noah's talents grew, before she made her choice. "This one," her finger tapped the corner.

"How did you know?" Noah asked rather theatrically.

"Am I right?" her high pitched answer gave away the fact she had guessed.

"It was a guess wasn't it?" Noah took the painting from her; he tipped it up and allowed the sunlight to play across the canvas.

"Yes, it was a pure guess," she confessed. "It really doesn't matter though. Sotheby's have already validated the provenance of the real painting."

"Good," Noah continued, "Let me just see if I have this right. The real painting, your painting, is going to be exhibited and sold at Sotheby's; but after the sale, you are going to substitute the forgery. The buyer takes it away, gives you half a million, and you keep your own Oleg."

"Yes I make half a million out of the deal."

"If that's what it makes?"

"I paid four hundred thousand for it, it will have appreciated during the years I've had it, besides the deal is that you get everything over the half a million mark. You must think it's going to make more."

"Okay," Noah placed the painting against his chest. "I have a proposition; it will make you another two hundred fifty thousand pounds. What do you say?"

"I'm listening."

Chapter Six

PORTRAIT IN VALENCIA (OLEG 2005)

St Tropez, France.
Tuesday, June 15.

THEY'D MOVED DOWN ONE FLOOR, TO A COMFORTABLE lounge, with a lived in sofa and a smell of jasmine.

Noah placed the two paintings on top of the battered old suitcase, "You told me one of the potential bidders has already seen the Oleg."

"Yes, in Geneva." Her tone was noncommittal.

"Do you think he would buy privately?"

"Yes," Senga said hesitantly.

"Okay here's the plan. I do two forgeries. Then, you sell one forgery privately." He handed her the first painting, and picked up the other from the suitcase.

"I could speak to my buyer in Geneva."

"Good. Sell it to him. Tell him half a million is a bargain. Then substitute the second forgery into the auction, so it's discovered after it's been sold. You get half a million for the first; I get anything over the top. You get the first two hundred fifty thousand from the auction buyer, I get everything above that."

"But I won't get any money from the auction buyer when it is discovered to be a forgery … and the police will."

"Forget about any police, I'll explain in a moment."

"But my buyer will know that he has a fake when the Oleg goes up for auction."

"When the scandal breaks at Sotheby's, that they had a fake in their auction, your private buyer will believe he has the real painting." Noah handed her the second painting.

Senga laughed, "Hey I don't want to mix them up."

Noah opened the battered suitcase on which they had rested, "Oh, it doesn't matter, they're both fakes." Inside the case the real painting sat on a blue silk cushion.

"These are both yours?" she held them out to appraise them.

"Yes, one for your man in Geneva; half a million; and one to substitute in the auction for another half a million, of which I get fifty percent. Now don't mix them up, you don't want to end up with one of my forgeries, seeing as how you can't tell the difference." his smile would have melted anyone's heart.

Senga thought about the plan, "What's this about a scandal at Sotheby's?"

"We let them test the forgery after the auction. It's a fake. Your first private buyer is assured his copy is real. Then you replace the fake with the real one. Sotheby's test again and end up with egg on its face. You approach the auction buyer, who is now convinced the painting is real, it was all a terrible misunderstanding, and you sell to him privately."

"The risk would be a second buyer would be scared off."

"There's always a risk at auction. You know who is likely to have bided. He will be over the moon when you deal with him directly. I just added a little bonus. If we work on half a million sale price, it is an extra two hundred and fifty thousand pounds for you; and you get to keep your own Oleg."

Senga smiled, she went through the plan again. "You really are the best."

"I like to think so."

Almost as an afterthought she asked, "What if my first buyer does the tests," doubt spread through her voice. "Surely he will do tests. The forgery won't pass the tests will it?"

"When he sees that a forgery was uncovered in Sotheby's, he will assume his is the real painting," Noah asserted.

"It won't pass the test will it?" Senga insisted.

"There are two types of x-rays used in art authentication. One, stereo-radiography, works the same way as a medical x-ray, sees beneath the skin. Two, autoradiography, which uses beta particles, sort of brings the painting out in 3D, and then they can measure the colour spikes to see if it matches with the paint used when the original was produced. Both methods are in frequent use, and both will show different things that would be missed by the naked eye."

"I'm aware of the different procedures, Noah. What I want to know is what will happen when they put your forged Oleg through the machine?"

Accompanying his message, Noah waggled his head, "Um; x-rays see through the different layers of paint. X-rays can show where touch-ups have been made, or where an artist has painted over something he already had on the canvas. In order to create the complete picture of all the layers, the rays pass through the painting and create a negative of darker areas on film. Think of it as reverse photography. After the rays are passed through the painting, old layers of paint can be seen, and the investigation can begin. An expert verifier can tell if it is consistent with the known preparation and painting methods of a particular artist. They ask, are the hidden compositions similar to the style that the artist used? In order to find these hidden paintings within a certain work of art, the technician will apply a certain amount of kilo-voltage. That's basically a measurement of how intense or weak the x-ray beam is. The more kilo-voltage applied, the more it reveals what's beneath the painting. The technique can be compared to changing the contrast on the TV, when it goes from white to black. The more kilo-voltage that's used, the better you can see what's underneath. It is said that a good radiographer uses the intensity of the kilo-voltage to paint a picture-"

"Noah!" Senga halted his flow, "will your forgeries stand up to that level of investigation?"

"Time will be on our side, the owner will be compelled to believe he has the real article when he sees a forgery in London. He won't check it."

"They will fail won't they?"

"If they use a Gilardoni Radiolite x-ray machine, my forgeries will fail."

"Shit!"

"But he won't have time to organise a test before the auction," Noah said reassuringly, "generally only art laboratories have use of that kind of machine. If he has a verifier with him, and he has an x-ray machine, it is likely they will only scan with *grenz* rays. With that machine the wavelengths are long, and less intense."

"Why would they only have an x-ray machine, and not a Gilardoni?"

The Gilardoni, is a big, and expensive piece of kit, not easily portable. They don't even have one at Sotheby's. That's how the mix-up will occur. Most likely your man will only have an ordinary x-ray machine."

"Will your forgeries pass an x-ray test?"

"Yes," Noah answered quickly. Senga thought it was probably a lie.

"How much time will I have?"

"Enough." Noah nodded, offering reassurance.

Senga thought the plan even more audacious then her own, certainly more risky, but she did need the extra money. The time scale was right. Currently she was a million down on the two point thee million she owed. The sale of the two forgeries would give her three quarters of a million.

She looked at the forgeries, seven hundred and fifty thousand would go a long way, but it wasn't enough, absently she said, "I don't suppose you have a Picasso hanging around do you?"

"If you're talking about the 'Pigeon with his peas', then no. I don't do anything that news worthy."

"But hey, what a scam that would be, reproduce the five paintings stolen from the Museum of Modern Art. And I am reliably informed you should refer to the *Pigeon* as the *Dove*."

Noah snorted in derision, "The Picasso is more affectionately known as the *Café*. Whoever took them has a real problem on his hands."

"Explain."

"No one will touch them. Only hope any thief has is to ransom them back to the museum."

"The police always catch them at the handover point."

"Exactly, so best just ring-up and tell them where they're hidden."

"You've done your homework," said Senga.

"I have to, a heist that big brings the heat all the way down to my level. The police and the Art Loss Register start to squeeze the market. Squeeze it like a whore squeezing my balls."

Senga looked at him with a disgusted look on her face.

""If it weren't for the whores I wouldn't have a sex life," Noah said lamely.

"You really do have a way with words don't you?"

"And the ladies." He winked.

Senga began packing the three paintings in the battered old suitcase; soon the look of mock disgust wore off, "Have you ever thought of painting an original?"

Noah smiled, and pointed casually to an array of canvases propped against the far wall. "I've done a few portraits and a few harbour views for the tourists. I keep them here to show the gendarmes something when they come knocking. But honestly if I sold them all for double their value it wouldn't pay the bills … I like to go gambling you know."

The suitcase locked with a resounding click. Senga was ready to leave. But she hesitated; she craved more time with this fascinating man.

"What's your favourite painting? She suddenly asked.

Noah looked genuinely taken aback, he blurted out an honest reply, which shocked him at how quickly he had given up his precious secret.

"Actually, it's a painting I've never seen."

Senga screwed up her face, "I'm intrigued, do go on."

Noah suddenly felt compelled to open up to this beautiful woman. Her green eyes sparked, her face glowed, her hair, constrained only by the antique ivory Toucan-billed hairgrip, spilled like a wild wave of excitement over her shoulders. Without hesitation he left the room, returning momentarily with another old battered suitcase.

Senga looked in judgement of the old case.

In response to her silent criticism, Noah said, "I don't like the new plastic cases. Collecting these is like a hobby to me, so many memories."

Senga felt her heart flip at his obvious affinity with old suitcases.

Noah flipped the latches. With reverence he opened the lid, and withdrew a folder. From within it he produced two pieces of age-weary paper, wax-sealed in air-tight plastic bags.

"These are just preliminary sketches."

Senga studied the detailed sketches of fingers, and hands. Each sketch was accompanied by calculations and ratios. She looked into Noah's eyes.

"Here it is," his voice caught. His hand trembled as he passed the second sheet to her.

The same calculations and ratios were written around the outside, in the same handwriting, but in the centre of the page, looking back at her, as bright and vibrant as if it had been drawn yesterday, was the face of a girl.

Suddenly Senga realized there was no face, no confirmation of it being a girl, just a beautiful pair of eyes looking back at her, looking directly into her heart. The symmetry was so feminine as to rule out any other alternative; these were the eyes of a beautiful girl, the eyes without a face, without a hint of corruption. The most beautiful thing she had ever seen.

Senga looked again at the calculations, and then she noticed the date.

"Is this real …genuine, I mean, you know, not a copy." The words tumbled from her mouth in a cascade of wonderment. Her voice was filled with the emotion of a new parent.

Noah nodded. Gently he took back the sketch. "He taught students, similarly as you would today, giving them ideas, helping them with the ratios etc. He drew these for a student named Bernardino Luini."

"He?" Senga's voice was thick with emotion.

Leonardo di ser Piero Da Vinci, born April fifteenth 1452, died May second 1519. He was an Italian polymath. A painter, sculptor, architect, musician, scientist, mathematician, engineer, inventor, anatomist, geologist, cartographer, botanist and writer." He paused for breath. "Often described as the archetype of the Renaissance man. A man whose unquenchable curiosity was equalled only by his powers of invention. Widely considered to be the greatest painter of all time and perhaps the most diversely talented person ever to have lived."

Senga gently manoeuvred Noah's hand so she could study the sketch again. Noah continued, she could have drowned in his voice.

"In 1506, Leonardo returned to Milan, to his studio in Porta Orientale in the parish of Santa Babila. You see I know all the details," he smiled. "This is the period his most prominent students studied under him. They included, Luini, Giovanni Antonio Boltraffio, and Marco D'Oggione." He felt the warmth of Senga's hand radiate up his body. These sketches are Leonardo's actual work notes; his cribs for his pupils."

"How did you come by them?"

He side-stepped the question, "There are other preparatory drawings from the same period. The mouth for instance has equivalent sketches. They are owned by Queen Elizabeth. The sketches reside in Windsor castle." He could see Senga wanted a direct answer. "How did I come by them? That's a long story. I reserve the telling of that tale for after a magnificent banquet."

"How can think of food at a time like this?"

"I'm not talking about food."

Senga let go his hand, "You really are incorrigible."

"Thank you." They both laughed.

Senga spoke in a far off tone, "So could these sketches be the ones actually used by Luini for *The Lady*."

"Yes, I believe so."

"But you've never seen it?"

"No one has, well at least for the last two hundred years or so, it was lost during the French Revolution."

"But …" Noah put his finger on her lips.

Senga pulled his hand away, "Why don't you paint it, claim it as Luini's lost work." As soon as she'd said it she regretted it. The look on his face was savage. Senga felt her cheeks redden with embarrassment. They both stood in petulant silence.

After a moment Noah shook his head to shift the melancholy. "I won't lie, I've often thought about what she would look like."

She turned to him, "Do it then. My contacts would validate it, your sketches would give it provenance." Excitement grew within her making the little freckles across her nose and cheeks stand out, like stars on a dark and sultry night.

"No, she is lost. If I forged her it would be …sacrilege. Luini only ever completed three portraits, his last, 'La Coloumbina' a woman named Albertina, from Vienna, hangs in Benson's London collection. His second was the tinted inferior reproduction of his original 'Portrait of a Lady' it resides in the National Gallery of Art, in Washington. The original and his best is gone forever."

"Have you seen the copy, in Washington?" Senga asked.

"Oh yes, many times. I superimpose the eyes onto the painting; I try to think which fingers he would have used. Have you seen it?"

"Yes, I worked for the New York Met for a number of years, I visited Washington; she's lovely." Senga looked at the sketch to imagine what the original looked like.

"I believe the smile would be a reflection of Leonardo's Mona Lisa; and even with the awkward arrangement of the fingers," Noah held up the 'finger' sketch. "I think you have to say that the original *Portrait of a Lady* was Luini's very personal homage to his teacher." Noah shook his head slowly, the smile left his face. "Call me superstitious but I just can't paint her …I once dreamt that I'd completed her. I saw her clearly, in here," he tapped his temple, "In my dream I saw she was beautiful. I instinctively knew, as one does in dreams, that it had taken me years to complete; but I was so very proud. I put my own signature on it; then as soon as it was done, I simply lay down and died."

"I can see why you're not keen on giving it a go. However

your painting would be worth more if you were dead." She viewed him with an enquiring eye.

"I don't intent to shuffle off this mortal cowl just yet."

"Your choice."

Noah shrugged, "And that is my favourite painting."

"Fascinating." Senga held up the sketch of the eyes without a face.

Noah wasn't sure if she was referring to the sketch or his revelation about the premonition of his own death dream.

"This sketch alone must be worth a fortune."

Noah took the sketch, and held it protectively, "It's not for sale. Ever!" He shook his head in quiet dismissal. He pointed toward the old suitcase containing the two Olegs. "I say go to Geneva. Sell the first painting, then get to London and prepare for the auction. But prepare your bidders for a private sale. Get as much as you can."

"I will. I'll be in touch."

"I'm sure you will." Noah executed a mock bow, still holding the Da Vinci sketch close to his chest.

Chapter Seven

THE JUST JUDGES (VAN EYCK 1430)

London, England,
Thursday, June 24.

HISTORY TELLS US THAT THE CITY OF LONDON HAS certain areas dedicated to specific types of business. Hatton Garden has been the epicentre of London's jewellery trade since medieval times. And so with the value of the merchandise at the forefront in everyone's minds, security is always tight.

The Art Loss Register is an ever developing, global computerized database, capturing data about lost and stolen jewellery, and works of art. It is an independent corporate off-spring of the New-York based, non-profit organization, International Foundation for Art Research.

With significant capital investment being needed to computerize the IFAR, the ALR was founded in 1991, and quickly established as a commercial company in London. It began earning fees from insurers and victims of theft. Its founding shareholders included insurance companies and auction-houses. Usually it was the epicenter of calm, but not today.

79

"We were developed so that our database is available to worldwide law enforcement agencies." Carrington ranted.

"I'm quite aware of our history," Forbes answered politely.

"Then why do you shun the police, and try to do everything on your own?"

"The police and Interpol had come up with nothing for three weeks."

"So you bullied a girl in the CCTV department to override the investigation?"

"I got the results." Forbes thought it pointless to go into detail.

"You compromised the integrity of an officer of the Guardia di Finanza."

Forbes shrugged.

"He might be your friend, Bill, and former army buddy, but he could lose his job over assigning national police computer time to your investigation. We have Interpol for that. For Christ sake Bill, use them."

"Point taken."

"Anyway, how did you discover the whereabouts of this Mosca chap?"

"It was in Minardi's report."

"No it wasn't; and how did you get an appointment to see Mosca?"

"I don't remember."

"And did you take a photograph from the crime scene?"

"I don't remember." Forbes responded calmly, there was no trace of the panic attack he'd had in the Verona office now.

"Don't you remember anything, to any of the questions?" Carrington asked.

"That's right," answered Forbes.

"What a coincidence, and I don't believe in coincidences, Bill." His face was getting redder.

"Neither do I, what a coincidence."

"Don't get clever with me, Bill, not unless you want to admit that memory-loss is a side effect of your PTSD, along with depression, hallucinations and schizophrenia, in fact all manner of mental-health issues are side effects. Anyone of which could get you thrown off this investigation, and for not reporting a murder, thrown into prison!"

"People suffering from stress often blot out memories that are the cause of their anxiety, it becomes a subconscious protector. And of course you know I've suffered from all of those symptoms; so why not memory loss?"

"So that's your response to the Italian police is it?"

"Do you think I'm making it all up?"

'Don't joke, Bill. With your condition the brain compensates by introducing humour, I understand that. Helps you make a joke out of the actual root-cause of the problem."

"I'm not thinking of going into stand-up."

"Really? You're wearing the right get-up." Immediately he felt guilty about bring up Forbes's bizarre taste in clothes.

"What? You're psychoanalysing my dress-sense?" Forbes knocked an imaginary piece of fluff from his Highland-green and blue check jacket.

"I'm deliberating whether it would be beneficial for you to have more therapy?"

"Beneficial for whom?"

"For you of course. Your mind is working against you, stopping you from getting ...better. You still need help, Bill. Your subconscious is protecting you. But you need to lower your guard to allow the psychologists to help."

"My subconscious is not subverting my actions."

"You went to a museum in the dead of night. In the morning a body was found, beaten to death. An empty photo-frame, with your finger-prints, and blood on it. Then we discover that you asked Giancarlo Minardi to run data through the police computer, to get information on the dead man, and all you can say is you don't remember anything."

"Wow Michael, you make it seem so black and white, what a just-judge you are. Do you think I killed Mosca?"

"That's how your condition works, Bill. Without you knowing it. If you don't agree to get help you'll be on medication for the rest of your life ...and be out of a job ...and probably in jail."

"Oh well if you put it that way. I'll go and see Doctor Hall." Forbes stood, intending to leave. Half way to the door Carrington asked, "What was in the photograph?"

Forbes was about to play the innocent and deny taking it, but Carrington shook his head, "It'll go no further, Bill."

Forbes walked back to Carrington's magnificent desk, and showed him the photograph. "That's Giovanni Mosca and Tommaso Buscetti. He stole the credit-card that bought the cutters that broke into the museum. That is LeCoyte Chellen, the man I consider to be the prime suspect in the theft."

"And those two?"

Forbes flipped the photo over. "Sotheby's contact? However, it's a two year old photo. Sotheby's have nothing to do with the Paris theft. I want to go after Chellen. I think he did it."

Carrington read everything on the back of the photo. "What's SENGAM?"

Forbes looked at the girl's face on the photo, he hoped she had nothing to do with the theft. "I don't know, yet."

Carrington sat back, and rubbed his fingers through his hair. "You didn't kill that man did you?"

"No, he was already dead when I got there. But, as neither of us believes in coincidence, I think he was killed because of his involvement in the Paris theft."

Carrington focused in the middle distance, after a moment he said quietly, "Make an appointment to see Doctor Hall when you've finished your investigation. I will confirm to the Italian police that you get memory loss when faced with trauma."

"Thank you."

"Keep looking for the paintings, but remember, you're not alone in your search anymore."

London, England,
Thursday, June 24.

THE DOORBELL RANG. SENGA WIPED THE SLEEP FROM her eyes, threw back the duvet and stumbled to the window, stretching the stress of the late night flight into Heathrow from her body. A Royal Mail van sat in the courtyard. The doorbell rang again. Senga grabbed her dressing-gown and went to the front door.

She peered through the spy-hole and instantly recognised the Hi-Viz jacket of the Royal Mail. She opened the door. The postman, of East European origin, held up a shoe-box sized parcel. "Parcel for you Miss."

Senga un-hooked the chain from the door, and pulled it open. Suddenly the postman thrust the box into her face. As her arms came up to protect herself, he dropped the box and pushed her back into the apartment.

Once inside, he single handily grabbed her throat. The pressure of his fingers shocked her. Her airway closed. In panic her hands seized his arm, but she was no match for his strength. She looked into his face, Turkish she decided. His eyes stared back with devilish intent.

With dread, she realized he was not alone, at his shoulder stood another man; with even more dread she realized that she recognised him, they had met only yesterday in Geneva. She remembered his name was Key.

He stood midway between five and six-foot tall. He wasn't muscular, but what he lacked in bulk he made up for in attitude. He had a hatefully thin mouth, and an abusive look in his eye. A mop of tight curly hair indicated he was not in the least bit, fashion conscious.

The Turk pushed her up against the wall. Key closed the door, flicking down the lock with wicked intent. He turned slowly, chilling the room with his stare.

He had been introduced to her as Head of Security for the Chellen Corporation, Senga concluded that part of his remit would include beating up anybody that upset the company's chairman, LeCoyte Chellen. As he licked his thin lips, Senga thought it would be a task that he enjoyed

With the door closed, the Turk pushed her back into the lounge, arms flailing Senga desperately tried to keep her balance, then with one almighty push, he threw her back onto the sofa.

Senga deduced she had really upset Chellen. As her head cleared she realized that he probably had enough influence to have the use of a Gilardoni Radiolite x-ray machine. The painting therefore had failed the test.

Her hands flew to her throat, as she tried to massage some life back into it, she took in a few massive gulps of air.

"Got your attention have we, Ducky?" Key asked.

Senga nodded an affirmative response. Key produced a rolled-up Sotheby's catalogue from his pocket.

"Mr Chellen would like to understand why a painting he bought from you yesterday is being advertised for auction in here." Slowly he opened the catalogue, and flicked through the pages. His eyes never left hers.

"Lot 247, Portrait in Valencia, by Casper Oleg." He dropped the catalogue on the floor, and stared at her, mouth wide open in astonishment, "We were shocked, shocked and stunned, please, Ducky, can you explain?" His mouth closed and formed an un-friendly smile.

Senga rubbed her throat, "It's a fake."

Key snapped his fingers, "Kill her."

The Turk took a step forward, Senga held up her hands to fend him off. "No, not yours for Christ sake, Mr Chellen has the real painting," the lie came easy to her, "The one to be sold at auction is a fake."

"You'll forgive me if I sound sceptical, Ducky." Key snapped his fingers again; "I would like the cheque Mr Chellen gave you please."

Senga inclined her head to the table, "It's in my bag." Just talking caused waves of pain to go through her throat.

The Turk looked in mock sadness at her as he tipped the

contents of her handbag onto the floor. He scooped up the cheque.

Key reached out and placed his hand on her chin, tilting it up, so that their eyes made contact. Senga shuddered with fear.

"I will be attending today's auction, Ducky. If they take you away in chains for trying to sell a forgery, I will forward the cheque to Holloway prison."

"Holloway," the Turk laughed.

Together the men stood to block out the light, all she could see was them; they dwarfed her. Her body shook in terror. Key straightened his tie, "However, if you succeed in selling the real Oleg …" he let the words hang, "Then my bloodhound here, Mr. Obit, will track you down and rip you apart. You see, Ducky, he has your scent."

The Turk leaned in close, and sniffed at her cheek. He grinned, spittle formed on his lips. It was a sight she would remember for a long time.

∘

Sotheby's Auction-house, London.
Four hours later.

"THE BID STANDS AT £350 THOUSAND. PHONE BID TO MY left," the Auctioneer pointed with his mahogany gable. The light caught on the diamond solitaire on his little finger.

A surreptitious right index finger lifted on the second row. With the eye of a hawk, the Auctioneer picked up the movement, noting the wrist was wrapped in Rolex.

"£375 thousand, to you sir," the Auctioneer looked over the audience, but kept the phone bidder in his periphery.

The girl with the phone in her hand, waggled her slender finger dismissively, and drew her hand across her throat.

The Auctioneer, waved the gable, like a cobra following a flute. Heads turned as a new hand, with an old wedding ring, rose above the crowd.

"£400 thousand, new bidder."

The Rolex rose again. "£425."

Wedding ring surfaced. "£450."

No movement, where was the Rolex?

"Are we selling?" No Rolex. The eyes of the hawk burned into the potential bidder. No movement. The Auctioneer raised the gable, "Fair warning, going once ..."

The Rolex lifted.

"£475, to you sir." A ripple of anticipation ran through the crowd. Hands nervously twitched on laps. Fingers drummed on knees. The Auctioneer tightened his grip on the gable, feeling the smoothness of the mahogany.

"Looking for five hundred thousand pounds." The diamond sparkled.

The wedding ring lifted. "£500 thousand." Then dropped like a shooting star.

The Rolex answered. "£525 thousand." All eyes turned. Palms got sweaty.

Unfalteringly the wedding ring soared above the heads. "£550 thousand."

The heads turned in unison. Rolex met their stare. "£575 thousand."

The bid shot across the saleroom, the wedding ring was

stubbornly thrust into the air. "£600 thousand." Hands came close to cheeks. Heads turned.

In the moment that your foot searches for a non-existent step, and you believe you are falling, it is the same sensation in a dream, right now the entire saleroom was filled with that same sensation. Heads turned, but nothing caught their eye.

Was it over?

"I'm bid £600 thousand. Are we selling?" The diamond sparkled.

Not even a twitch. It was over. The audience waited for the gable to hit the block with the same anticipation of the crowds at a public hanging.

"Going once, twice ..." The gable hit the block, the crack allowed everyone to breathe again, "Sold for 600 thousand pounds."

The silk-gloved hands of the porter placed the painting on a black velvet covered tray; and with a twist of his heels disappeared behind the curtains.

In the privacy of the corridor, the porter passed Senga. "Well done miss."

"Thank you," she croaked, her throat still hurt. She drew her silk scarf around her. She followed the porter, her heart beating louder than her heels clicking on the terracotta tiles.

It was just the two of them in the corridor, a world within a world. The eager muffled sounds of the audience were a long way off. There were no doors, or exits here, there was only one destination; the holding room, and Senga needed to carry out the first part of the plan and swap the paintings before they got there.

Senga knew that in the holding room, an expert verifier

waited to verify the seal that Sotheby's had put on the item before it went to auction.

Senga needed just one brief moment to swap the paintings. The fake Oleg sat in her bag, rubbing against her hip. All she needed to do was swap them over. Then the expert would fail to verify it, and the scandal would erupt, like champagne on a Grand Prix podium.

Senga knew that in Geneva, LeCoyte Chellen would be satisfied that he had just purchased the real Oleg, and that in the audience, Key and Obit would let her live.

"Porter?" Senga attracted him, "Could I just have one last hold of my darling little Oleg," the eyelashes fluttered.

"Of course, miss." With that sexy husky voice, how could he refuse her anything? Anything except a moment alone. She held the painting as they stood looking at each other like lovers about to part. Her mind screamed at him, *'Just turn around!'* But he didn't.

The holding room smelled of embalming fluid, the kind of aroma you get from an old Auntie's parlour.

The independent verifier sat behind a steel and glass desk. He wore a black pin-striped suit, and steel rimmed glasses. Senga smiled at him. She handed over the painting.

The porter confirmed, "Lot 247, Portrait in Valencia."

The verifier took it from her. He noticed she was very pretty, lovey hair, captured by an antique ivory Toucan-billed hair-grip.

"Thank you," he said, but thinking, *'That must have cost a pretty penny'*.

Moments expanded into minutes, breathing became laboured, and loud. Figures were checked. Accusing looks were offered.

The verifier looked at the porter, "Can we put this in the vault please?"

"Yes sir," he bent to pick it up.

"Why?" Senga asked sounding suitably startled.

The verifier removed his glasses, "The seal is incorrect."

"Oh my God!" Senga picked up the painting, "What does that mean?" Panic ripped through her voice, it croaked, it almost broke. Drama had always been her forte.

The verifier stood up, "Nothing for you to worry about. It appears the seal has been tampered with."

"What does that mean?" Senga asked. The porter stood in-between them, like a child witnessing its parents arguing.

"It means a second verification of the authenticity of the painting. I'm sorry I cannot discuss any further."

"Are you saying it's a forgery?" Senga asked with real conviction, the real Oleg lay heavy on her hip.

The verifier smiled, "That's not for me to say."

The porter took the painting from her trembling hands, "I better take this Miss. Senior Cassavanurnez will have to verify the painting," he slipped it into the black velvet pouch. It was identical to the one the real painting now sat in.

"Who? When?" she asked quickly. She had to swap it back before it got to the vault.

"Senior Cassavanurnez will need to do tests, which will be tomorrow now." He went toward the vault. Senga needed to swap the paintings. The verifier was already leaving the room. The porter had no distractions. He was at the vault. Senga needed to act now. He pulled open the vault door. The painting dangled in his hand.

"Wait!" she screamed. Everybody froze. She marched over to the porter and snatched the painting. "Get the manager!"

The verifier turned, "He cannot change anything. I have complete authority this side of the saleroom."

"Check it again," Senga thrust it into his chest.

"No," he pushed it back at her, "If you do not release this painting into the vault immediately I will call security."

The porter arrived at her side, "Just a moment sir, I think a little more tact is needed when dealing with the public."

Senga made her move; she pivoted, turning away from the quarrel between the two alpha males. She moved quickly toward the vault. Now was the moment to switch, and get the real one into the vault. The men were arguing behind her.

"It really doesn't matter, I'm sure this can all be sorted out tomorrow." Senga slipped the forgery against her case. She was just three steps away from the vault. The two men were still arguing. She un-clipped the lock, and tilted her case, the real painting began to slip out. All was going well. Two steps to the vault. She felt the men's eyes upon her. Her skin began to tingle, her heart thudded against her chest. She knew they could not see what she was doing.

One step away. She made the final step. She felt the painting release, it began to slide. He fingers gripped the forgery. Senga imagined everyone would be able to hear it slide out of her case; it was as loud as a sword being drawn from a scabbard, a sound as obscene as tearing silk. The noise consumed her.

"Miss Munreaux?"

Senga's head snapped around, she kept her body taught. The painting rested in her fingers. "Yes," she replied confidently.

With a sudden irrational fear of uniforms she watched, spellbound, as another porter strode across the holding room floor toward her. In the distance, the two men had stopped arguing, and were watching the new scene un-fold.

"Phone call for you Miss," his face was open and smiling, he took the forgery from her hands and marched into the vault, "I'll put this away. Better hurry, it sounded important."

The verifier and the first porter came toward her. She twisted, re-engaging the real painting. As she completed her turn, the catch closed on her case. Her face was frozen. She had failed.

"Are you alright Miss?" the first porter asked. She needed to go into the vault, think of something, quick.

The second porter came out of the vault; he began to close the heavy metal door behind him.

Senga's world began to dissolve; if the door closed she was lost. When Senior Cassavanurnez, tested the painting tomorrow, he would discover it was a fake. Senga would have to explain. The sale would not go through. She would lose the chance of getting the extra two hundred and fifty-thousand pounds. She would miss the fifth of July deadline. She would lose the helmet; she would lose her opportunity to get back with the man of her dreams. Her life dissolved around her and there was nothing she could do about it, just like when you watch an egg rolling off a table, she waited for the crash of the vault door.

It was at that moment, Charles Crombie, director general of Sotheby's marched into the holding room. With an air of superiority he separated the porter and the verifier, pointing an accusing finger into each of their faces, "Stop your bickering, while I establish the problem here. You!" he pointed to the porter at the vault door. "Leave it open, I want to see that painting."

Senga breathed a sigh of relief; her opportunity had opened up again. Her fingers clasped the case. The painting felt hot within it.

"I can assure you the seal has been tampered with," the verifier asserted.

Crombie was an imposing man, six-foot plus, with the body of a rugby player. His face was wrinkled and crinkled, like a bulldog's but his mind was like a steel trap. He arrived in front of Senga. Somehow she had to convince him to let her hold the painting, and then she could swap them over.

"Okay Senga, you go and take your telephone call, I'll sort this mess out."

She heard the words, but she could not accept the consequences. But, before she could react, his giant hands were gently ushering her toward the door. "Go on, don't worry about all this nonsense."

Senga let go of the case, she felt the painting slid back into position. As she walked in-between the porter and the verifier her fixed smile hurt. Like some music-hall villain, the verifier asked Crombie, "WIll the painting be safe in your vault?" his words mocked her need to get at it. Senga left the holding room without looking back.

"I'd like to think so; even I don't have the combination." She heard Crombie telling the verifier.

"Then how can you open the vault in the morning?" his voice challenged.

"The combination is randomly generated at our secure-"

Senga was all too quickly out of earshot, but it didn't matter, she knew where the combination was generated. Suddenly hope flooded through her veins.

She picked up the phone from the porter's table; she noticed her hand was shaking. "Hello."

"Hello Miss Munreaux?" the male voice pronounced it perfectly, Monroe (like Marilyn)

"Yes," she answered, she sometimes wondered if the riddle of her name was really worth it.

"It's Julian Pritchard, Christie's; I thought I'd find you at the saleroom."

"Yes … what is it, I was told it was important," Senga's frustration spilt over.

"Of course. I have some very exciting news about the helmet, and the British Museum."

Another piece of the jig-saw was about to fall into place, Senga composed herself, "Yes?"

"The British Museum, and by association the Government, will not be blocking your application to export the Crosby Garrett helmet. It's yours to take. Isn't that wonderful news?"

The rest of the conversation blurred into insignificance, although she did hear Pritchard reminding her of the deadline for payment.

"Yes, fifth of July, I won't forget." Senga put the phone on its cradle, and began to think how to extract herself from this stinking mess.

MOMENTS AFTER SENGA RECEIVED HER DEVASTATING news, William Forbes opened a routine ALR e-mail. He read that the Sotheby's duty verifier had raised a 'concern' after a sale. He scanned the text. "I require a second verification that *Portrait in Valencia* is genuine, after discovering anomalies with the seal."

Forbes opened the Sotheby's auction web-site. No mention of a potential forgery yet. Forbes smiled at the irony. The scandal was potentially harmful to the auction-house, but as he'd been looking for a reason to visit (after seeing the photograph), it was a most fortuitous incident.

Forbes scanned the on-line catalogue. He knew the painting would be safely closeted in the vault until an independent verifier had given his conclusion on the authenticity of the painting, which would be tomorrow morning earliest, ample time to fly in from Paris.

It had been five weeks since the theft of the five masterpieces. All he had was a photograph of LeCoyte Chellen, and two dead thieves, and a hint of another mystery with a beautiful girl with wild hair and heavenly eyes.

Forbes flipped through the on-line catalogue, he put his personal thoughts to one side. In reality, all he had was a two year old message saying, *Sotheby's contact*.

Suddenly, Forbes leapt to his feet, he grabbed his Highland-green jacket and ran from the office.

The image he'd left burning on the computer was a photograph from the auction catalogue web page.

The photograph showed the painting in question, *Portrait in Valencia* by Casper Oleg. It was being displayed by, quote 'A Sotheby's employee'. A female, with a beautiful smile, heavenly eyes, and a cascade of copper curls, pulled back from her face by an antique ivory Toucan-billed hair-grip. The catalogue legend detailed her name as, Senga Munreaux.

"SENGAM, the Sotheby's contact."

Chapter Eight

LE PRINTEMPS (EDOUARD MANET 1881)

London, England,
Thursday, June 24.

IT WAS A THANKLESS TASK, BUT SOMEONE HAD TO DO it. The Security guard had been on duty at the warehouse for ten straight hours; two more to go. He'd spent the last thirty minutes dividing his attention between *'Angry Birds'* on his mobile, and watching one of his monitors, where two fork-lift trucks, ferried supplies up from the dock.

The warehouse, as it was known to the art loving fraternity of London, was a very secure holding area for all the works of art in-between exhibitions. All bought items deemed too valuable to be on display in the owner's homes; and all art coming up for restoration, or sale.

Suddenly he saw movement on another monitor. He put down his mobile, happy for the distraction, and watched a small car drive into the car-park. It stopped, nose against the side of the quay. A figure emerged from the car, a Mini Cooper S. He looked up, and saw the figure approach for real. Even in the dark, and wearing a full length coat, he recognized the female form as it came toward him. The gentle sway of hips always brought promise.

He stood to attention (a practice retained from his years of military service). He smiled, he actually recognized her; it was Senga Munreaux the fit Scottish girl from Sotheby's New Bond street branch, he thought.

"Good evening Miss," he said.

"Hello …Sargent," Senga noticed the stripes on his shoulder. The gods were on her side, she'd actually met this security guard before, at the New Bond Street auction-house. "Pete, isn't it?"

"That's right Miss," Pete's chest swelled with pride.

"I need to access Mr Crombie's office." Her hip jutted, as she assumed a very sexy pose in the doorway.

"And you need the access code from the computer room?" he sucked in his stomach, and assumed a manly swagger.

"I'm afraid so. I sort of cocked up today, and need to put it right before 'Sir' gets in tomorrow." The soft Scottish burr, was like a warm whisky, which rolled around her throat.

Pete, totally under her spell, nodded cautiously, "Better be careful inside, Miss Munreaux, there's only the emergency lighting on at night."

Senga moved closer to him, she fluttered her eyelashes. "Could you come inside with me?"

"No," Pete cursed his devotion to duty, "More than my job's worth." He laughed at the phrase.

Senga breathed a sigh of relief; that was what she wanted to hear. At least she'd be on her own in the office. "Not a problem, Pete, I'll be extra careful, thanks for your concern. I have to go in tonight, or someone will have my arse." She maintained a dominant eye-contact, but her vulnerability was turned on full.

Pete thought about her phrase. His smile lit up the dingy security office. Without a second thought, he buzzed open the door.

Once inside the warehouse, she felt her first real pangs of fear. She was now involved in something she had never dreamed she would ever do; actual theft.

The events at the saleroom still seemed like a dream. The British Museum had refused to put up any money to keep the helmet in the UK. That meant she had to find all the two point three million herself, and it had to be available in, to all intents and purposes, ten days-time.

With the sale of the Oleg postponed, Chellen would be satisfied. He'd not done any tests. He'd only come to the conclusion he'd been sold a fake, because he'd seen the Oleg up for auction. Childishly Senga crossed her fingers, if she could just swap the paintings over. The independent verifier would confirm the Oleg was genuine. She would come over all enraged and indignant, withdraw the Oleg from the sale, than quietly approach the buyer and sell it to him privately, less commission. Sotheby's would just let everything drop, Chellen would be none the wiser.

But, to swap them, Senga needed access to the Sotheby's vault; and to get into the vault she needed the randomly generated combination from the computer held here at the secure warehouse.

Senga took several deep breaths to steady her nerves. The dull glow of the emergency lighting made the warehouse ghostly and very imposing.

"Just get to the computer room, and get the code." She pictured herself walking through the gates of Hell. Her feet seemed heavy as she lifted them. Her hands were shaking as she trailed them along the wall.

"Not far now, have strength my wee lassie." She recited a saying her father used to say.

The computer room was bathed in the same green glow as the corridor. Stupidly Senga attempted to turn on the light. It clicked uselessly, and she felt embarrassed at her mistake. Slowly she groped her way around the office. She sat at the desk. She pressed the start button, and fired up the computer. She fumbled on the keyboard, until the screen lit up her view.

The silence was oppressive, she'd already turned her mobile off in the car, not wanting any distractions, now she desperately needed company. Quickly she entered the password, and waited for the program to begin. Only the sound of her breathing broke the silence. She imagined her heartbeat could be heard all over the warehouse.

The darkness was kept at bay by the light from the screen, and the silence was kept from spooking her by the small beeps and clicks of her keystrokes.

A single ping announced the file was open, Senga's heart skipped a beat; she pressed the memory stick into the USB port. It would not fit in.

Although she knew it was symmetrical she turned it over to try the other way. The memory stick would not fit. Her breathing got faster; she felt the trickle of sweat on her neck.

Deliberately she pressed the stick into the port again. It engaged. Another ping confirmed the PC was transferring the combination. The program had generated a random combination that would populate the vault. Senga had the code to get into it. All she had to do now, was go back to the vault, open it, and exchange the paintings.

Her fingers shook as she pulled the memory stick from the tight USB port. Senga shut down the PC, all again was quiet, at last Senga relaxed.

"Hello!"

Senga screamed and threw her arms in the air. A beam of light flickered, and then shone brightly into her face, no doubt, illuminating all her fear, shock, and guilt.

The beam of light left her face and focused on the holder. Senga looked up at a bizarre figure wearing a tweed cap. As the beam of light fanned out, she noted he was wearing a beige trench coat, which swung open to reveal a heavy green looking checked tweed suit. "What are you doing here?" he asked.

Desperately she tried to remember her cover story. "I'm Senga Munreaux." She stood up and thrust out her hand.

"That's as maybe, but, what are you doing here?" asked William Forbes. He recognized her beauty even in this pathetic light.

"I work for Sotheby's," she pointed to her ID badge. "I'm downloading data for analysis."

"I work for the Art Loss Register," Forbes held out a business card, Senga took it in trembling fingers.

"I thought only the Director General could access the PC out of hours?"

Senga felt herself on the verge of panic. She summoned all her reserve, and came up with an off-the-cuff gem, "Mr Crombie asked me to download the data, as a personal favour to him." She tried to engender a look indicating sexual tension;

it came over as if she were suffering from stomach cramps; yet Forbes still thought her beautiful. Oh, how he wanted to touch her hair.

"I understand he's been busy today," Forbes nodded as if he'd accepted the story. "Better be quick then, I understand there was a scare at the saleroom today?"

"You can say that again," Senga began to feel more confident. Her mind still struggled with the idea of an ALR investigator at the warehouse, at night. She thought it much too coincidental, that her Oleg had prompted such a response. If it had, surely the ALR would be with Crombie. But, her cover story was that she was doing a task for the Director General. Christ! What would happen if those two men ever got together, she mused.

Her fear returned with a vengeance. 'What if the ALR man had already visited Crombie? They might already be on to her. Her eyes were wide with fear, but the semi-darkness masked her true feelings from the man with the flashlight, and the bizarre dress code.

The PC gave one final death ping. "All done," Senga said. She held up the memory stick, between her fingers.

Forbes's hand flashed out and took the stick from her. "Thanks I'll take that."

Senga made a half-hearted attempt to retrieve it, but inside she knew she'd lost it. The prospects were looking grim.

"I'd like to check your story with your boss."

She began to wonder if he really worked for the ALR, maybe he was another one of Chellen's men; sent here to discover the truth about the Oleg.

Forbes put the memory stick in his trench-coat pocket. "After you," he gestured for her to leave the office.

Slowly and deliberately she squeezed past him. She noted with satisfaction that he gave an involuntary gasp as they touched. All may not be lost, if need be she'd use her body to get the memory stick back.

As they walked down the corridor, Senga generated a better idea which didn't involve sleeping with the, so called, investigator. Pete, the security guard knew her, trusted her, fancied her. If she could raise doubt of this man's authority, she could get him arrested. She could get back her memory stick, and swap the paintings.

Before she figured out what sort of alarm she needed to raise, they came to the door. It squealed in protest as he opened it.

In the harsh glow of the security lighting that lit up the yard, Forbes saw that the girl looked terrified. Her vulnerability touched him, and slowly he extended his hand, gently touching her on the shoulder. His fingers brushed against her hair, it felt soft and vibrant, the antique ivory Toucan-billed hair-grip shone in the light. She jumped at his touch. He ushered her into the yard.

"It's okay, just take it slowly, we need to go to security before we leave." Forbes reasoned she was afraid of the dark, she was trembling.

"That's a beautiful hair-grip, you have there."

"Thank you, it's antique," Senga sensed her moment, keep him talking until they got to the security hut; then she would raise doubts about his authenticity. She'd even suggest sexual assault, as long as it got him off her back and the memory stick back in her pocket.

"Are you going back to the saleroom now?"

"Yes," Senga nodded, how had he guessed her next destination? It was obvious he worked for Chellen. If only she could just get to the security hut. The thought of Pete, military background, taking this country gent out appealed to her.

Then, all thoughts of salvation vanished.

Pete came to the door, and shouted, "Everything alright Mr Forbes?"

"Everything's fine thanks Pete," Forbes answered.

Senga's spirits sank, Pete knew him; which also meant he really was an ALR investigator. Senga looked directly at Pete, fingers crossed this might still work, she began to call-

Pete opened his mouth at the same moment; but the sound he made was inhuman. The muzzle flash from the gun lit up the dark night. Pete's head disintegrated. Slowly the body toppled backward, hitting the security hut, and dropping like a rag doll.

Forbes grabbed Senga, "Get down."

Senga had no idea what he'd said, because he was speaking in Croatian.

More shots rang out, peppering the ground around them. Senga broke free of Forbes's grip, if he was Chellen's man she had to get away. But in an instant he was on her, "Oh no you don't," he growled. He caught hold of her arm and guided her away from the shots.

At the crouch they ran across the quay. Another shot rang out; Forbes saw the flash of the bullet ricochet off the ground in front of them. He guided her in another direction. Fighting her attempts to shake him off, Forbes suddenly smelled the rotting vegetables on the streets of Bosnia. He cupped his arm around her neck.

"Please, you're hurting me," she screamed.

Forbes struggled to recognise her face, as his memories mingled again. He looked at Senga, but saw the face of a young Bosnian girl. Slowly she shrank away from him. She danced away from his grip, and ran into the middle of the street where a bullet took her life. "No!" he shouted.

The sound of another shot brought him back, he panted, struggling to take a deep breath. Senga looked terrified. He gripped her close to him. Was she really trying to get away from him, or was he holding on to her because of the memory of the Bosnian girl?

He focused on her hair-grip. "Antique, you say," Forbes's foreign words meant nothing to her. She struggled against him as he pulled her toward a double row of containers, "It's either me or them?

Senga looked at him, failing to understand what was happening; surely he was trying to kill her. He'd been holding her very roughly, but he seemed to be trying to get away from the shooting.

Their eyes met. This was real; someone had killed the security guard, and was actually shooting at them. "What's happening?" she asked.

The sound of diesel engines shattered their moment's calm.

"Change of plan. We're going for the car." They ran together toward her car. Reluctantly Senga went with him, at least he was speaking English now.

Senga turned to see two fork-lift trucks following them. "Change of plan." Forbes changed direction, heading back toward the containers, the trucks followed suit, the big diesels eating up the ground. The closest driver span the wheel, and the truck turned on its axis, he'd guessed their destination and was trying to cut them off.

"Shit, these guys are good." Forbes pulled her arm.

As the truck came over the rough surface the driver raised his gun and fired again. Bullets cut through the air.

Desperately Forbes pulled Senga along, he guessed this was her first time under fire.

Senga knew she'd never make it to the containers; she wanted to try her car. "Let me go!" she pleaded, her eyes wide with fear.

Forbes kept moving, "Not on your life, I want to know who you are, and who those guys are?" just a few more yards to go. He felt the truck closing in on them.

"I don't know who they are," Senga screamed, slipping on the greasy surface. The roar of the engine pounded in her ears.

Forbes could smell the diesel, and feel the heat from the engine. He knew it was almost on top of them, just a couple more steps to go. The wooden containers looked very close now. "Come on."

The tyres slithered, it had just gone over the greasy part, the engine screamed in protest, searching for traction.

With one last herculean effort, Forbes threw Senga behind the first row of wooden containers. Right by his side the first truck smashed into the front stack of boxes. The wood splintered from the impact, sending foot long shards of wood scything through the air. In the aisle behind the boxes, they continued to run, massive splinters spiralled inches behind them.

The driver lifted his forks, engaged reverse and turned back from the smashed container. Another box was pushed from the stack, it fell, splitting open like a ripened fruit.

Forbes and Senga ran down the teetering gauntlet of boxes. Beyond the first row of creates, Forbes heard the truck overtake them. They stopped running.

Forbes grabbed her by the chin, "Friends of yours?"

Senga looked back at him, she recognized a new menace in his eyes. Her already pale skin turned white. The freckles across her cheeks stood out in stark contrast. Forbes could plainly see she was terrified. He gulped in a lung full of air.

This was not a flashback, this was actually happening. Since first seeing her face in the photograph all he'd wanted to do was protect her, and pay homage to her beauty. Yet here he was accusing her of trying to kill him.

"They're not your friends are they?" his breathing was still heavy.

"No," Senga struggled to get just the one word out.

Forbes had naturally assumed he was the target, she had been the bait. He realized he was wrong, maybe she was the target.

The trucks drove up and down, just a couple of feet the other side of the containers. Forbes held her shoulders, "It's okay, stay with me, I'll get you out of here," he inclined his head, encouraging her to trust him.

Slowly she nodded, slowly she began to believe. She'd been torn between believing if he was trying to kill her, or if he was just an innocent bystander; whichever he was, she decided to put her trust in him.

Suddenly the smell of burning rubber assaulted their senses. Then the truck released its brakes. The truck hit a container on the top row, right next to them. The forks smashed through the box. The driver reversed and turned sending other boxes crashing down around them.

As soon as a space became clear the second truck skidded into the gap. The steel forks clanged against the shattered wood, and the driver began firing his gun into the dark shadows.

Bullets thudded into the box by her head. Senga screamed. Forbes grabbed her and backtracked along the row, "We're going back."

The container in front of them suddenly rose up, tilted and smashed down into the gap in front of them. It completely blocked their escape route. Senga screamed again. Forbes pulled her back into his chest, just as another box smashed onto the ground behind them. To each of their sides, the trucks were working feverishly to remove the thin screen of wood protecting their fragile bodies. Like demented robots in a low-budget science-fiction film, the trucks began clawing away at their protection.

Forbes looked around, there was no way out. Another box fell on top of the one beside them, smashing open. Its contents of broom handles spilled out, cascaded down, and rolled across the cold unyielding concrete. Forbes knew that when the next row of boxes went, they would be exposed.

The drivers were firing into the gaps at every opportunity. They had no intention of leaving the scene until both prey were dead.

Engines revved, and tyres squealed as the trucks worked to remove the containers.

As if to complement the action, adrenaline surged through Forbes's body, not since Bosnia, had he felt such elation. The memory stopped him in his tracks, but this time it was a good feeling. He checked his hands, not even a slight tremor, obviously Senga was doing him a power of good. There was no fear, no flashbacks, not even time to think what might go wrong. There was only time to think about saving Senga.

Forbes took off his green tweed cap, and placed it on her head. He slipped off his trench coat. Picking up a piece of spilt debris, he wedged a broom handle between the containers, and snapped it in two.

"Take your coat off," Forbes instructed.

Senga did so without question. Quickly he threaded the handle through the sleeves of Senga's coat.

Another box crashed down to the rear of their position, the steel forks invaded their space, intruding like a terrier sniffing for rats. Forbes knew they would be sitting targets in a matter of seconds.

"Listen to me," he looked deep into her eyes. Her mouth was open, and her breath came in husky pants.

"Keep close to the edge, keep your head down, and go for your car, I will draw them off." With danger all around them, Forbes found her demeanour very attractive; it suddenly troubled him to be this distracted by her beauty at such a precarious moment. "I'll get them, don't worry."

Another create smashed onto the ground, showering them in splinters. Senga stood like a statue, "Good luck," she said, her face covered in a light sheen of sweat. The tweed cap, sitting above her tousled dark copper curls, bobbed as she nodding to his instructions. But, it was her eyes that gave him confidence; they conveyed a trust akin to that of a child. Forbes felt compelled to protect her innocent beauty.

With a rush, he recognised this was the emotion he'd first felt when he saw her in the photograph. Senga smiled, because she knew what he was feeling.

Now he had purpose back in his life, his own weakness was forgotten; now he was back to his former self.

The final box was removed; as the truck withdrew Forbes pushed her through the fallen debris.

"Go!" he whispered, it was the loudest sound she had ever heard.

Senga scrambled around another fallen box, and set off at a sprint. The fear fell from her shoulders.

Wearing his cap and coat, she looked like Forbes, and on her right arm she held the broom handles inside her own coat, replicating the pair of them running for the car. To the drivers it looked as if the man was helping the girl to escape.

Both trucks span around and followed the decoy, billowing out clouds of exhaust fumes.

In their wake Forbes jumped over the broken boxes and scampered down to the ground. He needed a weapon and fast. At full tilt he bowed to scoop up two broom handles.

From his days on the playing fields of Eaton, he took hold of the first handle, and hurled it, as one would a javelin. The stick ricocheted off the steel cab.

The driver turned and saw an absurdly dressed man chasing him; wielding a broom handle like some demented Samurai warrior.

For a moment he could not believe what he was seeing. It was the ALR man chasing him. He had to decide what action to take; but it was that hesitation that would cost him his life.

Forbes was only twelve feet away when the driver decided to take him on. After all he had been instructed to kill him.

"Gun verses stick," he said, "Trained killer verses some namby-pamby art-teacher. No contest, mate." He stopped the truck. Forbes slashed at the cab with the broom handle, completely missing the driver.

As he jumped down from the cab the driver laughed. Forbes stood facing him with just nine inches of the handle remaining. The driver began to aim his gun, time was on his side. He would certainly enjoy killing this freak. The hours of manual labour he'd put in tonight, shifting box after box was about to be recompensed. He completed the aim.

Forbes thrust forward with the remains of the broom handle, then at the last moment, chopped down onto the man's wrist. The gun fell to the floor. "Shit," he said rubbing his wrist. When he looked up, he saw Forbes thrusting forward again. This time he completed the move. The sharp end of the broom handle penetrated the driver's throat. An incredulous look of disbelief spread across the driver's face as he died, squashed up against the throbbing beast of the truck.

As if by magnetism, the driver was held in place. Forbes watched the years melt away in the driver's eyes, his face morphed into that of a young Somali pirate. The boy, no more than fifteen had displayed the same look of disbelief, when, as he was climbing up the ladder of an oil tanker, William Forbes of the SAS had risen from the sea; and shot him with his Glock 16 pistol. Now, as then the eyes had remained fixed upon Forbes, as they drifted away to eternity. Forbes covered his face with his hand, but the vision would not go away.

Senga was sobbing and dangerously out of breathe as she

reached her car. Grabbing the handle she flung the door open. She threw off the trench coat and jumped in. With her heart pounding in her ears, she tried to put the key into the ignition, her hands shook. The lights from the truck illuminated the interior of the Mini. Senga turned and stared in frozen horror as the truck approached.

Her hands fumbled, and she moaned in frustration. The truck was much closer now. With relief the key engaged.

The engine started first time. She engaged reverse. The truck was upon her. Senga froze in terror, as the rear of the car began to lift up. Her hands went ridged on the wheel. The car tilted, and Senga screamed.

Her cry brought Forbes back to the present, he roared in frustration.

The truck tyres span on the ground as the driver pushed forward. Senga screamed, it was a long drawn out wail, akin to a child suffering a nightmare.

She looked through the windscreen at the cold dark water, it seemed to beckon her. As she felt the Mini lurch forward she pressed down on the brake. Her hands strained, pulling on the handbrake. Tighter, and tighter, but to no avail, the front wheels dropped over the side of the dock. The car body scraped along the ground as the Fork Lift Truck pushed it to the point of no return.

Physically and mentally, Forbes pushed the dead driver away from the truck, and jumped up behind the wheel. Looking up he saw the first truck pushing Senga's Mini over the edge. With grim determination he hit the accelerator. As the truck leapt forward, Forbes raised the forks, aiming for the cab.

Forbes watched in horror as Senga's car tipped over the edge of the dock. It began to slide.

Like a hangman, before sending their victims to their deaths, the driver's hand paused over the lever. Then in a cruel thrust, he pushed it forward and the forks lifted, and the car tipped into the dark water.

The action had taken only a few seconds, but it had fully engrossed the driver. As the Mini slipped from view, he turned to see a new danger approaching.

The forks on Forbes's truck hit the driver full in the side of the head, killing him instantly, and the two trucks collided, rupturing the diesel tank. Forbes jumped clear.

Ignited from the sparks, flames blossomed as the two trucks were immediately engulfed in a fireball.

Forbes rushed to the edge of the quay. With a feeling of helplessness he looked down into the cold water, the car was already submerged, its red tail lights fading fast.

His rage surfaced with a primeval roar. Moments ago he had promised to save the girl. He had felt stronger than ever. But, when it came down to it, he had failed. The *Somali-pirate* flashback had lost him precious seconds, and now she was gone.

Fear and indecision flooded through his mind and body. He reached for his pills. As the tears flowed, he took two, they tasted thick in his mouth.

With the loss of Senga at the forefront of his mind, he brought up the memory of her memory stick. It had been in his trench-coat pocket. Forbes surveyed the scene. His coat lay smouldering on the ground. Dodging the flames from the trucks, he ran to the coat, stamping on it to extinguish the flames. He felt in the pocket. She had given her life to get the information on the memory stick. The stick was gone.

"Looking for this?" Forbes whirled around to see Senga Munreaux, still wearing his tweed cap, holding the small plastic memory stick.

Instinctively, he held his arms open, and she ran to him, and with honest affection, melted into his arms. "What a cleaver girl you are?" The assertiveness was back. He took the memory stick, and eased it into his Highland-green and blue check trouser pocket. Was it the pills, or was it the girl. He kissed her protectively on the forehead. He knew which he preferred the taste of.

The flames scorched their clothing. "Come on, I think we should leave."

Her face opened into a delightful childlike smile. On impulse she reached up and kissed Forbs full on the lips, his hands slid from her shoulders, to the small of her back, and he pulled her into him.

Her mouth was open, and they kissed like lovers. Her tongue was eager, shocking Forbes with its strength. Her arms snaked around his neck, her fingers eager. But, almost before the kiss started it ended, Senga pulled away, and gestured to the water, "Our ride is gone," her tone heavy with embarrassment.

The moment of intimacy was forced from her mind. Everything she was risking her life for, revolved around getting her old lover back. Her current feelings were borne of relief, not affection.

Forbes watched the transformation, within a few seconds she looked in control again, gone were the freckles of vulnerability, yet still he draped the trench coat over her shoulders.

"It's okay, I have a car."

Senga looked around at the tangle of trucks, and the body on the quay.

"You were …" she struggled to find the right words to thank him, and convey her fear of the scene from hell they found themselves in, "Fantastic."

"You weren't so bad yourself." He flicked the tweed cap down over her eye. She giggled.

As they walked away, Forbes felt that the girl was everything the photograph depicted of her. With delight he realized he could still taste her, the affection was something that could be worked upon. Right now, reviewing the scene of carnage, he admitted he was not on his own in the search for the paintings.

Wherever he had been on this investigation, death had followed. His arm remained around Senga's shoulders, and he thought, although he wasn't alone in his search, maybe the odds had just tilted in his favour.

Chapter Nine

THE STORM ON THE SEA OF GALILEE (REMBRANDT 1633)

London, England,
Thursday, June 24.

WHILE NO THIEF CAN HOPE TO GET THE ACTUAL VALUE of a stolen work, even a small percentage of its real value can be substantial.

However, ownership of well-known art is easily tracked, and an unsophisticated thief may steal a piece of art only to find there are no buyers.

Most art of high quality is sold at auction, and major reputable houses such as Sotheby's or Christie's demand proof of art provenance.

Once provenance is proven, a code number or 'seal' is assigned to the work and the documentation.

One of the finest examples of Noah Coleman's talent was his ability to doctor the seals, but, of course anything that can be made to look perfect can also be made to look 'wrong' it was this anomaly that had alerted the verifier at Sotheby's in the verification of the Oleg, after the sale. The tampered seal now sat in the vault, on the forgery.

Unbeknown to Senga, the exact same anomaly was currently to be seen on the painting that resided her case.

Unaware of the anomaly, she still believed that all she had to do was swap the paintings, and the independent verifier would confirm the painting was real.

Senga now had the code to open the vault. She needed to affect the swap tonight while the code was still relevant to the combination, then she could relax, after the verifier confirmed the Oleg was genuine she would sell the second forgery in a very private sale. The world, and in particular, LeCoyte Chellen would think he had the real Oleg. The world, in particular Sotheby's would be satisfied that the matter of the forgery at the auction was hushed up.

Only one small obstacle now sat in her way, the memory stick containing the code for the vault was in the possession of ALR investigator William Forbes.

How to prize it away from him? Now, that was the question. She'd tried to palm it when she kissed him, but strangely she enjoyed the experience too much to be able to take it. Think girl, think.

At the heart of the Art Loss Register was its ever evolving database, the 'go to' bible for all art buyers, traders, and insurers. A result of its success was that every now and then someone needed to go and retrieve a work of art which was found to be in the possession of someone who had no right to the piece.

Instead of handing over the information to law enforcement agencies around the world, the ALR had started employing its own investigators some ten years ago. Its growth since then had been an important element of raising global awareness of art theft, which was instrumental in the international effort to halt the trafficking of stolen art.

Forbes had been the perfect choice for investigator. A background in art, a degree from Eaton, a hands-on knowledge of archaeology, digging in Iraq, and a ruthless streak acquired during his time with the SAS. But, tonight was the first time Forbes had killed anyone since joining the ALR, he was unsure of the spotlight he would now come under from the police.

Having escaped charges in Italy, he was not keen to expose his actions in London. Right now he wanted to understand if it was he, or Senga that were the targets of tonight's attempt on his life. If it were him, then he needed to understand if the girl was part of the Paris theft. If it was her, then he wanted to know what she had gotten into, with this forgery claim at Sotheby's.

It was almost eleven pm, when Forbes and Senga arrived at Sotheby's. In the time it had taken to come from the warehouse, Forbes had found doubts with his new found friend. He wanted to be sure she was trustworthy.

"Tell me again Miss Munreaux, why were you at the warehouse tonight?"

Senga was surprised by the question; she hoped her friendly demeanour had shaken him off the question; however during the drive she had revised her cover story.

"Couple of weeks ago, I bought the Crosby Garett helmet."

Forbes looked at her, trying to detect the lie, "I'm impressed."

She continued, "I thought the British museum would step in and make an offer, to ensure the helmet stayed in the UK. Earlier today I learned they would not be blocking my request to take it out of the country."

Intrigued Forbes gestured for her to continue, this seemed much more important than the five stolen paintings.

"I don't have the full two point three million, to fund the purchase. I thought I could make a quick profit, but I was mis-advised." She shrugged, "Anyway, I think I've found a potential buyer. He is willing to offer me the full two point three million. Naturally if I was seen to be selling such an important artefact so quickly after purchase ..."

"You might be charged with fraud."

Senga seized on the idea, "Exactly, that's why I needed to get into the vault and take my helmet back, tonight."

Forbes nodded, his hands lightly tapped the steering wheel, "With Crombie tied up with the potential forgery, you needed the code for the vault."

"Yes," she reached out and touched his hand, "I'm desperate, and I've got to access the vault tonight."

Forbes felt the first tingle of deceit course through his body.

"Who were those guys at the warehouse?" his tone was hard.

"How the hell should I know, thieves? For all I know, they could have been waiting for you," Senga's response came out a little too quickly, Forbes seized on her words.

"Hardly, I only went to the warehouse when I learned about the potential forgery claim from the saleroom today."

Senga undid her seatbelt, preparing to get out, but Forbes continued. "I agree they could have been planning a robbery, but if that were the case I believe they would have simply waited for us to leave. Instead they tried to kill us, I think they were waiting for you Miss Munreaux," Forbes pulled the memory stick from his pocket, "I think they were after this, and now I know what's in the vault, I understand why."

Senga felt sick with worry, had he seen through her plan?

Forbes looked at her. "I think they could be after your Roman helmet."

"Oh my God," Senga's shock was genuine, although she knew it was her they were trying to kill, she believed it was because of the Oleg not the helmet.

"Surely they couldn't expect to break into the auction-house, and steal the artefact?" No, she decided, the only plausible motive was to stop her accessing the vault and swapping the picture, the 'why' still eluded her.

Forbes held up the memory stick, "Here, you take it."

Relief spread quickly through her lithe body, like hot butter through a toasted crumpet. "Thank you, Bill."

"If I were you I'd sell that helmet as fast as you can. Now, go and get it; I'll wait here?"

Senga thanked every God, Saint, and idol she could think of, he was not intending to go inside with her.

AS SENGA CREPT PAST THE DIRECTOR GENERAL'S OF-fice she was surprised to see Charles Crombie, sitting like a judge presiding over his assizes. His face was etched with de-spair, she wasn't sure he'd seen her, so she stepped backward and peered into the office, "Charles?" Panic grabbed her, not in a million years had she expected him to be there. What would happen if Forbes came in now? How could she keep the two men from conferring? And more importantly how was she going to explain what had happened at the warehouse?

"Senga?" Crombie looked up, his shocked expression turning to relief, "Thank goodness you're alright. You must be cursing me for sending you that damned text?"

"Oh don't fret," said Senga, thinking '*Shit, what text?*' She suddenly remembered she'd had her phone switched off all night.

Crombie held her at arm's length, as if checking that all her limbs were intact. Then favouring the wrist on which he wore his Patek Philippe, he rubbed his weary face, stress was clearly at a high level. "What a dreadful day. Today we possibly auctioned a forgery. All those damned security measures, and yet this one got through; and then I hear someone tried to kill you."

Senga used her best maternal tone to steer the conversation, "We don't know if it's a forgery, there may be some perfectly innocent explanation as to why the seal was faulty-"

"There's only one reason why a seal is faulty," he ranted.

Senga's smile came assuredly from the knowledge that when the verifier looked at the painting in the morning, he would find the authentic painting nestled in the vault, "What time do you expect the verifier?"

"Who, old 'Caster van your knees' former painter and Spanish demi-god?"

"Yes, Senior Cassavanurnez," she corrected the pronunciation

"Whatever; he's already here, arrived just over an hour ago."

"When will he be examining the painting?" Please say the morning, say 'here' means in London. She prayed silently and swiftly to all the deities; but her knees began to buckle, as Crombie chipped in …

"He already has it."

It was at that precise moment when Senga knew life couldn't get any worse that the police arrived.

⁊♂℃

Nine hours later, Friday, June 25.

THE VERY KIND OFFICER HAD SAID SHE COULD LEAVE. Without needing to be told twice, Senga left the police station, she crossed the road in a dream. Time was against her, it was already, Friday, twenty-fifth of June. She had just nine days to get the money, and sleep was already a stranger.

All night she had gone through the events at the warehouse. Somehow she had to get the helmet from the vault before the news broke that *Portrait in Valencia* was a forgery.

Although that news would get her off the hook, temporarily with Chellen; the revelation of her trying to sell a forgery would finish her. It would only be a short time before she was identified as the owner of the forgery. Her job, her apartment, her life would soon disappear into the Thames, a bit like her beloved Mini Cooper S had last night.

She switched on her mobile. The fanfare announced texts and emails by the dozen, three messages from Crombie alone. She opened the latest one first.

'Gr8 news Painting verified REAL.'

Senga stopped dead, "Holy shit. How can that be?" She

was so lost in her thoughts that her attention had to be brought back to reality with a screech of brakes.

She gave an apologetic wave to the driver who'd had to stop to avoid hitting her. He, in turn mouthed an obscenity, and revved his engine.

Senga did a little hop skip and jump out of the way. Once on the pavement she turned to stare at the driver as his car accelerated past her. She was looking back, across the road at the police station when she saw a car pull up to the curb. The annoyingly short, curly haired, Mr Key leapt out, slamming the door behind him. He ran up the steps, two at a time. With no pause at the top he eased open the double glass doors and entered the police station.

Senga felt the panic rise within her. Real painting at Sotheby's meant real danger in the form of Mr Key and the sweaty Turk, Obit.

When she'd first embarked on this lifestyle choice, she knew there would be times when she would be in danger, but, she'd always thought that **he** would be there to protect her, but **he** wasn't in the picture at the moment.

Senga recognised the threat Key posed. Key was a killer who would carry out his orders and not think twice about it.

She took her bearings, and darted into the tube station. Fumbling in her purse she took out some coins, and fed them into the ticket machine.

Keeping one eye on the entrance, she bought a ticket, it would get her onto a train; she'd pay the excess later, if there was a later. She felt Key's presence.

She had only one chance, get to the platform, get on the first train, and get away from Key.

Senga ran down the escalator. Her progress slowed by a loved-up couple travelling arm in arm and tongues in each-others mouths. She looked back, toward the top of the escalator.

Key's, meerkat-like head showed through the crowd of faces, all of which seemed to be staring and pointing at her.

"Excuse me," Senga pushed past the couple, almost choking the girl in the process. She danced down the escalator with the skill of a slalom skier.

At the busy intersection, she joined a group of tourists looking for the Piccadilly Line. Using the group as a shield, she darted down the tunnel toward the platform proclaiming the next train arrival.

The warm fusty air that is unique to the underground hit her as she ran onto the platform. An eclectic mix of people were already jostling for the best spots, for the imminent arrival of the train. Senga weaved in and out of the crowd, looking for a vantage point to stay hidden. Looking behind her she stumbled into an elderly man, he shouted in protest. Stumbling, arms flailing, drawing attention, frightened and vulnerable.

"Sorry," she said hastily, hands outstretched in a peaceful gesture, hoping to placate the grumpy old sod. The crowd swelled against her, and she felt caught in the riptide of people adjusting to the commotion.

"Come with me," said a voice next to her ear, an arm firmly around her shoulder; grip like a python. Senga lost her balance as the arm pulled her backward. She saw the faces of two Oriental girls, deep in conversation. Senga tried to attract their attention, but they were too involved with each other to notice her plight.

The sudden whoosh of air, and squealing brakes announced the arrival of the tube train. The crowd pressed forward.

Once in the shadows, the powerful arm twisted her around, her face, now buried into his chest. A strong hand, eased into her copper curls, and twisted her face. "Do you know that man?" the voice whispered. She saw it was Key.

Senga twisted again, and looked up, into the face of William Forbes. He looked into her eyes. "His name is Robert Key; he's a nasty piece of shit, works for a guy called LeCoyte Chellen.

"Like in the Chellen Corporation?" she asked innocently.

Passengers were spilling from the tube train. Shoulders barged their way through the tight gaps in the crowd.

"Correct," Forbes continued to twist, keeping both of them out of Robert Key's sight line.

"Why would he be following me?" she executed a dramatic inhalation of breath, "You think he's after the helmet?" Senga made it sound innocent, the breathless throaty husk to her voice added to the illusion.

Forbes guided her into the departing sea of passengers emptying from the platform. They dropped in step, and bustled their way out.

"I don't think it's the helmet, Chellen isn't an artefacts man." His body swayed, weight shifted, carving a way through the commuters.

"Do you think it was Key at the warehouse last night?"

"I think it was Chellen's men, yes." Forbes scanned the crowd, making sure Key had not doubled back. Hundreds of faces looked back at him, all of them strangers. Then he saw the face of the man he'd killed with the broom handle.

The man he'd skewered to death on the quay by the Thames

looked back at him. The dead eyes looked directly into his soul. A putrefied hand reached out toward him. Forbes looked up at the tube station roof, but he saw the catacombs of Belgrade, heard the scurrying of rats, felt the closeness of death.

"What's a Dutch Telecoms giant got to do with … Bill?" Senga watched Forbes begin to sway. His face was deathly white. He looked like he was going to be sick. His eyes bulged. "Bill?" she put her hands on his shoulders.

Forbes looked around at the hundreds of faces, all beginning to decompose. The commuters turned into zombies, walking aimlessly toward him, rotting flesh dripping from their bones. He gripped Senga's shoulders, shaking her hands from him, he began to squeeze, she moaned in protest.

Senga's confused expression turned to real concern, she thought Forbes was about to keel over and faint. "Bill, are you OK? What is it?"

Forbes's legs turned to jelly, his memory tricked him again, and in a sickening flash he was back in the ransacked office in Verona. Mosca was pointing toward the photograph *"There's your evidence,"* the lifeless lips mouthed.

An African man, with kind eyes, and grey curly-hair, standing next to Forbes and Senga, asked "Is everything ok?"

Forbes looked at him. It was Giovanni Mosca. Forbes's hand shot out to fend the apparition away; he punched him on the shoulder.

"Hey man, what's your problem?" the eyes were suddenly hostile.

The words brought Forbes back to reality.

"I'm sorry, he's not well," Senga explained apologetically.

"Fucking nut job." He walked away, rubbing his injured pride.

Without further explanation, Forbes grabbed Senga's shoulders, "Chellen's men are everywhere." His was the voice of an alcoholic, no comprehension, no reason.

"Come on," Senga pulled Forbes by the hand; they stumbled along one of the arched passageways, stopping close to a busker, who was belting out an impassioned version of Lady Gaga's 'Bad Romance'.

"What the hell just happened back there?" Senga demanded

"I'm claustrophobic." He reached in his pocket for his pills.

Senga watched him knock back three small pills. Forbes rested, unsteadily against the wall. The cool tiles soaked into his head.

"How long have you been following me?" Senga asked.

Forbes smiled, it was quite infectious. "I'm not following you." He thought it best not to go into detail about his obsession with her in the photograph.

"This is all connected to a case I'm working on."

"Which is?"

"Come on, we can't stay here, Key could be coming back from the platform at any moment." Forbes began walking along the tunnel. Senga followed, she dropped a pound coin in the busker's cap.

They began up an escalator, "I think LeCoyte Chellen masterminded the theft at the art museum in Paris, back in May."

"The Picasso, Lady with the fan ..." Senga realized she was still holding his hand.

"That's right, and three others, biggest heist in art history." Forbes enjoyed the feeling. Commuters passed them going up, and others were descending; but all their faces were alive. His fear had subsided, his breathing regular. He thought it best not to tell her that he believed she was implicated in the heist, and that he thought her a suspect; and yet strangely he didn't want to let her go.

"And you're leading the investigation for the ALR?"

"Yes."

"So, what's the link to me?"

Forbes shook his head, but his eyes remained fixed upon her. Senga noticed how they twinkled. "All I can say right now is that there is a link. But I don't want to involve you," he held her at arms-length, "Please Senga, just get your pretty Roman helmet from the vault. Then I suggest you get as far away from here as possible." He pulled her close to him, "Do you have anyone you can trust?"

Senga immediately thought of Noah. "Yes I do."

"Then go."

"But what are you going to do? You're clearly not well."

"Don't worry about me. I'm going after Chellen."

"Do you know where he is?"

"Yes, he's in Helsinki, opening another gallery. I've interviewed him in his home in Amsterdam. He wasn't pleased to see me."

They stepped off the escalator. Forbes searched the crowd for Key, but his curly-haired head was nowhere to be seen, "He must have got on the tube."

So intent was he to recognise Key's face from the hundreds coming at him that he completely missed the seemingly innocent man in the grey ski-jacket that had travelled up the escalator behind them.

The man wore a matching grey woollen beanie-hat, pulled down to his eyebrows. The disguise was a must, but the coarse wool sure did itch the puckered scar forming on his head. The man slowly passed Senga and Forbes, listening intently to what the pompous Englishman was saying.

He did not look back, that would have been noticeable, he walked straight toward the exit. He didn't have to follow Forbes so closely now, he knew where he was going, Helsinki. It was the girl that he needed to keep a close eye upon. He recalled Forbes's words *"There is a link, but I don't want to involve you."* Too late bitch you are involved. *"Involved in my chain reaction."* The thought made him laugh.

Chapter Ten

THE WHITE DUCK (OUDRY 1753)

Nice Airport, France.
Saturday, June 26.

NOAH COLEMAN SLIPPED HIS WAYFARER SUNGLASSES into the top pocket of his dark-blue linen shirt, as he met her at the arrivals gate.

"You brought the Oleg?" there was more than a hint of stress to his voice.

"I'm fine thanks, good of you to ask."

"I can see you're fine, you already told me you were fine on the phone," he made a phone shape out of his hand, and put it to his ear, "You told me not to worry about you, I'm not. What I need to know is did you bring the painting?"

Senga inclined her head, "For what it's worth yes. I must have screwed up, mixed the paintings up. You've heard that the real one is in the vault in London?"

"You'd be surprised at what I know," Noah gave a nervous laugh and changed the subject. "What's this about you meeting an Art Loss Register investigator, do I hear wedding bells in the air?"

Senga gave him a look of disapproval, "When it was confirmed that the painting was real, Chellen sent someone to kill me."

"Things get a little hectic did they?"

Senga fought the urge to argue, so she felt satisfied in flouncing off. The breeze generated by her sudden movements was a welcome accompaniment to the heat of the Cote D'azure.

For the man with the puckered scar just above his hairline, the climate was much more acceptable here in Nice than it was in London. Like many other passengers in the arrivals hall, he was busy on his mobile phone, deep in conversation with his transport provider.

The girl with the antique ivory Toucan-billed hair-grip was an amateur, she had been easy to follow. Forbes, the so-called professional would be out of the picture until his Scandinavian trip proved to be a dead-end.

He smiled at the girl, ever since the theft in Paris, his life had been a series of un-connected events leading him to this moment. But of course he recognised them as part of his own chain reaction. He watched Senga, followed by the simpering timeworn man wearing faded old espadrilles.

"So this is the man you trust?" he quoted from the overheard conversation in London.

Noah and Senga walked right past the man.

"I just need one shot," he said to himself as they passed. Without any shutter noise, he altered the angle of his mobile and fired off a number of photos.

He scanned through them, "Just another link in the chain reaction."

Outside the welcoming sun shone in all its glory. As Senga

and Noah walked across the car-park, a jet announced it was leaving Nice, with a howl of power, Senga followed it, on its path to the sky, her anger mellowed.

"Yes, you could say things got a little hectic in London. That's why I'm here. I love it here, everything is so calm."

They crossed the six lane highway, and descended, via a stainless-steel, and mirrored elevator to the underground car-park of the hotel.

"That's mine," Noah gestured to a metallic, chestnut brown, Audi A8. A dark suited chauffer took her luggage, as Noah opened the rear door. "After you," He pushed her in.

LeCoyte Chellen sat in beige-leather luxury.

Senga thought she would faint. The one man she never wanted to see again, sat waiting for her, like a pale bloated spider in the centre of his web. Her body froze. Noah pushed her closer to him, as he squeezed in beside her.

Chellen was a few inches shy of six feet tall, his squat body made him appear soft and overweight, but his body was naturally large boned, so he was only slightly too heavy. His hair was the purest of blondes, straight and long pudding basin styled, but a shade that many Hollywood starlets paid thousands for. His eyes were a mellow blue, deep set in his rounded face. Chellen wasn't an Albino, but his colouring made people wonder.

As Senga sat by him, his eyebrows raised; they were however so fair and fine that in anything other than semi-darkness looked like he had none at all.

Chellen always liked to be lit correctly to minimize the effect his pale skin had on his visitors.

Because of his body shape, Chellen always imagined that

people who didn't know him would dismiss him as being harmless; he'd once heard someone liken him to a 'fat white duck'. That was a big mistake; people who made mistakes around LeCoyte Chellen would swiftly be brought to task, meaning which he often overcompensated for their mistakes with cruelty beyond reason.

Senga could feel the body heat that he generated, she could smell the expensive sandalwood aftershave and the freshly laundered shirt.

"Let's take a ride," Chellen waved a finger at the chauffer. "We're not going far." The accent was American, but tinged with a memory of Dutch.

Senga made a move, but Noah leaned in close, and made a disapproving noise in her ear. His eyes drilled into hers, and although he spoke to her, the words were directed at Chellen, "She has the painting, surely there's no need to go anywhere else?"

"I want it to be more private," Chellen's voice was clear and lyrical, he lent into Senga, she felt his minty breath on her skin, "When she explains why she thought she could get away with cheating me out of half a million pounds?"

Noah sat back. Senga could smell his aftershave too, the mid-tones were difficult to pinpoint as they were mixed with fear.

"Please, you know it was a misunderstanding, you were never meant to be disadvantaged." Noah appealed.

"So you say."

Senga unexpectedly felt claustrophobic, she wondered if this was how Forbes had felt in the underground station. She panicked and made a sudden movement toward Noah's door.

Where she was going, or what she hoped to achieve she didn't know; she only knew that she had to get out of the moving car, because just as Forbes had thought he was going to die in the underground; that's what she thought would happen to her here.

Chellen grabbed her shoulder, and forced her back into the seat. His other hand arced around and his fist smashed into her solar plexus.

Her body cried for air, she struggled to take a breath.

"Don't ever think you can con me, and walk away."

"She's frightened!" Noah offered.

"She should be. I really hope you can both convince me that this was some awful misunderstanding. I don't enjoy seeing people get hurt," he sighed, "But then again we all have to do things we don't enjoy." Chellen grabbed Senga's chin, forcing her face towards his. "You try to get away again, and I'll make you wish you were dying of cancer."

The Audi glided along the highway. They sat in private-glass seclusion, hiding from interested onlookers.

"You have so much to answer for, Miss Monroe, or is it Munreaux? I had a visit from a man called William Forbes, from the Art Loss Register, he asked lots of stupid questions about the Paris art theft. Now," Chellen interlinked his fingers on his lap, "Where do you suppose he got my name from?"

Senga flinched at the mention of Forbes's name. The danger was increasing by the minute.

Noah tried to smooth the tensions, "You're a famous art collector, a dealer in fine art for a hobby. You own twenty-five art galleries around the world. We've just witnessed a theft from

133

Paris that's taken the art world by storm …obviously the ALR are going to question you."

"He came to my home. He set foot in Villa Kavel," Chellen leaned around Senga, and looked directly at Noah, "Where my mistress lives."

Noah tilted his head, indicating how embarrassing it must have been.

Chellen examined his fingernails, "I don't like my personal space invaded." He said menacingly.

The Audi dipped into another underground car-park. The lighting was inadequate, but it was good enough to show Noah that the place was empty, except for a silver Renault Megane parked across a number of parking bays.

The Audi glided to a halt. The chauffeur got out. Senga heard him pop the trunk.

Senga looked at the Renault. She winced as she saw the sweaty Turk from London get out. He held a black canvas case, just like the one in the Audi's trunk, the one she kept the painting in.

The chauffer and the Turk swapped cases. The Audi's trunk slammed shut.

"There now, tell me about the mistake." Chellen pronounced every word.

Noah began to speak, "I was asked to …"

Chellen cut him off with a swift gesture of the hand, "Not you, her."

Senga cleared her throat, "As Mr Coleman was about to say, he produced a copy of the Oleg for the original owner, for insurance purposes. The owner instructed me to sell the painting. I felt it was in his best interests to sell privately, so I contacted you. He felt he could get more at auction, so entered the Oleg at Sotheby's."

Chellen cut in, "And the paintings got mixed up?" his mouth opened in mock surprise, "Get out!"

Noah opened the door, the Turk pulled it open. Noah slid from his seat, pulling Senga with him.

From the interior, Chellen instructed, "Give it to her!"

The Turk's hand disappeared into his jacket. Senga knew it would come out holding a gun. As the hand withdrew, Senga closed her eyes.

Noah coughed. Senga opened her eyes, the Turk presented her with the crumpled cheque for £500,000. Roughly he pushed past her, sniffing at her hair as he went, then he disappeared into the back of the Audi. The engine fired up and the car drove out of the car-park. Noah and Senga stood alone.

"That went well." Noah rubbed the back of his neck.

"What?" she attacked him with the canvas case, swinging it in a wide arc, Noah stepped out of the way, his hands tried to placate her. "Listen to me, and stop trying to smash the Oleg."

Senga stopped. She looked at him as if he'd gone crazy.

Noah explained, "The only way I could get Chellen to swap the paintings was if he believed you had the real one."

"That was the real one, I couldn't swap it in London; no wait the real one is in London, that was a fake?" She screamed in frustration, "Oh, I don't know!"

"Chellen bought the real Oleg from you in Geneva. I told you it didn't matter which one you put in the auction."

"Chellen had the real painting?" her knees gave way.

"Yes, after all he did pay five hundred thousand for it. But he thought it was a fake. He knows the one at Sotheby's is a fake, therefore he reasoned the one you had was real."

"How on earth do you come to that conclusion?" Senga raised her hands to the heavens, "The Oleg at Sotheby's has just been declared authentic."

"No, the two examples you had were my forgeries."

"You shit, I went through hell doing all that swapping ..."

"And you failed. I couldn't take the chance, and I knew that if you knew what I had really planned, you'd never have agreed to it. No matter what happened in London, Chellen had to believe that you had the real painting. This was the only way I could think for you to get everything you wanted."

"So Chellen didn't do tests on the painting, or he'd have known it was real?"

"Tests were done in Geneva the day he bought it."

"I'm lost."

"The results said it was a fake," Noah opened the Renault's door, "Get in, I'll explain."

⁓⌀

DRIVING FROM NICE TO ST TROPEZ NORMALLY TAKES in the region of ninety minutes. You take the N7 which runs inland, and records your registration plate on six cameras; or, if you are a forger and your partner has just conned someone out of £500,000 you can take the 'bord de mer'.

The coast road takes a little longer and a lot more concentration, but the views are worth it.

Noah Coleman eased the old Renault around the hairpin-bends with the confidence of a racing driver, this skill however was lost on Senga, but as the journey unfolded and Noah confessed everything, she had to reluctantly admire the other genius he possessed.

"I was impersonating Juan Cassavanurnez, the man Chellen, and Crombie, had employed to do the tests, I confirmed one painting was a fake, and the other one real."

"Key and that smelly Turk almost killed me because you said the painting at the auction was real, what would have happened if I got caught?"

"You didn't, but you did fail to swap them, good job they were both fakes."

She mulled it over in her mind again, each time she'd gone through the deception she'd come up with another question, which Noah had handled with the skill of the master forger he was.

Now she blurted out another annoying anomaly, "How did you fool Chellen and Crombie into thinking you were Cassavanurnez?"

"How well do you know the old Spaniard?"

Senga thought about her answer, "Only by reputation. I've seen him working, but he keeps himself to himself."

"Never actually met him then?" he glanced at her.

"More like never spoken to him, and please keep your eyes on the road."

"Neither had, Chellen or Crombie until the other night."

"But how ..."

Noah chuckled, "Everyone's seen him. Everyone knows what he looks like, but no one really talks to him when he's working, except me."

"How?" Noah anticipated the question and gave a detailed answer.

"I bumped into Cassavanurnez at the Guggenheim in Bilbao, a couple of years or so back, he gave me his business card."

"Why would he want to do that?"

"I was pretending to be someone else."

"Okay, that figures."

"I copied his card, got some printed out, and sent them to various auction-houses, offering my services. However, I did change the telephone numbers, and email, and website address."

"But?" Senga started, but Noah held up his hand-

"My phone is on divert to Cassavanurnez's real telephone number, so after a slight delay, all calls go through to him. However I can intercept, and ask what the call is in connection with. If it's mundane I say, 'Connecting you now'. If it's interesting, I become the old Spaniard myself."

"How do you know where he's going to be at any time?"

"I phone his office and enquire about his availability."

Senga thought it through, "Brilliant." She felt humbled by the simplicity of the plot.

"Of course when the timing is right, I just turn up and make my expert decision."

"So you were in Geneva and you went to the auction-house." She knew it was so but she repeated it to let it sink in.

"Yes," he smiled and nodded, keeping his eyes on the twisty road, "I had to be there before you cocked it all up."

"Hey, someone tried to kill me the other night, I think it was Chellen, and then Key came after me, after I was released from the police station," Senga heard the words but realized the motive had just disappeared.

"No, you've got it all wrong. By then we had had a little chat, and the story, you so brilliantly remembered had been sown. I told him you were bringing the original to him. I know he wanted you very much alive."

"Even if it was to kill me himself, if we proved to be liars."

"He's a very nasty man."

"What about Key?"

"Him too."

"I mean about him following me."

"Key was probably looking out for you, trying to protect you and the painting, from the real killer."

"Then who the hell is trying to kill me?" An idea popped into her head, the thought hit her like a cold shower. Senga realized that the one consistent element in all her near death experiences had been William Forbes.

Forbes had asked a lot of questions, but hadn't offered any real answers about why he'd turned up out of the blue at the warehouse, or at the tube station. Noah's voice brought her back to reality, and threw in another candidate for her assassin.

"Do you owe anybody any money? I know that's the most common reason that people come after me …that and standing them up for dinner," he added quietly.

Senga thought about the £2.3 million she had to pay Christie's in eight days. Her face dropped.

Noah did a double take, and instantly understood the problem, with gusto he slapped the steering wheel, "Ha, I knew it. I bloody knew it. You do owe money. How much do you owe?" he waited for the answer.

Senga pursed her lips; her fingers drummed a quick tattoo on her thigh. She took a deep breath, and slowly exhaled, "Have you heard of the Crosby Garett Helmet?"

∽✤◯

Helsinki air-space, Finland.
Saturday, June 26.

WILLIAM FORBES LOOKED OUT OF THE AEROPLANE window at Finland's glorious landscape. He had always thought it was a land designed on the themes of forest and water, from the wilds of Lapland, to the inspiring lakes of the East, and the archipelagos of the South-West, Finland was full of interesting contrasts; the midnight sun, and the long dark winter nights. Who knew what awaited him in Helsinki?

Carrington had been edgy about the trip, especially after the complaints Chellen's company had lodged after Forbes's interview in Amsterdam.

Forbes had asserted that Chellen was the prime suspect, "He knew the man that bought the cutters used to break-in to the museum. Robert Key, the Head of Security for the Chellen Corporation, was following Senga Munreaux, the Sotheby's contact, the morning after an attempt had been made on her life."

His argument was compelling, and it had won him the approval of the Interpol officers assisting in the investigation. Forbes was about to find out just how much Chellen knew about the Paris theft, in … he checked his Tudor wristwatch, "Four hours."

The city of Helsinki is spread out across a number of bays, peninsulas, and islands. The inner city occupies a southern peninsula with a population density of 3,050 inhabitants per square kilometre. It ranks as sparse, compared to other European cities.

Forbes felt that downtown Helsinki had a very 'old-town' feel about it, with very old buildings stretching along-side tram lines and paved streets.

As he drove out to the suburbs the buildings became more modern, separated by patches of un-touched forests – that contrast again.

Forbes drove along the narrow Central Park Road. The snow had turned to sleet, and slid from the windscreen-wipers easily, as the car cut through the slush on the road.

The road stretched to the Northern border of Helsinki, and was noted for being an important recreational pathway. For miles, the only recreation that Forbes could see was the graffiti, squeezed onto every urban wall. He shook his head in disbelief, "That's just not art."

$$\mathcal{O}$$

Place aux Herbes, St Tropez

NOAH PARKED THE RENAULT IN THE LIVELY SQUARE that had been the centre of activity for the inhabitants of St Tropez for centuries. Located just one street behind the Quai Jean Jaures, and a little way past the Office de Tourisme, the Place aux Herbes is a busy little enclave of vegetable, fruit, and flower stalls. Even at this time of day, the produce managed to stimulate all the senses.

Noah bought a large bunch of Lilies. He held them loosely, as he and Senga trekked through a maze of back streets.

"Why do you need flowers?"

"They might just keep us alive long enough to get a meal."

"Where are you taking me?"

"To one of St Tropez's best little restaurants, don't worry it's tucked away in the heart of the old quarter, no one will find us."

"Chellen's not going to be there is he?"

"Oh no, someone much worse," His smile was supposed to convince her that his comment was supposed to be a joke.

Chapter Eleven

Boy in the Red Vest (Cezanne 1895)

Place aux Herbes, St Tropez, France.
Saturday, June 26.

THE BEST TABLES AT THE 'AU CAPRICE DES DEUX' ARE inside, in a section to the left of the small bar just as you enter, or, better still, if you don't want to hide from the world, you can sit at one of the outside tables, where you can watch the evening stroll by.

Senga read the hand-painted sign, "Au Caprice des Deux," her expectations took a nose dive.

"Trust me, you'll love it, wonderful clientele."

There was no electric lighting inside, and the candles on the tables had yet to be lit, but the aroma from the kitchen made up for it. Senga began to relax.

"Noah Coleman, I'm going to kill you!" Daisy came out of the kitchen, eyes wild with rage, "You stood me up, now, where were you ..." she saw Senga, her rage intensified, her index finger extended like a knife blade; she waved it under Noah's nose. "What's she doing here?"

Noah produced the Lilies, "Daisy, keep the noise down," he

143

whispered. She brushed away the flowers, "Noise, I'll give you noise." Daisy looked at the diners in the restaurant, "He stood me up last night. No word all day, today, now he shows up with 'Sorry Baby' flowers, and a pretty city girl." The couple on the nearest table put down their cutlery, and shook their heads at Noah.

"You see everybody agrees with me," Daisy snatched the flowers and put them on the bar, "Get them in mineral water!" she instructed the barman. She turned back to Noah, her finger wagged aggressively in his face, "You going to pay for this meal?"

Noah produced his most disarming smile, "Of course."

"Sit down."

Noah looked at a table to the left of the bar, but Daisy pointed to the other corner, "Over there."

Noah took Senga to the table, they sat obediently. Senga suddenly realized that during the whore's rant, no customers complained, nor was she approached, or reprimanded by the manager. "Who is she?" Senga whispered.

"Daisy? She owns the place. Head Chef."

Senga's mouth dropped open, "I thought she was a whore."

Noah's smile wrinkled his eyes, and he struggled to make his answer seem normal. "Well, she likes to supplement her business with a little pleasure. She's very good."

"At which job?"

"Hey, careful now," Noah said in hushed tones, "She's a very good friend of mine, and I usually eat for free."

"And you tolerate what she does for a living?"

"Of course, it's a very good restaurant."

"No, I mean the other work."

144

"Of course, you can't keep loved ones on too tight a leash, besides our relationship allows me a certain freedom to ...wander, when I want." Noah lay his hands, palm up on the table.

"Jesus, you do have a way with words." Senga refrained from saying anything else, because Daisy was walking toward them, her eyes and ears were as sharp as knives.

Noah answered, "True, but you're the one who's in trouble ..."

Daisy pulled up a chair, "Trouble? She looked at Noah, then, judgementally, back at Senga, "You pregnant?" she sat in-between them.

Senga replied in an angry whisper, "Certainly not."

Daisy turned to Noah, "Then it must be money, do we have anything tied up in her?"

Senga noted the word 'we', and marvelled at their relationship. Noah shook his head, and then gave a reassuring wink to Senga.

Daisy looked at Senga, her eyes widened; "How much?"

Senga answered openly, "I need to find a million pounds by this time next week."

✑◯

Helsinki, Finland.

FORBES SAT ON A LARGE COMFORTABLE SOFA, WATCHing the antics of the beautiful secretary, who was trying to determine if he was gay, or if he might be interested in her.

She had positioned herself such, so as to make sure he was able to see her long legs beneath the desk.

Of course it was his clothes that had prompted her decision

to test her theory. Her decision to tease would have been a natural preoccupation, she was very attractive, and so this was her way of exerting her power over those that came to see LeCoyte Chellen.

Forbes watched her nylon clad legs making over-exenterated movements. Silently he cursed his choice of clothes, '*I wish I hadn't worn this damned red waistcoat.*' His hand was in his pocket, his thumb ran down the edge of his business card, should he just present it to her, and stop all these games, and have her refuse him, or should he remain professionally aloof, and have her thick he was gay.

Her phone bleeped, she took it in her slender hand. Her mouth was moist as she spoke, she looked directly at him, sexual tension; right there in the eye contact. She was indeed lovely. '*What a tease.*'

"Mr Forbes? You can go in now."

The door was opened by a golden-haired heavy, with a look of Dolph Lundgren about him; mind you all big blond guys in Scandinavia have that look.

Forbes entered the plush, pine and leather office.

Behind the desk sat, head of security, Robert Key.

"Sit down Mr Forbes, how can I help you?"

"My appointment was with Mr Chellen." He unbuttoned his jacket. The red waistcoat peeked out.

"I'm afraid Mr Chellen is otherwise engaged, I hope I can answer any questions you have?" he relaxed into the comfort of his boss's chair.

As his curly-hair touched the leather headrest, Forbes had a brief flash of Key's flesh melting from his face. Instantly Forbes could smell the fetid air of the tube station. He squeezed his eyes tight shut, and grasped the arms chair.

"Have you lost weight since we last met, Mr Forbes?" Key noticed the prominent cheek bones that weren't there in Amsterdam.

Forbes's eyes flew open, he ran his tongue over his dry lips. "I like to keep in shape."

"I can see that Ducky. Now, what do you want to discuss with Mr. Chellen?"

"Mr Chellen is an art collector of some repute. I'm interested to understand if he has been approached with information pertaining to the Paris art theft." He stuck his thumbs in the red waistcoat pockets.

Key lent forward, "The Chellen Corporation has already cooperated with Interpol, and local police forces. We have explained that, in the unlikely occurrence, we are contacted by anyone with information pertaining to the Paris art theft, or the whereabouts of the five stolen paintings, that we would pass on the information," he paused, "Immediately. But I must impress on you that Mr Chellen is head of a global telecommunications company, his art collecting is no more than a hobby ..."

"He owns twenty-five galleries around the world. He sponsors numerous art colleges."

"Is Mr. Chellen a suspect?" his tone became harder.

"All that information is in the public domain," Forbes answered quickly.

"But you checked it out?"

"Yes."

"But you have already spoken to Mr. Chellen at his home."

"And you complained."

"Not me personally, but Mr. Chellen was very upset by your insistent questioning, I ask again, is Mr Chellen a suspect?"

"Do you believe the Paris theft was undertaken by a lone thief, just chancing his luck?"

"I have no opinion."

"Who do you think would specify the *Café* as a target?"

"I don't know." Frustration crept into his answer.

"Do you think the paintings were stolen to order?"

"That seems more realistic, from what I've read."

"What's Mr. Chellen's view?"

"I don't know, he hasn't discussed it with me?"

"But you would know if he was thinking of purchasing an expensive work of art; for the purposes of security, of course."

"Of course."

"Is he?"

"Is he what?" Key rested his hands on the desk.

"Thinking of buying another expensive work of art?"

"I don't know, you'd need to ask him that yourself."

"I'd like to but he won't see me; that's why you're here, to fend off awkward questions about art theft."

"Stupid questions about art theft ... Is Mr. Chellen a suspect?" Key shouted.

"Ask Interpol."

"We have, they say he isn't. Only you keep coming forward and stepping on our toes. Only you keep following Mr. Chellen around the world. Stalking him, I believe that is the correct term nowadays."

"Do you have an opinion on who stole the paintings?" change of tack.

"No, but I would imagine that any thief would want to get something from the theft."

"But those paintings could never be sold on the open market."

"Of course not."

"So they'd have to go to a collector."

"If you say so."

"Surely an intelligent man like yourself cannot believe that a new collector, a Saudi, or a Chinese for example would began a collection with stolen works that cannot be displayed."

"Probably."

"So we both accept the collector has a number of paintings in his collection already."

"If they were for a collection."

"Why else would they be taken?" Forbes asked quickly. Key realized he'd been suckered in. "I really don't know Ducky," he spoke slowly, trying to regain his composure, "You're the expert in stolen art, why do paintings usually get stolen?"

Forbes gave a stock reply, "Collateral, currency, ransom. But usually for a private collection."

"Mr. Forbes, no matter how you dress this up, the Chellen Corporation has not received an invitation to purchase the stolen paintings."

"Perhaps you never intended to buy them. Ever since the theft, Chellen has been unavailable. I'm on to him. Tell him that when you report in."

"Tell him what?"

"Tell him, I think its LeCoyte Chellen."

"That did the theft?"

"Let him work it out."

"Mr. Forbes, I don't know what you are implying, but I promise you, if you continue this line of enquiry the ALR, and you as an individual will be hearing from the Corporation's lawyers."

Forbes felt that Key was angry enough to let something slip. He decided to probe some more. "I'm sorry Mr Key, but there is hard evidence that Mr. Chellen is implicated in the theft. So far we've been asking about the actual thieves trying to sell the paintings to Mr. Chellen, as a collector. The next time we speak, it will be about Mr. Chellen ordering the theft to take place, and never intending to pay the thieves for their work."

"Two art thieves bludgeoned to death since the theft, it's hardly a smoking gun is it."

Forbes shrugged, "That depends."

"Depends on what, Forbes? The police believing you? Everyone thinks you're crazy. Just what evidence have you got?"

Forbes thought about the photograph, he thought about Buscetti's cremated body in the getaway car; he thought about Mosca's beaten in body in the museum in Verona, "I'm not divulging anything to you. I want the organ-grinder, not the monkey."

"Then we have nothing further to discuss Ducky."

Dolph, held the door open.

As Forbes left the office he stopped in front of the secretary's desk, he placed his business card in front of her. "Write your number on there, I don't leave Helsinki until late tomorrow."

The girl wrote quickly, and handed the card back to him.

"I'll call you at eight."

She looked nervously back to the office door but it was already closed. She smiled and nodded, "I'd like that," her lips suggested she would.

Forbes descended in the elevator, this was more like it. Just like the old times, bluffing the bad guys, getting the girl, coming under fire, and getting vital information under interrogation. Key's words echoed in his mind. He knew he was on the right track. How else would Key know that there had been two deaths? The killing in Marseille had been reported as a fire. The fact that Buscetti had been killed by a blow to the head, prior to the fire had not been made common knowledge.

Forbes examined his business card. The girl's name was Katja, and her number was very legible. Forbes knew instinctively what had swayed her decision, yes; he was very pleased with his decision to wear the red waistcoat.

❧ᴄ

Place aux Herbes, St Tropez, France.
Saturday, June 26.

NOAH SPOKE QUIETLY, "SENGA, IF WE'RE GOING TO help you I think you have to tell us the whole story, you're going to have to tell us who you owe the money to."

"A million pounds," Daisy nodded in collaboration, she moved her chair closer to Noah, "That's a lot of money."

Senga composed herself, "Five years ago I went on holiday, I met and fell in love with a man in Chamonix; a little too easily you might say, but still it happened."

"It happens," Daisy validated, fussing with her clothing.

"He flattered me. Told me I could do anything I wanted to do, could go anywhere I wanted to go, be whoever I wanted to be …and he could make it happen quicker, if I went to work

151

for him," Senga took a drink. "In the cold light of day I figured he must have been talking about drugs or prostitution-" Senga looked at Daisy, "No offence."

Daisy looked bewildered, "None taken."

"I packed up, and left during the night, probably because I wasn't sure if I trusted myself to say no ..."

Daisy looked at Noah, and shrugged.

Senga noted the exchange, and continued, "Anyway a couple of days after I got back to London, I was contacted by a firm of Head Hunters. They told me that Sotheby's wanted to talk to me. I did the interview, got the job, got on the career ladder, and at the beginning of 2006, headed off to the Hong Kong office, my holiday romance completely forgotten."

Daisy looked at Noah, the stone setting in her eye, with a flick of her hair she commented, "She's been to Hong Kong. You promised to take me to Hong Kong, Sharky."

Noah tried to calm her, his face conveying a look of real interest in the tale.

Senga continued, "Couple of weeks after I got there, an amazing find was brought to my attention. The seller was a Mr. Remmert van Braam ..."

"The master!" Noah interrupted, his breath escaped in a low whistle.

Senga acknowledged the remark, "Indeed, although of course I didn't know him at that time," her eyes flicked from Noah to Daisy, the name meant nothing to her. "Remmert, indicated that if I didn't delve too deeply into the provenance of the newly found painting, which was undergoing extreme scrutiny, that I would be able to earn enough money from 'the find' to buy a Ferrari by the end of the month."

Senga lent forward, and whispered, "His comments made me look at the provenance even more closely; but I could find nothing out of order, honestly, so I passed it. The painting and ownership was declared, authentic."

Daisy too lent forward, her tone was dark, "Go on."

"A week after the painting sold at auction, for four million dollars, I received a thank you gift from Remmert, a small cabinet painting. His note suggested I put it up for auction in Berlin. I did, it made one hundred and twenty-five thousand euros."

"So you bought a Ferrari," Daisy asked expectedly, her lips were already pursed.

"Yes," Senga replied rather guiltily.

Daisy glared at Noah, "I have to drive around in a five year old Renault Megane. By the way Noah, where is my car?"

Hurriedly Senga continued, "There was no further contact until the middle of the year. When it came, it followed the same procedure, verify a find as authentic, receive a gift, sell it, and get rich. It happened every couple of months until the beginning of 2007. Eighteen months since I'd had my holiday romance, he walked back into my life."

"Only now you had your own money, I hope you made him beg," Daisy, interjected.

Senga shook her head, "He asked how I'd enjoyed working for him since I'd been in Hong Kong?"

Daisy snorted, "You told him to go fuck himself?"

Senga gave no answer, her eyes made no contact.

Daisy spoke accusingly, "You slept with him?" her voice was at soprano pitch.

"2007 was a fantastic year, I was transferred to the Met, in New York."

Daisy's jaw dropped, "America-"

"Go on," Noah tried to hurry the story along.

"Then, van Braam asked me to get him into Bartholomew House ..."

Noah clarified to Daisy, "Sotheby's restoration house."

Senga nodded, "It's nothing more than an art studio in New York ..."

Noah closed his eyes, and inhaled, drawing on a memory. His left hand covered his eyes, he began to moan softly, "Oh no."

"What is it?" Daisy asked.

"On November the third, 2008, a painting called *Suprematist Composition*, a work by Kazimir Malevich, set the world record for any Russian work of art," Noah recited, his fingers dropped to cover his mouth.

Senga's haunted face turned toward Daisy, "The most expensive work sold at auction that year, sold at Sotheby's in New York City for just over Sixty million U.S. dollars."

Noah continued, Daisy looked suitably astounded, "Far surpassing his previous record of seventeen million, set in 2000. The painting, as I recall had been damaged, and was restored at Bartholomew House."

An age passed before Senga finally answered the unvoiced question. Her voice sounded thin and frail, "van Braam took the original."

Noah exhaled, "Genius."

Daisy asked, "I take it this van Braam guy is a better forger than you?"

Noah looked shocked, "He might have been once, but not anymore."

"Why?" Daisy asked

"He's blind," Senga interjected.

"Oh, that's a shame, what happened?" Daisy asked.

Noah replied in a matter of fact tone, "Somebody informed on him, and he had a nasty accident trying to escape from the police."

"Aargh!" Said Daisy, "who would have done such an underhanded thing?"

"It was me," answered Noah.

Daisy looked genuinely shocked, "Why'd you do such a thing? Her voice rose to a high pitched squeal. Noah winced at the onslaught he knew was to come.

"I wanted him out of the way," he looked at Senga, "I wanted to do a deal." He looked as Senga, "which led to the Oleg venture, so all's well ... I had no idea he would try to run from the police." He defended.

"He was 65," Senga added as if his age would have precluded him from the thought of running.

"Senga and I met shortly after. Senga just made three quarters of a million pounds, and I got three hundred and fifty thousand." He dipped an eyebrow in Daisy's direction.

"I've still got to sell the second one."

"No problem, it'll be a breeze."

All were silent. The sound of the dishes in the kitchen filtered through to them. Senga looked guilty. Daisy looked happy, thinking of her access to Noah's cash. Noah looked deep in thought.

"You said you needed a million," Noah spoke to Senga. She nodded.

"You'll have three quarters from the sale of the two Olegs,"

Noah's eyes narrowed, "you have to pay two point three million next week. That means you already have five hundred and fifty thousand put aside for the helmet."

Senga looked sheepish, "Fifty thousand is my own. I borrowed the other half a million."

"Who from?" Noah's tone vented his frustration.

"Her boyfriend, obviously," Daisy chipped in. "The helmet is for her boyfriend, they've had a spat; she thinks that by giving him the helmet it will get her credit cards cleared."

"She owes him half a million … hang on. What is the name of this sex-god you met in Chamonix?

"Yeah," said Daisy, "I'd like to meet someone I can argue with, and get kicked out of bed with half a million pounds."

Senga took a deep breath, "Chandhok Nahmad."

"Holy shit!" Noah threw his eyes to the heavens.

Daisy asked, "Who?" but Noah was already groaning.

Senga blurted out, "I didn't know who he was …he was charming."

"Why hasn't he just killed you?" Noah asked.

"I gave him collateral for my five hundred thousand."

"What did you give him?" Noah pointed an accusing finger at Senga.

She shook her head, her hands went to her face to hide her shame. Noah grabbed her wrists, "What was it?" Noah asked.

"Sharky, leave the lady alone," Daisy defended her new found friend.

"What have you given Nahmad as collateral worth half a million?" Noah ignored Daisy's request.

"Madame X."

"Oh shit, this just keeps getting better." Noah pushed back his chair, it whined across the floor, like a child in a supermarket.

"What?" Daisy asked, "Who's this Madame X?" Her head turned from face to face, but got no reply.

Noah stood up, attracting worried glances from the other clients. He spoke quietly to the two women. "No wonder he's after you. Christ he makes Chellen look like a Sunday-school teacher."

"Who's Chellen?" Daisy was ignored.

Senga was confused, "I don't see why he's the one that's after me, I conned Chellen out of half a million. We got six hundred thousand out of the auction buyer, or will do. But Chandhok has Madame X, and the Sargent is worth ten times the helmet."

"It's a forgery!" Noah spat out the words.

Daisy placed her hand on Senga's arm, she pleaded for calm with Noah.

"Can someone tell me who this Madame X is? Who's the Sargent? And who the hell wears a helmet these days? Or is it some kind of Gimp mask?" silence fluttered down around them.

Chapter Twelve

MADAME X (JOHN SINGER SARGENT 1884)

Place aux Herbes, St Tropez, France.
Saturday, June 26.

NOAH RECITED, "JOHN SINGER SARGENT WAS THE most successful portrait painter of his era. However his most famous painting was the first he ever exhibited."

"Like his debut album," Daisy understood her own metaphor.

"He painted an extra-ordinary portrait right at the beginning of his career, something, for those times was very risqué. He hoped it would win him fame …it did, but not in the way he imagined."

Daisy winked at Senga, indicating that she was about to learn something from Noah's description. Senga smiled, and hid the fact she knew all the details.

"Sargent approached Virginie Gautreau, a famous society beauty, and wife of a French banker. She agreed to be his model for the painting."

"Nude?" Daisy asked expectantly.

Noah shook his head, "Sargent chose the pose; her body

boldly faces forward, while her head is turned in profile, a posture of both contention and sanctuary."

Daisy re-enacted the pose, "Like this?" one eyebrow rose theatrically.

"Absolutely," Noah confirmed.

"Yeah, very sexy," Daisy proclaimed to both.

"When this beauty, with her hour-glass figure, and ivory complexion, was put on display at the Paris Salon in 1884, it created a scandal. The public were shocked by her low cut dress, and deathly white make-up."

"I get the picture, it was like a sex-tape." Daisy said understandingly.

"They were outraged by the fact that one of her dress straps was hanging off her shoulder, a sure sign of impropriety."

Un-noticed by Noah, Daisy checked her own dress strap.

"The scandal caused Virginie to retire from society. Later Sargent painted in the shoulder-strap. He too left Paris after the scandal, but always maintained the portrait was the finest work he'd ever painted."

Daisy looked at Senga, "She sounds sexy! What happened to her?"

"Oh she got painted again by Sargent. Even did the pose again seven years later for Gustave Courtois, and then again for, what would be her favourite painting, Antonio de la Gandara."

"They did the same pose painting again? So there's more than one version of this Madame X painting?"

"That's right, the third one was done in 1897, and it was very well accepted."

"Then how do you know that Chandhok got the real one?"

"They're all real. Sargent's first one, is the famous work. It's not uncommon for an artist to paint more than one version of a painting, Da Vinci painted a second version of the Mona Lisa, you know," Senga chipped in.

"Do they know where the second one is?" Daisy asked hurriedly.

"Yes, it hangs in the Louvre," Noah replied.

Daisy narrowed her eyes, and prepared to launch a verbal assault.

"It's true, the first version is known as the Isleworth Mona Lisa, it's owned by a consortium in Switzerland." Senga smoothed the waters.

"He painted two Mona Lisa's?" Daisy raised two fingers.

"Yes, both in 1503." Noah answered.

"And they're both real?" The voice started to raise again.

"Yes," Senga joined in, "there's actually a third painting in St Petersburg. It was bought from an American family at the end of the 18th century. It hung in KGB headquarters for years."

"Three Mona Lisa's? But which is the real one?" Daisy asked, a confused smile drifted across her lovely face.

"They're all real, but the one in the Louvre is accepted as the one that was Da Vinci's best version."

"And they're all real?" Daisy asked again.

"Yes, radio-carbon dating proves they were all painted by Leonardo. All are confirmed as having the right primer layer and containing the same pigments and baritone sulphate."

"How do they do that?" Daisy asked, looking from Noah to Senga.

"Multi-spectral cameras that reflect the layers of paint," Senga responded. Daisy looked bemused, so Senga simplified the statement, "X-ray machines."

"Oh, I get it," Daisy looked satisfied.

"Sargent sold Madame X to the Metropolitan in 1916," Noah got them back on track, only to be de-railed by Senga.

Senga interjected, "And it's been hanging in the Met for the last 94 years."

"It's a forgery." Noah asserted.

"How can you be so sure?" Senga asked.

Noah's hand slapped his chest. "Because I did it,"

Daisy's eyes opened wide, Senga's mouth dropped open, "Does Chandhok know?"

"Yes," Noah replied sarcastically, "I did it for him. He has the real one."

Senga dropped her head into her hands and began to sob. Daisy leaned over and put a protective arm around her, "Why did you borrow the money off him?"

"She didn't borrow the money. The money was her cut for delivering the painting from the Met."

Daisy looked confused, she asked uncertainly, "But why would this man Chandhok want a painting, if he knew it was a fake?"

Noah looked at Senga, urging her to complete the story, "The truth now."

Senga sniffed back the tears, "The money was my payoff for getting the Met to lend Chandhok a painting for his exhibition in Hong Kong."

"I bet he wasn't expecting Madame X was he?" Noah asked.

Senga shook her head, "No, he was expecting a Pollack; but there was a mix up with the restoration schedule, and at the last minute the Sargent became available. I made the decision to switch," she shrugged.

"You'd already had the money by then?"

Senga nodded, "I had to pay you a retainer for the Oleg."

"He wanted his money back, didn't he?"

Senga nodded through the tears, "We had a big fight. I left, I thought the helmet was the way back into his life." She banged her fist on the table, "I thought he'd have loved to exhibit Madame X in Hong Kong."

"But it was the one painting he didn't want to see."

"So, did he send it back?" Daisy asked, still stroking Senga's shoulders.

"He can't. They will discover it's a fake. He'll face an investigation. The last thing Nahmad wants is the ALR poking around in his private galleries. He'll have to send the real painting back, after the exhibition."

"So how come, they didn't discover it was a fake before?" Daisy asked.

"Remmert van Braam," Noah and Senga said together.

"So van Braam, got the paintings through museum security; but now he's blind, he can't help this guy Chandhok anymore," Daisy thought about the problem, then burst out laughing, "No wonder he's trying to kill you. You took his money, and you stiffed him with the painting."

Noah's hands caressed the table, "He's lost you. He's about to lose Madame X. Your face keeps popping up at auction. First the Crosby Garett helmet, then the Oleg-" Noah stood up, his hands covering his mouth; he sucked in a lung full of air through his fingers. "The helmet went for way over the estimate. I bet he was the one bidding against you."

Senga suddenly looked serious; she shook off the tears, "So what do we do now?"

"We?" Noah and Daisy answered in unison.

Senga's eyes darted from one to the other. "Yes *we*! Surely you realize that van Braam will have told Chandhok, who informed on him?"

"How would old Remmert even know it was me?"

"You said it yourself, with him out of the way, you're the next best thing. It wouldn't take long for the penny to drop. I bet you've been compared to van Braam, ever since you did Madame X, am I right?"

Noah nodded proudly.

"And now that we've been seen together-" she let the comment drift.

Daisy chipped in, "Get a buyer for the gimp-mask."

"Roman helmet," Noah corrected.

"Helmet then, just sell the damn thing and give him his money back."

Senga shook her head, her voice, when she spoke was full of emotion; "I don't think it's the money he wants."

"You better give him what he wants then lady, cause I sure do want to visit Hong Kong before I die."

Noah suggested, "Why not just front it out. Go and see him, throw yourself at him, and ...you know," he simulated the sex act, much to the amusement of other diners at the other side of the restaurant.

Senga sounded exasperated, "He's trying to have me killed. I don't think giving him a blow job will get me back in his good books."

Daisy began to speak, but then thought better of it.

Noah made a decision, "Okay, we need to think of something

else." The darkness of the night was truly formed before their plan was decided.

❧

Helsinki, Finland.
Saturday, June 26. 19.30hrs.

PIZZA IN HAND, FORBES BROWSED THROUGH THE Chellen Corporation website. After the slip by Key, Forbes was convinced that Chellen was behind the Paris theft. He searched for a confession on every page.

Forbes scrolled down the diverse holdings of Chellen's empire.

He needed to do something to fill in the time before he phoned Katja.

'New Acquisitions.' The Corporation was growing so fast that the new information had a web page of its own.

"New acquisitions," Forbes took a bite of Pizza. "He would never be able to show the paintings to anyone else." Forbes went to the page, and scrolled to the date of the theft. "So he would want to keep them close."

The twenty-first of May. "It would have taken a while to plan." He went back to March. "What did you buy in March?" Forbes knew he would want to keep the paintings close to him. He dismissed, the American acquisitions.

"Paris! And Munich!" the only two acquisitions in Europe since March. Forbes returned the Pizza to the box. "And where have you been frequenting since the theft?" Forbes switched to another website. This one was funded by Euro News. Forbes knew Chellen had been in Amsterdam, with his mistress, but where else had he been? The site showed photos of Chellen at various functions.

"What the fu-" Forbes read the review under the photo, Forbes cross-checked the dates with the Corporation site. Then he clapped his hands together.

"So although you own a multi-million dollar apartment in Paris, you were seen in the company of two punk singers, leaving a well-worn hotel north of the city. They're young enough to be your daughters, you old perv," he counselled.

The article continued that, Chellen had bought an old bakery in Goussainville, for his protégés 'Reflectionz' (sensational singing twins – the article called them).

The bakery was to be turned into a recording studio. Forbes flicked back to the corporate website. The financial accounts confirmed that the Chellen Corporation had purchased a number of buildings in the Goussainville area.

As Forbes packed his bag, he made a call to the airport, "Do you have availability on the next flight to Paris?" he waited expectantly, "Yes, I can make that," he glanced at his Tudor wristwatch, it was 20.03hrs.

ৎ৫〇

French airspace.
Sunday, June 27. 02.00hrs.

WILLIAM FORBES HAD CURSED HIS LUCK DURING EV-ery minute of the flight from Helsinki. He knew that Katja would be in no doubt he was gay. The pain he felt was more than physical, he ran his palm over his new haircut, and wished he could make a phone call from the plane explaining his predicament. He'd gone through a lot of anguish in plucking up the courage to speak to her, the Munreaux girl had certainly given him a new confidence. Now he was destined to be alone again.

Forbes chastised himself, it had been his intention to only think nice thoughts during the flight, but Katja and Senga had crept inside his head; and not having either them frustrated him.

He looked forward to the next couple of days, because soon he would have to confront LeCoyte Chellen, and get up close and personal if he wanted that confession. Forbes settled back into his seat, and imagined finding the paintings.

As the seatbelt sign lit up, he knew the paintings were within his grasp.

St Tropez, France.
Sunday, June 27.

NOAH COLEMAN HAD ALWAYS LIVED BY THE PREMISE that he would not look to prolong the days in this life, by adapting to a diet, or cutting out wine; but instead he would actively use every hour he was given on God's earth to seek out and indulge in pleasure. He had always assumed this meant not tying himself to one woman.

If fame and fortune, glitz and glamour had not waved its magic wand on St Tropez, one wondered how the town, little more than a sleepy fishing village, might look today, and it was that vision, pretty much now, how Noah and Daisy had viewed the harbour as they had wandered around the charming waterfront without a care in the world; the sun warmed their hearts and their bodies.

Last night's conversation with Senga, had somehow cemented their relationship. Noah realized that he wanted the whole world to know about his relationship with Daisy. Everything felt so right with her in his life. Their backgrounds and baggage melted away. He hoped she felt the same.

Together, they strolled around the narrow streets and marvelled at the baroque architecture. They ate lunch on the great seawall that once surrounded the port. Daisy played at being a soldier, marching along the battlements on the original fortress which once protected the town from pirates.

For lunch, Noah plumped for the pan de cazón, a tortilla dish of baby shark, topped with fried beans, onions and epazote herbs. Daisy was happy with the owner's recommendation of Kachin-amba, a shrimp delicacy with coconut, served with applesauce.

The daylight hours had been filled with conversations neither of them could recall, and the night had been filled with lovemaking neither would ever forget. Knowing that they were soon to be parted brought them closer together.

Now that his bag was packed, he was dreading the time he was going to spend away from her, even more than dreading the task that lay ahead of him.

St Tropez, France.
Monday, June 28.

NOAH LISTENED TO DAISY SINGING IN THE SHOWER. IF Senga could get them on a flight, this would be their last day together for a short while. For the first time he even felt a little uncomfortable about her hobby, or profession, whichever way you viewed it. He even felt a pang of jealousy about what she might get up to during the time he was away. With that image in his head, he was already looking forward to coming home.

The whore, and the forger, their lifestyle was certainly unique. Noah decided then and there, that should he return with his life intact, he would give up living outside the law. Maybe it was even the right time to leave the French Riviera altogether, maybe it was the right time to take Daisy to Hong Kong.

Noah and Senga were going to shout at the devil. They were going to rattle Chandhok Nahmad's cage. They were going to make him an offer he could not refuse.

⨏◯

THE MISTAKE OF FOLLOWING THE CHESTNUT BROWN Audi, when it emerged from the second underground car-park had cost the man with the puckering scar just above his hair-line, an entire day.

Now, he sat in the stop, start morning traffic crush approaching St Tropez. His mind was relaxed, yet focused. The photo-shoot at the arrivals-hall had paid dividends. A seemingly un-connected link in his chain reaction had resulted in a name and address.

168

He imagined what the night would hold for him, the promise excited him more than the scarlet Ferrari he was following, and much more than the girls sauntering along the pavement.

∽✍◯

Goussainville-Vieux Pays, France.
Monday, June 28.

GOUSSAINVILLE, WAS A ONCE QUIET FARMING VILLAGE, 30 kilometers north of Paris. Inhabited by the bourgeoisie from the 17th century, it returned to a more rural environment after the revolution, silencing the guillotine blade once and for all.

Quiet and calm remained until the international airport of Roissy-Charles-de-Gaulle opened for business in the early nineteen seventies.

When construction on the airport began, the town shifted its center a few kilometers from what is now called the Vieux-Pays, to the older community of Goussainville. Some near sighted developers even bought land, hoping to cash in from the airport, but they soon put it back up for sale.

Although a few diehard townsfolk continue to live in the area, those who did not want to bear the omnipresent sound of planes taking off and landing simply packed up and left.

The town became deserted over a few short months. Remaining at the heart of the ghost town is a bakery named *Le Manoir*, converted from an old mill, and a hotel, formerly a coaching-inn modernized at the turn of the 19th century, named *Auberge du Raisin*, it sits upon the skeleton of a once grand 16th century bourgeois chateau. Both buildings overlook the town's renaissance church, which residents took great pride in restoring over the years.

Le Manoir looked more like a fairy castle than a conventional bakery. Made from local stone, the building imposed itself upon the devastated landscape like a polished jewel. Above the upper floor windows, turrets and spires pointed toward the clouds; gently jostling with faint wisps of smoke from the chimney, drifting toward the sky.

To the side of the building, rotating in the swollen river, a bedraggled water-wheel fought in vain to keep the rushing water at bay.

It was just a fleeting glance, as Forbes drove past, but it was enough to convince him that as a recording studio it was adequate, but as a hiding place for the paintings it was perfect, total seclusion, and isolation, but just thirty minutes north of Paris. Forbes felt buoyed.

The next building was the hotel. What a disappointment!

Forbes turned off the road, and bounced over the un-even surface of the car-park.

The *Auberge du Raisin* was advertised as a true 'home from home'. Just ten cosy rooms housed within an historic, charming structure. "Nestling amid spectacular rural French scenery," Forbes threw down the leaflet. As he opened the car door an A320 airbus, rushed over his head shattering any semblance of rural tranquillity.

As he dropped his bag on the lumpy bed, a cloud of flea-powder blossomed into the air. Another roar of jet power rattled the windows in their frames.

Most of the noise from a modern jet originates from the fan at the front of the engine and not the exhaust. At takeoff, the tips of the fan blades can exceed the speed of sound, at that moment a series of shock waves transmit forward from the fan. Even at lower power settings, the fan blades create a lot of noise, especially if the inlet is pointed in your direction. Forbes was in no doubt which direction the planes were pointing when they came over his room.

This was not a good place to return to after a day of sightseeing, especially for a billionaire art impresario and two sexy punk protégés young enough to be his daughters. Forbes could smell the paintings, deep down in his soul he knew they were hidden at *le Manoir*.

In the quiet between breathless landings and roaring take-offs, Forbes felt, rather than heard a beating thump. He went to the window. The view from the rear of the hotel was no better than the front. Ramshackle outbuildings fuzzed the view. Somewhere beyond his vision he was sure he could hear an old bilge pump. He tilted his head and filtered out all other sounds, trying to pinpoint the noise. Another jet screamed overhead like a wailing banshee.

"No wonder they all left." The quiet between planes was just long enough to allow the beat of the pump to enter his consciousness, "I hope that's not going to go on all night?" Forbes went down to dinner.

Chapter Thirteen

COUNT LEPIC AND HIS DAUGHTERS (DEGAS 1871)

St Tropez, France.
Monday, June 28.

HIS FINGERS MOVED FROM THE HARDENING SCAR JUST above the hairline, to the contraption that was clamped on his face. He flicked the switch to night-vision, and scanned the darkened windows.

He entered through a rear, ground floor window, it whined like a cat on heat; but there was no sign of response.

Silently he walked through the hallway, listening softly at each door for signs of life.

On the first floor his patience paid dividends. He heard the contented sounds of breathing. Carefully he threaded a small tube beneath the door. It had two functions, at the end of the tube was a small thermal imaging camera; along the outside resided a bi-metallic strip which detected how much carbon dioxide was present.

He looked at the tiny screen, the CO_2 readout allowed him to determine there were two people in the room. *'Lucky Noah,'* he thought.

Soon he stood beside the bed, and completed the last link in his chain reaction. It had started on May the nineteenth, in the Museum of Modern art, Paris, it ended as he administered the poison via the hypodermic needle into the neck of Noah Coleman; his death was silent and quick.

Noiselessly he traversed around the bed. He raised the hypodermic again, a spray of poison burst forth like a fountain. As he manoeuvred his head to get a better look at Senga's neck he realized something was wrong. Gently he pulled down the sheet to get a better look at her face, he inclined his head to view her innocent beauty. With a silent rage coursing through his body he realized this was not the woman he'd seen with Coleman at the airport. This was not the woman that Forbes had been with in the underground station. He lent over the sleeping woman, and studied the face of the dead man lying beside her. The man was not Noah Coleman.

❧◯

THE PUMP HAD WOKEN HIM AGAIN. VARIOUS GROANS and settlement had lulled him to sleep, the jets had been constant but acceptable, but it was that damned pump that had jerked Forbes out of a fitful, jet filled dream.

He imagined himself in Africa, the tribal drums thudding through the jungle air, this though was not a P.T.S.D. induced flashback, it was just a genuine associated dream state. He interlocked his fingers behind his head and smiled. The closer he was getting to the paintings the stronger he was becoming.

Everything about this dirty little run-down hotel told him that Chellen was using the girl singers as cover. They had all stayed here, he wondered if they'd slept in this bed; all of them. He pulled a face of disgust, and tried to think of Senga to brighten his mood.

The thump, thump, thump of the pump droned on, in the morning he would take a look at the offending item, and find out just what was being pumped out.

The desire to do so was almost as compelling as breaking into the bakery and finding the five stolen paintings. Another jet soared overhead.

⁓∅◯

SUDDENLY DAISY BECAME AWARE THAT SHE HAD TO wake up, her senses dragged themselves from slumber …and then came the panic.

Something was stopping her from breathing. Her eyes could not open. Frantically she moved her hands up to her face.

She felt something covering her, moulding itself over her eyes, her nose, and her mouth. She performed an uncoordinated body pop, and brought herself upright, the duvet slid from her naked body.

Her hands clawed at the objects on her face. It felt like plastic. She tried to scream, but realized her mouth was sealed shut. She wiggled her tongue between her lips. It tasted sticky, like duct tape. Who the hell had she brought home last night!

Her fingers clawed at the tape over her mouth, the glue relaxed its grip and the tape came away. She pulled at the pieces covering her eyes. The tape lifted, and she peeked out beneath the tape. It was then that the blow whacked into her face, she saw bright stars …and then nothing, as she slid from the bed onto the floor, unconscious.

When she next became aware, she heard a crackling sound. There was light beyond her closed eyelids. Her head throbbed from the blow, like a wine induced hang-over. Daisy opened her eyes.

It was her bedroom, but it was out of focus, her vision was blurred. Daisy tried to move her hands, but they were restrained at her sides, tied to a wooden kitchen chair. The plastic seat-pad sucked at her naked buttocks. Fear flooded through her body, she began to whimper. She tried to move, but realized her legs were also tied, to the legs of the chair. The tape hurt her legs, and wrists.

With rising panic, she became aware that the crackling noise was her own breathing.

"It's just a cheap plastic bag," a voice came from behind her shoulder. It was so close it made her shiver. Suddenly she became aware of her nakedness. Not being able to cover her nudity made her feel ashamed. Goose pimples shot up her arms.

With a grim understanding Daisy knew the reason for her laboured breathing was due to a clear plastic-bag over her head. She squirmed on the chair. The bag was taped around her throat.

"Shit, I should never have let you stay over." She mumbled through the tape. With sad realization she assumed that her client was responsible, "Just my luck to land some kind of hom-icidal manic."

His hand seized her chin, and turned her face toward the bed, "Just so we're clear."

Daisy saw the body of her client in the bed. Before she could scream, the voice spoke again, "You have approximately two minutes of air, don't waste it." The hand detached, and her head fell forward. Now, she was completely confused.

"Who are you?" she mumbled.

"Stay calm. I just killed the man you were sleeping with." The voice was slow and deliberate, it sounded like an adult talking to a child.

"Oh, Jesus!" Daisy panicked, if her client was dead, just who the hell was doing this to her, and why? She fought against the tape holding her to the chair.

She jerked her head from side to side, but the effort made her dizzy. The lack of clean oxygen was already affecting her.

"You have about one minute now." His hand came over her shoulder again and touched her cleavage. She felt, for the only time in her life, embarrassed, and vulnerable.

"Your heart is racing. Please calm down and answer my questions. Just nod or shake. Do you understand?"

Daisy nodded her head. Her voice screamed within her body, it stopped just behind her lips, trapped in her muffled mouth. The effort drained her, she felt hot stringing tears well up in her frightened eyes, and then slide fearfully down her cheeks.

Daisy took in some stale air, and choked, although the cough would not come, the room began to spin.

"Nod for yes, shake for no, do it, and all this can stop." The voice was full of hope. His hand remained over her shoulder and on her sternum.

"The man in your bed, was his name Noah Coleman?"

Daisy shook her head, bright stars of light fought with the blackness to come.

"Do you know where Mr Coleman is?"

Daisy nodded. The movement was small.

His hands moved over her face. He squeezed the bag, and cut a small hole in it, just in front of her mouth, "There, I told you."

Daisy sniffed in some fresh air. Desperate to control her sobbing and urge to cough, she gulped in the life giving oxygen, widening her nostrils. The relief of feeling the air rushing into her lungs made her feel like crying.

Cutting through her joy, he spoke again, "I'd like to take the tape from your mouth, but I'm afraid you'd scream." Daisy shook her head quickly, but the voice continued, he was lent close to her now, both hands on her shoulders. "If you scream, I will have to kill you. But, I want answers to my questions …and I hate to see you so distressed." He nestled into her body, his head close to her ear. "Okay, I'm going to ask you questions, Nod for yes shake for no, understood?"

Daisy nodded again, it seemed she was fighting for a privilege she already had. She knew this man would have no compunction about killing her, no matter what he said, but she had no choice but to comply.

He needed only a basic understanding of Coleman's whereabouts to determine his own actions, he wanted to see her face when she answered, to be certain she wasn't lying, and see the fear in her eyes, but that would mean putting the goggles on again, and that meant itching his scar.

"Do you know where Noah has gone?" he asked, Daisy nodded.

"Has he gone with the woman?" Daisy nodded, she knew that bitch was bad news.

"Have they gone to meet William Forbes?" The name meant nothing to her, Daisy shook her head.

The man understood, Coleman and Munreaux only had a limited number of options.

"Have they gone to Paris?" Daisy nodded.

"Are they going to meet Chandhok Nahmad?" Daisy felt relief flood through her body. She nodded enthusiastically.

His face was next to her ear, "Good, that's all I need to know," his voice was like a lullaby. His body moved, she saw the shadow, then saw his bulk coming in front of her.

He knelt, he was humming a tune, but Daisy did not recognise it. She did not recognise him. She smiled in anticipation of being released.

His fingers worked delicately over the plastic bag, smoothing it over her mouth. Deftly he applied a piece of duct tape over the hole.

Daisy's eyes widened in the horror of understanding she was going to die, his widened in ecstasy.

He inclined his head, and smoothed her hair with his gentle fingers. "Most people don't have what it takes to kill another human being," his voice was melodic; "I do, that's what makes me special." The man touched his puckering scar. He recalled the fight with Buscetti. He reached down and stroked her naked thighs.

"And you are special too, you are so beautiful." He smiled at her while revelling in the memory of killing the driver in the field of sunflowers. He remembered it was these very hands that had snapped the man's neck; he looked at his hands dispassionately, professionally. His hand went instinctively to Daisy's throat, encased in duct tape. "We are going to have such fun together. I wasn't meant to meet you, but fate has brought us here tonight, just another link in my chain reaction." Slowly and gently he rubbed her thighs and throat. He recalled how his fists had pummelled Mosca in the office in Verona, knowing that Forbes was walking toward them, he relaxed in the memory.

Daisy felt the room begin to spin, her breathing was becoming shallow, and with the sound of his hypnotic voice in her ear she began to black out.

Surely it could not end like this, surely Noah would save her. Noah? Where are you now? She entered a dark tunnel.

"You are lucky to be with me tonight, I will take care of you." His hand moved down, and rested between her breasts, he felt for her heartbeat. "That's good, it's much slower now, soon it will be over ...then we can play." He thought back to Buscetti, his body burning in the car. "Would you like to play?" The heartbeats grew slower. He waited almost expecting her to respond, but instead her head fell forward. His fingers kept their pressure on her body until her heart stopped beating.

He removed the night-vision goggles, "That's better."

The first part of his fixation had been satisfied with her death. Now his mind forced other wicked thoughts down through his body into his fingers and tongue, as he lent forward to lick her body.

Hotel Auberge du Raisin,
Tuesday, June 29.

BREAKFAST DID NOTHING TO IMPROVE FORBES'S OPIN-
ion of the hotel. There were more chips and cracks in the crock-
ery, than choices of preserves on the stained and battered
menu.

The elderly woman that booked him in the night before
brought a stainless steel pot of coffee. Her appearance matched
her surroundings. There were pulls, snags, and small holes in
her black cardigan, which suggested she was a cat owner. Her
shoes displayed the dull beaten leather look that was reflected
in her weathered face.

He perceived that he would gain no information from her,
but had no option but to try.

With an extravagant turn of the head, he made a comment
to her in passable French, "I would have expected the hotel to
be full."

Her glazed expression did not change, "Why?"

Forbes assumed she would not have heard of the twin-sis-
ter girl group (he himself had only gathered the salient facts
on Sasha and Justine, by 'googling' for *Reflectionz* information
the previous night), "I understand you had some famous guests
stay here recently."

"Sasha and Justine?" her voice whistled a lisp on the letter 'S'

Impressed by her knowledge he nodded. The old woman
continued, "They are not my guests, they are my patrons." The
lisp was strong.

"They own this place?" Forbes could not hide his shock.

A nod of the head accompanied the famous Gallic shrug for an affirmative answer.

Forbes made the quantum leap that the purchase of the hotel had come as a result of their new found singing career, it was the only link he could come up with, combined with the Chellen Corporation's purchase of the bakery. His question seemed naïve, "So they just bought it?"

The old woman tilted her head back and cackled, the sound was a mixture of mirth and evil, much more annoying than the jets. Her thin lips drew back to make a gesture faintly resembling a smile, but achieved nothing more than revealing to Forbes that she had some teeth missing. Suddenly the sound stopped, her eyes fixed onto his, "No, Monsieur, not bought it, no. They inherited it. A relative died."

"Oh I see," Forbes answered, although he didn't see how it fit in with his understanding of the events. The old woman continued to stare at him.

Forbes felt she was hypnotising him. The knowledge she had imparted had embarrassed him, and suddenly he felt the need to turn away from her enquiring face. It seemed she was interrogating him, instead of visa versa. Averting his eyes to her waist, he noticed an object that he could fix his attention on.

In her movement to laugh, the black cardigan had ridden up her body to reveal an object protruding from the waistband of her skirt.

Fascinated by its appearance, Forbes recognised it as a fan. Unable to contain himself, he pointed at it. "That's," he wanted to say 'interesting', but his lack of translation only allowed him to say 'A talking point'.

The old woman clasped the black lacquered fan with her

bony fingers, and slowly withdrew it. "It's a very rare antique," she said, the whistling lisp giving a sing-song lilt to her words.

Suddenly there was an undeniable pride in her voice, "Justine and Sasha persuaded monsieur LeCoyte Chellen to give it to me, as a thank you for the good service in the hotel," her smile glowed.

"How do they know LeCoyte Chellen?" It was a lame question, exposing the need for the information he was desperate for. He felt ashamed of his inability to keep the important elements to himself, and allow the old woman to talk freely.

All those years training in interrogation, wasted on an old woman with a fan. If she were working with Chellen, she would be in her element telling the likes of Key about the strange breakfast conversation she had had.

The old woman tilted her head, as if to better recall the memory, "I can remember the day well, Mr Chellen had just purchased the *Le Manoir*," she turned toward the bakery, as if the stone wall were transparent. Her crooked finger pointed with unnerving accuracy at the fairy-tale building down the road.

"His company is converting the bakery into a recording studio. Sasha and Justine were helping him to understand what equipment he needed to buy."

"I'm sure they were. I think I'll visit *Le Manoir* today. So, you've actually met Mr Chellen?" Forbes couldn't believe how amateurish he sounded.

"Oh course, he is a lovely man." Her head wobbled with pride.

Forbes thought she was going to cackle again, and thanked God when another jet screamed above them cutting out the dreadful sound.

"Will that be all?" The interrogation was over, he'd blown it.

"Yes, thank you," Forbes busied himself breaking open a stale roll. The old woman shuffled away from his table stuffing the fan back in her waistband.

Momentarily she turned and, pointing through the thick stone wall of the kitchen, said, "He set up the pump, you know ...Lovely man."

Forbes found himself looking blankly at the stone wall.

"To clear the water out of the cellar, the river, the flooding, the global warming, it will be the death of us all." She left the dining room.

Forbes bit into the stale roll, perhaps his interrogation training had paid off after all, because he'd just got all the information he needed.

The paintings weren't in the bakery, they were here, in the cellar. The bakery was just a red-herring, something to woo the twin owners of the hotel.

Chapter Fourteen

The Maharajah Dunleep Singh
(Charles Duncan Beechey 1852)

Gallery 'Defence', Paris.
Tuesday, June 29.

LA GRANDE ARCHE COMPLETES THE LINE OF MONU-ments that form the famous *Axe historique* running through the very centre of Paris.

The Arche seems to be slightly out of line, but it is actually turned at an angle of 6.33° for a very specific reason. With the metro station, RER station and six lane motorway situated directly beneath the Arche, the angle was the only way to accommodate the structure's substantial foundations. From an architectural point of view, the turn only emphasizes the depth of the monument, it has been suggested that the structure looks like a four-dimensional hypercube projected onto a three-dimensional world, which said, it does look fantastic.

Underneath, and hidden from view it boasts a pre-stressed concrete frame.

To the naked eye, the Arche is covered in glass and Italian,

Carrara marble. All in all it is the perfect setting for an exhibition of Art.

Noah Coleman looked sophisticated in his charcoal Yves Saint Laurent suit, it was something that hardly ever came out of the closet these days, but it still fit reasonably well.

As he approached the lavish reception desk, the Indian girl in the expensive uniform thought he cut a fine figure of a man. "Good morning, welcome to Gallery 'Defence' how may I help you?" she had a gold tooth, and a pretty smile.

Normally Noah would have commented upon this, and begun to flirt, but as he hadn't lived in England for more than ten years, and was dressed head to foot in French couture, he was unaccountably annoyed at being addressed in English. *'Senga must look very English'*, was the only explanation he could think of.

He pressed his hand against his chest, and in his near perfect Breton accent, proclaimed, "Good morning; Noah Coleman," He gestured to Senga, "and Miss Munreaux, to see Mr Nahmad." His smile was compelling.

"Do you have an appointment?" Her eyes sparkled with power, her smile as false as a toupee on a windy day.

Senga lent forward, "Just tell him I'm here, he'll see us!"

"Miss Monroe, was it?" her lashes fluttered.

Senga turned on her heel and went to appraise the Sylvia Antonsen feature in the centre of the exhibition area.

With acute frustration she gestured for Noah to accompany her. This action negated any protestations by the girl on the desk.

Senga extended her hand, and loudly proclaimed, "Her art is so full of colour."

"Yes," Noah answered sarcastically, pressing into her side.

"Note how she particularly uses the white hues," she raised her eyebrow, inviting Noah to comment, as the girl picked up the phone to ring 'upstairs'.

Noah agreed, "Charming."

Senga continued oozing over the display, much to the chagrin of the receptionist, who, without the power to put them down, was forced to make the call.

Senga shook her head, sending shimmering waves of copper curls dancing over her shoulder. Noah noticed the antique ivory Toucan-billed hair-grip, stark in contrast.

"Antonsen, enjoys the focus and balance, that only white can bring to a painting."

"Whatever," Noah replied quietly.

"What I love is the fact she is not overly textural and painterly. I believe Sylvia creates interest simply by building up the thin glazes ..."

"I believe you're making it up."

"Sometimes," she looked at Noah, "over a **thick** ..." her smile was intended to hurt, "layer of paint."

"Which results in such a rich effect," Noah added with a flourish.

As if by magic a beautiful Indian girl had presented herself at their side. Her jet black hair was cut short; feathered forward in the style of a 1930's Berlin cabaret singer.

Without introduction she stood close to Noah, and gazed into the middle distance, offering her own thoughts on the merits of Sylvia Antonsen, "Her Danish heritage is still an influence ...you can see it best in her Acrylic contemporary paintings." She turned and smiled, Noah was hooked.

"I feel she produces paintings of such calm, the atmospheric scenes are-" Noah tried to engage her, but Senga cut him off.

"Atmospheric?" Senga muscled in between them.

Noah continued without acknowledging Senga, "Such remote flat landscapes, how she imagines such a vision, I'll never know?" His hands moved hypnotically, his words were soothing. The expert prose was meant to impress and infatuate, "Especially the one with the lone boat in an uninhabited marshy area," he smiled.

The girl looked at him, mesmerised.

Senga couldn't believe what she was seeing, he was flirting with her.

The girl extended her hand toward the elevator, "Please, come with me. Mr Nahmad will see you now." She led them to the elevator.

"Down boy, stop your flirting," Senga cautioned.

"If it wasn't for the flirting, I wouldn't have a-" they stepped into the elevator.

In the bright artificial light, Noah could see she was even more stunning than he'd first appreciated. She wore a soft white, pure silk blouse, neatly tucked into a shimmering pair of black spray-on trousers. The gold pieces she wore at her neck and wrist were both tasteful and expensive. Noah appraised her body, just as Senga had appraised the Antonsen piece.

She smelt of orange blossom. Her lips were full and expertly coloured to complement her skin tone.

"My name is Mohini," her voice was as pretty as she was. Her dark brown almond shaped eyes were straight from a Disney animation.

"Will you be staying for the exhibition?"

"Yes," Noah allowed the silence to act as an invitation. He continued to look directly at her, after all, eye contact was so important during these opening moves. But, Noah was also wise enough to use his surroundings to his advantage, and took in the reflection of her perfectly rounded bottom, in the mirrored wall.

Senga could see she was leading him on, responding to his advances, *'This will end in tears',* she thought as she watched Mohini look back at Noah from under her long lashes. Traditionally the look would be interpreted as submissive, but her body language, especially in the company of Senga, was confident and challenging.

Noah was intrigued. The shrill ping of the elevator announced their arrival at floor 23. His face dissolved into a smile as he gestured for the two women to leave the elevator before him.

Senga strode away, but Mohini stopped and asked Noah, "I've never been to Paris before; I'm looking for a little something to remind me of this beautiful city." She made the invitation sound very exciting, by adding mischievously, "Do you have any suggestions?"

Senga recognised the pitch, and answered before Noah could respond, "The souvenir shop?"

Mohini looked at Senga, she recognised the dark fury of jealousy; this was something she had not been briefed about.

"Of course, how silly of me." Quickly she turned to Noah, "I don't suppose you have time now to take me? ..." she let the question fade, and then added subtly, "Whilst Miss Monroe meets with Mr Nahmad?"

Senga needed to act quickly, she knew Noah was about to

take the bait. The last thing she wanted now was to be alone with Chandhok, it would destroy their plan.

"Maybe later, but right now Mr Coleman will be accompanying me in our meeting. Now if you'll excuse us?" She grabbed Noah's arm and pulled him away.

"Of course," Mohini turned, and walked away, it was one of the most seductive movements Noah had ever seen.

"I'll collect you later?" Noah offered.

Mohini looked back over her shoulder, "I'd really like that."

Senga growled at him, "How can you think of sex at a time like this?"

"It's a gift!"

∿◯

THE DOOR TO THEIR LEFT OPENED, REVEALING A SMALL Indian man, wearing rimless glasses and a huge smile. "Miss Monroe!" his pronunciation of the old Scottish name was perfect. His oil black hair, cut with an air of Eton, his smile open, and affectionate.

"Prakash, how lovely to see you again."

"Lovely to see you too Miss Monroe, please come in."

Once they left the corridor, and stepped into the office, all traces of reality were gone.

Prakash led them through a world adorned in the style of a Maharaja's palace. Sitar music played unobtrusively in the background. Even the aroma, was pure India, heady and seductive.

The wall to their right was decorated with a traditional *Gombi Thotti*, or *Dolls Pavilion*. Hundreds of traditional dolls from the nineteenth and twentieth centuries stood to attention on luxurious dark wooden shelving.

Standing in front of this priceless collection, was a wooden elephant howdah, decorated in 84 kilograms of gold, it rested upon a lavish royal-blue and gold-leaf rug.

Noah followed the line of the room, along the back wall, where seven golden canons; one-eighth scale models of the real guns that stood in front of the Mysore Palace rested in regal devotion.

Prakash beckoned them closer. Noah noticed the room was split in two sections by the ornate head of an elephant, full size, its trunk and bejewelled tusks resting upon a golden, carved tree trunk.

The elephant head served as a gateway into the main part of the room, which finished with a full floor to ceiling window over-looking the Yaacov Agam Fountains, and the bronze sculpture of *La Défense de Paris* by Louis-Ernest Barrias.

"Impressive," Noah whispered.

The pavilion office was covered in beautiful geometric patterns, created by using shining glazed tiles, emulating a traditional *Diwan e-Khas*, or hall, as used by the Maharaja for private meetings.

Sitting on a rattan lounger, looking out over the city was Chandhok Nahmad. Prakash cleared his throat as way of announcing the presence of the guests; then in silence, he bowed and backed away.

Noah recalled everything he knew about the dangerous tyrant sitting before him,

Born in 1968, into an upper middle class family in the village of Sarai Mir; Chandhok's father was an advocate by profession.

However, Chandhok's privileged education came to an abrupt halt after his father died in a road accident.

Rather than complying too the 'Riches to Rags' career-path set before him, Chandhok began selling paintings by local artists on a busy street corner in the European sector of the town. Initially his percentage supported his family. But soon trade increased, and he left for Delhi.

Here he supplemented his income by working as a taxi driver. After only twelve months he shifted his base to Mumbai, the financial capital of India.

In Mumbai the demand for western art outstripped the desire for locally produced paintings. Nahmad diversified.

As his notoriety and retail empire grew he became a target of the local underworld; but instead of acquiescing to their demands, he joined forces with the gangsters that were intending to harass him.

A ruthless rise to power followed. At the age of 25, Chandhok Nahmad successfully defended himself on the charge of murder.

Everyone in the underworld knew he was responsible for killing Bollywood film directors, Rajiv Rai and Rakish Roshan, but the un-bias and certainly un-bribed jury decision was final.

After this, he was untouchable. Linked only loosely to various murder and extortion cases; his reputation as an Art Dealer grew with the romantic appeal of a Caribbean Pirate; and by the time he was thirty, he was a multi-millionaire. His association with organized crime had largely been forgotten, thanks to a very clever PR whitewash.

He travelled extensively throughout Europe, buying works of art for export to India.

It was during this time that he secretly began to recruit a few very talented forgers to supplement the number of 'old masters' that were being offered to the emerging markets. During the next four years his personal fortune doubled, and his art empire grew.

Nothing stood in his way, and no ever said no to him, that was until a steamy après-ski night in Chamonix.

Like a tiger, he uncurled himself from the lounger. His hair was longer than she remembered, but his eyes still held the animal magnetism she had remembered for every heart aching moment of every day since she first met him.

His voice was laced with honey, his body moved with the mesmerizing weave of a cobra.

"Hello Agnes, have you come to give me my money back?"

TO THE REAR OF THE AUBERGE, THE THUMP, THUMP, thump of the pump drew him through the ancient outbuildings. Everywhere was damp, mould on the walls, mud on the ground. Barely able to hide his excitement, Forbes stepped over a worn threshold, and slipped on an ice like layer of gooey mud. He steadied himself, appraising the building. It looked like an abandoned stable, no roof, just walls. Above he could see the Lufthansa, from Munich was making its final approach.

"No pump in here, so where's this cellar?"

Moving cautiously he looked beyond the rear of the stable, there was nothing but fields, all the way down to the river. "Where's that bloody pump?"

Then he saw the pipe, a blue python hiding in the grass, it looked as if it dropped into the middle of the field, but as he got closer, he saw the hole from which the pipe was sucking water. "Why would you have a cellar out here?"

Forbes peered into the hole, the pump continued to throb. The bright blue pipe lay on an old wooden staircase. The worn steps descended into darkness. Forbes could just see the water. It looked as if there was a good four to five inches of foul smelling river spillage covering the tangle of debris at the foot of the stairs.

Forbes scurried into the hole, quickly disappearing from the view of anybody glancing across the field. He stopped above the waterline, and looked at the pump. It was a state of the art piece of kit. "Somebody wants this place dried out, why?" he peered into the darkness.

The water was seeping from a rent on the far side, thirty or forty small waterfalls oozed foul-smelling water between the sodden earth, and the rough stone blocks that had become dislodged over the years. Because of their age and the increase in the water table, they now lay like Christmas presents around the tree. Toxic mould crept in, around the tear in the wall, offering an aroma closer to a sewer than a cellar.

Already the excitement was flowing out of him, there was no way Chellen would have allowed the paintings to be stored here.

Forbes crouched, holding back the memories of the Belgrade catacombs as he sized up the dimensions of the underground room. "If it was a cellar, it was a bloody big one," he said. He was pleased the ceiling was higher than in the Belgrade tunnels, if only it wasn't so wet.

He crouched down, just above the water. From this perspective he began to appreciate the dimensions of the room. In his mind's eye, he imagined the cellar, filled with racks of wine, stored with food, and salt, etc.

If the wall which had burst had been an outer wall, then the dimensions of the chateau on which this was under would have been immense. He imagined the stables, and outbuildings, being behind the chateau, which would mean they were midway between here and the Auberge. The Auberge must have been built much later, and had nothing to do with the cellar; he'd just assumed the buildings belonged to the old hotel.

The staircase cracked and groaned beneath his weight. As

his eyes became accustom to the darkness, he saw what could pass as wine racks.

"The wine cellar," he announced. Another jet screamed overhead.

The floor was littered with shattered pieces of wood. He picked up a piece, and poked at the tangle that lay beyond him. The unmistakable jingle of glass came back at him, along with a muddy plume of gas.

"There's no paintings down here my friend, no one's done anything other than set up the pump." Then something caught his eye. "Unless-" Forbes stepped off the staircase. His foot dipped into the water, it came up to his ankle.

As he shuffled his feet around, he brushed against the added danger of broken glass. He moved cautiously through the cellar. The debris he was stumbling over was obviously from the broken wine racks, long ago used to serve the chateau. He followed the blue pipe to its mouth. Eagerly it sucked in the water. Forbes looked at the wall. A wet tide mark was clear at the height of his chest.

"Could all this have happened in the last six weeks?" Forbes desperately wanted to believe that Chellen had hidden the paintings here in the cellar, and then the wall had collapsed, so he needed to pump it dry, "That's just rubbish," he dismissed the idea quickly; and yet the wall that he was looking at seemed different in its construction to that at the entrance to the cellar. The stones seemed smoother.

"He set up the pump, you know ...Lovely man."

Forbes found himself looking at the stone wall.

"To clear the water out of the cellar, the river, the flooding, the global warming, it will be the death of us all."

The old woman's words came back to him. LeCoyte Chellen, multi-billionaire, head of the Chellen Corporation; and art collector extraordinaire, was funding the clearing of water from a redundant cellar, close to a hotel owned by two young singers, for whom Chellen had also purchased a recording studio.

"It's just wrong, it doesn't make sense," Forbes said forcefully. "The stolen paintings are here …why else would he be interested in this flea bitten dump, and be bothering with two singers?"

He stepped over another piece of broken racking. Everything was dropping into place. Chellen hid the paintings here, immediately after the theft. They'd be close enough to Paris so that he could see them at will; but then came the investigation, the attention from Forbes himself; and then the wall ruptured. If only he'd checked the website before, if only he'd trusted his gut feeling, and not given in to Carrington's 'play it by the book' instructions.

Forbes thought about the senseless deaths, a result of Chellen trying to cover his tracks; and all the lost time Forbes had spent chasing around Verona and Helsinki, when the paintings had been here all along.

"I always thought it was Chellen." Distracted and angry, Forbes misjudged his step, and slipped, he put his hand out to stop his fall, but the wood splintered at his touch. He felt the splinter go into his palm as he fell.

The cold water soaked into his clothing. Freezing cold water trickled down his neck. The embarrassment of his position hurt more than the pain he could feel radiating from his right knee.

With clarity of thought he realized it was too dark to attempt a detailed search. He would need to come back with a flashlight. Painfully he got to his feet. Left hand and right leg were practically useless.

Despondently he began wading back, favouring his good leg, unable to put any pressure on his right, the muddy water sucking at his shoes. He touched the shelving at the foot of the stairs, mustering the effort to climb out-

It was then, he heard the voices from above. Forbes froze. One male, one female; the whistling lisp gave away the identity of the old woman with the fan, and her words quickly identified her co-conspirator.

"Oui, Monsieur Chellen."

Forbes was stuck, he had nowhere to hide. Time stood still. A jet screamed overhead, descending into Charles de Gaulle, Forbes took the opportunity to step back into the darkness; he felt the past close in around him. A rotten piece of racking touched his neck, his good hand shot up to hold the teetering pile of shelves in place, if he moved; it could all come crashing down. Time ceased to exist. It was then that he felt the thing touch his hand.

It was the faintest of touches, as if a feather were being drawn over his skin. Forbes visualised the rat, mouth open about to bite. Unable to resist the repulsion, he lent forward and snatched his hand away. As he did so the cat hissed loudly, and leapt from the shelving. It jumped from one piece to another, scattering the wood fragments as it went. Forbes watched the cat bound up the stairs. His relief was tangible.

"Hello pussy," the old woman whistled.

Chellen asked, "And he said he was going to the bakery?"

"Yes, as I told you."

"I will instruct my men to look for him there. I'll send someone

to keep guard here. When he returns, phone me immediately. Do you understand Madame Aspasie?"

"But of course," she whistled.

The voices began to fade. "On no account allow him to come out here."

"As you wish Mr Chellen."

Chapter Fifteen

Woman with a Fan (Modigliani 1919)

Gallery 'Defence', Paris.
Tuesday, June 29.

AGNES? WHO THE FUCK IS AGNES? NOAH BLURTED.

Nahmad threw back his head and roared with laughter, then went suddenly silent, and viewed Noah like prey, "Didn't work out the riddle then?" he looked at Senga, "What sort of a relationship do you to have then, not telling him your real name …tut, tut, tut."

"Relationship? It's nothing like that," Senga was affronted.

Nahmad's face became cold, "Tell me how it is then, Agnes?"

"The relationship is purely professional."

Nahmad guffawed again, "He's a forger, he lives with a whore, it just doesn't get much more professional than that does it?"

"He knows about Madame X," Senga's smile was victorious.

"Of course he does, he painted her for me," Nahmad looked her directly in the eye. She felt her face blush.

"Good isn't it?" Noah quipped, trying to get one of them to blink.

Nahmad turned on him, "Unless you've got my money in hard cash, shut-up, or I'll have you killed."

Prakash, the small ineffectual man with the rimless glasses took out a large silenced pistol from his jacket. His smile was still open an affectionate, but the gun made him appear cold and sinister.

Nahmad turned back to Senga, his finger inches from her nose, "Give me a reason not to kill you both."

Senga smiled seductively, "Keep us alive, and we can get the fake Madame X returned to the Met without any difficulty. No scandal, no investigation, no consequences." It was her trump card, the plan's success rested upon it beating anything Nahmad could bring in to play.

Senga and Noah had constructed the plan on the basis that Nahmad had lost the services of van Braam, and had no replacement. Noah would offer his services in the guise of Cassavanurnez, and work with Senga to verify the authenticity of the fake. Senga waited for Nahmad to understand the implications of her statement. She began to smile, soon he would be back in her debt, and she would be back in his arms.

"I can get it back in the Met any time I want. I'll just pay off the new verifier."

Senga looked crestfallen, quickly she disintegrated, "I don't have your money," their eyes met, "Not yet anyway, I'm working on a new buyer for the helmet," she enthused.

"The helmet won't attract anything over one-million. It was me bidding against you in London." His smirk hurt her like never before.

"Why?" she pleaded.

"If we're ever going to get back together, I want to be sure you understand your place. Treat this as a lesson," Nahmad smiled.

"Is that it?" the anger stated to rise in her voice.

"And the next painting you get for me you do out of love. No incentive." His head inclined waiting for an answer.

Senga backed away, her mouth opened, and her temper broke-

Noah cut in, "Now don't be too hasty." He stepped in-between them.

Prakash aimed his gun, "Don't move or I'll shoot."

"Sorry," Noah raised his hands, and stepped back.

Senga turned to him, "Don't let Prakash speak to you like that!"

"He's got a big gun," Noah replied, hands still high in the air.

Senga shook her head, her rage was boiling over. This had been a bad idea coming here. She looked at Chandhok, suddenly she was un-sure if she ever wanted to be with him again, she thought about William Forbes. She turned to Noah, "He's just trying to scare you."

"He's doing a good job," Noah replied nervously.

Senga recognised the situation needed defusing. She let out a charming laugh, it was infectious, her eyes lit up, she placed an arm around Chandhok's shoulder. "So that's it? One little job without payment, and all this ..." her other arm gestured around the room, "These threats of death, they all stop, is that it?"

"I hope so," Noah offered, hands still raised.

"A cessation of all hostilities between us?" Senga asked, her face close to his.

"Why not? With Remmert van Braam out of the picture I need the pair of you to keep my 'business in business."

"Are you offering me a job?" Noah asked, his hands lowering. He turned his head to allow his 'good' ear to pick up the response instantly, "Eh?"

Nahmad snorted, and then puffed out his chest. "I'm offering you your life …And the ability to live it in the lifestyle you've always dreamed of."

"You're still talking to me right? Noah asked.

"Yes," but his eyes looked at Senga, "If it's what you want?"

"Well, I'm certainly up for that," Noah's smile was constructed of relief. He looked at Senga, and saw she wasn't going to play ball.

"Hey, 'Sharky' don't forget he tried to have me killed the other night, spit-roast on a fork lift truck …" Her words simply ruined the vibe.

It was Noah's turn to try to defuse the situation, "Are you absolutely sure it was Chandhok?"

Senga nodded her head sarcastically, but Nahmad cut through her performance.

"I've never issued an order to have you killed."

Prakash lowered his gun, and shook his head in confirmation.

Noah looked at the little man with the big gun, "I think you can put it away now, we're all on the same side." Prakash remained un-moved.

Nahmad waved a hand in dismissal. Immediately, Prakash put the gun away, only his smile remained.

Senga faced up to him, "Two of your trained bully boys, tried to spear me with fork-lift trucks, shoot me, and then pushed my

Mini into the Thames. I think that says you instructed someone to kill me."

Nahmad took a step back, raising his own hands he proclaimed, "Not me."

Senga looked at Prakash, Noah, and then Nahmad, "Shit, then who's trying to kill me?"

Nahmad clapped his hands, "Let's try to figure it out over lunch."

Noah asked, "Any possibility that Mohini could join us?"

Senga slapped his shoulder, "Think about Daisy!"

"I am, that's why I want some female company." Noah turned, and began walking away. He was unable to see Senga's disgusted reaction. She shouted after him, "You're a real sexual dinosaur."

"Thank you very much." Noah replied, a genuine smile covered his face.

Senga looked at Chandhok, his face was hard, masking his true feelings; he asked, "Do you want me to have him killed?"

Prakash's hand went back to his jacket, the smile was expectant.

Senga turned on her heel and followed Noah from the room, "Perhaps after lunch."

FORBES HUDDLED IN THE DARKNESS, HOLDING HIS left hand to his chest, it was throbbing like hell. He began thinking, *'If Chellen is desperate enough to send men out to guard the cellar; I think the paintings are here for sure.'*

Forbes reasoned there would be no opportunity to come

back later to search. It was now or never, there was no escape, his car was in the hotel car-park for all to see; it was just a matter of time until they tracked him down. He knew that when he came out of this stinking hole, he couldn't run, so, he better have all the answers. He also thought that if he had a big enough bargaining chip he might just be able to talk his way out of here; well five priceless masters would certainly do the trick. As quietly as he could, he waded back across the cellar floor.

Stumbling over shattered wine racks in the dark is not the most efficient way to search for the most expensive items ever stolen, yet Forbes knew he had no time for finesse. He was almost hopping when he fell again.

He went down heavy, and knew he'd damaged his ankle. With or without the paintings he doubted he would be able to make it back up the staircase.

He sat in the filthy water. He was so close, and yet so very far away. Reluctantly he knew he was going to have to admit defeat.

In frustration he hurled a piece of wood against the wall, it smacked into the stone blocks with a resounding thud. In the seconds that followed, he recognised that the sound was not one he would have expected to hear.

Forbes searched for another piece of shelving, he hurled it against the wall, a few feet from where the first had hit; it thudded against the blocks, then splashed into the water.

"Fuck!" the profanity slipped out of his mouth as he realized that the sound had been different.

"Different stone, different sound, this is it!" Favouring his better leg, he limped over to the wall. "Please God, let this be it!" Bracing himself against the cold wet stones, he painfully drew himself up. He rested his cheek against the dry wall, then, levering himself away, he drove an elbow back against the wall.

Keeping a hard fought balance he moved along the cellar wall, testing its resistance. The second strike, made him see stars, the ankle and knee, were burning, and his hand had swollen to twice its size. Gauging his own strength, he thought he had just a couple of goes left in him, he hit the wall again, nothing.

The broken-glass ground beneath his shoes, he steadied himself. Falling rather than pushing he smashed into the wall again, this time he felt it give.

"Yes, yes, yes." He was almost crying with relief. Slowly he pushed against the stone. He felt it grate against the one below it, tiny pieces of mortar drained from it, like sand pouring from an hour glass.

He grasped a short piece of shelf, and used it like a chisel to scrape the mortar away from the wet stone below, where the water had softened the mortar.

Quickly he was able to isolate the stone, it stood outlined against the four that surrounded it.

Forbes put his shoulder to the stone, and pushed. His ankle screamed in protest, his knee burned, and popped. He pushed again. He pushed for all the times he'd been traumatised since Belgrade, for all the times he'd seen the apparitions of zombies, the walking dead; all the times he'd been incapable of moving. For every pill he'd ever taken, for every flashback; he pushed.

Digging in like an English rugby prop, in a last minute scrum against the French, he pushed.

Forbes felt the stone move.

Frantically he felt about for something to stand on. He

dragged a piece of racking over and wedged it against the wall. Favouring his good leg, he climbed on it, and pushed again. The stone moved, it actually moved. Then the racking gave way and he dropped into the water. The pain soared through him, he screamed, but the sound was drowned out by another jet leaving for far-away shores.

Breaths coming in short, frustrated pants, he braced his hands against the wall and pushed. It gave anther inch. He couldn't get any higher, he didn't have the strength to move anymore; this was his only route to the paintings.

He was sweating freely, his ankle hurt like crazy, but he kept pushing. With a rush of air, and a crash that must have been heard all the way back to the Auberge, the two stones above the one he'd been pushing fell away from him. They crashed down onto the ground, beyond the wall.

Forbes thought his heart would burst, he grunted and panted, unable to move. Eventually he put his good hand over the lower stone and stretched up to look inside, the darkness was all consuming.

"Brilliant!" he whispered, and took out his mobile. With shaking hands he hit a key, and allowed the light from the screen to illuminate what lay beyond.

He felt like Howard Carter at the tomb of Tutankhamen.

The area was small, he could see its entirety. This had been an alcove, no more than ten feet deep. Against the back wall he saw something square, it was covered in, what looked like cloth. To the side, hessian sacks were neatly stacked, but none of it looked like a recent placing.

Forbes put the mobile in his mouth and hoisted himself over the lip of the hole. The air was squeezed from his lungs, he wriggled, and squirmed the top half of his body over the stone, and balanced on the edge. Taking his mobile, he extended his arm, pressing the key he allowed the light to illuminate the alcove.

He could see now that it wasn't one structure, but rather three. They looked like trunks, piled one on top of the other.

A deep rumbling laugh alerted him to a new danger, male voices sharing a joke. Even from his position he recognised the reverberation of footsteps coming down the old stairs.

Forbes put the mobile back in his mouth, and pulled himself further over the stone. The splinter dug into his palm, he bit down onto the mobile. There was no alternative he had to go in.

He'd perfectly understood the dimensions of the secret room, so he tumbled headfirst into the darkness with utter confidence, preparing for a paratroopers roll; he crashed into the floor, his shoulder hitting the stones that had fallen free of the wall. Pain shot through his body. Pain squeezed itself out through his closed eyes; it dripped down his cheek in silent agony. The men were in the cellar now, Forbes heard them kicking the debris at the foot of the stairs. They had no desire to search any further.

He spat out the mobile, rolled over and clutched his leg. Obviously he was soaked, but he still recognised the ooze of blood coming from another gash on his shin. Fighting back the tears of pain, and struggling to hold back the tell-tale scream, he sat alone in his dark tomb listening to Chellen's men exchanging comments in rapid French.

He could not make out their words because of the swishing of the water, and the snapping of rotten wood masking their intent. The noise and the search seemed to go on forever. Then the water stopped swirling. The wood stopped splintering. The stairs creaked. The voices subsided. Except for the pump, all was quiet. After a minute, which seemed like an hour, Forbes began feeling around in the darkness for his mobile.

His fingers touched the hessian sack, it felt old; it felt as if whatever was in it had been dead for a long time. Forbes's fingers traced up the rough material, he heard it clink, metal on metal.

Everything felt old, everything smelled of dust, and decay; but at least it was dry in here. He backed away from the sack, sweeping his hands for the mobile. It was obvious this was not the hiding place of the five stolen paintings, but it was very obvious this was a room that had been bricked-up to conceal the contents; and it had been done a long time ago.

Forbes felt a new thrill taking hold of him. He allowed himself the luxury of thinking what could be inside the sack; silver, gold? Maybe there would be a wealth of fabrics and clothing in the trunks. Tentatively his hand reached out again, and prodded the sack, his nerves craving the tinkle of metal. His fingers closed around the rough neck. He dragged it toward him. Whatever was inside settled with a satisfying metallic clink?

Forbes sat shivering, and bleeding in the dark secret alcove; he had no chance of getting out, and no chance of escape. It was then that his mobile rang.

≈℘◯

CHANDHOK PROPOSED HIS TOAST, "TO SUCCESS."

Noah and Senga readily raised their glasses in salute. "Well, I'm certainly pleased you two have put your differences aside. It's nice to have all that un-pleasantness behind us," Noah drank from his flute.

"I'm glad I didn't have to shoot you." Prakash said unconvincingly.

"So am I." Noah replied.

"But it doesn't tell me who is responsible for trying to kill me?" Senga blurted out.

"Tell me exactly what happened," Nahmad put his arm around her shoulder.

Senga looked back at him, her confidence was growing with every sip.

"Last month five paintings were stolen from Paris,"

"Go on." Nahmad nodded in confirmation of the fact.

"The motive and perpetrator remain elusive from the police."

"Of course, what did they hope to achieve? What can you do with something you cannot sell?" Nahmad offered, they all laughed sympathetically at the statement.

Senga continued, "Bill Forbes is heading an international team of police, and Interpol, for the ALR."

Nahmad, sniffed distastefully, "Yes, I have discussed the theft with Mr Forbes."

Noah raised his eyebrows expectedly. But Nahmad, pre-empted the question.

"No, Mr Coleman, I had nothing to do with the theft."

Noah gave a hearty nod confirming that the thought had never even so much as crossed his mind.

Senga took another sip of champagne, her mood was improving, "Bill thinks LeCoyte Chellen is behind the theft."

"You'd get short odds on it being him," Noah said quietly.

"Bill was following his leads, when he came across me."

"What leads were they?" Nahmad asked, his tone becoming terse. He noticed Senga was calling the buffoon, William Forbes from the ALR, Bill. She certainly seemed familiar with him.

"He wouldn't tell me."

"When did he inform you of this …connection to the theft?"

"The first time we met," her hand reached for her flute, her voice was becoming dreamy with the memory, and she wondered how he'd gotten on in Helsinki.

"Before or after someone tried to kill you?"

Her hand stopped reaching, "After."

"After he helped you escape." Nahmad offered.

Senga nodded, her innocence showed through her eyes.

"At a time when you would be very vulnerable and susceptible to his suggestion." Nahmad dabbed his mouth with a white linen napkin.

Senga continued nodding, it wasn't the first time the thought had crept into her mind.

"And the following day he suggested you go to France …"

A single nod.

"Straight into the arms of Chellen, confirming your belief of his guilt."

Senga wasn't sure how much Chandhok knew about the Oleg scam, so she continued to nod, providing assurance that she believed every word he was saying.

Nahmad looked pleased with himself; he knew Senga enjoyed him taking control. He clicked his fingers. "Please Agnes, will you ring Mr Forbes, and let us all see where he is now, I think we should all like a word with him."

WITHIN THE GLOW OF THE PHONE, FORBES COULD clearly see three grey trunks, his mind did somersaults as to what they held. He guessed that the sacks contained the family silver. He scrambled to the mobile, placing it close to his lips, "Forbes."

"Hi Bill, Senga here, just wondering how you got-"

"Where are you?" he interrupted, his voice breathless.

"I'm in Paris ..."

"Thank God. Listen, I'm in real trouble-"

"Are you hallucinating again?" Senga asked, genuine concern poured from her question.

"No, this is real. I need you to come and help me." He sniffed.

"Where are you? What's that noise?"

"Goussainville, the ghost town north of Charles De Gaulle."

"What the?"

"Never mind all that, I'm staying at the Hotel, *Auberge du Raisin* ..."

Senga gestured for a pen, Nahmad handed her his Mont Blanc.

"Address?"

"It's the only place in the town that's got any living people in it. Now, for God sake don't let anyone see you coming. I'm trapped in a sort of underground cellar, out in the middle of the field behind the hotel, on the way to the river. You can't miss it, there's a blue hose running into it, and a terrible thumping noise coming from within."

"Is this to do with Chellen and the paintings?" Senga asked confidently.

"It was," he didn't know how to describe what had happened, "Are you alone?"

"Why do you ask?" Her reply was hesitant, but Nahmad encouraged her. "No, I'm with old friends."

"Thank God. You'll need to bring help in order to get me out of here."

"Can't you just shout for help?"

"No, Chellen has men looking for me. They're guarding the entrance."

"Okay, I'll bring someone."

"Is it the man you said you could trust?"

"Yes," Senga looked at Noah.

"Good, oh and Senga, better wear some old clothes, it's really dirty and wet down here."

"Okay."

"Oh, and Senga? …Come quickly."

"Okay we'll be there within the hour. Bye."

Her voice cut off, the phone went black; the darkness consumed him again. The thumping of the pump was like a mother's heartbeat. Forbes clasped his legs close to his chest.

The dilemma was acute. Should he open the trunks now, or wait until Senga arrived. The pain from his knee and ankle, told him he would not be able to lift the trunks. Even if he could, he himself would need support to get out. Senga's friend, would then need to make three trips to extract the trunks. The place would be swarming with Chellen's men by then.

Forbes decided he had to see what was inside. He climbed up the trunks. He pressed the key on the mobile. He looked at the locking mechanism.

Placing his thumbs against the rusted catches, he opened the top trunk.

Chapter Sixteen

PORTRAIT OF A LADY (LUINI 1525)

Hotel Auberge du Raisin,
Tuesday, June 29.

IN THE POOR LIGHT, IT LOOKED AS IF THE TRUNK CON-tained curtains. But as Forbes touched them, he realized the curtains had been used to wrap something.

Carefully he pulled out the first bundle, it was too heavy to be just curtains.

"How long has this been here, since the revolution?" He be-gan to un-ravel the package. The cool smooth feel of porcelain filled his hand. He pressed the mobile key to allow the pale light to play on the figure. He marvelled at the delicate figurine, "Girl with a flower basket, Christ, it's an original." Could this be what Chellen had been searching for?

Forbes's fingers traced the exquisite curves. Reverently, he placed her on the ground, and hopped back to the trunk. He pulled out a second and third bundle, carefully un-wrapping the items they contained.

Cautiously he placed the figures on the ground, he aimed his mobile, and began to take photographs.

In the utter darkness after the flash, he stumbled back into the trunks. He began the routine of feeling for the bundle, un-wrapping it in the dark, and then lighting it, placing it on the ground, and photographing them.

As time passed, the excitement grew within him, even the throbbing of the pump and the injured leg and hand could not lessen his mood.

He placed the empty top trunk on the ground. His fingers undid the second set of catches. He felt the edge of the bundle. Understanding what it must contain, he laid it on the floor, and continued to dig back into the trunk.

Every now and again, he would open the bundles, just to make sure everything was in order.

At the bottom of the trunk, Forbes felt for the edge. He judged that this bundle was different to the others; it was much bigger, flatter. "A painting?"

The outer wrap, was obviously a curtain. He balanced it on the corner of the open trunk, he un-folded the bundle.

Sandwiched between the two early 19th century linen drapes was an oil-skin wrapped package. Forbes flicked on the mobile. The package was tied with a fine horse-hair braid. Momentarily he stopped to admire the handy-work,

"Whoever did this would have been proud."

Forbes looked at the drapes, he saw the gay golden flowers blossom over the dark crimson background, and then he con-centrated on the oil-skin package, "Probably a family portrait."

It had lain undisturbed for 150 years. Wrapped in the oil-skin package, tied with braid made from the finest horse hair.

Forbes noticed his hands were shaking as he untied the

braid. Carefully, almost with religious reverence he un-wrapped the package.

Even in the darkness, he recognised the familiar proud relief found on many frames. Forbes held his breath, he traced his fingers over the canvas. The texture and ridges sent pulses of anticipation racing up to his brain.

His heart was beating in time to the pump as he raised the mobile phone high above his head. With deliberation he struck the key pad.

"Let there be light."

The light shone down onto the painting. A jet screamed overhead.

Unlike other famous works of art, it had never been established whom this carefully painted portrait represented. Luini's own copy had featured a beautiful woman named Albertina, from Vienna; but the original remained anonymous.

"Oh my God," Forbes whispered breathlessly, he recognised the likeness instantly. Logic and reason told him that this painting resided in Benson's London collection, yet here it was.

As the silent tears trickled down his face, he admitted to himself that he was looking at Luini's original portrait of a lady, the original painting inspired by the tutorage of Leonardo Da Vinci.

His hands shook, Luini's original painting rested within them. The real lady stared back at him. She wore a dark grey gown, decorated with a white embroidered chemisette, and yellow head-dress. In her right hand she held a marten, whilst her left hand touched the long necklace to which a jewelled cross was attached.

A green curtain formed the background, focusing the

attention on her face, on her eyes. The eyes fascinated him. In the shimmering light, the eyes drew all of his attention. A man could become lost looking into those eyes.

The beauty of her face eclipsed the copy he'd seen in London. The beauty of the painting eclipsed any work he'd ever seen before.

He wanted to turn off the light, to conserve his battery, but he was unable to pull away from her, unable to look away from her eyes. It hadn't taken the rest of the portrait to take away his breath; it was the eyes alone, the eyes without a face that had captured his heart.

Forbes thought about Senga Munreaux, she would be here soon, she would share in his discovery. The feeling felt good, it was a feeling he wanted to last for ever.

NOAH PARKED THE CAR. THEY'D BOTH CHANGED OUT of their finery into dark-grey security uniforms, supplied by Nahmad's exhibition staff. Senga had her wild copper curls tied in a neat bun, crushed inside a base-ball cap.

They walked in from the river; there were no trees to use as cover, but then again there were no people to see them.

"I thought Forbes said there were people looking for him?" Noah asked.

"Yeah, but there's not many places to look, they might be home having a croissant and coffee," she replied sarcastically.

"That's got to be the hotel," Noah pointed.

"Come on then." They marched over the field.

The 'thump, thump, thump' of the pump accompanied their arrival at the cellar entrance.

Senga led the way down, arcing her powerful flashlight around the cellar.

Noah was at her shoulder, "Where is he?"

Senga phoned his number, it rang in the darkness. "We're here."

A breathless rasping voice came back at her, "Did you get past the guards okay?"

"Its fine, nobody saw us," she looked at Noah and shrugged her shoulders. The line went dead.

"He suffers from hallucinations?" Senga tried to explain the caution about guards, "I think it's P.T.S.D."

"Oh, does he have pills for that?" Noah asked innocently.

"Apparently."

"I'm over here," Forbes waved his mobile through the hole in the wall.

Noah saw the light, "There he is." Carefully they picked their way across the floor. Once at the wall, Noah lifted Senga up, to peer inside.

"Bill?"

The porcelain figure of the flower girl was thrust into her face, breathless with exertion, Forbes whispered, "Quick take this. There are two more."

The second and third came through rapidly.

Senga looked at the porcelain pieces, "They're beautiful, what else have you got in there?"

The rasping voice came back from the darkness, "Wonderful things, it's like a fairy-tale world in here."

The clanking heaviness of a hessian sack appeared. Noah

took it, and placed it on the ground, the water, and mud sighed in protest.

With an outpouring of effort, Forbes's torso appeared at the gap, he squeezed himself through the hole." Pull me through, but mind my legs, I'm hurt."

They manhandled Forbes to the ground. The thump, thump, thump, of the pump, muffled his cries of pain.

"What the?" Noah noticed a length of fine, horse-hair braid, tied to his ankle.

Almost hysterically Forbes grabbed the braid and started pulling. Senga helped, and a moment later the oil-skin package appeared at the hole.

"It's okay, I've got it." Forbes held the package close to his chest, his eyes were maniacal. He began to sob, as he slid down the wall.

"The guy's gone cuckoo," Noah whispered.

"Bill, it's okay, we're going to get you out of here," she smoothed his newly short hair-cut. Secretly she approved.

Noah picked up the sack, and went for the package. Forbes held it tight, "Back off!" he snarled.

"Okay, big fella," Noah smiled, but gave a look to Senga, indicating that he thought Forbes had gone stark raving mad.

Senga knew he had problems, she remembered how he'd acted in the tube station, she looked worriedly at him, "Come on Bill."

Forbes looked up, he wriggled his hand in his pocket, and thrust his car keys into Noah's hand, "You can drive."

Forbes, clutching the painting to his chest hobbled through the cellar, Noah, holding one of the figures, and the heavy sack followed. Senga, holding the other two porcelain figurines brought up the rear.

The sun had started to dip toward evening, "How long was I in there for?" he asked, but as neither knew when he'd gone in, Senga said, "Just a couple of hours, now don't worry we'll get you to hospital."

"No! We have to go to the museum." Forbes, bedraggled and bloodied, looked like a madman. Noah took control, "Museum, no problem," he winked at Senga, indicating he thought Forbes had gone mad.

Blinking the darkness of the cellar from his eyes, he was amazed to see the path to the Auberge was clear. Without pause he hobbled toward the car. The journey seemed to take an age. Every step was agony. He gripped the painting tightly, every step was heavenly.

"Keep a look out for Chellen," Forbes cautioned.

"Sure," Noah humoured him, theatrically he looked around.

Senga bundled him into the rear of the car. Noah engaged the key, and the car eased out of the car-park, un-molested by Chellen's men. As they drove south out of Goussainville, Forbes allowed himself the luxury to relax, "Take me to the Museum of Modern Art," and still clutching the painting to his chest he collapsed.

They hit the Périphérique, a good thirty minutes before the accepted rush hour began, which meant the flow of traffic was about 30mph. Noah hit the cruise control, "It is said, that if travelling at the legal speed limit, it takes around thirty minutes to complete a full circuit of the Périphérique,"

"Really, what time of the day is that?" Senga looked at the crush of traffic all around them.

"Apparently it's the same time as you can see the pigs flying." A Renault van honked his horn at a speeding kamakazi scooter rider. The youth didn't even bother to acknowledge the rebuke.

"The speed limit is just 45 mph, for all us humans," Noah shouted his advice to the fast disappearing suicidal candidate. "What do you think 'Stinky's' got in the package."

"Something good; the porcelain is fantastic," she enthused.

Noah noticed the flashing blue lights in the rear-view mirror. He checked his speed, and felt confident that the fast approaching Police entourage would soon sweep past them.

"Do you think he could be behind the theft, and the attempt to kill me?"

"Who, Chellen?"

"No," she inclined her head to the back seat.

"Stinky? No way, he's completely gaga, couldn't organise a piss-up in a brewery. No, your mate, Chandhok is just messing with your mind. Trying to deflect the attention from himself, and easing the way for you to get back into his bed." With frightening noise, the sirens penetrated the car. Senga looked back as they approached. She smiled at Noah, hoping to convey the message that the Police posed no threat. Noah smiled back, conveying he understood what she meant. Neither smile convinced either of them.

"Maybe Chellen went to the Police, about Forbes in the cellar." Senga muted. The first motorbike slipped past them, but the second, dropped in line beside them. The patrol car tucked in behind them.

"You might just be right." Noah began to slow down.

"What if they're bogus, could be Chellen's men."

"They'd have stopped us at the hotel, if that were the case." Noah pulled over onto the hard shoulder, and stopped. "Hey stinky, the Police want a word with you." He shouted to Forbes.

The police cordoned off the vehicle. The officers approached them, guns drawn. The traffic on the Périphérique gave them a wide berth.

The officers gestured for them to get out. Noah and Senga obliged, hands raised. Forbes slid from the back seat, and rested against the car.

An officer raced toward Forbes, helping him to the floor. Two other officers, separated Noah and Senga from their stricken friend.

After they had been patted down for weapons, a hook-nosed man approached them. By the car, Forbes was receiving medical attention. Noah scowled at the way this was going. Forbes may be behind this little charade after all.

"Could I have your name please sir? The man looked like a bird of prey. Another officer was reciting the registration number into his radio.

Noah figured it was the car that had alerted the police, Forbes's car, but as he had been driving … "Noah Coleman." Noah recited his name loud and clear, he wanted to be sure no one mistook him for Forbes.

The thin faced detective nodded, then formalized his stance, he cleared his throat, and then in clipped English, said, "Noah Coleman, I am arresting you for the murder of Miss Danese Kantargo."

Noah heard the words, but couldn't understand why they were being spoken.

Senga asked, "Who?"

Noah replied automatically, "Daisy."

Forbes shouted over, "Who's Daisy?" as one of the uniformed officers handcuffed Noah.

Senga answered from a lonely place, "She's Noah's partner."

"He killed her?" Forbes asked. They led Noah toward the patrol car.

"No she was alive when we left."

The hawk-like detective approached Senga, "You were with Mr. Coleman?"

"No, she was with me," Forbes shouted.

"Noah!" Senga shouted, as they pushed him into the car. Noah looked back at her, but for once he was lost for words.

The detective asked Forbes, "He did this to you?"

"No, I fell in a river; he was taking us to the hospital."

The detective nodded toward Senga, "Mr. Nahmad sends his regards, his thin lips spread, in an attempt at a smile.

Senga answered absently, "Thank you."

The detective bowed, "I would like to take the opportunity to introduce myself. I am Detective Gerrard DeFocault."

Absently Senga responded, "Thank you," it was obvious the Police had been informed about who was in the car, and their understanding of her relationship to the informant, and it was apparent who had done the informing; Nahmad. Did this mean he was behind the theft, the attempt on her life, the killing of the security guard in London? Senga felt lost, she watched Noah. With mounting sadness, he sat in the back of the patrol car in abject disbelief that he was being arrested.

DeFocault addressed Forbes, "You have sustained a number of injuries Mr. Forbes; I will send for an ambulance."

Senga's mind whirled, Nahmad, had told them the identities of everyone in the car.

Forbes's mind was in turmoil, he didn't want to leave the painting unattended for even one moment. Then, Senga gave him a way out.

She asked, "Can I accompany Mr. Coleman to the police station?"

"But of course," Defocault gestured for an officer to assist Senga to his car.

Forbes raised his voice, "There's really no need for an ambulance, but could I ask that an officer drives me to the Museum of Modern Art?" he waited in hope.

DeFocault weighed up the situation, someone would have to drive Forbes's car. "Why not." He snapped his fingers, looking for a volunteer.

Noah Coleman felt numb. Deep inside his heart, he hoped there had been some dreadful mistake, but sitting just under the surface of reason, he knew Daisy was dead. He began to piece together the events that would have had to have transpired to allow the Paris Police, to know his exact whereabouts, and why he was the prime suspect in a murder enquiry.

The conclusion he came to was Forbes; who was now being helped back into his own car. Noah let his head fall back against the seat, wondering how he could get out of this predicament, and kill William Forbes.

Chapter Seventeen

EYES WITHOUT A FACE (COLEMAN 2010)

Paris, France,
Thursday, July 1.

THE TAXI PASSED THE 'RADIO FRANCE' BUILDING, THEN turned onto the *Pont de Grenelle.* Stopping at its centre, William Forbes paid the driver, and turned toward the steps. He held the rail as he hobbled down to the river, partly because of his injuries, and party because of the stiff breeze from the Seine.

Two nights in hospital, having lumps of wood removed from his hand, stitches applied to a gash in his leg, an icepack on his knee and tender love and affection to his sprained ankle, had seen him discharged this morning, and eager to see Senga, reference an oblique message she'd left at the hospital last night. The weight had dropped from his body, leaving him with the eager, haunted look of a predator.

He made his way under the bridge toward the statue of Liberty, his shoes crunching on the gravel. He wondered why Senga had chosen such an out of the way spot for their meeting.

Slowly and painfully he passed a number of small brightly

coloured tents strung out between the massive pylons of the bridge, testament to the ingenuity of the homeless.

As he came out into the sunlight, he saw Senga leaning against the barrier, looking out over the river. Her long copper curls blowing in the breeze.

Face turned slightly in profile, as if she was listening for his approach, Forbes saw the antique ivory Toucan-billed hair-grip, stark against the darkness of her wonderful hair. He stumbled forward, the ankle still hurting like crazy, the swelling still hampered his progress. The pain extenuated his limp across the rough ground. Soon he would understand the meaning of her guarded message.

As he approached, the shock of the gun pressing against his neck made him stop dead. He began to raise his hands.

"Keep perfectly still!" the voice came from behind, distorted in the wind. Forbes remained motionless, as the girl at the barrier turned and took out the antique ivory Toucan-billed hair-grip, and took off the copper coloured wig. With her other hand she fluffed up her own brass-blonde hair, and then saluted Forbes. Her gesture was ironic, because she held a look of pure hatred in her eye. As she walked past she tossed the wig and hair-grip onto the bench that sat in front of the statue.

They were alone now. Suddenly the pressure of the gun was gone from his neck, only to be replaced with a crashing star-filled blow which dropped him to his knees. Forbes cried out in pain, the knee exploded again, undoing all the good work of the last day. His ankle gave way and he crashed to the gravel. Forbes started the healing process by rubbing his head where the gun had hit him, as he clumsily began to get to his feet.

"Stay where you are, scum." The statue of Liberty formed an all-consuming background to Noah Coleman.

"Noah?" Forbes whispered, "What the hell are you doing? Where's Senga?" Colman adjusted his grip on the gun. Forbes thought he looked mad enough to squeeze the trigger. If Coleman were the man trying to kill Senga, he'd driven her straight into his arms, "What have you done with Senga?

"She's safe, safe from you."

"From me, why what have I done?"

"You killed my Daisy."

"What? Are you crazy? I don't even know her, why would I?"

Coleman moved back a pace, he held the gun steady, the action made Forbes believe he was about to shoot.

"Wait!" he shouted his voice, and strength beginning to return, "I haven't killed anyone."

"Senga said you killed two guys in London, killed them like a real pro."

"They were trying to kill us."

"Senga says you thought they were working for Senga, which means you're after her." Noah's face was full of rage, "And you came after her again, in St Tropez. But she'd gone, so you killed Daisy."

"No!" Forbes brought his legs around in front of him to ease the pain. "You've got to believe me. Let's talk. When did the police say she was killed?" Forbes was stalling for time.

"Tuesday night."

"I was in Helsinki, I can prove it." Forbes put his hand inside his coat.

"Stay very still my friend." Noah stepped forward, placing the gun against Forbes's forehead.

Forbes brought his hand out of the coat quickly, brushing his knuckles against the gun, he grabbed it and twisted, clamping his other hand on Noah's wrist, then he snapped back in the opposite direction. Noah felt the pain spread through his whole arm. Instantly he let the gun fall, Forbes caught it and aimed it directly at Noah's groin.

Noah brought his knee up to kick Forbes, but Forbes back flicked with his good leg and sent Noah crashing down.

Noah twisted as he fell, landing on his back, Forbes rolled over elbowing him in the face. The cheek immediately bruised. Forbes scrambled to his feet. Noah got to his knees; but now Forbes held the gun, "Now it's my turn, what the hell's going on here Coleman?"

"I came to kill you."

"Well that's not going to happen, so let's understand why we're really here."

"You killed my ...friend."

Daisy?" Forbes wanted confirmation.

"Yes."

"No, no I didn't. Now, you're going to tell me what you've done with Senga."

"I told you she's safe; she doesn't ever want to see you again."

"Why?"

"Because you're the man behind the Paris theft, and you're the one trying to kill Senga."

"Bollocks, stop talking crap, Coleman. I'm not the villain here ..." Forbes let his words sink in. Slowly he lowered the gun, and limped over to the bench. He sat heavily next to the wig. "Look, I'm truly sorry about your wife. But I promise you I had nothing to do with her death."

Noah and Daisy had never married, but Noah felt very comfortable with his choice of words. Keeping his eyes on Forbes and the gun, he got to his feet and joined him at the bench.

The two men sat in silence in front of the illustrious statue. A long, heavily laden barge slowly chugged past them.

Noah started to explain, "You have to see it from my perspective."

"And just what exactly is that?"

Noah composed himself. "You appeared at the Sotheby's warehouse without any good reason. Senga was attacked. You told her to go to France, to me. Then Daisy was killed in my bed."

"Does Senga really trust you?"

"Yes," he responded, thinking about all they'd gone through.

"Then so should I." Forbes placed the gun on top of the wig and hair-grip, "Best not forget to take that with us."

Noah picked up the antique ivory Toucan-billed hair-grip. "Yes, it's worth a fortune." He put it in his pocket.

"How on earth did we get here?" Forbes asked.

"Sorry about your head," Noah pointed to where he'd hit Forbes.

"Sorry about the cheek."

"Oh it's nothing, I thought you were going to shoot me in the dick."

They both laughed.

"Where did you get the gun? It's real state of the art."

Noah thrust his thumb back toward the bridge, "The young lady's pimp lent it to me."

"You know some very colourful people."

Noah reflected on his words, then looked at Forbes's Highland-green check suit, and red waistcoat, "you included." Both laughed again.

"I take it the police let you go? I mean you haven't escaped or anything have you?" Forbes asked.

"They let me go last night, after they'd figured out that I couldn't be in two places at the same time." Noah laughed, and then winced as the muscles in his cheek twanged with the effort. "Sorry, I really thought you'd killed Daisy."

"Well it all fits, if you look at it from one point of view."

"So what have your investigations turned up? Help me to see this from your view."

"Lots of circumstantial evidence, but nothing fits. It's like a jigsaw puzzle, without the picture on the lid."

Noah looked deep into Forbes's eyes, "Tell me what pieces you do have, I'm pretty good at jigsaws. I can often see what should go into the gaps."

"And that's a skill of yours is it?" Forbes asked sarcastically.

"Yes, I'm a forger. I see everything in a different perspective to how you would see it. I have to forgo the luxury of conception and fit in the facts as the originator of the work saw it. I always have to think as if I'm someone else. Like a character actor."

Forbes nodded, "Okay."

"When you look at a problem, you only see it from your point of view, through your own eyes. I look at it through the eyes of Picasso, or Pollack, Luini, or Da Vinci."

At the sound of Luini's name Forbes straightened up, but Noah didn't notice, he continued, "You try to put yourself into the mind of the perpetrator, whereas I have to remove myself and my influences from the work that I do."

Forbes took a deep breath, "On May twentieth, five paintings were stolen from the Museum of Modern Art."

Noah became attentive.

I was tasked with liaising with and following up on the efforts of Museum security, the local police, the national police, and Interpol. They were getting nowhere, so I interviewed a number of art-dealers, and collectors. Some with a background that lent itself to perhaps making me think they were in some way implicated ..."

"The usual suspects, I believe they're called." Noah eased the way for Forbes's admission.

"Correct, as you can imagine there are a very few men rich enough, or who possess the desire to own something that no one will ever know they own. Whoever has the paintings can never tell anyone they have them. And for a collector, having people know that you have something that they don't is all part of the fun."

"Who do you suspect?"

"LeCoyte Chellen, I've always thought it was him."

Noah pulled a face confirming he would be high on his suspect list too. "What about the Russian, Kerim Beynachinski?"

Forbes nodded, "Yes he's on the list as well."

"I'd love to take a look in his private galleries in Murmansk." Noah cut in enthusiastically.

"And then of course, there's Chandhok Nahmad."

Noah's smile was fast and furtive, "Thoroughly nasty piece of work that Nahmad fella."

"Then, maybe only a hundred or so collectors would be

brave enough to mount such an audacious theft for one, but not all five."

"Small time thief, looking for a big profit?"

"No, any potential buyer knows the work is stolen. Any attempt to advertise the stolen goods risks someone contacting the ALR, or Interpol."

"Why is your money on Chellen?"

Forbes looked across the Seine, "Art theft is usually for the purpose of resale or ransom,"

"Artnapping!" Noah interjected.

Forbes nodded, "But, when I worked at Bonham's, Chellen had one of his paintings stolen from one of his galleries, way back in 2004. The painting came up for auction a year later. The sellers showed provenance, that pretty much proved their family ownership, and that the painting was looted from Amsterdam during the Nazi occupation. They were selling the painting to allow a young family member to receive medical treatment, a real sob story. Anyway Chellen, blocked the sale and got them arrested for the theft. He dragged the action through the courts for months, until the young family member died. Then he dropped the case."

"What a bastard."

"He had enough money to save the child's life ten times over, he could have just bid, and won the painting back. But, there was something about his manner, he's such a big horrible, Dutch slug ..."

"Can you have a Dutch slug?" Noah asked.

"You've seen him?"

Noah nodded, thinking about the journey in the back of the

Audi. He recalled how he'd hit Senga. "I know of his appearance, and reputation."

"Mix that with the ability to destroy a family, kill the heritage, and allow a child to die; then you have someone who could easily own five priceless works of art, without ever needing to show off about it. That family stole the painting, not for profit, but in order to save a life; Chellen is capable of taking a life, that's why I think it's him."

"Is there any real evidence to support your theory?"

"When I interviewed him in Amsterdam, he was so smug. He was definitely hiding something." Forbes thought of the Luini painting in the cellar, maybe that was the secret he was hiding, he dismissed the thought, it had to be Chellen.

"We found the getaway car, with the charred remains of a known art thief inside. The man's partner in crime was found beaten to death in Verona. These men were responsible for stealing a credit-card, which was used to purchase the cutters which were used to break-in to the museum. A photograph linked them to Chellen." Forbes took the photograph from his pocket.

"It's Chellen, and Senga, together with the two art thieves. There's such a perfect symmetry to the photo don't you think?"

"Definitely." Noah instantly felt uncomfortable about Senga and Chellen's previous meeting.

"Turn it over, on the back it confirms Senga was their contact at Sotheby's. That's why I turned up at the warehouse. I wanted to interview Senga Munreaux, about her connection to the art theft. And the rest you know."

"Not exactly," Noah pointed at the photograph, "How did you know to find Senga at the warehouse?"

"On my arrival in the UK, I contacted Sotheby's. They told me she could be found at the warehouse, collecting the vault code for Charles Crombie, the Director."

"So you went directly to the warehouse?"

"Correct."

"When you met her at the warehouse, did she confirm the reason for being there?"

"Yes-"

Noah cut in, "Did you believe her?"

Forbes thought for a moment, then shook his head, "At the time no, but later she confessed, and told me the real reason she was there."

"Which was?" Noah held his breath for the reply.

"She wanted to get her Roman helmet out of the vault," Forbes answered.

Noah breathed a sigh of relief. His involvement in the subterfuge with the Oleg was unknown to the ALR. Good, somethings were best left unsaid.

"After the attack, what did you do?"

"I took her back to Sotheby's."

"But you didn't go inside with her?"

Forbes wondered how he's deduced that fact, "That's correct, I stayed in the car, and tried to get verification about her and the Crosby Garett helmet story. Before I could do anything else the Police arrived."

"So at that point you still thought she was involved with Chellen, and the Paris theft?"

"Yes, it was a possibility."

"Go on,"

"When she was released by the police, I followed her. As she left, Robert Key arrived at the station."

"Chellen's head of security?"

"That's him. He began tailing her. A man like that only gets his hands dirty on the most sensitive of Corporation matters. However she is involved, I figured Chellen was tying-off the loose-ends, and getting rid of everyone in the photograph. I thought it best to get her out of danger. I wanted her out of harm's way until I'd questioned Chellen again. Interpol informed me Chellen was in Helsinki. So I told her to go to someone she trusted."

"But Chellen wasn't in Helsinki, was he?" Noah knew he'd been in Nice.

"How do you know that?" Forbes became suspicious.

Noah tapped a finger against the side of his nose, "He wasn't was he?"

"No, but Key was, and under interrogation he let slip a number of things linking the Corporation to the two dead thieves."

"And that confirmed your theory that Chellen was behind the theft?"

"Yes."

"How did you trace Chellen to Paris?"

"I reasoned that Chellen would want to be close to the paintings. I looked at his recent movements and acquisitions."

"And that took you to a cellar in Goussainville,"

Forbes nodded, he spread his hands, "That's my story, sorry there are a few pages missing."

"Not missing, just sticking together," Noah licked his finger and thumb, and then rubbed them together, "Just need a little friction to open them up. Chellen could have been looking smug because of his acquisition in Goussainville. Nice find of silver and porcelain by the way."

"Your right, he was definitely searching for what I took from the cellar."

"The painting?"

Forbes nodded.

"Whatever you got, he's going to be furious that you took it from under his nose. Chellen doesn't like being made a fool of," Noah spoke from experience with the Oleg, "Okay, let's take Chellen out of the Paris equation. What evidence links Beynachinski, or Nahmad to the paintings?"

"Nothing, they've both got cast iron alibis. Do you know I'm no closer to getting them back now than I was a month ago?" Forbes looked dejected.

"On the contrary from what you've told me, I now know who masterminded the theft, and I know where the paintings were hidden, with a bit of luck they might still be there."

"That's great news," Forbes sounded skeptical. He looked at Noah, who looked worried, "If you have all the answers why are you looking so worried?"

"I'm worried about how deeply Senga is involved."

"Yes, that's my concern too. So what do we do now?"

Noah got up to leave, he held out his hand, for Forbes to take. "We're going to ask her some questions, in front of her boss, Charles Crombie; you've never actually met her boss have you?"

PART TWO

Artists

Chapter Eighteen

BERNARDINO LUINI (1481 – 1532)

Museum of Modern Art, Paris, France.
Thursday, July 1.

THE JOURNEY FROM THE ILE DE GRENELLE, TO THE
museum at the Troccadaro, had been one of grim discovery
for William Forbes.

Coleman had explained about the previous and potentially re-kindled relationship between Senga, and Chandhok
Nahmad. Naturally he omitted all references to forged paintings, Madame X, Senga's participation in fraud, and Nahmad's
offer of employment to Noah to join his entourage of forgers.

During the one-sided conversation, Forbes had slipped
deeper and deeper into depression. But, the feeling of helplessness was nothing to that which Noah was about to experience.

As they arrived, a line of Gendarmes held back a small
but determined crowd of reporters. The taxi pulled into the
museum, amid TV news vans, and government vehicles. The
buzz of excitement grew as they got out.

"They've found the paintings," Noah exclaimed, but Forbes
shook his head.

"Something better," his smile was un-shakeable.

Reporters rushed in, "Kaylee Dean, Sky News. How long have you been searching for the painting?" Flashbulbs exploded, as they made their way to the door. Forbes ignored the question.

Museum security staff formed a cordon around them, and under a barrage of questions, lights and excitement the two men rushed inside.

Noah was halted by a hand on his chest, thrust out by a small man.

"Who's this?" the small man asked, looking at Forbes. His piercing blue eyes and sober charcoal suit gave off a frosty welcome, compared to the near adulation from the reporters outside.

"Search him." The Parisian accent demanded. Two uncompromising security guards rubbed their hands over Noah's body.

"Easy boys, he's with me." Forbes said quickly.

"It's okay, if it wasn't for the body searches, I wouldn't have a sex life." Noah winced at their roughness.

Forbes addressed Girard, "This is Noah Coleman, he's …"

"This is the man arrested for murder!" Girard stepped back, and indicated the guards should overpower him. "Seize him."

Forbes waved the guards away, "Steady on, he's innocent."

"So you say." Girard encouraged the guards to continue.

"Call, DeFocault if you want it corroborating." Forbes muscled in.

"He doesn't have to," DeFocault pushed between the guards, waving them away. "Mr. Forbes, you are looking much better than when we last met."

"Thank you Detective; would you please explain to Monsieur Girard that Mr. Coleman is not wanted for murder."

The thin faced detective smiled sourly and shrugged toward Girard, "It was a miss-understanding."

Reluctantly Girard accepted Coleman into their group un-restrained; he brushed an imaginary piece of thread from his jacket, avoiding eye contact.

"With the developments of today, it is necessary to be careful."

Forbes straightened his Highland-green jacket, and pulled down his red waistcoat. Coupled with the reaction of the media outside, and the paranoid security inside, Forbes asked, "I take it, its genuine then?"

As if the movement might kill him, Girard gave a slight shoulder shrug, followed by a sour-lipped nod, "Preliminary tests confirm the age, but that is all."

Noah looked at Forbes, but before anything could be discussed, Girard turned and walked away. Forbes began to follow, with Noah and DeFocault hot in pursuit.

Noah fell in step with Forbes, "Who does Napoleon think he is, head of security?"

"His name is Daniel Girard, and he is head of security, but he thinks he's God."

"That figures. So, if they haven't found the famous five, what's 'genuine' enough to attract this circus?"

"You'll see," Forbes smiled.

With a single gesture of his well-manicured hand, Girard brought the group to a halt. "In there," he pointed toward a metal door, which seemed out of place in the old museum.

Forbes pushed through the door, and marched down a

well-lit corridor, Noah and DeFocault, trailed behind him, side by side, Girard bringing up a frustrated rear.

They stopped by a large observation window (large enough for all four to stand side by side, without touching).

Inside the room two figures dressed in blue Tyvek paper coveralls had their backs to the window, their bodies seemed distorted by the all-encompassing uniforms. At the far side of the clinically white room two other similarly dressed figures stood to attention.

They were all masked, only their eyes were visible, but their shape was of stark contrast. One reminded Noah of the Michelin Man.

The figure next to him, raised a gloved hand, and waved. Noah had no idea who was the intended recipient.

Suddenly Michelin Man became animated, he wobbled forward. The two figures with their backs to the window suddenly became aware they were being observed. They moved away from the object they were working on.

Noah's reaction to the sight they revealed shocked everyone, he fell against the window, hands and face pressed up against the glass.

"Dear God you've found her." The eyes, the fingers, the abstract sketches, were all assembled in front of him.

There on a canvas not ten feet away from him was his holy grail.

In living colour, the lady looked back at him.

"You recognise her?" Forbes asked.

Noah nodded in response, not trusting himself to speak.

"Senga said you'd be pleased. Come on let's meet the team."

In the observation room's dressing facility, Michael Carrington was the first to remove his mask, his friendly features beamed as he thrust out his warm hand, "Well done Bill, let me introduce you."

Michelin Man was next, when unveiled he turned into Pierre Cornette de Saint-Cyr Paris, the rotund Director in chief of the Museum of Modern Art. "C'est magnifique, I'm so happy to meet you Monsieur Forbes."

The next, and smallest member of the team came through the air-lock, and removed the paper hat with a flourish, revealing a mass of copper curls, "Hello boys, glad to see you settled your differences," Noah kissed her on both cheeks, handed her the antique ivory Toucan-billed hair-grip, and stood back, arms outstretched, in a 'You know best' gesture. The pretence was cutting him up inside, he desperately wanted to trust her, but the evidence kept piling up.

Forbes cut in, "He was going to shoot me; did you know that?"

Senga made a dismissive hand gesture, "Don't be silly, the gun was for his protection."

Noah echoed, "Don't be a silly Billy." He looked at Girard and DeFocault, and commented, "They're just joking about the gun." But no one was looking at him now. The final figure came through the air-lock.

Juan del Marco Enrique Cassavanurnez removed his hat and mask, he let out a long whistle and said one word, "Exquisite."

Everyone began to talk at once, but the old Spaniard raised his hands and calmed the assembled with a slow fanning motion. "The tests are not complete by a long way my friends, but results from the preliminary scan suggest the work is from the right period."

DeFocault whispered in Noah's ear, "You're a very lucky man, Monsieur. A lot of people thought it was going to be a forgery."

"Why?" his heart was beating like the pump in the cellar.

DeFocault shrugged, and brought his hawk like face close to Noah's "Because we found certain paintings and drawings in your house in St Tropez. A man with your talent, involved in the greatest art find of the century, it is too much of a coincidence to ignore."

Noah whispered back, "Everything in my home is genuine, there is no intention to commit fraud, so I hope you are taking real good care of my work, any damage, and I will sue. Now, I think you should be concentrating on who killed my wife, and less on my talents. Go and do your job and let me be impressed with your talents." His smile ended the conversation. At least the chat explained to Noah why he had been included here at the verification.

From the silence that existed between the two men, they heard Cassavanurnez, comment that he would like to go straight to the projection.

∾ℰ◯

IN ONE OF THE LECTURE THEATRES, CASSAVANURNEZ began to speak in front of a large projected view of a small section of the painting, "Magnified fifty times, you see here the dignified suavity that is the most characteristic of Luini's works," his fingers danced in the air, like a child describing rain drops. "The strokes are constantly beautiful, with an exquisiteness which depends, at least as much upon the loving self-withdrawn expression, as upon the mere refinement and attractiveness of the form."

Trance like, Noah answered, "It is that quality of expression that appears in all of Luini's works. Whether secular or sacred, it instils the latter with a peculiar religious grace, not an ecclesiastical unction, but with the devoutness of the heart." Everyone turned to look at Noah.

Cassavanurnez gave a small cough to attract their attention to the projection, "Well said my friend, I take it you are the museum's expert on Luini's work?"

"You could say that," Noah responded.

"Have we met?" Cassavanurnez asked.

"No sir, I have not had the honour before today," Noah shrank away from his gaze.

Cassavanurnez moved the camera, focusing now upon the eye; Noah felt a huge rush of emotion. "Luini always creates the head, the face, the eyes, in the style of Leonardo, but with more beauty, but less subtlety, less variety of expression," he pointed to the eyes, "here you see he has a somewhat dry style. This is exactly what I have seen in the 'Pieta', which hangs in the church of the Passione. It is another quality, another signature which distinguishes this example as consistent to other works known to be by Luini."

The camera panned out, to reveal the entire face, "Although his execution never quite equalled that of Leonardo, Luini's work does exhibit the impetuous style of the rapid stroke, but here ..." his fingers danced again, "We see boldness, not a hint of negligent brush work, as is usually associated with a rapid worker."

"As depicted in 'Crowning of Thorns', which he painted for the college del S. Sepolcro." Noah chipped in.

"Exactly, please tell the group why this fact is important."

"Because the work contained a large number of figures, the college decided to pay him 'one figure per day' they estimated it would take him over one hundred days to complete."

"And every figure demonstrates this stroke work ..." Cassavanurnez added.

"Yet it only took him thirty eight days to complete," Noah concluded.

Both men were smiling, they were positively loving describing the most intimate of details of Luini's work.

Senga glanced between the two men, and instantly noticed enough similarity in appearance for Noah's impersonations to be very convincing. She observed the body language, and thought even now they could pass as brothers. The Spaniard was older by about ten years, a little fuller in the face, with a more receding hair line, and much greyer hair; but, Senga felt that with the right stage make-up, Noah could easily pass for Cassavanurnez in the right circumstances.

The Spaniard continued to enthuse about the uniqueness of Luini, "His method was simple, the shadows are painted with pure colour, laid on really thick, while the lighter shades are of the same colours with a thinner layer applied ...maybe even mixed with a little white."

Pierre Cornette de Saint-Cyr Paris, asked, "Is the pigmentation of the period?"

"From what I have seen of the painting, yes, most certainly."

Girard asked bluntly, "When will you be able to say conclusively that this is a genuine Luini?"

"Only after the x-ray tests."

"Will you use the Gilardoni Radiolite x-ray machine?" Noah asked.

"Of course, x-ray testing is common practice among art authenticators. Not only does it establish authenticity, it unlocks secrets beneath the visible layer of the painting. We will see preparatory sketches, changes to the composition, and many other clues to determine the consumable origins."

"Consumables?" Girard asked.

"Canvas, wood, glue, paint pigment, minerals, need I go on?" Cassavanurnez seemed to be growing tired of Girard's tiresome questions. Forbes smirked at the little man's discomfort.

Girard saw Forbes's shoulders moving in mirth. "What's the matter Forbes, do you need to take another of your pills?" he goaded him, "I congratulate you on this lucky find, it's such a shame that lady luck has not offered you the same good fortune, in finding the five stolen paintings taken from this establishment …You are still on the case, are you not?"

Forbes turned slowly, and glared at him through violent eyes, his fists shook at his side, his lips snarled.

Cassavanurnez tried to defuse the air of confrontation, "During this period, lead was a primary component in white paint. The tests will show if the right amount of lead is present in the paint …perhaps we should break for coffee?" the tension remained high.

Sensing the danger, Senga linked arms with Forbes, and directed him away from any potential arguments, "Tell me Bill, what we can expect to see when they put it through the machine?" she asked.

"I'd like to rip his face off and see what's underneath."

"Maybe you could hold that thought, while your boss, and the whole world is looking on?"

Cassavanurnez dropped in line with them. "When we looked at Picasso's 'The Old Guitarist' we saw that the man started life as an old woman, with the head bent at a different angle. Also," the old Spaniard gave a hearty laugh, "There was a cow, looking over the shoulder."

Pierre de Saint-Cyr Paris joined them at the table, champagne flutes had already been filled. Cassavanurnez was in full flow. None but Senga noticed how Noah was watching, and listening to how the old Spaniard was communicating.

"The El Greco painting 'A Spanish Grandee' showed a layer of still-life beneath the old aristocrat. Can you imagine that, a bowl of fruit no less?"

No wonder no one actually engaged Cassavanurnez in conversation, he was an unrelenting bore. "Fascinating, please excuse us," Senga, offered a flute to Forbes, and led him away from the old Spaniard and the un-suspecting de Saint-Cyr Paris and Girard. She wandered over to a distraught looking Noah.

"So what was all that about you trying to kill Bill?"

"I thought he'd killed Daisy." Noah had so much sadness for Daisy, and so much concern as to how much Senga was involved in the Paris theft that his sad tone was not false.

"And now you know for sure he didn't?" her smile was angelic.

"Yes," he wanted to shake her. If she was lying; it would either kill him, or he would kill her. He glanced at Forbes, looking to understand what he was thinking, clearly, his thoughts too were about killing; an uncompromising stare was etched on his face. However, who was the intended victim Noah was unsure of at this moment.

"So, I'm safe in his company then?" Senga tried to buoy the mood.

"I believe so."

"Good," Senga, snuggled into his arm, she felt safe in-between these two men, safer still knowing that they were both on the same side, just maybe with their help she could break free of her reliance on Nahmad.

She knew Noah was feeling sad at the loss of Daisy, but she had no idea about how much his mood was affected because of what he suspected. Noah did nothing to reciprocate the gesture of friendship.

Forbes gave a quick cold smile to Noah. Today, he should be feeling on top of the world. The Luini find, especially from under the nose of LeCoyte Chellen, was a fantastic achievement, and yet he felt sick with apprehension. Noah's validation of his thoughts, reference the missing paintings had been beneficial, but their absence kept him from celebrating, and souring the taste of today's champagne. But, the potential betrayal by Senga hurt the most; he could not rest until he knew the truth. Forbes scanned the room looking for someone to trust. Carrington raised a flute in his direction.

For the moment he was the undoubted star of Michael Carrington's ALR; this had been their most significant find to date. Yet, unless a breakthrough with the missing five masters came soon, he thought his career as an ALR investigator may soon be at an end.

Coleman was looking at him, he gave a cold knowing nod that conveyed his intentions.

Forbes knew he was right. Yesterday he had dragged him from a flooded cellar, this morning he'd intended to kill him, undoubtedly the influence of Senga Munreaux was the root of the problem. Forbes looked at her now, the copper curls dark against the antique ivory Toucan-billed hair-grip. Absently she touched the grip, repositioning it to pull back the luxurious locks from her pale face and dark almond eyes; he so desperately wanted to trust her.

But, Forbes now knew of her links to Chandhok Nahmad, and that Coleman thought her involved in the Paris theft too; the room began to spin, would he ever be able to trust her again.

As the champagne flutes were being refilled, Forbes watched DeFocault, his connection to Nahmad needed to be investigated once the bubbles had settled. He then settled a murderous gaze upon Girard, the scheming little coward, whose job he had taken at the ALR, trust him? "No-way."

"What?" Senga asked, pulling the antique ivory Toucan-billed hair-grip from her hair, she shook her glorious mane in front of him, then threw it back, before re-applying the grip, "What did you say, Bill?"

"Nothing ..." Her beauty fascinated him; her deceptions cut him deeper than any blade.

Senga wondered what had actually transpired between the two men this morning. She had readily agreed to Noah's request to get Forbes on his own, after all, now that she understood that both Nahmad and Chellen were innocent of trying to have her killed, the obvious candidate had been Forbes. But Noah seemed happy with the answers he had been given.

Senga looked around the room, her life was fast falling apart; she thought she wanted Chandhok, and had undertaken desperate measures to win him back, but having met Forbes, she no longer felt that way. Now she was being forced down a route she could not control. Chandhok had proposed it would be one painting without any money, but she could be trapped into providing him with works for a long time.

Someone had tried to kill her; someone had killed the delightful Daisy, she still owed money to Chandhok, she owed millions to Christie's, which needed paying in four days. And then, to top it all off she'd conned Chellen out of half a million pounds, if he should ever get the painting tested; she shuddered at the thought. "Excuse me guys, I need to ..." she smiled and left the room.

Chapter Nineteen

JOHANNES VERMEER (1632 – 1675)

Museum of Modern Art, Paris, France,
Thursday, July 1.

SENGA ALLOWED THE DOOR OF THE SMALL WASH-
room to slam noisily behind her; she leaned against a washbasin, and checked her tired drawn face in the poorly lit mirror.
The museum was old, and the provision for women then was
not as necessary as it is today. The room smelled of cheap
disinfectant, and stale soap.

It had been one hell of a day, after one hell of a nightmare
night. After Noah had been released, he recounted the details
of Daisy's death. His words, shocked and disgusted her, her
heart went out to him, he looked older, and frail.

As the early morning sun had crept through her window she
finally admitted Daisy's death was her fault, and that she had
probably been the intended victim. If they had not travelled to
Paris, she would have been there when the assassin called.

Nahmad, Chellen, Forbes, potential killer names tumbled
from her reflection. So much deceit, so many lies. Last night,

Noah was convinced that Forbes was responsible for Daisy's murder, today they seemed like best buddies.

She recalled the early morning phone call from Charles Crombie, "Senga, darling, a wonderful find has just presented itself in Paris. Would you like to pop along to the Museum of Modern Art and represent Sotheby's at the initial verification? Your old friend, Juan Cassavanurnez (his pronunciation had much improved) will be doing the initial tests, and has asked for an assistant. As you're already swanking around the City of Lights I thought it too good an opportunity to miss? It will be a fantastic occasion, and if it's authentic, could be history in the making."

How could she refuse? And of course when she saw the painting ... she recognized the eyes immediately, Noah's sketch of Da Vinci's eyes without a face, she knew the importance of the find, she knew where Bill had found it, and who had been searching for it. "Chellen, oh shit, this is all going to end in tears."

She searched her reflection to see if all the lies she'd told could be seen. Bill and Noah were acting so strangely toward her, it was as if all their trust had evaporated. She rubbed at the dark circles under her eyes.

The door opened, and in the reflection she saw Noah and Bill enter the room.

Senga turned, "I think you'll find this is a Ladies only establishment?" the smile on her face was of genuine amusement, which quickly turned to embarrassment and then fear as they approached.

"Good, then we won't be disturbed," Noah's voice was flat and strangely menacing.

Forbes came close to her, "Noah and I had a nice little chat today, confirmed a few facts, and threw about some theories. Now we want to ask you some questions."

Senga looked to Noah, hoping to gauge what they'd chatted about; surely he would have kept Madame X a secret? She wondered what else.

"Okay, fire away." The forced smile hurt her cheeks. She thought Forbes would lead the questioning, but it was Noah that began.

"Let's go back to basics, blank canvas if you like. Forbes here is looking to recover some stolen paintings. During the course of his investigation he discovered a link between you and LeCoyte Chellen-"

"Ah yes the mysterious link, did he tell you what it was, Noah, I asked but he never told me," she turned to Forbes, "You were reluctant-"

Noah interrupted, "Not now Senga, you listen, and then you can provide some answers. Bill went to London to interview you; but before he could have a word, someone tried to kill you both. Let's examine the real reason behind the attempt on your lives, and discover who's behind it."

"Yeah, glad to," Senga said weakly.

Forbes asked Noah, "Do you think the attempt on our lives was to do with my investigation, or Senga's Crosby Garett helmet?"

"That's what we're going to find out," Noah's smile was reassuring.

"Good," Senga added, her voice firmer now, she folded her arms in defiance to their bullying.

"Bill, did you go to London just to interview Senga?" Noah asked.

"Yes, I knew she was linked to Chellen, I wanted to establish if she was involved in the Paris theft."

Senga began to remonstrate, but Noah held up a halting hand, "All in good time, we're just putting some background strokes on our blank canvas."

Senga rested back against the basin, her arms folded tightly across her breasts, her breathing hard to control.

"How did you know where to find her?" Noah asked.

"I telephoned Sotheby's. They told me she was at the warehouse."

The alarm bells began to ring in Senga's head; she knew his explanation was un-true, because no one at Sotheby's knew she was there. With a dread fear she realized that Forbes **was** the killer.

"Senga, when you returned to Sotheby's, you alone met with Charles Crombie?"

"That's right ..." subtly, she tried to distance herself from Forbes.

"How did he react at seeing you?" Noah asked.

"Shocked at the news someone had tried to kill me, pleased that I was alright," Senga realized that Noah was leading her. Good old Noah, he'd kept quiet about the Oleg forgeries, and the frauds from the Met; she relaxed a little, and allowed her mind to drift back to the night, and the words Crombie had used, "He was stressed out, said he was upset, and that I must be blaming him for sending me to the warehouse."

"Why exactly was it he sent you to the warehouse that night?" Noah asked.

'Wow' what a curve-ball question she thought. It was only the next morning that Senga had discovered the text from Crombie. After a moment's hesitation and fear, she relaxed again, marveling at how brilliantly Noah had guided her through the questioning, he was obviously trying to trap Forbes. "Mr. Crombie text me, and asked me to go to the warehouse to get the vault codes for him."

"But when you went back to Sotheby's after the attack, Cassavanurnez had already been given access to the painting."

Senga's mouth dropped open, it was something she'd not considered; especially as she had been unaware that Crombie actually wanted her to go to the warehouse in the first place.

Noah turned to Forbes, "What reason did Senga give you, for why she was at the warehouse?"

Forbes's answer was clear and concise, as if he were answering under oath in a court of law. "Senga told me she had been instructed to go to the warehouse by Charles Crombie, with the aim to release the vault for the Oleg to be examined?"

"Did you believe her?"

"No."

"Did you probe her?"

"Yes, later she confessed that the real reason for being there was to get the code to retrieve the Crosby Garett helmet."

"Were the assassins already present when you arrived at the warehouse?"

"Yes, masquerading as workers, preparing a load on the quay for shipment."

"Senga, when you arrived were these assassins present?"

"Yes, same as Bill just described."

"Okay, let's add some colour to our canvas. A security guard was on the gate. If the two workers had been bogus, he would have known, do you think?"

Both nodded slowly in agreement.

"So why were they there?"

Senga answered, but it sounded like a tentative question, "To kill me?"

"What was their motive?" Noah waited for an answer.

Senga shook her head in defeat; Forbes was reconsidering everything he'd deducted so far. "If they were there to kill you, why not do it when you arrived?"

"Think back further than that, Bill. Go deeper, to the next layer of paint, why were they there at all?"

Senga asked, "To kill Bill?"

Noah shook his head, "Bill only went there because he'd been advised that you were there. The killers were already working like beavers, moving boxes up and down the quay."

Forbes took up Noah's train of thought, "They killed the security guard. If they'd been after the helmet, the attempt would have been after you'd got it from the vault."

"So they needn't have been there at all, forget about the helmet."

"But it would be the same scenario if they were after the Oleg." Senga chipped in.

Forbes rubbed his hand over his short hair. "They weren't put there for me, but they only tried to kill you, after I turned up."

"Why try to kill us at all, all we had was the code for the vault."

Noah flexed his fingers, "Time to put the foreground on to our canvas. From what you've both said, they were there, working, known to security before either of you turned up. Probably before you even knew you needed to go to the warehouse."

Senga understood this to be true, her reason for going only came about because she couldn't swap the paintings.

"So why were they there?" Noah asked

"They were guarding the warehouse," Forbes said quietly.

Noah blended more colour onto their canvas like the true artist he was.

"They didn't try to kill Senga when she first arrived," he held up a finger, "They had been accepted by the guard on the gate," a second finger went up, "But they turned into killers when the man investigating the Paris art theft turned up out of the blue, to meet with Senga Munreaux." Noah spread both hands wide. "Why were you really there Bill?"

"To interview Senga about the Paris theft."

"And that's what you told Crombie on the phone?"

Forbes nodded.

"What time did you receive the text, Senga? Not when did you really read it, what time did Crombie send it?"

Senga pulled out her mobile, and scrolled down the screen, "Nine o'clock."

Forbes cut in, "That was after I spoke to Crombie."

Noah, unsurprised said, "Bill, get out your photo, and show Senga the link between her, Chellen and the Paris thieves. Show her why you thought there was a link to Sotheby's."

Hong Kong.

The moment Forbes took out the photograph.

SOFTLY IN THE BACKGROUND, A RADIO PLAYED TRADI-
tional music; various plucked and bowed instruments accompanied flutes, cymbals, gongs, and drums, hardly catchy, but
barely irksome.

The young Chinese girl carefully placed the small china cup
on the jade inlay at the center of the occasional table next to
his chair.

Remmert van Braam smiled as he heard the scrape of
china on jade. Since the accident his other senses seemed to
be heightening.

"Tea-time already?" he asked, quickly placing his large dark
sunglasses over his burn-scared face.

"Yes, although I was not sure if you were sleeping?" Gently,
the girl guided his hand to the cup. Even at his venerable age,
she appreciated the softness of his skin.

"I was lost in a memory, thinking about my work."

"Your paintings?" she asked in heavily accented English.

He tapped his temple, "In here, I can still see them; I can
still imagine the strokes of the brush."

"You were a great artist?"

"I was, but no one ever recognized my work, I was always
pretending to be someone else."

"Why was that?"

Speaking in Cantonese, he explained, "Artists such as Van
Gogh, Gauguin, Manet, Sisley, and Renoir, only reached fame
after their deaths, and have always been prone to the forger's

attempt to copy their style. I would pretend to be them, to make money," momentarily he laughed at the memory.

She saw the sadness return to his face, the acute embarrassment of his new disability.

"Tell me more venerable father," she asked, even though she had heard the story many times before.

"Forgeries, are nothing new. Copies of paintings have been passed off as examples of the real thing, for profit, from as early as the sixteenth century, and it is always so much better, when the real artist cannot be questioned in order to validate his own work."

"I see," her tone was soft.

"How was it? The Cantonese?" he asked.

"Very good, your pronunciation has improved again."

"Less Mandarin?"

"Yes, soon no one will be able to tell it is not your native tongue."

"Thank you Xin (pronounced Sheen), you are most kind."

"Please continue your story; it is good to practice your words."

His blindness was something he was still getting used to. His fingers curled clumsily around the cup, the heat warmed his hand. "It was in the months leading up to World War Two when forgers became extensively busy, fulfilling the age old prophesy, 'Supply and Demand'. Even before the German army was poised to invade Europe, Nazi leaders had set out a plan to plunder the famous oil paintings, and recognized works of art belonging to their political opponents. This plan, when reviewed by Hitler, was quickly extrapolated to include privately owned pieces belonging to Jewish families living in the path of the advancing army."

Remmert van Braam took a sip of the tea. "Preempting the invasion, prominent figures from within all communities began employing forgers to copy their works. The previously shunned artists quickly took up their brushes in order to satisfy the wishes of the anxious owners. Soon, forgeries hung in museums and chateaux. The owners knew the works would be taken, but the loss would be at a fraction of the value of the real thing, and they would keep their precious art hidden until the Hun was admonished."

"You were a forger artist, like these men?"

"Yes, Xin, my reputation was mighty." van Braam thought back to the golden days of art forgery …

"The Nazi leader accredited with the grand plan for the theft of the old masters on such a grand scale, was Herman Goering.

As the third Reich advanced, he became so obsessed with paintings by the established masters, that he formed his own extensive collection."

"He stole them for himself?"

"Yes. Shortly after the invasion of Holland, Goering was contacted by a man named Han Van Meegeren; he said he was willing to trade a painting by Vermeer, for an assurance that his family history would not be exposed. After a clandestine midnight meeting, Goering came away with *'Mary Magdalene washing the feet of Christ'*, and Van Meegeren's family were declared non-Jewish. Goering took the piece back to Berlin." van Braam laughed again.

"What happened venerable father?"

"Jan Bredius, the most knowledgeable specialist on Vermeer's works, said there was no doubt the painting was authentic. Goering kept it in Berlin. It was recovered at the end of the war by America's 'Monument's Men', and shipped back to Amsterdam. Van Meegeren was arrested on the charge of treason, selling Dutch cultural property to the Germans. That carried the death sentence." van Braam chuckled to himself as he took another sip of tea. "While in prison, Van Meegeren confessed that he had in fact forged the Vermeer. During the long hours of interrogation that followed his confession, police and art experts became convinced that the Vermeer painting was a fake." van Braam thought about the scandal that news must have brought; how, Van Meegeren, peeved at being considered an inferior untalented artist, had embarked upon the illegal pastime of copying the masters, and fooled the established critics.

"Van Meegeren told the investigators that fooling the art experts, who had scorned his own work, had been his revenge. He told them about a number of other forgeries that he had completed prior to the invasion. He did however stop short of telling them who had the real paintings at the time." van Braam continued to chuckle to himself as he took another sip of his tea.

It was never established how many other forgeries Van Meegeren had actually produced over the years.

Soon after his prison term began, the world press reported that Van Meegeren had died of a heart attack. In truth, along with his wife and baby son, they had slipped quietly away from Holland, for a new life in Paris.

Form an early age Van Meegeren's son, Remmert, had demonstrated an extraordinary talent for painting. Even now at the age of sixty-five he was, within a very private fraternity, until his recent accident, still acknowledged as the world's greatest forger.

"Mister Van Meegeren was a great artist."

"Yes, he was. Thank you for listening Xin, you are very kind."

"It is my pleasure Mr. Remmert," Xin answered. She'd guessed long ago that the baby son, and her employer were one and the same, but she'd never asked. That would be impolite.

Remmert van Braam finished his tea, its bitter taste was something he had already become accustom too.

Without deviation, he replaced the cup on the center of the jade inlay.

Xin took the cup, and allowed him to return to his memories.

Here in his new world of darkness, daydreams about his childhood and about his work, almost satisfied his desire to see again in colour, almost, but not quite.

van Braam remembered growing up in post-war Paris. The war, it seemed had had no effect on the art market in the city of lights, and trade blossomed despite economic restrictions.

With the return of peace, the French capital became the main art trading center of the world, attracting an emerging new school of painters.

In his mind's eye he conjured up visions of the new offerings to the art world; the expressionism from Picasso, Braque, and Matisse, the surrealism of Dali.

The new eccentric contributions to art were throwing the established buying markets into turmoil. Customers, new and old, and so-called connoisseurs were not sure how to accept the new wave, so there was still a demand for the old masters, and therefore still a market to exploit for the Van Meegeren School.

By the mid-sixties, van Braam was studying under his father, along with several other renowned art forgers, David Stein, Elmyr de Hory, and Real Lessart. The school, his father had often remarked, was of similar structure to the great studio of Da Vinci in Milan.

One day they were visited by the prominent gallery owner, Fernand Legros-Braam, who was not opposed to selling fine art reproductions with forged certificates to a growing international clientele.

A former ballet dancer, Legros-Braam, had just sold one of Van Meegeren's forged Vermeer's to Arthur Meadows, owner of the General American Oil Co. in Texas. This single transaction opened the door to the new world.

Legros-Braam, and Remmert, posing as his son, visited America, with ten creates of forged works. When asked by US customs about the nature of their business, Legros-Braam explained they were going to sell some fine art reproductions.

Eager to determine whether Legros-Braam was trying to cheat them out of the import duty, US customs impounded the works, and drafted in art specialists to determine their true value.

So good were the forgeries from Van Meegeren's school, that the specialists verified the works as originals.

Legros-Braam, gladly paid the half a million dollar import duty, and set about selling the 'real' old masters, complete with US customs certification to an eclectic mix of buyers.

Unbeknown to the world at large, a vast number of forgeries from Van Meegeren's school were being sold to an unsuspecting customer base. Back in Europe, Picasso authenticated one of his own paintings; it was actually painted by David Stein.

When Van Meegeren died, Elmyr de Hory, left the school and went to live in Ibiza. There he produced, hundreds of forgeries, including works which were actually signed and authenticated by the Dutch artist Van Dongen.

Apparently, Van Dongen was so short of money near the end of his life, that he gladly endorsed the fakes for a percentage. These paintings were shipped to the States and sold by Legros-Braam and Son, as genuine Van Dongens.

The nineteen sixties was a dark time for the art world. It was not uncommon for genuine artists to repudiate some of their own work, simply because critics had given them a negative review, or they'd made a loss at auction.

Italian master, Giorgio de Chirico, produced some backdated 'self-forgeries' to profit from his earlier successful career, whilst denouncing his later paintings, hanging in public and private collections as forgeries.

Maurice de Vlaminck refused to authenticate some of his own works simply because he did not like them anymore.

"Happy days," Remmert rested his head back against the chair. When thinking about his life's work, he became filled with pride. "It was so much easier before x-ray machines, and spectrograph technology, they have all but eliminated the market. I really think my world is over now."

In 2008, the Art Loss Register had issued a public statement, warning potential buyers in America that forgeries produced by the students of the Van Meegeren school accounted for nearly fifteen percent of all works put up for auction, they titled the statement, 'Buyer beware'. Privately, they believed that many of the originals, combined with works removed before the Nazi invasion of Europe were locked away in private galleries.

There was even doubt that some of the genuine works looted by the Nazis, and stolen by the Russians at the end of the war were actually real. The new tests would prove authenticity, but the paintings needed to be found before that could happen. van Braam wondered where those paintings had been kept for all these years, "Probably in Moscow," he mused.

Remmert van Braam knew that times were changing, forgeries of art, were becoming more difficult to pass the authentication tests. His world, was coming to an end, his life was almost over.

In his new world of darkness, devoid of light and shade he knew he had just one more masterpiece to complete before he could go to meet his creator.

His hands gripped the arms of the chair as he contemplated his last action on earth. He intended to kill the man responsible for killing the light of his world.

To that end, he was going to use his former employer, Chandhok Nahmad. He was going to exploit his knowledge of Nahmad's master plan and force him to bring Noah Coleman into striking distance.

"Keep your friends close, and your enemies closer!"

Chapter Twenty

MARC CHAGALL (1887 – 1985)

Museum of Modern Art, Paris, France,
Thursday, July 1.

WILLIAM FORBES HANDED THE PHOTOGRAPH TO Senga. She screwed her face up at the memory, "Monaco Grand Prix 2008, Lewis Hamilton won."

"Thought that Lewis winning would have been a joyous occasion for any Brit?"

"It was, but for me the day was a disaster."

"What Monte Carlo, being a guest on Chellen's yacht?"

"It's not Chellen's yacht. Sotheby's hired it for the event. Chellen was our guest. As you can see his hands were all over me. All day long, he had a disproportionate view at what was on offer."

"Do you know the other men in the photograph?" Forbes asked.

Senga looked at the picture, wide smiles, and expensive sunglasses greeted her. "The guys at either end were security, they came with the boat. I've no idea about their names, but this one ..." she tapped the photo, "kept asking for my number.

He was Italian, I think. He was fascinated about my name; kept spelling it out every time he came close to me." Senga pulled a face at the mock tough guy pose in the picture, "Tight tee-shirt, bulging muscles, brains in his pants, not my type." She smiled at Forbes, and handed it back.

"Their names are Giovanni Mosca, and Tommaso Buscetti."

"The men you suspect carried out the theft?" Senga said quickly.

"That's right, so when I saw Chellen with his arm around the waist of…" Forbes turned over the photograph, to allow Senga to see what was written on the back, "his contact at Sotheby's-"

"His what?" Senga read the legend, "Monaco 08, Sotheby's contact, S.E.N.G.A.M." Shaking her head she pushed the photo away, "The Sotheby's contact is Crombie."

"Charles Crombie?"

"Yes," she turned the photo over and dabbed her finger over the fifth figure, "Charles Crombie."

Forbes closed his eyes, if the ground could have opened up and swallowed him, he would have welcomed it.

Noah appeared at his side, "Crombie, the fifth person in the photo, and Senga's name spelled out on the back by some musclebound Italian stallion. That's the real link," Noah took the photograph, looking at it at arm's length, "Crombie would have known you were leading the ALR investigation into the Paris theft … let's just suppose, for one moment, that Crombie was holding the five stolen paintings in the London warehouse. He had his security guards patrolling night and day. Everything is fine, no one has any idea he has them hidden in London. The heat is firmly on LeCoyte Chellen, you're looking in France, and Finland, Interpol is looking up its own ass, and the Paris police are just concentrating on looking good. Crombie is in the clear; then … out of the blue he gets a phone call from you, asking to speak to Senga Munreaux about the Paris theft. The panic button gets well and truly pressed." Noah lent back against the washbasin, "Crombie sends you to the warehouse, where his trained killers will take care of you. When he speaks to his men to give them their orders, they inform him that the lovely Miss Munreaux is already there. Crombie, of course has no idea why Senga would be there, unless …she knows about the paintings, and is intending to assist the ALR investigator to find them."

"So he gave the order to have us killed," Senga whispered.

"He must have been in a right state, don't forget he was tied up at the auction-house with a forgery, entertaining Cassavanurnez. Imagine his surprise when you walked into his office late at night."

Senga put her hand over her mouth, "He sent the text to provide evidence to the police as to why I was there, a reason to divert their attention about us looking for the stolen paintings."

Forbes asked, "Are you suggesting that Crombie stole the paintings?"

Noah waved his hand, "No, the man that killed Buscetti and Mosca, he's your actual thief."

"Who's he working for?"

"We'll have to come to that later."

"You think it was the same killer?" Senga asked.

"For sure. But he was not responsible for trying to kill you in London that was Crombie." Noah replied.

"How do you come to that conclusion?" Senga asked, worried about the connection to the Oleg, and Madame X, and the Crosby Garett helmet.

269

Forbes interrupted, "Whoever killed Giovanni Mosca did it for a different reason from when he killed Buscetti."

"What's that got to do with anything?" Senga asked.

"Mosca was killed in Verona, at his place of work over three weeks after the theft. If he'd been hired by the mastermind, they would have known where he worked, conversely, if Mosca thought they knew where he worked, he wouldn't have been there, at night, on his own, meeting with you. Buscetti was killed at the handover site, very quickly, very professionally, and disposed of in the same manner," Noah responded, "Whoever killed Mosca was after information, just like with Daisy. Whoever killed all three is also looking for the paintings."

Senga's jaw dropped, Forbes's lips went tight, he could see all too clearly now the picture that Noah had so expertly painted for them.

"It was a double-cross. Mosca wasn't hired to do the Paris theft." Forbes said.

"No, he was Buscetti's man; together they intended to rip off the real thief."

"Whoever killed Mosca, saw you, and followed you to London, where you presented him with Senga," Noah explained.

"He must have overheard me telling her to get out of London, and go to someone she trusted."

"Why would he follow me and not Bill?" Senga asked.

"Did you say where you were going when you left Senga?" Noah asked.

"Yes you did, I remember you saying you were going after Chellen in Helsinki." Senga added.

Forbes rubbed his hand over his face, "Well whoever he is, he knew Chellen wasn't in Helsinki, so he's well connected.

He knew I was on a wild-goose chase. He followed Senga, followed you both down to St Tropez, where he intended to kill you both."

"Why was he after us?" Senga asked.

"Because the real thief had the paintings stolen from him, and now he, and the mastermind behind all this wants them back. He saw you two as rivals."

"He didn't get any information from Daisy," Noah said quietly.

Senga put a reassuring hand on his shoulder.

"Now we're all together in Paris, he'll be watching us." said Forbes.

"But we still don't know where the paintings are?" Senga said.

"I think Crombie still has them in the warehouse in London." Noah said.

"Let's go and find out." said Forbes.

"But quietly, yes?" said Senga.

Forbes erupted, "Absolutely not, if we're going to catch this killer, we need to let him know where we're going."

"We're not going to capture him, I'm going to kill him," Noah explained, "he doesn't know where the paintings are; he can't help you get them back."

"No, but he can tell us who organized the theft." Forbes declared.

"What good will that do anyone? Buscetti and Mosca intended to take the paintings from the killer; it got messy, Mosca got away, and gave the 'priceless five' to his contact in Sotheby's, Crombie, for safe keeping, that's the link. However, with both Mosca and Buscetti dead, Crombie has inherited a fortune. He'll distribute them through his channels. Now let's get this psycho bastard."

"Okay, so if Crombie still has the paintings, and the killer, the real thief is looking for them, Crombie will know that, so, what's he likely to do short term?"

"He knows we're all here, all excited about finding the Luini, now's his best chance to move them on."

"If he thinks he can get away with this, he's dreaming."

"Let's go wake him up." Noah said, holding the door open for Senga and Forbes to storm out of the washroom.

AS THE THREE CAME THROUGH THE GRAND HALL OF the museum, Chandhok Nahmad removed his Persol sunglasses. He waited for Senga to get within touching distance, before saying, "I see you've spoken to Mr. Forbes, as I suggested."

Forbes and Noah stood at her shoulders.

"That's right," she said submissively.

"Shall we press charges?" Nahmad asked.

"No, he's not responsible for trying to kill me," her voice a little more assertive now.

"Good to know the truth. So, we are finished with these people," he stretched out his hand to guide her away.

"Not yet, I'm still anxious to complete what we started."

Nahmad's hand went to his heart, "Then you will be mine again."

"The expression is, 'and then I'm all yours' I think you'll find."

Nahmad held out his hands to stop Senga brushing past

him, "When you finish your task, I will expect you to join me, I thought ...Monte Carlo, now that the petrol heads have gone. I trust you've not forgotten my proposal?" He held out a hand for her to touch.

Senga fought to control her reply, she glanced at Forbes for strength, and then triumphantly she responded, "We'll see!"

Nahmad glared back, the bond he'd thought they shared seemed tenuous. The developing relationship he detected between her and Forbes was clearly more advanced than his jealous mind had calculated.

Forbes broke the uneasy silence that had descended on the group, "Why are you here, Mr. Nahmad?"

His dark eyes left Senga's beautiful face and focused upon Forbes. How different he looked, from when they'd last met, when Forbes interviewed him about the five stolen paintings. Nahmad looked at them; they both seemed stronger, mentally and physically stronger.

His face broke into a cheeky smile, "I have come to view the wonderful find."

"How do you know about it?" Forbes asked.

"I was invited here by my friend, Monsieur Girard."

"If he's your friend then keep your hands off the lady." Forbes took Senga by the arm, "Come on we have a plane to catch." They pushed past.

As Noah drew level, Nahmad spoke in a strong commanding voice, loud enough for Forbes and Senga to hear. "I'm sorry to hear about the death of your lady friend, Mr. Coleman. As your employer I would like to say, take as much time as you need, meet me in Hong Kong for the exhibition, shall we say by the end of next week."

Noah barely turned his head to acknowledge him, "We'll see!"

As they progressed along the corridor Forbes turned to Noah, "He thinks he's your boss?"

"A lot of people have made that mistake." Noah shrugged his shoulders.

❧◯

THE VOICE WAS HOLLOW AND WITHOUT ACCENT, IT CAN sometimes be that way on a long distance call through a decoder. The precautions were annoying, but it was essential not to have the call traced, or be the victim to some lucky Interpol eavesdropper, or internet hacker.

"They're booked on the next flight to Heathrow. So are you."

"That's very efficient," the man ran his finger along the length of his puckered scar. The action was almost second nature to him now.

"Please make sure you get the exact location of the merchandise before killing anyone else."

The man winced at the comment, recalling the moment life had drained from the Italian in Verona, and the hope poured from Coleman's woman in St Tropez.

He became aware his finger was tracing the scar again, quickly he brought his hand down and pointed an accusing finger at the telephone. "Don't forget Buscetti was your choice."

The rebuke was swift, "And you said he wouldn't be a problem."

"He wasn't, I killed him without breaking a sweat. I enjoyed watching him burn."

"Shame you didn't see his friend coming."

The hand shot back to the scar. The sound of the baseball bat striking his skull replayed again. The blow would have killed a normal man, but it only knocked him unconscious. Mosca's second mistake was not closing the container doors, he'd appreciated the fact that the fire needed oxygen, but it had allowed the man to crawl out of the inferno. "He paid the price," he recalled the joy he'd felt at beating him to death him in Verona.

"Eventually." There was a hint of disdain.

"The delay was down to you, as I said Buscetti was your choice, I could have gotten us a driver without any aspirations."

"I wanted someone who Interpol would believe was responsible for the theft. I apologize for the man's aspirations. Now, let's not bicker."

The man felt a flare of anger, "I will recover the paintings, that is what you still want isn't it?"

"Yes, more than anything, well almost anything," the voice laughed at the secret meaning to his words.

"I'm sorry for not getting Coleman in St Tropez."

"Maybe you did not take his life, but you took something very precious to him, I hope he is suffering too."

"I'll get him in London."

"Get the paintings first …then you can kill Coleman."

"And the girl," his reply was just a little too quick to be professional, but his desire to kill another woman was overwhelming.

"So the copper-haired vixen has aroused you? Have you already fantasized about killing her?" The voice conveyed no pleasure in the words, the intention was to stimulate the desire to get the job done, but the response from the man shocked him. He expected banter, but he got pure evil.

"The thought of killing her excites me."

The decoder removed all emotion from the response. "Get the paintings, and she's yours. I distilled my life's work into that theft and the consequences. Let's not let some two bit Italian muscleman take away the ultimate prize."

"I better go, I have a flight to catch," his finger traced the scar as he put down the receiver.

Impressed that he'd been booked onto the same flight, the man with the scar now seethed in frustration. The queue shuffled forward slowly, as the result of another useless countermeasure to a fictitious terrorist threat.

He'd seen the unholy trio of Munreaux, Forbes, and Coleman, deep in conversation, coming out of the executive lounge. No doubt their tickets were first class.

Security apologized for the delay, and sent him down the boarding tunnel.

Senga's mobile rang, "It's her," she answered the call, "Hi Poppy."

Primrose Parsons had been known as Poppy since University. Certain staff members at Sotheby's called her *Prim and Proper* Parsons, but never to her face. As Charles Crombie's personal assistant, Poppy would certainly be able to shed some light on his current whereabouts, and future plans. It wouldn't do to run into him at the warehouse.

"Good morning Senga, oh sorry it's afternoon where you are. How is Paris? How's the holiday?"

The comment said an awful lot about people's perception of her movements since her near death experience in London.

"It's all lovely thanks. Is Charles about, I need to catch-up with him."

"Sorry to spoil the surprise sweetie, he's at the airport now, he's coming to see you."

"To see me? Why? She pressed loud-speaker to allow the others to hear the reply.

"Well not you specifically today, but I'm sure he'll take you out to dinner."

"Poppy, why's he coming to Paris?"

"He's meeting a couple of buyers, very hush; hush."

"Oh wow, what's he selling?"

"I'm not privy to that, but I do know he's been sorting through some old stock at the warehouse recently, sorry, didn't want to remind you of that awful night."

"Any idea on the artists he was looking at, I might be able to hazard a guess at what he's going to sell."

"I heard him say, 'contemporary artists' though he's not looking to sell, the buyers are looking for exhibits for an exhibition, in Hong Kong, I believe."

"Chandhok Nahmad's exhibition?" Senga's pitch was high.

"Yes, I heard his name mentioned."

"Is he meeting Chandhok in Paris?" She tried not to be pushy.

"No, it's not in his diary."

"Buyers names?" Forbes whispered.

"Who are the buyers he's coming to meet?" Senga asked.

"Senior Rossini, and Monsieur Pierre Lachaise. Do you know them?"

"Er, yes, where's the meeting taking place, I think I'll crash it, force him into taking me to dinner tonight," a sparkling laugh accompanied the comment.

"Oh, it doesn't say. Strange. Still it's at four thirty."

"Okay, Poppy, listen, if he rings you, can you ask where the meeting is?"

"Sure, I'll tell him-"

"No, don't tell him I called, I want it to be a surprise; make him feel guilty about not contacting me."

"Okay sweetie, chat soon. Bye."

Senga finished the call, then looked at Forbes and Noah, "He's coming to Paris, with un-named paintings to exhibit in Chandhok's exhibition. He's got a meeting with a Mr. Rossini, and a Mr. Pierre Lachaise, buyers that I've never heard of, either through Sotheby's, the Met or Chandhok's empire. Have you ever heard of them?"

Forbes nodded, "Yes, but it is Père, not Pierre. Père Lachaise is a place not a person."

"It's a cemetery, a famous one too, but not one you'd take paintings to, to place in an exhibition." Noah chipped in.

"And I suppose Rossini is buried there? Senga asked.

Noah furrowed his brow, "Well he used to be for a while, and then he went home." He took out a coin and flipped it, "Heads or tails?"

"Heads," Forbes responded.

"Heads it is then, who do you want to go after?"

"We'll stay here; Senga is going to be of more use with Crombie and Nahmad than you."

"I'll go to London, see if the paintings are still there, and establish what other stuff he took from the warehouse."

Both men knew that was how the responsibilities were always going to be divided. Forbes would never have plumped for London, believing the paintings were coming to Paris, even though his credentials would have gained access to the warehouse easier than Noah. But, with the eyes of the forger, Noah had got what he wanted too. In London, the man that killed Daisy would be following them. This was an opportunity not to be missed.

"Okay, give me your ALR Identity card; that will open the warehouse door for me."

Forbes handed over his card, it was a clever idea.

Senga explained the change of plan to airline staff, and after a brief conversation, she and Forbes headed out of the airport.

After they'd gone, Noah walked calmly through the tunnel and boarded the plane.

Chapter Twenty-one

LEONARDO DA VINCI (1452 – 1519)

London, England.
Thursday, July 1.

RELUCTANTLY, IAN DOWNER, THE MANAGER OF Sotheby's riverside secure warehouse welcomed Noah Coleman into his office. As they shook hands, Downer silently cursed his luck, *'five minutes later and I'd have been gone'*, he thought. The golf clubs were stacked neatly in the trunk of his car.

The production of the ALR Identity card at the gate had persuaded security to call Downer, and with gritted teeth, allow him a meeting.

Fortunately for Noah, Downer's preoccupation with getting the meeting over as quickly as possible meant he did not examine the Identity card too closely.

"My PA should be able to help you with anything you need," he pressed the intercom, and asked, "Kirsty can you come in?"

"This is Kirsty," Downer's cockney heritage was hidden beneath the façade of the Sotheby's position.

Noah stood up, "Hello Kirsty, I'm William Forbes, Art Loss Register."

"Oh wow the man that killed the two robbers."

With a growing feeling of embarrassment, Downer remembered where he'd heard the name before; the prospect of golf today was looking more fragile than ever. "Can you get us a drink please; I'll deal with Mr. Forbes myself," his smile grew.

"Coffee Mr. Forbes?" her eyes were flirting.

"Why not, milk and two sugars," Noah flirted back.

With coffee on the table Noah got to the point. "Can you access a list of the paintings Charles Crombie took with him to Paris?"

"For the Hong Kong exhibition?"

"Yes that's right."

"No problem, but he didn't take them to Paris, they were air-freighted to Hong Kong," his fingers danced over the keyboard. The printer buzzed and spat out a sheet. "Twenty three paintings, apparently Mr. Nahmad is looking for artists that have been overlooked by the public; he wants to understand why people don't like contemporary." Downer pulled a face, while his mind told him, *'this guy killed two hit-men. They say he skewered one of them through the neck with a broken broom handle, and now I'm saying words like contemporary.'*

"That's a great warehouse management system you've got there; could you get it to show me all the deliveries you've had in here since May twentieth?"

After a few deft key-strokes, "Forty-two deliveries," *'fuck, I'm sat next to a killer, talking about deliveries'* he thought.

"How many of those are still in stock?"

More keying, "Twenty-nine."

"Is that normal?"

"Yeah, this is a warehouse." The Oxbridge accent almost completely disappeared, as he tried to man-up with the killer.

"How many of the receipts from May twentieth went out in the last four days?" Noah asked.

The fingers went to work again; just moments later came the terse reply "Five." Downer passed the single A4 sheet over.

"I wouldn't know what to look for; does anything strike you as odd?"

Downer's cockney accent was becoming stronger; some words were a more difficult interpretation than some of the French locals encountered during his self-imposed exile in St Tropez.

"This one's strange; in so much as it was in the same location all the time it was 'ere." Noah had to incline his head to fathom out the words.

"Why is that odd?"

"This warehouse is computer controlled; it decides where a package will be stored. Being in the same location, since the day it came in means it never went to auction, or wasn't given a value – we store by value."

"Who's the customer?" Noah asked

"Dunno," all semblance of upper class was gone now.

"Is that normal?"

"It is in this case."

"Why?" Noah straightened, frustration flowing through his body.

Downer could feel a broom stick being thrust into him at any moment, "It came in by hand, and was taken by hand." There was no 'H' in the sentence.

"So can you check who signed for it?"

"Oh shit," Downer stared at the keyboard.

"Well?" Noah asked.

"Blimey, it was taken by Charles Crombie."

ℒ◯

Paris, France.
Thursday, July 1. 16.30hrs.

THE PÈRE LACHAISE CEMETERY IS LOCATED ON THE Boulevard de Mènilmontant, in the Eastern quarter of Paris.

Within its one-hundred and sixteen acres, a little over three-hundred thousand bodies are buried, with the ashes of an additional four-hundred thousand souls, stored in the columbarium.

The taxi pulled up opposite the Phillipe Auguste Metro station. In awe, Senga and Forbes looked at the pale grey stone façade of the grand entrance, Senga un-folded the guide-book, purchased at the airport.

"I'll take that." He plucked it from her hands.

"I can read a map," she said defensively.

"No, I mean, you stay here, I'm going in alone."

As Senga began to protest, Forbes pressed his finger to her lips, "I need to take it from here, on my own, and after all I know what Crombie looks like now."

"Bill ...be careful." She noticed that he'd definitely lost weight, he looked better with the short hair too, and his eyes looked more focused. Perhaps the killer in him was being re-awakened, perhaps he didn't have to be careful after all.

"Me? Ex-SAS no problem."

"What about … you know your problems with tunnels."

"I'm not claustrophobic," he began, but decided not to go into to detail, "Besides, I'm not planning on going underground."

"But you're still taking the medication?" she asked uncertainly.

"Belgrade was a long time ago, I'm over it." Forbes knew that to recount the true horrors of the catacombs in Belgrade, would give her nightmares too. He walked away, without looking back, "Just stay here," he disappeared through the giant square gate.

Once within the walls of this city of the dead, he glanced at the guide-book. Without one, you could easily get lost on the many paved roadways which meandered through the array of monuments.

Forbes glanced at the more extravagant sculptures, erected by the city's wealthiest families, as he strode along the main thoroughfare. The road was wide enough for two vehicles to pass each other with ease. To each side of the road, a neatly trimmed grass bank rose to border a cobbled, tree-lined pavement. The grave markers here ranged from simple headstones to lavish family tombs.

Rambling in-between the many spectacular works of art, Forbes observed a number of tourists, and tapophiles, strolling along the leafy avenues, taking selfies by the various gravesites of famous individuals. Jim Morrison lay over to the right, but Rossini's tomb was away to the left.

Père Lachaise is the resting place of many individuals of world renowned, and as such make the cemetery a very popular tourist attraction.

When he saw the tomb, he was reminded of the Dr. Who Tardis; the monument was nearly twelve feet square, and over eighteen feet tall; an immense imposing grey-stone structure, with a single step leading up to two dark reddish-brown latticed doors. Light was able to permeate through the structure, highlighting three fresh bouquets lodged in the lattice work, just above the round door handles.

With an air of despondency, Forbes saw that there was no meeting taking place. He checked his Tudor wristwatch; 16.33hrs. He wandered over to the monument and read the legend, declaring this to be the resting place of the musician, and composer, Rossini.

Inside the monument he noticed some torn-up sheets of paper nestling among the scattered leaves on the floor; one sheet looked like a bill of laden. He saw today's date on it. Forbes grasped the door handles, and pushed.

Pain, like never before coursed through his body in the form of an electric shock. Forbes felt himself falling to the floor, which he noticed looked to be made of brass.

Prakash jogged over to the tomb. Having turned off the power, he quickly manhandled Forbes into the confines of the lattice cube. Depressing a small mushroom shaped button, the brass floor began to descend. Within moments a cool stone shaft surrounded them.

To the accompaniment of what sounded like a toilet flushing, the brass platform continued to drop. Twenty feet below ground level it came to a cushioned halt.

As Prakash dragged Forbes along a dark passageway, the sound of rushing water cascaded through the ancient lift shaft.

Built in 1888, in classic arch, with bricks, the passageway

resembled an old metro tunnel, its darkness was gothic and uninviting.

Forbes became aware of the sound of running water. With difficulty he raised himself up onto all fours. It was dark, and damp, and he was underground. The horror of Belgrade came back to him sharply.

He began to shake, his breathing became shallow and hurried. He climbed to his feet, and fumbled for his pills.

"Still need the pills to stop you from pissing yourself?" The beam of light caught him directly in the face. Forbes covered his eyes with his hand.

The light waved in front of him, "Go on, that way …I have a gun, so please no heroics," Prakash ordered.

Using the damp wall for support he began to stumble down the passageway. The bricks were damp, but provided a solid wall between the passageway, and thousands of bodies, buried on the other side.

"At least they're all dead," Forbes whispered.

"What do you say?" Prakash asked.

"Nothing," Forbes swallowed his pills.

At the end of the passageway a door barred any further progress. It had a very old looking lock and latch arrangement.

"Just lift the latch, it's not locked."

Forbes lifted the latch and the door opened. The room beyond was nearly fifty feet in length, and almost half again in width It was well lit and crammed full of hi-tech gadgets, TV screens hung on one wall. Opposite, in contrast hung a Monet.

The room seemed to be interlaced between modern surveillance kit, and examples of Art nouveau.

His head was still spinning from the reaction to the nearness of the corpses, and the memory of the tunnels. His hands were burnt, from the electric current which had pulsed through the door. No wonder there was no sign of a meeting in the cemetery, all the action was below ground.

The kiss of the gun against his neck brought him back to the present, although his body was still shaking, and his knees were week.

"Sit on the chair, hands on your head." The gun knocked him forward.

The sound of running water began to stabilize, as air replaced the water gurgling through the pipe work. The noise was all consuming, all he needed now were the flesh-eating zombies, to make the party complete.

"You are correct, Mr. Forbes, the method of entry is water driven. The room and the lift were designed in 1888. A bi-product from the pumping station at Etampe, all very 19th century, but as you can bear witness, the surveillance and the electrified doors are very 21st century."

Forbes looked at the CCTV monitors, images of all the approach views to Rossini's tomb stared back from all angles.

Prakash said, "We thought you were on a plane to London."

"Who's we?" Forbes asked.

"Not forgotten me already have you?" said Chandhok Nahmad. Suddenly he appeared standing in front of him. "Was he alone?"

"Yes sir," answered Prakash.

"Shame, I thought you'd have brought my woman with you." He abruptly felt the need to explain his relationship, "Agnes and I go way back."

"Agnes?"

Nahmad gave out a raucous belly laugh, "Oh dear not quiet in the inner circle yet are you?"

"You mean Senga?" Forbes asked

"Yes, Senga Montreux, or Munreaux, or whatever she likes to call herself. I know her as plain old Agnes Monroe. I knew her before she was corrupted."

"Corrupted by you."

"Yes, I broke her in, you could say."

"I think you'll find she's moved on."

Nahmad clapped his hands, "Moved on, oh that is simply delicious," suddenly the smile dropped from his face, "You didn't let her go to London with that whore-loving good-for-nothing gambler did you?"

"I told you, she's moved on."

"Oh, so she's had him too."

Forbes shook his head, "I didn't mean that."

"Touchy!" Nahmad turned to Prakash, they both laughed. "Once she has finished with you, and paid her debt, she will come back to me. She cannot resist my charm."

"You don't think she still wants to associate herself with a sewer rat like you, do you?"

"This isn't where I live." Nahmad gestured to the TV screens.

"It's where you belong!"

"You don't like my lair?" his face distorted theatrically.

Forbes took a slow look around the room, ostensibly to answer Nahmad's rhetorical question, but secretly to look for a means to escape. "Not really."

"In 1887, the Italian composer, Gioachino Rossini's remains were moved to Florence, but the crypt, still dedicated to his memory, remained empty. Some enterprising guillotine dodgers decided the space could be used to provide temporary sanctuary if the peasants ever decided to spit out their cake again. When the Nazis strolled in forty years ago, a number of valuable works of art were safely stored in here."

"The rest is history," quipped Forbes.

"Very good Mr. Forbes," Nahmad turned back toward the monitors, "History indeed."

"Is Charles Crombie, late for his meeting?" Forbes asked.

"Such an inquisitive man, aren't you. First time we met you were looking for five stolen paintings, now you're looking for the director of Sotheby's," Nahmad waved a finger, "You should learn to relax more. Take some chill pills." Nahmad laughed again.

"Yes, take some pills," Prakash lent forward, "You get it, pills?" he put his fingers toward his mouth, imitating swallowing pills.

Forbes recognized they'd done their homework on him, the information had probably come from Girard. He looked down at his hands, they'd stopped shaking. "You still think Crombie will be bringing the five stolen paintings?"

"You think Crombie stole the paintings? Does this mean Mr. Chellen is off your list?" Nahmad's jaw dropped open, emphasizing a mock look of utter amazement, "You were convinced Chellen was behind the Museum theft."

"Crombie wasn't behind the theft, Crombie inherited the paintings after a double-cross."

"No honour among thieves then? And this double-crosser, just gave the paintings to Crombie, on a whim?"

"He has them now, yes."

Prakash stood in front of Forbes, "Not true."

"What would you say if I told you that I know for 100% sure, that Crombie doesn't have the paintings, what would you think then?" Nahmad walked beside the monitors, "Are you a betting man Mr. Forbes?"

"No."

"Ah, not like that fool Coleman, he's a betting man."

Prakash gestured to Forbes to get his money out, "Wager!"

Forbes, so wanted to smash the little man's face in. Forbes got out his wallet, and produced a twenty-euro note, "This enough?"

"That's perfect, come on." Nahmad walked to the far end of the room. Prakash followed, poking Forbes in the back with his gun.

"You know, you're a very irritating little man?"

"But I have the gun." Prakash smarmed.

Nahmad opened the door to what looked like a storeroom, "You're looking for Crombie, Forbes?"

"I'm expecting him here, yes."

"I bet you he's already here, come take a look."

Forbes stopped walking, recognizing that they intended to put him in the storeroom.

"Come on Mr. Thomas Doubting."

"That's Doubting Thomas," Forbes corrected. Prakash hit him across the back of the neck with the gun, and forced him forward.

Forbes stumbled to the door, the room beyond was dark, but emitting a loud hum.

Nahmad flicked on the light. Forbes recognized the generator, providing the power to the main room. Around the walls, he saw saws and other rudimentary cutting equipment. But it was the floor that took his attention.

Hundreds of rats tumbled over each other, in a scrum in the center of the room. As the light registered on their brains, they darted toward their hole in the wall. Funneling in to get out of the light. As the final wave of disgusting scuttling furry bodies disappeared, Forbes saw a much more horrific sight.

In the center of the room, lay the bloodied heap of a man.

Nahmad took the twenty-euro note. "I win, here is Mr. Crombie. I don't think he was enjoying his last meal in Paris." Two more rats ran out from beneath his pin-striped suit jacket, nipping at the bloodied stumps of his fingers as they darted past. "But they are enjoying him."

Forbes felt his chest tighten, the memory of Belgrade came flooding back. He looked at the corpse, expecting it to get up and come screaming at him at any moment. Involuntarily he took a step back.

"No, you go in." Prakash pushed him forward.

The years of treatment melted away, he was back in his nightmare; only this time there was no Minardi to save him. Forbes stumbled into the room. He noticed the heavy cables extending from the generator. Some snaked along the wall, one came into the center of the room and was attached to a tripod. The video camera was aimed at an ancient workbench, the top of which had been cleared off. On top of the bench, a powerful light stood next to a black carbon tube.

"Alas, poor Crombie, his demise was necessary."

The last time Forbes had seen a tube like that, it was over the shoulder of the man stealing the paintings from the Museum of Modern Art. He took strength from knowing the five priceless works of art were not more than twelve feet away from him.

"Why did Crombie have to die?" Forbes asked.

"He was attempting to blackmail me," Nahmad answered quietly.

"It was an inspired attempt," prompted Prakash, the light reflecting off his rimless glasses.

"Indeed, perhaps Mr. Prakash should bring you up to date. After all, he has followed the Paris theft almost as closely as you."

"Thank you." The little man smiled openly, his teeth were very white and very even. "When you visited Mr. Nahmad, after the theft, we were all very interested to know who would have been responsible for such an audacious theft. I followed your investigation, and conducted my own research. I believed the death of Buscetti was a little too staged. I believed he was intended to be the fall guy."

Forbes felt his strength returning, perhaps the pills were working after all; he must remember to tell Dr. Hall at his next appraisal appointment.

"Such a theft, such skill in extracting the paintings. No alarms, no security. Such a choice of art. One man on his own, he had to be an expert. Buscetti, on the other hand, got caught on CCTV stealing the credit card, which bought the cutters. No, not the style of our thief."

Forbes, unable to resist nodded his head in agreement. "And all the time the trail was pointing to LeCoyte Chellen."

Nahmad added, "Like yourself, I thought such a crime could only have been orchestrated by a private collector. Until Buscetti's burnt body was discovered I thought the paintings would never be seen again. But the car and the thief? Found together in Marseilles; smelled of a double-cross to me."

"The real architect wanted the world to think Buscetti was the thief, and the paintings had been destroyed in the fire." Forbes probed.

Nahmad nodded in agreement, "Then Crombie contacted me. Somehow, he had stumbled upon information about a long-term project I am putting together. He suggested some artists that I might like to exhibit in Hong Kong. We talked, but his conversation soon turned to the paintings he had acquired. He suggested I buy them from him, and he would forget all about my project." Nahmad smiled guiltily, as if admitting he'd been caught out.

"Acquiring the paintings not appeal to you?" Forbes asked.

"Simply knowing what Crombie knew, compromises my organization."

Forbes marveled at the scale of Nahmad's proposed project, if owning the five priceless masterpieces was not bait enough, it must be something big. "Yet, you now have the five paintings." Forbes nodded toward the black carbon tube.

A rat emerged from beneath Crombie's out-flung arm, its snout covered in blood. Once exposed to the light, it scurried to the hole in the wall, and disappeared. All three men felt a fleeting revulsion.

Nahmad waved his hand, indicating that it was nothing. "Yes, I have them, although I will return them in due course."

Forbes thought about his choice of words, "Your chief forger, recently lost his sight."

Nahmad bowed slightly, acknowledging that Forbes had almost cracked the puzzle.

"Coleman!" Forbes exclaimed. "Without a forger, you had no ability to copy the paintings, you didn't want anything to jeopardize your big project, whatever it is; but now you've bagged Coleman, he can copy the five paintings, and you turn a hefty profit."

"We set about snaring him by using Agnes," Prakash explained.

Forbes felt the twist of the knife again, as Senga's involvement became clear.

"The Roman helmet, was too good an opportunity to miss."

"Explain?" demanded Forbes.

"I lent her the money to purchase it." The lie was white, the pretense was necessary, even though he intended to kill Forbes; he did not want to give away any details of his big project.

"But, then we had a lovers spat, and I bumped up the bids to make things difficult for her. I hoped it would mean she and Coleman needed to get imaginative."

"But you tried to have her killed?"

"No, not me; and Agnes knows this now. The man behind the attempt on her life was Crombie. Suddenly the ALR investigator turns up on his doorstep, with Agnes, seemingly willing to help you find the paintings."

"Bastard!" Forbes looked down at Crombie's chewed face.

"Crombie panicked after the killings at the warehouse. He confided that Mosca had left some paintings in his trust, but now that Mosca was dead, he insisted that I buy them, and his silence. Only after Coleman agreed to work for me did I agree to buy the paintings; but of course I could never trust Crombie to keep quiet in the future. Besides the real thief is still out there. I put two and two together when I heard about the death of Coleman's woman."

Prakash continued, "The real thief is trying to retrieve the paintings. He killed Buscetti, when he tried to double-cross him, but Mosca must have got in-between them. Anyway, whoever masterminded the theft still wants the paintings. The thief began trailing you, you led him to Agnes, then Coleman, and now back here to Paris. If a man like that had gotten hold of Crombie, Mr. Nahmad's project could be dead before it begins."

"The thief believes you are the best chance he has at recovering the paintings."

Forbes felt strangely proud of the accolade.

"When Agnes and the forger came to me, two days ago, I encouraged them to seek you out, hinted that you may have been behind the Paris theft, and therefore responsible for trying to kill Agnes. I did it for one reason only, and when I saw you all together at the museum earlier, I was hopeful that we would get sight of the thief."

"And capture him," Prakash smashed the gun handle into his other hand.

Forbes raised his hand to stop the flow, "Crombie was selling you the paintings, why do you want to know who stole them originally?"

"So I can sell them on to him." Nahmad thought it obvious.

Prakash added, "For a profit."

"I thought having Coleman arrested for murder, would flush them out, but your discovery of the Luini worked just as well. I must congratulate you on your find by the way. I'm sure LeCoyte Chellen is furious."

"I do hope so," Forbes gave a genuine smile.

Nahmad picked up the carbon tube. Instinctively Forbes knew now was the time to strike, the five masters were only a few feet away from him, temptingly close, yet just out of reach.

"Well our catch-up has been fascinating. In a perverse way I'm glad you found out the fate of the paintings," he held up the tube, "Before you died."

As Nahmad walked past, Forbes held out his hand, the carbon brushed his fingers. Prakash cocked the hammer on the gun, "That's close enough."

Nahmad stopped and studied Forbes, "You know, your obituary is going to be a damn good read. Ex SAS soldier found the lost Luini painting 'The Lady' and captured Radovan Karadiz in the catacombs in Belgrade; shame about these." He wiggled the tube. "Tell me, do you still have to take the pills at night to help you sleep; and do you still have nightmares about what happened down in the dark tunnels?"

Forbes shook his head. Understanding the movement to mean no, Nahmad said, "Shame, thought they might have been able to say it was the pills that made you do it?"

"Do what?" Forbes asked.

"Kill Crombie, and take your own life." Nahamd looked at Prakash, "shame the rats can't have their fun with him first."

Forbes knew he meant for Prakash to shoot him before the rats had a chance to eat him alive.

"Well, goodbye Mr. Forbes, I'm off to Hong Kong."

Chapter Twenty-two

AMEDEO MODIGLIANI (1884 – 1920)

Paris, France.
Thursday, July 1, 17.30hrs

PRAKASH AIMED THE GUN AT FORBES, "GET OVER BY the generator."

Without protest, arms down by his side, Forbes ambled over to the generator.

Convinced the fight had gone out of him, Prakash took great pleasure in sitting on the chair behind the bench; the sharp tools fanned out behind him like a headdress. His lips parted in anticipation; Forbes was put in mind of a python about to devour its prey.

"Such a sad end for such a brave warrior. Well no matter," he sighed, and tightened his finger on the trigger. "Nearly time for you to die, tell me Mr. Forbes, do you have any regrets in life?"

"Yeah, I wish I'd had the Sancerre with my lunch today."

Prakash frowned, "I had Sancerre with my lunch."

What a coincidence, Forbes seized on the comment, he knew he'd have to use every trick to get out of this, "Yes I know you did, we've had you under surveillance for weeks. There's enough gendarmes up there to kill you nine times over, or whatever your religion demands," Forbes laughed, "Nahmad will already be in handcuffs."

"Don't fuck with me." His eyes narrowed.

"I'm not, take a look at your CCTV." Forbes inclined his head.

Prakash was about to go and look, when he realized Forbes was bluffing.

"Very funny."

"I like to think so, you have to get up early to fool you."

"So you thought you'd got up early did you?"

"Well, I had a lot to do today, and I haven't had lunch yet."

"Been a busy boy haven't you, and all before lunch too. There has been no surveillance on us, has there?"

"Better pull that trigger now or you'll never have the chance." Forbes put some steel in his voice.

"You think you are so clever, discovering the link to Crombie."

"I did that before breakfast."

"Tell me Mr. Forbes, what are you going to do for tea?"

Forbes did not reply, he looked deep in thought. Prakash became pleased with himself, believing the Englishman was lost for words.

But Forbes was simply calculating his last-chance life-saving move, his eyes narrowed.

Simultaneously he noticed two things, firstly a nut had worked loose from the generator; it lay innocently on the floor. The second was a movement, it generated quickly, out of the corner of his eye; he adjusted his balance. "Well before tea, I thought watching you die would be a good bet."

"I thought you weren't a betting man?"

"Only when the odds are in my favour."

"That, I'm afraid will just not happen," with great deliberation, Prakash aimed the gun and crooked his finger, so that it squeezed the trigger. "Such a tiny movement, needing almost no effort." Prakash inclined his head, the light reflected from his glasses. "No more bets, our little chat is over."

The movement Forbes had noticed, moved again. The rat ran across the floor. Prakash was drawn to the grotesque shape, and for an instant he froze. That was when Forbes made his move.

His shoe caught the rat, and propelled it through the air, tumbling as it went toward Prakash. The little man obliged Forbes by doing the natural reaction of flinging up ones arms to fend off the attack. Forbes took a deep breath and watched it all happen in slow motion. The rodent flew toward him.

The rat landed on the workbench, Prakash pushed his chair back, and jumped up, fear spread across his face. It darted back and forth, and then came to a halt at the edge, close to his crutch. Prakash glanced over at Forbes, and instantly felt ashamed. Forbes had seen the look of terror, he had the emotional advantage now, but Prakash still had the gun.

Forbes pointed to the floor. Prakash followed the finger. With growing horror, he saw more rats running from the hole in the wall; the light, it seemed, held no fear for them anymore.

Forbes stood, unaffected by the scabby rodents as they scurried across the floor. The balance of power had shifted, after all this was something he'd been through before, in Belgrade.

In one swift movement, he scooped up the nut and hurled it at Prakash. It hit his thumb, crushing it against the handle of the gun. Prakash jerked his hand back, and impaled his hand on the teeth of a saw blade. He screamed in pain. The teeth dug in, lacerating his hand. He dropped the gun.

Forbes vaulted the bench, aiming his kick at Prakash's chest. When they both straightened up, Forbes had the gun.

Slowly he backed away toward the door. The rats now covered the floor like a cheap carpet. At the door Forbes fired three shots into the generator. It fizzed and yelped like a beaten dog, then fell silent.

Immediately the lights dimmed, and a moment later they all went out, plunging the storeroom into utter darkness. The black was absolute, crushing and cold. Forbes voice cut through the blackness, it was clear and chilling, "You were quite right Prakash; I won't see you die." Forbes shut the door, sliding the bolt through the latch.

From within the room Prakash shouted, "Forbes, you have to help me."

"No I don't," he shouted back.

Prakash's voice held more than a hint of hysteria, "You cannot leave me here."

"Yes I can."

The darkness was complete. Prakash stumbled forward. Totally disorientated he fell over the outstretched leg of Crombie, Prakash's lacerated hand gave way on impact, and his chin hit the floor, bursting open. Prakash rolled over onto his back, he lay there gasping for breath. The noise was interrupted by a scuttling. The rats sniffed the blood as it dripped from his wounds.

Bravely they moved closer to the prone body, Prakash waited, his nerve endings tingling in anticipation.

When the first rat sank its teeth into his hand, he screamed. Then a second bite caught him between thumb and the fleshy webbed part of the palm. Prakash pulled his hand away. The flesh ripped. He struggled to his knees, the shrill screeching of the rats filled the room with noise.

The next rat bit his ankle, Prakash fell forward. In the darkness, their claws and teeth hooked into his flesh, latching onto his clothing for a better grip. With disgusting ease they began to climb over him. Under the added weight he struggled to his knees.

He felt a rat running on the small of his back. Panic spread through him, he dived to the floor and rolled over squashing the rodent into the stone-flags. The pain of the bites and the whine of their screams filled his world. His leg twitched in a forced reaction to shake another set of sharp teeth from him.

A particularly large rat, fat on the putrefying flesh of his own dead brothers was flicked up in the air, in the darkness it arced and landed with a heavy thud, on his chest. He rat smelled the blood from the wound on his chin, and it launched itself at his throat. Its teeth sinking into the soft perfumed flesh.

~✒◯

THE HAZY EVENING SUNLIGHT FELT AS BRIGHT AS ANY-thing he'd ever seen before, as William Forbes burst out from the tomb doors. He was alone.

"Senga!" he screamed. He began to sprint to the front gate.

Visitors looked at him as he ran irreverently through the cemetery. At the massive stone gates he stood alone.

Breathing hard, he span around, looking for the copper

haired beauty to appear. "Senga," he growled. Some people looked at him, believing him to be drunk, others, pretending to be consumed by their own lives ignored him.

Rage consumed him. The pressure had risen quickly, like milk heating in a saucepan, boiling over, in a frothy effervescent fury, uncontrollable and indiscriminate in its blame. "Senga!"

When he thought Senga had betrayed him he'd felt anger, but when he discovered she'd merely been a pawn in Nahmad's plan, his rage against the Indian had seen no sanctuary. Now she was gone.

The palpitations began to steal oxygen from his lungs.

He rested against the wall, rolling his head against the cool stone. Frustration overcame him, and he slid to the floor. Her loss was more than he could take. He covered his head in his arms.

"Well, goodbye Mr. Forbes, I'm off to Hong Kong."

Nahmad's words came back to him, driving the depression from him. He knew that Nahmad had taken her, he knew he had to get her back.

A new strength coursed through his body. A new purpose to his life.

William Forbes suddenly knew that he would rescue Senga, and if he got the chance, he would kill Chandhok Nahmad.

Chek Lap Kok Airport, Hong Kong.
Saturday, July 3.

TALL, WAFER-THIN, WITH SUNKEN CHEEKS, AND TO-
bacco blond hair, the current head of the ALR, HK office, and
former British civil-servant, Leighton Stonehouse, watched the
passengers flow through the arrivals-hall.

He enjoyed picking out the first timers to the province, as
they looked around in awe at the new terminal.

Visitors to Hong Kong often found the fusion of cultures
both fascinating and engaging. The new international airport for
instance is constructed on the site on a largely artificial island,
reclaimed from the islands of Chek Lap Kok, and Lam Chau.

The thirty-two executive lounges in the airport are the
only public rooms where smoking is still allowed, this suited
Stonehouse and his colleague, the Chinese government official, Mi Wai. Both men smoked with obscene swiftness.

Wai, was a barrel-chested bull of a man, his hands were
callused with thick stubby fingers that seemed incapable of
performing a western 'hand-shake'.

The difference in their stature and manner was something
of comedic genius.

As Stonehouse scanned the arrivals-hall with the eager-
ness of an eagle looking for lunch, Wai gave off the air of a
man who would rather be anywhere else than here, with the
pending responsibility of playing nurse-maid, and interpreter to
the art-expert, William Forbes.

"Here he is," Stonehouse waved an extended broomstick
of an arm. Forbes refreshed from the long journey as only a
serviceman can be, bounded over to the lounge.

Forbes was immediately amused by their different stature. Stonehouse, was a thin and willowy chap, who dwarfed Forbes's six feet. His beige linen suit had seen much better days, and his attitude for a diplomat, even an ex-one, was poor, a definite throwback from the old colonial rule. Forbes opened his memory bank to recall if they'd ever met before.

"Ah, Forbes, good to meet you; this is Mi Wai, he is a Government official, and will act as your interpreter whilst you're conducting your investigations here."

"Hello," Forbes replied, problem solved, first time meet for all concerned. Forbes thought the powerhouse of a man must be bored ridged with the thought of translating all the questions and answers for an art investigation.

Wai's mental status soon manifested into a facial tick, every time he tried to prize his tight fitting shirt-collar away from his powerful neck.

Access to Hong Kong is now via a causeway through the historic village of Tung Chung, which has expanded into a modern town.

Gone are the days when every local would pray every time a 'Jumbo' skimmed over their houses to land at Kai Tek.

Stonehouse's voice matched his appearance, it was thin and reedy, and it came with the annoying habit of him smoothing down his tobacco stained moustache every time he spoke. It was going to be a long journey.

Forbes put his bag in the trunk, and jumped into the passenger seat of Wai's Toyota. Wai sat behind the wheel with an inscrutable look on his face. Stonehouse was in the back talking about something or other.

But some things about the island never change, Hong Kong

is a vibrant city with a contagious sense of energy. Situated on the southeast coast of China at the mouth of the Pearl River, visitors love to see the Chinese traditions running in parallel with fantastic modernity.

The Toyota cruised along the harbour front's dazzling 'Avenue of Stars' then zipped down Temple Street and zig-zagged up Nathan Road's glittering Golden Mile. Wai and Stonehouse seemed so pre-occupied that they missed the pretty girls milling around the entrances of the stylish restaurants, bars and clubs of Knutsford Terrace.

Ultimately, whilst other Oriental cities try to wrap you up in an artificially created surrounding, Hong Kong allows you to experience life and culture at its most exotic, atmospheric best.

Soon they were amongst the hi-rise skyscrapers that dominate the skyline. The hotel made up for the moronic banter in the car.

Cocooned in the heart of the bustling Tsim Sha Tsui region, the *Peninsula Hong Kong* has long been hailed as one of the world's finest hotels.

Forbes was unable to stifle a smile as he saw the hotel's celebrated fleet of Extended Wheelbase Rolls-Royce Phantoms, outside.

Built, some would say born, back in the glamourous 1920's, the legendary 'Grande Dame of the Far East' still continues to set hotel standards worldwide, offering a blend of the best Eastern and Western hospitality, in an atmosphere of un-matched classical grandeur and timeless elegance.

Wai reluctantly drove the anonymous Toyota into the drop-off zone. As Wai waited by the car, Stonehouse took Forbes by the elbow, and had a quiet word.

"This is all going to end in tears my dear fellow, just you mark my words."

"You're wrong, this will be the greatest day the ALR has ever had. I'm going to recover the five paintings stolen from Paris."

The bell-boy took Forbes's suitcase into reception.

"You may have had some luck finding the Luini, but what makes you think the famous five are here?"

"It's my investigation, I'm working from reliable information." Forbes refrained from telling him any details about Nahmad, and the kidnapping of Senga. He observed a helicopter coming in from the airport, but refrained from asking why they couldn't have taken that quicker route.

Together with the Rolls Royce's and the helicopter shuttle service, Forbes felt buoyed with a sudden rush of British pride, even though the cars were now German owned, and the helicopter's birth place was Italian.

"I don't know whether you think you're Andy McNab, or James Bond, but this is China, and he's in charge." Stonehouse rolled his eyes toward Wai, who was kicking stones by the car. "If you have evidence that the famous five stolen paintings are here, why not let the police handle it?"

"I want to remain in control, I don't want the suspect bribing the locals."

Stonehouse scanned the reception area of the hotel, all uniforms and marble, how the hell had Forbes got booked into here? He smoothed down his moustache and said, "La Pastorale, by Henri Matisse is my favorite, I really do think that letting the police handle this case is my best chance of me ever seeing it again."

"Have faith old chap, I'll get them all back, the Picasso, the Leger, the Braque, the Modigliani, and the Matisse."

"Carrington has faith in you, I do not. If you step out of line the Chinese will crucify you. Whilst you're on Chinese soil all your actions must be approved by Mr. Wai. You cannot do anything without government approval, and for God sake don't make any accusations against a Chinese national, they'll stir-fry your balls and make me eat them."

"Well that's something I don't want to even contemplate." Forbes quipped.

"Be serious Forbes, if you screw this up we'll never be allowed to conduct business here again. Hong Kong will become the black-market capital of the world, a bootlegger's paradise in an Oriental era of prohibition. Do I make myself clear, Forbes?"

"Perfectly, Mr. Stonehouse." Forbes took an instant dislike to the man.

Wai approached with the air of an unpopular schoolboy. Stonehouse turned on his most condescending voice, almost wringing his hands to appease the government man. "Michael Carrington has instructed me to take personal responsibility for this investigation, so please be advised, I want a status report, six o'clock, every evening."

Forbes nodded in humble compliance, knowing it was totally unnecessary to have an interpreter, and the only reason he'd got Wai with him, was to speed up the passing on of information to the Chinese government. Stonehouse was right, every scrap of information would be used as a stick to beat the ALR at any future opportunity.

Above and beyond any damage to the ALR's reputation, Forbes understood that Stonehouse thought Forbes's presence in Hong Kong was potentially damaging for his own personal career, and that was why he was going to such lengths to rein him in. A daily report and a government interpreter were certainly shackles which would need careful manipulation.

Mi Wai bowed, "Will this be all for tonight?"

"Sure, it's been a long flight, what time will you pick me up in the morning?" Forbes asked politely.

"Is nine o'clock sufficient?"

"That will be perfect."

"Of course I will be expecting-" Stonehouse enthused.

Forbes walked into the hotel without a backward glance,

"Forbes?" Stonehouse shouted.

Forbes checked his Tudor Heritage, "I'll be phoning you at six, tomorrow," and walked straight past check-in and headed for the bar.

He had heard that the Peninsula's rich interior was every bit as spellbinding, as the colourful tapestry of the Hong Kong world which every lucky guest left outside, when one venture into the hotel. Forbes now felt blessed with that luck.

"Thank you Michael, get ready for the expense account from hell."

Forbes's phone buzzed. "Hello!"

"What the hell is going on, where are you?" Noah sounded angry.

Forbes knew the best defense was attack, "Where am I? Where the hell were you when we needed you? Nothing, no call, no update from London. I thought you'd turned Judas on me, and thrown your hand in with Crombie."

"Why would you think that?"

"Cut the bullshit Noah, what happened in London?"

Noah was stunned by the viciousness of the comments, he chose his response very carefully, in order to placate his colleague, and subdue his own suspicions. "Crombie has the paintings. He took them to Paris. What did you find out from the meeting?"

"What about the other paintings, what's the story on them?" Forbes wanted to keep him off guard for as long as possible.

"Twenty-three works by new, and contemporary artists were sent first class to Hong Kong."

"Why?" Let's see just how much you will divulge about your new employer.

"If you ask me, Crombie is doing a deal with Nahmad."

"For Christ sake, Noah, he's selling him a Picasso, why would he be interested in a deal with new artists?"

"Get real, Forbes, the stolen paintings are worthless, nothing more than trading collateral."

"Okay, so what do you think about this long term deal with Nahmad?" Forbes wondered if this had anything to do with Nahmad's big project.

"I've got no idea."

"Really, I thought you were working for him?" Forbes sipped his Gin and Tonic.

"He wishes, he made me an offer of employment, I'm still considering it." Noah thought it best not to divulge information about Senga's involvement in his forging of works pertained from the galleries.

"What are the options for Nahmad?" he swirled the plastic rod around, in the glass.

"He could forge the paintings, then should any of the new

artists make it big, he'd have a ready-made treasure trove of early works."

"He'd need a master forger for that."

Noah side-stepped the trap, "He has one, name of Remmert van Braam, heard of him?"

"Yeah, I understood he'd been incapacitated. Some 'two-bit' grass ratted him out, and turned him in to the police." Forbes let the words strike home.

"I wouldn't know." Noah replied without hesitation.

"Apparently there was an accident when van Braam was making his escape, the old guy is blind now."

"Well!" Noah exclaimed.

"I heard Nahmad just got a replacement for the old Dutchman."

"Really?"

"Yes, then I put two and two together with his comments to you at the museum."

Noah struggled to come to terms with just how much Forbes really knew. He decided to change the subject. "So did you see Crombie in Paris?"

"You could say that."

"For Christ sake Forbes, did Crombie have the paintings?"

"Yes, he had them."

Noah shouted, "YES!"

"But he doesn't have them anymore." Forbes added quickly.

"Oh," Noah's mood dropped, "Who does?"

"Nahmad."

"Then why haven't you called the police?" Noah asked curtly.

"He tried to kill me, and he has Senga, he kidnapped her from the cemetery gates."

"Shit, are they still in Paris?"

"No, he's debunked to Hong Kong."

"Then we need to get to Hong Kong, and quick."

"It could be dangerous if we travel together, there's still a certain killer on our trail. Our names would be on the passenger list …we'd be sitting ducks."

"Unless we use false identities." Noah said simply.

The words stopped Forbes in his tracks, his free hand soared to his face. "Of course, that's how we'll find the killer."

"I was only joking, Bill, you'd never get on an international airline now, unless all your details match …" Noah's voice trailed off.

Forbes cut in, his voice was measured and clear, "The killer followed me to London, from Verona. Then he went to Nice, after Senga. Maybe he even followed you to Heathrow. Either way, we could get his name from the passenger lists."

"You can't get airlines to hand that information over."

"Leave that side of it to me."

"Good, real or bogus name, we'll have him."

"Then we get a lead on who masterminded the Paris theft. I suggest you get your ass out to Hong Kong pronto."

"I'm on my way."

"Hey, Noah."

"What?"

"Don't talk to any strange men on the flight."

"Yeah, very funny."

Chapter Twenty-three

WILLIAM HOLMAN HUNT (1827 – 1910)

Hong Kong.
Saturday, July 3.

THE VINYL-SKINNED PORTER LED FORBES TO HIS TWEN-ty-fifth floor Grand Deluxe Harbour View suite, his smile was wide, and worthy of a tip.

Strangely, once inside the suite, the porter just bowed politely and left, without extending his hand. Forbes frowned in confusion as the man left, "Strange." He strolled into the opulent dining room. "Very nice."

Suddenly he became wary, experiencing the overwhelming feeling that he was not alone. He heard the soft muffled sound of running water, his mind flashed back to Nahmad's underground lair. Without conscious thought he palmed and swallowed another pill.

He approached the bathroom door, a pale light seeped from beneath it. He grasped the handle. Fighting back the vision of hundreds of rats dining on the exposed extremities of Crombie and Prakash, he pushed the door open.

A wet warm luxurious damp covered him in calm as he entered a relaxed world of scented bath oils.

Through the corner floor-to-ceiling windows, Forbes scanned the 270° panoramic view of the harbour, and twinkling lights of the Hong Kong skyline.

His eyes were drawn to the foreground, where languishing in the opulent Jacuzzi bathtub, drinking chilled champagne, sat Noah Coleman.

Forbes knocked against the door to attract his attention.

Noah opened his eyes, "Bill, I hope you didn't tip the bell-boy, I've paid a two-hundred dollar a day retainer, or rather Michael Carrington has."

"I am lost for words."

"I know, it's fantastic isn't it. Daisy always wanted to come here, I thought we'd do it in style."

"I just spoke to you on the phone. I thought you were in London."

"Yeah, I thought you were in Paris, seems we were both holding something back."

"When did you get here, how did you know to come here?"

"Simple, when they told me the other paintings were being flown direct to Hong Kong, I figured Nahmad would be coming here too, and therefore I figured you'd be in hot pursuit."

"Why didn't you tell me you were here, on the phone?"

"What and spoil the surprise?" Noah put down his champagne flute, and began to lever himself out of the tub.

"Wooah! No, you just stay there, I'll get myself a drink."

Dressed in hotel slippers and a white fluffy robe, Noah joined Forbes in the lounge.

Forbes asked, "How did you track me down to the hotel, and

gain access to my room?" His shoulders sagged, "You booked it didn't you?"

Noah ignored the question feeling an apologetic reply was beneath him. "So where's that shit Nahmad got Senga?"

"He has a villa," Forbes pointed across the bay, "Over there, high on the hill."

"Okay, you're SAS, let's go storm it."

Forbes looked up from his laptop, "I was thinking about a more indirect approach." His fingers danced over the keypad.

After a moment a slow jerky image appeared on the screen. A dark, rich Italian accent came through the speakers, "Ciao, Bill."

"Gianni, good to see you."

"Hi," Noah stood behind Forbes.

Forbes made the introductions, "This is Noah Coleman; Noah this is Captain Giancarlo Minardi, of the Guardia di Finaza."

"Fraud department," Noah commented quietly.

"Yes, I thought you've be familiar with it," Forbes mocked.

"Good evening," Minardi waved from the screen.

Forbes asked, "Do you have any information?"

Minardi lifted some sheets of paper, "Yes, everything you asked for. Thank God for the Interpol computer."

"How did he ...?" Noah began, but Forbes silenced him with a wave of his hand.

"Okay, passenger lists, Verona to Heathrow, Heathrow to Nice, and Charles de Gaulle to Heathrow." He fanned through the lists.

"Shit, he was on the same plane as me," Noah ran his fingers through his damp hair.

"Okay, in total 1506 passengers. 1470 checked out on the first run to the satisfaction of the airline security criteria. All their tickets were bought with credit cards that have a history longer than your bar bill in Sarajevo."

"What does that mean?" Noah asked.

"We both served with NATO in Bosnia," Forbes offered.

Minardi explained, "I owe this man my life, but he owes me more than one thousand Marka for a night we shared with some-"

"Thank you Gianni. Please continue with the analysis."

"Okay, I tell you another time. So, we only need to do a second sweep on 36 passengers. Twenty of them had no credit rating, or driving license."

"Suspicious?" Noah asked.

"No, they were children, or had never flown before. Of the final 16, four were recently married, first time for their new passports. Four were airline security. Five had diplomatic immunity, don't worry they all check out with their Embassies."

"That leaves three," Forbes felt the excitement rise.

Minardi held up a single sheet. "Okay, Verona to Heathrow, William Hunt, 38 years old, born in Glasgow. He flew out of Verona on the same flight as you, Bill ... However there is no record of his entry to Italy. He has a credit card, but there's been no activity on it for the past six months, and there's no record of him having a driving license."

"Could have been in prison, drink driving? He is from Glasgow," Noah mused.

"His ticket was purchased fifteen minutes after yours. It was purchased on a company credit card."

"What company?" Forbes asked.

"A yacht crew management firm called SAMSON. I checked it out; and on the surface, Mr. Hunt could be genuine. Yacht crews could be at sea for a number of months, so the six month inactivity on his card is not un-common."

"Buscetti and Mosca worked as security on a yacht in Monaco," Forbes said quickly, "Let's have the second name."

"John Everett, aged 37, born in Southampton, England. His ticket was purchased just after Miss Munreaux decided to go to Nice."

"Was it the only one bought after hers?" Forbes asked.

"There were twelve actually, but Everett's was the only one bought by SAMSON."

"Nice have yacht crews too," Noah offered.

"At this stage I think you should see the departure desk photographs," Minardi held up a photo.

The screen showed a Caucasian man, big strong, athletic build, late thirties, sensible hairstyle, black hair, striped tie.

"He doesn't look Scottish," Noah remarked.

"Why, cause he's not wearing a kilt?" Forbes responded, "Let's see the second picture."

Minardi held up the second photograph. Spiky hair, white tee shirt, black leather jacket.

"Shit, he looks like Arnie in the Terminator," Noah commented, "I'll be back." And with that Noah left the room.

"Simple enough disguise, it could be the same man," Forbes added, "What about the third name?"

"Gabriel Rossetti, same age, but born in Rome. The M.O. was exactly the same, SAMSON purchased a ticket, ten minutes after the three of you booked to go to London."

"Has SAMSON purchased any tickets to Hong Kong last couple of days?"

"No ..."

Suddenly Noah arrived back at Forbes's side, "Check the Hong Kong flight passenger list; tell me if any of these names appear."

"Welcome back," said Forbes, leaning out of the way.

"James Collison," Noah began, Fredric Stephens ..."

Minardi looked up, "There's a George Stephens."

"That's him, check his background, get his photo up," Noah ground his fist into his palm.

"Thirty seven, born in Cardiff," Minardi scrolled down the list for the photo.

"How do you know those names?" Forbes asked.

"In 1848, William Holman Hunt, John Everett-Millais, and Dante Gabriel Rossetti formed a group known as the Pre-Raphaelite Brotherhood."

"Like a boy band?"

"No, this was a group of English painters, despite Rossetti's name, he was born in England. The three founders were soon joined by Dante's brother, William Michael Rossetti, along with the renowned poet, James Collison. They were completed by Fredric George Stephens, and Thomas Woolner, to serve as agents for change in a seven-member 'Brotherhood'."

"It was sinister?" Minardi asked.

"No, the group's intention was to reform art by rejecting what they considered to be the mechanistic approach first adopted by the artists who succeeded Raphael and Michelangelo."

"You're not talking about turtles are you?" Forbes asked comically.

"Fuck off; listen, they believed that the classical poses and elegant compositions of Raphael in particular had been a corrupting influence on the academic teaching of art, hence the name Pre-Raphaelite."

Minardi held up the photograph, "I think, despite the history lesson, he's on to something."

Forbes and Noah studied the picture, "Same build."

"Different hair, different clothing style."

"That's easy to change; and he keeps his face away from the camera."

Minardi asked, "Do you think he has seven different identities?"

Forbes answered, "It's a distinct possibility, but what it does tell us is that whoever is in charge at SAMSON has a real interest in Pre-Raphaelite artists."

"A good knowledge of art, a link to yacht crews, this is promising," Noah chipped in.

"Gianni, what can you find out about this company?"

"Okay, give me a minute."

Noah paced behind Forbes, "They objected to the influence of Sir Joshua Reynolds, the founder of the English Royal Academy of Arts. They called him, Sir Sloshy. To the Pre-Raphaelites, sloshy meant anything lax, or rushed. They wanted artists to return to painting in the style of abundant detail, intense colour, and complex compositions as in the Quattrocento period in Italian and Flemish art ..."

"Got it!" Minardi, called from the screen.

"Thank God," Forbes responded.

"Just trying to educate you, I may be a forger, but I know my stuff." Noah put his hands on his hips, "And I got us this suite."

Minardi read the details, "It's a bona-fide company, and their website proclaims they have been in existence in Europe since 1960. SAMSON operate out of Monaco, Saint Tropez, Barcelona, and Malaga. Worldwide, they provide crews for luxury yachts, in Barbados, Key West, and Freeport. Cape town and Macau."

"Who owns them?" Forbes asked.

"That information could take me a little longer to establish. I'll call you as soon as I have the answer."

"Thanks Gianni, speak soon, ciao." Forbes closed the connection.

Noah was emphatic, "The killer is in Hong Kong, we have his description, I say let's flush him out."

Forbes remained calm, "I say let's get Senga first."

"Are we going to do this on our own?" Noah asked, having doubts about his ability to overcome a trained killer by himself. The man in the photographs had the look of an athlete about him. He was obviously very resourceful, and relentless in his pursuit of the paintings.

Noah appraised Forbes's build, ex-SAS. Senga had told him how he'd killed the two hit-men on the quay in London. He decided that Forbes was a trustworthy confederate in the job of getting revenge for Daisy, and rescuing Senga, and recovering the paintings.

"Yes just me and you, I don't trust my new-found colleagues to play fair."

"What do we do about recovering the paintings?"

"I'm glad you said that; that's where you come in."

"Me? How?"

"Take as much time as you need, meet me in Hong Kong

next week, that's what Nahmad said to you in Paris; so you see you already have a way in. In fact he's expecting you."

"You want me to visit Nahmad?"

"Yes."

"Even though he tried to kill you in Paris, and he's got Senga?"

"Yes, he has the paintings, and we're going to get them back."

Noah sat down.

"Let's draw up a plan. We have four objectives. One, rescue Senga. Two, get the paintings. Three, identify the mastermind behind the Paris theft, and bring him to justice. Four, kill Nahmad."

"If you're talking revenge, there's a fifth objective, kill the man that killed Daisy."

Forbes recognized the pain in Noah's face, he knew it came directly from the heart. Whatever the past, whatever his involvement with Senga and Nahmad, Noah Coleman had been tossed into the middle of this investigation without as much as a by your leave, and here was here now offering assistance. Slowly Forbes nodded in compliance. "Five."

Chapter Twenty-four

VINCENT VAN GOGH (1853 - 1890)

Hong Kong Convention Center (HKCEC)
Monday, July 5.

BUILT ALONG THE VICTORIA HARBOUR FRONT, THE Hong Kong Convention and Exhibition center, employs lavish motorized covered walkways to transport the majority of its 140,000 visitors per day, to and from the center.

Linked to nearby hotels, and commercial buildings, the automated tracks resemble blood pumping around the heart.

Within the complex, 850 staff administer the event co-ordination for six massive exhibition halls, with two smaller convention halls built on the sides to give the impression of a bird about to take flight.

A six thousand seat theatre is surrounded by ten-thousand meeting rooms.

To the rear of the building, sits a car-park for thirteen hundred cars, and fifty articulated transports.

On any given day it could be said that the building is the heart of Hong Kong Island.

Noah Coleman approached the girl from behind. She was

bending over a desk conversing with a colleague, but he recognized her all the same.

"I think we met in Paris."

Mohini jumped up and turned to face him, her face resembled a startled doe, eyes wide, mesmerized by a car's headlights. "Mr. Coleman! How very pleasant to see you again," she exclaimed.

"Enchanting," he sniffed her perfume, "Will you be accompanying me to see Mr. Nahmad again?"

"Do you have an appointment?" the smile never changed.

Noah shook his head very slowly, "I don't need one; I'm on the payroll."

Mohini went around the desk and tapped on the keyboard. The monitor pinged, and she glanced at the screen. "So you are. It will be lovely to see more of you."

"I was thinking the same myself."

"Follow me."

"Gladly."

Mohini led him across the giant reception area and through into the exhibition area. Her body moved with grace and eroticism, Noah wondered how she would avoid him over the coming days.

CHANDHOK NAHMAD, STOOD ADMIRING THE LATEST OF the many oil paintings to be hung in the vast exhibition hall. As Mohini approached she gave a delicate bow, and introduced Noah.

"Good to see you Noah, I'm so glad you decided to take up

my offer." He noticed Noah watching Mohini walk away, "You won't be sorry, I can promise you."

"There was really no other choice," Noah resisted the urge to punch him in the nose.

To his side, a grizzled Chinese bodyguard took in every detail of Noah's body language, but after a moment he relaxed accordingly. His hands disappeared into the wide sleeves of his dark blue tunic.

"Another new starter?" Noah gestured toward the hard looking bodyguard. Probably the Chinese equivalent to an ex-SAS soldier, or maybe even a Shaolin Monk.

Nahmad glanced at the man, "This is Tien; Tien has been with me for many years. He studied and trained as a Shaolin Monk."

"No Mr. Prakash then?"

"Alas, Mr. Prakash is no longer with us."

Noah knew better than to push it.

Nahmad spread his hands, and gestured they walk, "What's your first impression?"

"Magnificent, but then I knew it would be, your exhibitions are always famous for their works."

It was then that Nahmad brought up the subject Noah so desperately wanted to explore, "You've heard from Agnes?"

Now was the time to keep calm, "Don't you know?" Noah lent close to a painting and examined a brush stroke, keeping up the façade would be difficult.

"Know what? Please enlighten me Mr. Coleman, you know I have strong feelings for Agnes."

"After we met in the Museum of Modern Art, Michel Carrington wanted the three of us to go to London, follow up a lead on the stolen paintings. Just before boarding Forbes and Senga ran off."

"Ran off?" Nahmad asked, hiding his own knowledge was easy.

"She said she was going to resign from Sotheby's; apparently Crombie was in Paris, he had a meeting with you, I assumed it was about these wonderful contemporary paintings."

"You are misinformed, Sotheby's sent the paintings directly here; I haven't seen Crombie for months. What about Forbes?"

"That love sick puppy! He ran off after Senga," Noah lent close to Nahmad, "I think she told him she was coming back to you." He winked.

Nahamd grinned like a lottery winner.

"Such a strange choice of artists in this section, what made you choose them?" Noah walked down the line of paintings.

Nahmad caught up with him, "Tell me Noah, what makes Singer Sargent's version of Madame X more valuable than yours?"

"Sargent painted it." He examined another work, pretending to be preoccupied.

"But songwriters don't always have the most success with their own songs, sometimes another artist does a better job. Sometimes the remake of a film is better than the original, so why not with a painting?"

"I put nothing new into the work."

"Sargent was a very talented artist, but so are you," Nahmad gushed.

"Thank you."

"The canvas was probably no more than fifty dollars, the actual paint, not much more. The time spent with the subject probably the same time as you spent with the picture. So, why would someone pay one-million pounds sterling to own the Sargent, and cast aspersions on anyone who owned your version?"

"Because of his notoriety?"

"Exactly, because of the story that surrounds the actual painting."

"I didn't know the interview questions were going to be so hard."

"Noah, you've got the job. You have the talent, I'm just ascertaining your worth to my empire."

"You know what I can do." Noah let him believe he was getting frustrated.

"I know what you can do, I'm trying to understand what you are capable of."

"What are you talking about?"

"I want to make sure you see this position as a long term commitment."

"Are you offering me a pension?"

"You are aware that Van Gogh only sold one painting during his lifetime."

"Red Vineyard at Arles, always good for a point in a pub quiz."

"As you say. While alive he was not even considered a great artist. Critics largely ignored his work until after his presumed suicide in 1890. He first exhibited in the late 1880s. His reputation grew among friends, but art critics, dealers, and collectors tended not to care for him. After his death, memorial exhibitions were mounted in Brussels, Paris, The Hague, and Antwerp. But only in the early-20th century, were there retrospective exhibitions in Paris and Amsterdam. When the critics exalted his work in New York in 1913, there was a noticeable impact on the public. By the mid-20th century, Van Gogh was seen as one of the greatest and most recognizable painters in history."

"Very informative, where's my studio?"

"Which of these artists will become famous, and which will die in poverty?"

"Not necessarily in that order."

"Ah! At last you begin to understand. Tell me Mr. Coleman, which of these paintings is better than the other?"

Noah checked the painting closest to him, "Each has its own uniqueness, and none are badly painted. Each artist has an extraordinary talent, I suppose it just depends on which ones you actually like." Noah raised an eyebrow.

Nahmad shook his head, "Not so Mr. Coleman, it's the ones which we tell the people they ought to like. We tell the investors which artists to invest in, the ones that will soar in value. These days we put the greatest significance in value, not in art. That, Mr. Coleman is what has a direct relevance to the artist and his circumstances."

"Point well-made Mr. Nahmad."

"More people have seen your Madame X than have actually seen Sargent's original. No one goes away from the exhibition feeling cheated."

"Thank you," Noah took a bow.

Nahmad glanced over at the contemporary works spread out in the exhibition, "Who is to say which of these excellent works will become the most valuable in the future?"

"Agreed, we can't predict the future."

Nahmad made no attempt to answer. A sly smile spread

across his face. He pointed to an abstract work that could pass as a futuristic city skyline. "This is by Richard Hastings, if you are an art lover, and love abstract oil paintings, many galleries offer excellent works, yet serious collectors are only clamouring after Hastings's offerings these days."

Noah inclined his head, "Hastings is very skilled; I have to admit."

"Art lovers," Nahmad interrupted, "of abstract oil paintings understand the skill an artist needs to provide the vision to achieve such a work. However, lovers of landscapes believe the finished article could have been produced by a child. Yet with half the world thinking abstracts are awful, Jackson Pollock was an influential American painter, a major figure in the abstract expressionist movement. During his lifetime, Pollock enjoyed considerable fame and notoriety, unlike Van Gogh. So I ask again Mr. Coleman, what makes a painting desirable?"

"Art is a very personal thing, I get enjoyment out of painting in certain styles, I understand that art lovers can enjoy one style of painting, and not enjoy other styles."

"You miss the point, Pollack was regarded as a recluse; he had a volatile personality, and struggled with alcoholism. He died at 44 in an alcohol-related car accident. Van Gogh died at 37, supposedly suicide, although the gun was never found."

"What's your point, Nahmad?"

"Collectors of abstracts will pay large sums of money for examples that collectors of portraits would believe were worthless."

"That's a valid point."

"I'm glad you agree, that's why Hastings has been working for me these past two years."

A frown spread across Noah's face, "I don't understand."

Nahmad threw his head back and laughed, "The era of the forger is over, well almost. Now it's all about the hype. You can create a masterpiece out of elephant dung; you can get people to buy a pile of bricks. Create the demand, create the master-pieces that people want, and you create the demand for the supply. The key to fame and fortune is balancing the gap. Your version of Madame X may very well be technically better than the original, but because Sargent didn't paint it, it's worthless, but suppose we found other works by Sargent?"

"Now of course, they'd be worth ..." and then the penny dropped, "Hastings is producing new work, specifically for you!"

"Correct. He is becoming a desirable artist because I'm making him one. I'm drip feeding the world glimpses of his talent, his pain, I'm letting them decide should he become an alcoholic? Should he cut off part of his ear?"

"Drive up the desire for his work."

"Drive up the price."

The awful truth was beginning to dawn on Noah. The real reason Nahmad had twenty-three new, contemporary artists hanging at his exhibition. His mouth went dry, but his palms began to sweat.

"You're going to kill them."

"Not all of them, just the ones that the investors take to." Nahmad ran his finger down the frame of a Sexton landscape. "Jack Sexton was born in San Francisco in 1964. He studied at St Martin's School of Art, California. Today Jack Sexton has established himself as an evocative painter of landscapes and urban scenes." Nahmad wandered over to another of his ex-cellent works, "This is a pretty gritty description of a New York ghetto. Note his use of broad brush, see how he uses colour to create bold and clear vistas of the city. Almost abstract, yet clearly, New York. He is my Andy Warhol. Warhol was 58 when he died, he'd been making a good recovery from routine gallbladder surgery at the New York Hospital before dying in his sleep from a sudden post-operative cardiac arrhythmia. It was widely known that Warhol delayed having his gallbladder problems checked, as he was afraid to enter hospitals and see doctors. You see another accident. Van Gogh's suicide, Pollack's car accident."

"You're saying Van Gogh, Pollack and Warhol were killed to bump up the value of their work? Come on Chandhok that's madness!"

"No it's business. Sexton's strong and confident brush-work successfully record the essence of his subjects, be they landscapes or urban scenes. I'm told Sexton produces highly textural oil paintings full of light, shade and atmosphere ...I'm going to kill him, when the time is right."

"He's on the payroll too, I guess?"

Nahamd nodded.

"You're not selling the perks of working for you very well."

"Don't be afraid you are not seen as an artist, no offence."

"None taken. Listen, I'm a forger, not a killer, why do you need me?"

"Come with me," Nahmad waved him forward, they went to the elevator, and dropped in sumptuous silence.

Back on ground level the mechanical walkway transported them along at an enhanced speed, within three minutes they emerged onto Queens Road.

Towering above them, at an impressive height of six hundred

and eighty eight feet, was the jewel in Chandhok Nahmad's Oriental empire.

The imposing fifty-eight story 'World-life' building had risen from the ground, between 1997's handover and the millennium celebrations. Built with a unique semi-circular floor plan, the approach looked like a lagoon on a tropical island.

The impressive front entrance, on the 'ground-floor' did nothing more than carry commuters through another elaborate exhibition area, packed with limited edition prints of famous works of art (available to buy at reception). Onward and up-ward, via a set of velvet-smooth steel and glass escalators, passengers arrived at the third-floor reception area, with their appreciation of art, and understanding of what was in vogue, firmly set in their minds.

From the reception area, workers and visitors alike, were directed to their ultimate destinations with the efficiency of a small airport.

The building itself was set into a hillside so steep, that the entrance to the building's underground carpark, was from Kennedy Road, on the 7th floor.

Below that level, small, simple apartments were available for employees.

The 17th floor marked the top of the lower level, here was an exclusive spa, swimming pool, and gymnasium, these all housed in traditionally designed buildings on the 'roof'.

Above that, the shape of the building became more con-ventional against the hillside behind it. A square skyscraper occupied the rear right-hand third of the semi-circle. The front two corners were how-ever sculptured to house the panoram-ic-view elevators, which rose and fell like plumes of water. In all, this part of the building gave the impression of a gigantic waterfall, plummeting into the lagoon by the traditional buildings on the roof.

"It's not much, but I call it home," Nahmad explained to Noah as they entered the fantasy.

Laboratories and offices occupied the thirty floors of the square tower, then the building changed shape again.

With the right security clearance, it was possible to get to the forty-eighth floor, either by internal or panoramic elevator, but beyond the 48th, only personal guests were permitted.

The journey to the 48th had been rapid, accompanied by music as forgettable as a wet Wednesday in November.

The entrance was called 'Sky-lobby', it was futuristic in the extreme, with access to the Heli-pad. Noah quipped, "It's a bit of a trek."

"Not if you're as rich as I am." Nahmad replied dismissively.

The final ten floors evolved into a circular pencil-thin high-rise sculpture, culminating in a lightning bolt shaped communications rod.

Nahmad pressed the 56 button. "The fifty-seventh floor had been ear-marked to be a revolving restaurant, but I decided to have it as my own personal living quarters. The apartment, gives me a unique view of the entire island, with a 360° rotation every three hours."

"Essential for anyone as rich as you are," Noah goaded, "And the fifty eighth?"

"It's where I sleep."

"Does it revolve?"

"No."

"Slipping aren't we?" Noah watched the panorama opening beneath him.

"Don't concern yourself, you'll never get an invite for a sleep-over."

The elevator stopped at the fifty-sixth floor.

The fine aroma of oil gave away the purpose of the room they were entering. "This is my private studio," Nahmad gently pressed on Noah's arm, "You wanted to know why I need you? Before I show you what is in here, I need to know about your relationship with Agnes."

"Purely professional, I can assure you."

"That was never in doubt, Agnes has very exacting standards. What I want to know is ...what was the professional nature that brought you two together?"

From years spent at a poker table, Noah knew that the art of bluffing was crucial to success, and yet in the world of forgery and confidence tricks, keeping as close to the truth was essential in pulling off a great big, fat lie. They entered the room.

"Senga commissioned me to copy one of her paintings, *Portrait in Valencia*, by Casper Oleg."

"Of course, we were all shocked by the scandal at Sotheby's," he rubbed his chin, "Let me guess, you sold a forgery to LeCoyte Chellen."

"Very good," Noah was impressed, but he didn't show it.

Nahmad continued, "Forbes always believed Chellen was behind the Paris theft. He thought Agnes was tied in to Chellen, so he went to London to interview her," he looked at Noah for confirmation, "I'm right I know it. Now, Agnes could not confide in Forbes about the Oleg, so she used the Crosby Garett helmet as her reason for being in the warehouse that night. Am I right?"

Noah nodded, a smirk of admiration twinkled in his eye. Nahmad continued, buoyed with the reaction, "Agnes told me that Forbes rescued her from Mr. Key in London," he clapped his hands, "the link to Chellen would have been overwhelming. Forbes sent her to see you, keep her away from Chellen's goons," he began waving a finger, "But you knew Chellen wasn't involved in the London attack." Nahmad paced, "...There were two forgeries!"

Noah nodded in agreement, but his face was a blank canvas.

"Chellen wanted Agnes alive, he knew she had the real painting, which you then gave to Chellen."

"Sold to Chellen," Noah corrected. He omitted to tell him that it was a forgery that they'd sold him though.

Now Nahmad was impressed, "Brilliant, but surmising the attempt on her life had nothing to do with the five paintings stolen from Paris, or the Oleg, you surmised it must be in connection with the helmet. Then Agnes told you about me. You made the connection to Madame X, and thought I was trying to kill her. So you brought her to Paris to bargain for her life. Very noble, Mr. Coleman."

"It was only when you tried to influence us to believe Forbes was behind the attempt on her life, that I became confused."

"I want her back." The statement sounded honest.

"What about the helmet, the fee was due today."

"I paid it," his hand was dismissive, "But I'll leave it in England, it's not important. Getting you here was important."

"So we come back to the question, why do you need me?"

Nahmad wandered across the floor, touching various

canvases. "Poor old Chellen, the big fat white slug of a man, he almost pulled off the find of the century. Sniffing around those two young girls for the lost Luini painting, fraternizing with the old crone at the hotel, she was the grand-daughter of the staff at the chateau when the family got the chop, did you know that?"

"No, how come you know so much?"

"Being rich, it's like being in a very exclusive club. Still, Chellen's reputation was what put him under suspicion, and allowed Forbes to snatch the painting from under his nose."

"The Luini, the Oleg, the helmet; you're avoiding the elephant in the room, Mr. Nahmad."

"Crombie confessed everything in Paris, it was sheer luck that he became the keeper of the paintings. The real thief intended to kill Buscetti, probably an accident, and make it look like the paintings had been destroyed. Buscetti intended to double-cross the thief. Mosca ended up with the five masterpieces, the only person he knew that could hide and potentially sell the works for him, was Crombie. Then Mr. Mosca got himself killed, and Crombie saw the opportunity to muscle in on my big project."

"Killing Hastings and Sexton, and the others?"

"Yes, if the details, and my involvement ever got out ..." Nahmad shrugged.

"So we come back to square one, I'm a forger not a killer, why do you need me?"

"You know I killed Crombie." The statement shook Noah ridged, he'd imagined this whole Hong Kong job offer was about forging the works of the contemporary artists that had come from Sotheby's, but Nahmad's confession had put paid to that, now it seemed he wanted Noah only to silence him.

The best form of defense was attack, "Yes, and so do the ALR, they also know you took the five stolen paintings from Crombie, and you have them here." Noah was just about to demand their return, and the release of Senga, when Nahmad took another lungful of wind out of his sales.

"No they don't," he shook his head, "They know nothing of the sort, if they did the police, and Interpol would be speaking to my lawyers right now." He banged his index finger on a desk. "Only Forbes knows that Crombie is dead, only he knows that I have the five stolen paintings. Forbes didn't tell the police, or the ALR, but he did confide in you. He instructed you to come here and get close to me, and arrange to get him in here, so he could rescue the paintings. Now why would he be so foolish as to believe that I won't just kill you? What's his bargaining chip?"

"We want Senga released unharmed." Noah stood at his full height, and bellowed out the instruction.

"I don't have her!" His face was indignant, but then his eyes became sad, "Do you know, I really thought you'd come to work for me?"

"I wanted to, before I knew you were intending to kill two up and coming artists. I'm not looking for that type of work."

"Just what is it you are looking for Mr. Coleman?"

"I'm looking for a pattern in an abstract world."

"You can find it here working for me?"

"As an accessory to murder?"

"No! As an artist."

"Knowing what you're intending to do to artists will give me nightmares."

"No, knowing what I have told you will keep you close to me. You know you can never leave?"

"It will make me dirty."

"It will make you rich, or at least it would have." Nahmad stormed over to a door almost ripping it off its hinges as he burst through into an adjoining studio.

In the wake of his whirlwind departure, Noah followed, like a plastic bag in the vortex.

Inside the studio, the light was fantastic, not as vibrant as St Tropez, but none the less spectacular.

In the center of the studio stood five blank canvases, beyond them an artist's table, under which a grey tarpaulin covered something bulky. Next to the table stood a Gilardoni Radiolite x-ray machine. On the table itself, amidst an array of pots and tubes of oil, stood a long slender black carbon tube.

Nahmad marched to the table, unscrewed the lid, and up-ended the tube. The five stolen paintings poured out into his hand. One by one he unrolled them and carefully laid them on the table, fanning them like a pack of cards.

Noah looked on in reverent awe.

Nahmad gestured to the paintings, "I want you to copy these." His hand brushed over them.

Without thinking, Noah joined him at the table, his fingers dared to touch the Picasso. Light as a feather, his fingers traced over the Matisse, "Nudes on a hillside, Magnificent."

"Only you have the skill to copy them, but do you have the courage?"

Noah took in the Hong Kong vista before him, the modernity of the buildings, the tradition, and history of the landscape. He reached out a trembling hand and touched the edge of the

Picasso, suddenly he felt weak; "It would take me two years, maybe three to complete such an undertaking." Shocked that he was even considering the task he moved his hand away from the canvas.

"I knew that's why you needed me. I know that's why you revealed your plans about the artists, to keep me faithful, but I didn't come here to copy the paintings, I came here to secure the release of Senga Monroe."

Nahmad became angry, "I've told you, I don't have her; I didn't kidnap her. Anyway what were you going to do? Grab the paintings, then look in every room to find her? Then carry her off on your white stallion? The days of colonial rule are over in both India, and here."

"If I have the paintings it will flush out the man that killed Daisy."

"But we can do that together Noah," lovingly he stoked the paintings, it was as if he were attempting to bring them to life.

"Forbes wants the paintings back, you weren't part of the original theft, he'll take that into consideration; he's a decent man."

"And he wants the scalp of the person who took them, and the mastermind."

"Yes, of course."

Namad came around the table and clasped Noah by the shoulders, "Then we can give him everything he desires. You have twelve months, after the exhibition finishes, to complete the task. That's nearly two years. Do it Noah! Copy them. Everything you and Forbes desire will be done."

"Two years, is that when you plan to kill Hastings and Sexton?" The words made him feel sick.

Nahmad thought it was a good time to be honest, "If all goes according to plan, it will be a good time to bury bad news."

"Forbes knows you have the paintings, he knows you killed Crombie."

"And I take it he thinks I kidnaped Agnes too?"

Noah nodded in reply.

Nahmad puffed out his chest, "Let me propose an honourable solution to him, as you say he is a decent man, and one that I can make his goals come true."

"Go on."

"Give me a copy of each of the paintings within two years, and I will give you Agnes ..."

Noah's eyes opened wide, he was about to speak, but Nahmad silenced him, "...and the killer, and the mastermind. One will lead to the other. Forbes can have them all."

"I want to kill him, not bring him to justice."

"My associates are more than capable of facilitating that request."

"And the paintings?"

"Forbes can find them, in two years-time, what do you think he would say to that?"

"So you do have Senga ..." the rage flared up inside him.

"No, I did not kidnap her. But I will find her, I promise you this," he inclined his head, "Noah, only you can do this work for me, and only I can give you and Forbes what you are looking for."

"The killer and his boss?"

Nahmad nodded.

"You know who it is?"

"I will find him, let's face it I have the organization and

338

resource to expose him. Please, speak with Forbes, and then begin your work," He tickled the paintings again.

"I want to be there, when you find Daisy's killer, and I want to be sure Senga is safe!"

"I think that will be inevitable."

It was only then that Noah fully understood where Nahmad thought Senga was. "You think the killer has Senga?"

Nahmad nodded, "The killer knew you were in Paris, Senga disappears …"

Noah suddenly understood why the killer had not materialized in London. In that moment he understood that the relationship Nahmad and Senga had enjoyed would make the finding of her a very real proposition.

"How do we flush him out?"

"I propose to offer the paintings to the killer, ostensibly, the mastermind would still want to have them."

Noah shook his head, it came back to the old question, "What do you do with five paintings you cannot sell?"

Nahmad, looked him directly in the eye, "You offer them as collateral for the woman you love."

"I think that might just work."

"Then there is no time to lose, will you copy the paintings?" Nahmad scooped down to pull back the grey tarpaulin, "I took the liberty of bringing your tools." Five battered old suitcases looked back at him.

"My babies," he said, referring to the suitcases.

"You will be able to afford new ones, when this task is over."

"Why would I want to do that? I love these old suitcases."

Chapter Twenty-five

PABLO PICASSO (1881 – 1973)

Hong Kong,
Monday, July 5.

THE MAN WITH THE SCAR GLANCED AT WILLIAM FORBES, his dark glasses hid the movement so well, that to the casual observer, no movement was discerned.

Forbes looked agitated, he was pacing along the dock in front of the mock-Edwardian pier terminal. He turned abruptly just under the clock, and came back again, lips pursing, fingers twiddling. The taking of a pill was automatic.

The electronically controlled bells began to toll. The man with the scar knew that the electronic sound had been designed to replicate the tone of the original Edinburgh Place ferry pier bells.

The Star-line attendants began to gather at the water's edge, preparing for the arrival of the ferry.

It was the second ferry to arrive since Forbes, and subsequently him, had taken up their positions. Forty five minutes to be exact.

The 'voice' had been correct, after Nahmad had acquired

the paintings in Paris, he had returned to his exhibition in Hong Kong, pulling Forbes and Coleman along in his wake.

Nahmad would hold the paintings in his fortress-like sky-scraper, waiting for the replacement forger to enter his web. The vacant position would have been offered to Coleman in Paris.

Forbes would be waiting for confirmation that the paintings were at the World-life studio, before storming the building with the local police, or attempting to use his old SAS skills and steal the paintings by stealth.

Either action would of course be superfluity. As soon as Coleman confirmed the paintings were there, both he and Forbes could be killed.

The man with the scar wanted to know only if Coleman was coming to the pier, where he could kill them both, or if he would be killing them separately.

He saw Forbes lift his mobile to his ear. Momentarily he wished he were closer, so he could listen to the conversation. But, wishing for something was the trait of a weak man. Whatever eventuality, the man with the scar had his plan. The next link in his chain reaction would be soon; and then he could have the woman.

It was Coleman's name on the mobile, but it was Nahmad's voice in his ear.

"Good day Mr. Forbes I hope you are well?"

"Where's Coleman?"

"Mr. Coleman has decided to accept my offer of employment, he will be remaining here for a while."

Forbes felt the anger rise, but it had little direction and

focus, "As soon as this conversation is over, I'm contacting the police."

"Please Mr. Forbes do have some patience. I have a proposition for you."

"Spitting out your demands will have no effect on my decision."

"Not demands, Mr. Forbes, a proposition. I have five very beautiful and valuable paintings in my studio."

"Stolen paintings I believe."

"Correct, I understand you are looking for them."

Forbes felt a moment's confusion, "Of course."

"Good, here's my proposition. Visit my exhibition, free entry naturally. Return to your hotel, eat a sumptuous dinner with some fine wine, and then return to Paris. There you will discover the body of Charles Crombie."

"Or what's left of him."

"No matter, I will give you directions as to where the body can be found, well, as you say, most of him."

"Why move him?"

"I want to continue to use the tomb. Now, evidence will have been planted on the body. You will follow the clues and track down the paintings. You will become a national hero." Nahmad was careful not to reveal the timescale he planned for all this to happen.

"How long do you plan this charade to go on for? I don't want to be chasing the paintings for a moment longer than I have to."

Nahmad seethed inwardly at Forbes's understanding that there would be a delay in finding the paintings. He needed to divert the attention, "I have men tracing the original thief; the man that has been following you."

"The man that killed Daisy, Buscetti, and Mosca?"

"The very same. Once we apprehend him, he will soon give up the name of the mastermind behind the Paris theft. I believe that is something you also want?"

"I don't need your help to find him."

"Oh but I think you do, Mr. Forbes. Your investigations took you only to the door of LeCoyte Chellen. You have no idea who was behind the theft."

"And you do?"

"Mr. Forbes, I am offering you, the ALR, Interpol, and the Paris police, the name of the mastermind behind the world's most costly theft. I am also giving Mr. Coleman the opportunity to rid the world of the killer that murdered his wife …and I am offering you all the glory."

"In exchange for immunity for murdering Charles Crombie."

"If you like."

"And the price for this, would be the time it takes for Coleman to copy the originals. I assume it will be fakes that I get back."

"No, I can assure you it will be the genuine items. Face it Forbes, I'm offering you the solution to everything you need, on a plate. I just ask for a little time."

"To produce forgeries."

"Time to get hold of the killer."

"I told you I can deal with him."

"I doubt it Forbes, I doubt you could face him without a belly full of pills. Why can you not see that my proposal would solve everything?"

"Because you've not mentioned the one reason I want you dead."

"You refer to Agnes, I assume?"

Forbes felt physically sick. Senga was his main reason for coming to Hong Kong, killing Nahmad was his motivation, getting the killer and the paintings would be the cherry on the top of the cake.

Forbes knew that Nahmad was using Senga as blackmail for Noah to copy the paintings, and during that time, he would be playing detective on the other side of the world. When he finally discovered the paintings, and the original thief, and the mastermind, all links to Nahmad would be severed.

"Forbes, give me your answer."

"Don't hurt her."

"Good, I'll take that as a yes. My people will contact you in Paris."

"Okay, you win."

"Oh, and Forbes, make sure you haven't eaten anything before finding Crombie's body." The line went dead.

Forbes wandered dejectedly along the pier, his world was crumbling around him. Nahmad was right, he had no idea who was behind the Paris theft. The Chellen connection, had been a pure fluke, and the Luini find just a short stay of execution. Coleman had deserted him.

The man with the scar fell in step behind him.

The imagined attraction with Senga, had been just that, she was probably with Nahmad by choice. "That bloody Roman helmet." He'd trusted her, he'd lied for her, and all he'd got in turn was hurt. He'd come to Hong Kong like the man he used to be, an SAS officer, with remit to kill. Except he wasn't that man anymore. He was an Art Loss Register investigator. Paintings had been stolen on his watch, and now he was allowing one of the world's most corrupt art impresarios to forge the paintings and lead him around by the nose, until the time was right for them to be found again.

Forbes wanted to be on his own, but the ferry had docked, spilling hundreds of people onto the jetty, they swarmed like ants through the channels and out onto the busy streets.

In their rush they knocked into Forbes, but he didn't notice their touch. He just wanted to go back to the hotel and lose himself in a bottle. Perhaps some more pills. Perhaps a bottle and some more pills. Maybe it was time for that.

The man with the scar stepped closer behind. The crowd began to mass as they reached the gateway onto Man Kwong Street.

The man raised his hand and touched his scar, then neatly side-stepped an elderly lady; only two people separated him from Forbes.

The constant hum of chatting and the noise from the traffic on the street disguised the sound of the blade detaching from the handle. Quickly he pushed past a European businessman. Only a girl in a pink jacket separated them now.

Forbes, lost in thought, walked on, his back presented a perfect target. The man with the scar knew exactly where the knife would enter his body.

Hurriedly the girl in the pink jacket moved left, and pushed past the dawdling Forbes, his shoulder felt the impact, then returned.

In one elongated double-step the killer moved in behind him. Children screamed, mothers pacified, businessmen argued, the traffic honked and revved everywhere. All around them people were jostling for position, the old wrought-iron gate was just ahead.

Everyone slowed, and funneled into the gate. The noise level grew, the killer's heart rate rose slightly. To kill out in the open, with hundreds around him was exciting, not the same excitement that he got being up close and personal, but it would suffice until he got his hands on the girl. Suddenly he thought about the copper-haired girl. His mind went into overload, then he felt pressure on his arm. The man with the scar used his elbow to push an old man with a drooping moustache from angling in to him.

Simultaneously he lifted his left arm. His hand was no more than an inch from Forbes's neck. One more step, and he would clasp his left hand around the throat, in a mock greeting, and then plunge the knife deep into him.

Unexpectedly Forbes stopped moving, he'd bumped into the man in front. Forbes began apologizing, but the momentum of the killer, being carried along by the crowd took him smack into Forbes, his left hand brushed against his ear, the touch would be unusual, and Forbes would be confused. Now was the time.

With their bodies pressed into each other, and the crowd still surging forward through the gate, he plunged the knife forward, at exactly the same time the man with the droopy moustache, who he'd pushed away with his elbow, decided to push back into him, and go for the space which had opened. The knife brushed against the man, slashing between his third and fourth ribs.

With a piercing scream the man jumped back, arms flailing, trying to detach himself from the searing pain in his side.

The scream, and the touch of flesh on his ear jolted Forbes back into real time, he pivoted to face the noise.

The man's eyes were wide, the moustache droopy, the hands, and side leaking blood. Forbes saw the knife.

The blade accelerated, striking like a snake. In the crush of the crowd, Forbes brought both hands down, cross-blocking over the attacking wrist. His fingers wrapped around the hand that drove the blade forward. The relentless push of the crowd inhibited him from gaining the momentum he needed to twist the wrist. Together they were swept along.

The droopy mustached man had gone down on his knees, whimpering like a puppy begging for food.

Around them others began screaming. People pushed back against the tidal wave of passengers pushing into the gate, but the force was too great, the next wave forced the front of the crowd into the back of the man with the scar.

He was being crushed on both sides, hands reaching out, probing, some to help a fallen man, others to squeeze past the incident. The killer stepped closer to Forbes. His hot breath steamed onto his cheek.

They looked into each other's eyes. The dark lenses obscured the intent. The knife hand was withdrawn. Forbes stumbled back, fighting for his balance. Immediately the attacker's left hand crashed into Forbes's face, the palm hitting his jaw, the index finger seeking his eye.

Forbes twisted his body, tucking his chin into his chest. The finger turned into a claw and began to rake, but Forbes opened his mouth, and bit down on the first finger that entered it.

The man with the scar gave a short sharp yelp. He thrust forward with the knife, but the press of people removed any force.

An elderly man wrapped his thin arms around the killer in a heroic gesture. A portly woman, smashed her vegetable bag down over the blade. Their voices boomed as one, their sense of justice enraged by the large powerful knife-wielding attacker in their midst.

The crowd surged forward, sweeping over Forbes, he lost his balance and grip on the finger in his mouth. He allowed the crowd to carry him away. Just once more did he see the blade searching for him, then it was lost in a sea of clothing. Every voice was loud every limb flailing, every face getting closer.

Weak fists and hands were slapping the attacker, his sunglasses became dislodged, angled over his face. Forbes stared into the eyes of the man he had seen in the airport security photographs. You can disguise everything else, but you cannot disguise the eyes.

Although their bodies were separated, their eyes remained locked.

As they spilled out onto the road, they were carried away in opposite directions by the tide of people. Washing them up onto the sands of different shores. As the people drew back, like a retreating wave, Forbes saw the attacker throw off the elderly people that had attached themselves to him.

He shook them like a dog shaking off water, they flew into the street, knocking a cyclist off his bicycle. A car slithered to a stop, and a moped ploughed into the back of it. Horns blared reaching a crescendo of noise.

Pinned back by a wave of small Chinese intent on getting

away from the scene, Forbes watched helplessly as the attacker rolled over a car bonnet, punched a female cyclist, and jumped to the other side of the busy street.

Another car drove into a stationary vehicle in an attempt to miss the woman who had fallen from her bicycle.

The crowd changed their focus, and began to assemble around the accident. The exhaust fumes began to plume around them.

Drivers were stopped, bumper to bumper, foiling any attempt by Forbes to follow the killer.

As a cloud of exhaust gas drifted by, Forbes saw that the man had disappeared. All around him faces were looking up at him, he felt disorientated. The killer could be anywhere. Forbes span around, looking for the killer.

He wiped his mouth, smearing the blood over his chin. The faces were looking at him again, but this time in fear. Forbes felt that it was he that was transforming into to a zombie in front of their eyes. He stumbled backward, groaning. Every voice seemed to be talking at him, every face turned toward him, every heart demanding that he find Senga, and put these demons back in hell, where they belonged. Where was the killer?

The hand clamped down on his shoulder, spinning him around. Forbes expected the sting of the blade at any moment, his eyes squeezed tightly shut. But the pain did not come. He opened his eyes.

"You must not leave the hotel without me. Look at what happens. I must be with you at all times, how else can I protect you," Mi Wai stood in front of him.

"Come, my car is close. Mr. Stonehouse has requested you phone him, quick sharp. He has a very important message for you." The powerful man bustled his way through the crowd.

Chapter Twenty-six

HENRI MATISSE (1869 – 1954)

World-life building Hong Kong,
Monday, July 5.

HIS FIRST LAYER OF DISGUISE WAS GONE, IT WAS bright without his sunglasses.

The man with the scar looked out over a sea of oriental faces, He'd jogged two blocks from the ferry terminal, but his height, and obvious European features meant he was visible, and identifiable.

A raised hand hailed a taxi, his other hand, with the bloodied finger stayed casually in his pocket.

The man with the scar, slipped off his jacket, and slipped into the back of the car, immediately becoming invisible.

The taxi-driver was pleased to welcome his passenger, the destination address was at least forty minutes away. The taxi pulled out into the stream of heavy traffic.

The man with the scar wrapped a handkerchief around his finger, then turned his jacket inside-out, and pulled out a small tin of make-up, so began his latest disguise.

As the taxi accelerated along Kennedy Road, the passenger lent forward, "Stop here." His American accent was Mid-West.

"But we are not at your destination."

He waved a number of notes, which was all the driver saw in his dirty rear-view mirror, the taxi pulled into the World-life car-park entrance.

The man with the scar emerged from the taxi, slipping the reversed jacket over his shoulders. He walked to the entrance, calmly, hair parted centrally, scar covered; eye-brows darker, safe in the knowledge that none of the passengers from the ferry terminal would ever recognise him face to face.

With confidence he marched across the lobby, and straight into the nearest elevator.

At the twenty-third floor, along with two Japanese ladies, decked out in white laboratory coats, he left the elevator. With the natural grace of a tiger, he approached the highly polished reception desk. The two ladies whispered to each other about how attractive he was, and how attracted they were to him.

In heavily accented German he declared, "Good day, my name is Thomas Woolner, I believe you have a package for me." His smile was charming, but the girl on the desk knew instinctively he was off limits, she could always pick out a gay man.

"Of course," she flashed a smile, and checked her list. She squatted, then sprang up holding a light blue fabric bag.

"Danke," he took it, and returned to the elevators.

Once inside he pressed the number seven button. As he waited, other passengers joined him. The receptionist, if ever questioned would respond truthfully that Mr. Woolner had taken the bag and left the building.

"As the elevator began to drop, he reached out and pressed number twenty one. The doors slid open. Swinging the bag as he walked, the man with the scar crossed the floor, and entered the male restroom.

Here it was cooler, with the smell of disinfectant adding to the cleanliness.

Once inside a cubical, he opened the bag, and lovingly stroked the objects within. He took off his shoes, the jacket, and the trousers. Then he took out the objects. Quickly he put them on the seat, pausing only to lick the blade of the eight inch hunting-knife. Senga's face floated in front of his eyes.

He squeezed the bag deep inside the wastepaper-basket. He left the restroom, wearing a dark grey suit, clutching the matching chuffer's cap in his right hand, to disguise the small piece of cloth covering his wounded finger.

The new official disguise in place he punched the button for the forty-eighth floor. He checked his watch, "Bang on time," there was no accent in his voice.

He watched the numbers light up as he travelled toward the paintings.

Various passengers joined him on his journey, but none really took any notice of the hired help.

'Almost there,' he thought to himself. The disappointment of missing Forbes at the terminal was already pushed to the back of his mind.

Cautiously he walked through the 'Sky-lobby', past the Heli-pad, toward the smaller elevator in the core of the tower. He was on his own now, no hollow metallic voice to drive him on. Paris seemed a long time ago, but soon he would be reunited with the paintings he had so lovingly cut from their frames.

Just like when he was waiting to be picked up outside the museum, he knew this was the most dangerous part of the plan. He observed, and glanced away from all the cameras.

A very attractive Indian girl was sitting at the reception desk, beyond the glass door, he approached with the caution of a chauffeur not really knowing where to go.

Mohini looked up and smiled …

REMMERT VAN BRAAM'S MOTORISED WHEELCHAIR felt as light as a feather. Xin squeezed the trigger, and gently pushed the old man into the elevator.

It had taken a lot to persuade Chandhok Nahmad to allow such a visit today, but the amount of work which van Braam had done over the years, and therefore the amount of evidence he had amassed had tipped the balance.

As van Braam imagined the day unfolding, he began to get excited, this after all would be his last act, and in time it would define his life, and put to rest all his anger.

Coleman was in Nahmad's employ, and, he summarized was about to copy the paintings. The man that had taken his sight had also taken his job.

He spoke softly in Cantonese to Xin, as the elevator rose, "Matisse's separation from his wife in 1939, added to his anxiety about the direction of his work. After major surgery in 1941, he, like me was confined to a wheelchair."

Closeted with the music and the smell of polish he felt his stomach flip as the elevator rose.

"Matisse turned to paper cut-outs, this while sitting was

manageable and offered new potential for expression. Paper cut-outs symbolized the synthesis of drawing and painting. He used the technique to design the stained glass windows for the Chapelle du Rosaire in Vence, France. With the help of his assistants, he too was able to continue working through his illness." His hand reached up to Xin, he was thankful that he had her to assist him.

"Very good, I closed my eyes, I could not tell you were not Chinese," Xin rubbed his shoulder.

Another goal achieved, van Braam kept his rage under control, this was not a time to let personal feelings get in the way; this was business.

AS THE MAN WITH THE SCAR APPROACHED MOHINI'S desk, he was about to speak when he heard the ping of the elevator, he turned and saw a pretty Chinese girl pushing an old man in a motorised wheelchair. Surely his job of getting past the reception desk had just been made easier …

As they came level with him, he smiled at the girl, and began to keep pace at their side, as they approached the glass door, he lent forward quickly and said, "Allow me," the accent was perfect English.

Mohini looked up from her desk. She saw Remmert van Braam in his wheelchair, being pushed by Xin his pretty Chinese assistant, they were accompanied by a large athletic man; he looked like a swimmer, but Mohini failed to put a nationality to the man.

Concern rushed through her body, she had been told to

expect only two visitors; and then she saw the chauffer's cap, and instantly assumed the big man was van Braam's chauffer.

Mohini approached the trio, "Welcome, Mr. van Braam, you are early." His black sunglasses obliterated nearly all the scaring on his face.

Xin smiled back at this stunningly beautiful Asian girl.

van Braam recognised the voice, "Mohini, my little princess, come close to me," he held out his hands. She obeyed. van Braam devoured her pomegranate perfume, "You smell gorgeous,"

Xin smiled at the chauffer, whom she assumed was part of Nahmad's staff, sent to accompany them.

The man with the scar said nothing, and nobody challenged his right to be there.

"We have missed you so much," Mohini walked with them toward the core elevator. "This will take you directly to the fifty-seventh floor, Mr. Nahmad will welcome you personally when he returns." As the doors closed, she waved at them, then realized how stupid the motion was, as the former employee was now blind, he would not have been able to see the gesture of friendship. She stood back and watched the elevator rise.

The numbers lit up, charting the progress of the elevator, Mohini began to walk back to her desk, when she turned she noticed the number fifty-six was still lit.

Concern flowed through her again, she sat at her desk and contacted the studio.

The former Shaolin monk, Tien answered the call. "Hai."

"Tien, please can you check out in the corridor, I think Mr. van Braam is outside, he appears to have stopped at the wrong floor. Mr. Nahmad was very clear that under no circumstances should Mr. van Braam be allowed to visit his old studio; especially with Mr. Coleman in residence."

"I will check."

"You must put them back in the elevator, we don't want anyone seeing what's going on in there." Again Mohini felt silly about using the word 'seeing'. Reluctantly Tien moved away from the Gilardoni Radiolite X-ray machine. Nahmad had long ago understood how crucial it was to own this machine; essential for producing photographs of the layers beneath the final picture of the actual painting to be copied.

Noah Coleman worked the machine with a natural grace. He hardly noticed that Tien was leaving him on his own.

The *grenz* rays were capable of detecting and separating five layers of paint. Noah would photograph each, and then have to paint an exact copy of each layer, in order to build up the complete painting. Only by going to this degree of forgery, could one hope to satisfy the verifier, during the authentication process.

Noah laid out the photos on the table.

Tien stopped, caught in two minds, his instruction had been clear, "Don't leave Coleman alone with the paintings." It had come directly from Nahmad; but he knew he must also investigate the intruders in the corridor, and belay Mohini's concern.

In an awkward sideways shuffle, which the monk, made look elegant, he eased his way to the first door. Without a second glance, he keyed in the code. The door un-locked.

Noah looked up. Tien looked back at him, "Stay where you are; touch nothing." He continued through the outer studio.

Noah looked back at Tien, concern etched across his face, "You're not supposed to leave me."

Tien heard the buzz of an electric motor. He opened the outer door, and observed three people approaching. van Braam, in his wheelchair he recognized, but the small woman, and the large man he did not. They turned and stopped at the door.

Noah looked beyond his Shaolin guard, and recognized the eyes of the man he'd seen in the airport security photographs, "Tien, shut the door!"

Tien hesitated, but the chauffer did not, he raised his pistol, and shot him dead.

The suppresser made a tell-tale 'puff' noise as the bullet exited the barrel, and tore into Tien's skull.

Xin screamed, her hands shook in front of her face. The man with the scar turned the pistol on her, and fired again. She dropped to the floor. Silence, like the pool of blood from her wound spread out around her.

van Braam spoke, "What's happening?"

Noah felt the rage spread through his body. Without conscious thought he raced toward the door, he carried no weapon, just the desire to strike out at the man that had killed Daisy. As he stepped over Tien's body, the killer turned to van Braam, he answered the old man's question, "The bodyguard is dead, and it looks like Coleman is X-raying the paintings."

Noah heard the words, but their meaning made no sense, until van Braam nodded, "Take me to them," excitement filled his voice.

The killer aimed his gun at Noah, and guided van Braam into the studio.

"Oh fuck," the fight left Noah's body in one gigantic wave of emotion. In an instant he knew that van Braam was behind the Paris theft, and Nahmad had probably set him up.

"Hello Noah, it's so good to know that you are here. It will make taking the paintings back all the more satisfying."

Noah frantically searched for a weapon, but van Braam interrupted his thoughts, "Get the paintings."

Noah ran into the inner studio, he closed the door, but after two shots, the killer kicked it open.

As he entered, Noah was stuffing the paintings into the black carbon tube.

"And what are you going to do with that, eat it?" The killer mocked.

"Get me the paintings!" van Braam shouted.

"Coleman has them in the tube."

"Get it!"

The man with the scar, covered Noah with his gun, "Do it now, or I'll prize it out of your dead fingers."

"Come on, come on!" van Braam shouted.

Reluctantly Noah presented the tube to van Braam. He held it close to his chest, as one would do with a child, rescued from the path of an oncoming vehicle.

"Okay, get me out of here, we have what we came for."

"What about Coleman?" the man with the scar asked, "Shall I kill him?"

"No," the evil twisted lips came up with a better option, "Cut off his hands."

The man with the scar, felt inside his waistband, and pulled out the hunting-knife. With slow deliberation he approached Noah.

"Most people don't have what it takes to perform an

amputation on another human being," his voice was very melo-dramatic, "But I do, that's what makes me special."

"You killed Daisy," Noah said through trembling lips.

The killer stopped, the look was hesitant the knife and the gun remained steady, "Was that her name?" He resisted the urge to touch his scar, but revelled in the memory of her death, "Yes I did. She tasted very nice."

From nowhere, Noah fired out a punch which smashed into the killer's face. He shook his head, and smiled, "Is that the best you can do?"

"No this is," He fired another rocket of a punch into the man's face, but this time the killer blocked it. In an instant, he poked the gun barrel into Noah's solar plexus. Noah staggered back, stumbling into the table.

"Weak old man," he said. Without respite he jumped on him, clubbing him to the ground. "I don't know what that sexy woman saw in you?" He placed the gun on the table, and took hold of Noah's left forearm, gripping it in a vice-like hold, forcing it flat on the table.

Noah tried to break the hold, but couldn't. He kicked out, but the killer lent his weight into him, kneeing him in the spine.

The crook of Noah's elbow was jammed against the table His body crumpled on the floor beneath it. The killer crammed in behind him.

"Is he left handed?" the killer asked.

"What are you doing?" van Braam asked.

Holding up the hunting-knife, he said, "Cutting off his left hand." The man with the scar was smiling now.

The sting of the hunting-knife blade cut into the top of his wrist. Noah squirmed in panic. The killer brought his knee up into his armpit.

"Keep still." The skin split open.

Noah twisted his body, and tried to pull his hand away, but the man with the scar was much too strong.

The blade sliced into his wrist. The killer drew the knife back across his arm, as one does when slicing bread. All his strength was focused on exerting pressure on Noah's arm.

Noah screamed in pain.

van Braam's voice cut through the torture, "You took my eyes, Mr. Coleman; I think this is only fair."

Noah felt the knife cut deeper, feeling the blood flowing from the wound, Noah sucked in the pain, and shrieked out a cry of agony.

The killer exerted more pressure, on his forearm as the knife began to saw into the bone.

With a sudden clarity, Noah focused his attention to where the killer had put the gun.

In one last mighty effort Noah pushed himself up off the floor, his thighs burned, his calves screamed, but he continued upward, dislodging the killer.

As he toppled over the table his right hand wrapped around the gun.

The killer stopped the sawing motion. "Is this for real?"

"No, this is for Daisy," Noah brought the gun across his body, "Fuck you!"

The quiet 'puff' of the bullet discharging seemed very loud to Noah.

The bullet ripped off a chunk of the man's ear, but he did not waiver. Instead he lifted the knife, and in one act of defiance stabbed down through the back of Noah's hand. "Fuck you!"

Noah was pinned to the table. His finger squeezed the trigger in panic, a second bullet tore through the man's bicep. A third shot buried itself in the wall.

van Braam shouted, "What's happening?"

Noah homed in on his voice, aimed and squeezed the trigger. Bullets four and five, missed completely, but the sixth buried itself into van Braam's right shoulder. The old man screamed in shock. He clutched the carbon tube, and shouted "Get me out of here."

The killer elbowed Noah across the back of his head. As he crumpled on the table he lent in close to him, blood dripped from his torn ear, "Your woman tasted wonderful." In a flash he plucked the gun from Noah's hand. He backed away and busied himself manoeuvring van Braam's wheelchair.

The killer new that his words to Noah were worse than the pain form his wounds, they would stay in his mind for the rest of his life.

Noah tried to move, but the pain, and the loss of blood made him weak.

Helpless to move, skewered by the knife, Noah watched defencelessly as the killer pushed van Braam from the studio. Slowly he crumpled to the floor.

Daisy's killer, the thief of the paintings was getting away, pushing an old blind man, and there was nothing he could do to stop them.

AS THEY TRAVELLED DOWN IN THE ELEVATOR, THE MAN with the scar, held the rest of his handkerchief up against his torn ear. His other hand attempted to stem the flow of blood from van Braam's shoulder. "We may have trouble leaving the building, sir."

"Give me my phone," he gasped.

The man with the scar, reached into van Braam's jacket and withdrew the mobile.

The old man fumbled with the buttons, then spoke in hushed tones, "I need you now." He dropped the phone onto his lap, "Just get us to the Heli-pad, do you think you can do that?"

The killer smiled, again the 'voice' had thought of everything. "Sure, no problem," he put a new magazine in the gun, "I'll even have enough bullets for that cute Indian girl on the desk."

"You're a sick bastard ..." the doors opened, as they did, the man with the scar came face to face with William Forbes.

van Braam recognised that the elevator had stopped moving, "Come on we have to get to the Heli-pad,"

Forbes stepped into the elevator, and tried to take the black carbon tube from van Braam's grip, "I'll help you with this."

"What? No, let go." He brought both hands around the tube, protecting it from the unknown intruder.

As Forbes struggled to seize the tube, the man with the scar brought the gun up, and pressed it against Frobes's head, "Back off Forbes."

"Forbes?" van Braam shouted, he tightened his grip on the black carbon tube, his head shook from side to side, refusing to let it go.

The man with the scar pressed the button on the chair and

tried to wheel van Braam out into the Sky-lobby. Gun arm out-stretched, gun tight against Forbes's head they started to move out of the elevator.

Forbes refusing to let go of the tube, body bent double, arms interlocked, squeezed his body against the side of the door.

"We're not going anywhere. You didn't think we'd just let you walk out of here, did you?" The electric motor screamed in protest.

The man with the scar looked directly at Forbes, "Most people don't have what it takes to kill someone in cold blood ..." he lifted the gun away from Forbes's head.

Forbes returned his stare, "Give me the gun." He held on tightly to the tube, as the doors pressed against his ribs, and the chair pinned him against the wall.

"Give me the gun, you can't escape from here."

"Not alive maybe but I don't care about dying, but if I have to go, you're coming with me." The movement was small, but the noise was loud, in a single second the killer refocused his aim on Forbes, and squeezed the trigger, but it was the loud shot from Mi Wai's pistol that propelled the bullet into the kill-er's heart before he could complete the squeeze. The killer released his grip on the wheelchair, which fell silent. The gun slipped from his hand, which clattered on the floor. He fell back into the corner of the elevator. His head fell forward, hair parted revealing his puckered scar.

Forbes looked at Wai, "Thanks for that."

van Braam unscrewed the top from the black carbon tube.

"I told you Mr. Forbes, I am here to protect ..." but it was in that moment that van Braam pulled out a flare, and detonated the lime-bomb.

The flare gushed with flame, a flash so bright Forbes and Wai were momentarily blinded. van Braam pushed the flare inside the carbon tube. The flames roared out of the open end like a rocket motor, scorching van Braam's face. Globular pieces of explosive splattered all over the old man, melting his sunglasses and face alike. The flames igniting his clothing. His scream was loud, but short lived.

Wai's reaction was lighting fast, he fired two shots into the burning body of van Braam. The burning tube fell from his hands. His skin began to blister. His hair caught fire, and within a moment he was incinerated.

Forbes dashed forward and upended the tube, the lime-bomb spilled out, Forbes kicked it away. The burning canvases poured out, bright flames eating the material, devouring the oils, killing the very life of the paintings. As they watched the fire demolish every fibre it touched, all that was left was ash.

They had been created by geniuses, looked upon in wonder by thousands, coveted by many, and in one moment of insanity reduced to ash by one.

Wai began to stamp on the larger pieces of canvas, but the explosive stuck to his shoe and ignited again. Forbes took off his Highland-green jacket to smother the oxygen from the fire, but it was a lost cause. The explosive ate into the carpet, igniting the fibres. Instantly the fire-alarm sounded, and the sprinklers began to pour down a chilling cascade of water.

Chapter Twenty-seven

FERNAND LÉGER (1881 - 1955)

World-life building Hong Kong,
Monday, July 5.

WILIAM FORBES SAT BACK AND ALLOWED THE WATER to wash away the tears from his face. The flames extinguished quickly under the deluge. Mohini turned off the alarm, to allow themselves to think again. The water dripped, then it stopped.

Wai looked at the charred remains of van Braam. The devastation of the burned canvases combined with the torrent of water from the sprinklers left the paintings in a formless mushy shape on the floor.

"Where is Noah?" Mohini asked.

Forbes leapt into the elevator and pressed fifty-six. The doors closed behind him, shutting out the madness. As the elevator rose, Forbes checked the pockets of the dead man with the scar.

So much death and destruction. Dazed and confused, Forbes walked along the corridor, his clothes dripping wet, his shoes squelching on the carpet.

Outside the studio he came across the body of a young

Chinese woman. He wiped away more tears, he wasn't sobbing, just devastated by the loss of life caused by van Braam's insane plan.

At the door of the studio another body lay torn apart. Forbes wondered if the entire plan of stealing the paintings was only to entice Noah here so that van Braam could kill him. As he walked across the studio, he wondered what was in store for him beyond the door.

Forbes pushed open the door, and saw Noah hanging from the table. A massive hunting-knife skewering him. He could see the deep cut in his wrist, which seemed to be holding together by no more than a thread.

"Oh God," Forbes bemoaned another death.

It was then that Noah's blood soaked head moved, his eyes opened and in hushed tones he said, "van Braam was behind the theft." The eyes stayed open, eyes without a face, eyes only with hope.

For a moment Forbes thought it was another hallucination, another nightmare of talking corpses.

Forbes felt the room begin to swirl, he fell down; "Will this ever stop?" he screamed. For two years he'd been plagued with these visions.

He looked into Noah's eyes, they blinked.

"You're alive!"

"I hope so," Noah replied.

Forbes lifted his weight, Noah moaned with agony.

"It was van Braam," he whispered.

"I know, and it was your phone call to Stonehouse that led us to him. Stonehouse passed your message to me, that's why we're here, mob handed."

"Good."

Forbes fumbled in his pocket for his mobile, "Mi Wai, get some medical assistance up to the art studio on 56."

"On our way quick sharp."

"It's okay, Noah, help is on the way."

"The man that killed Daisy," he gestured toward his hand. Forbes lifted his body to ease the strain of the ripped flesh. "He did this to me."

"Hang in there buddy, help's on its way."

"The paintings ..." Noah said through gritted teeth.

"It's okay, we know everything." He didn't know how to tell him they'd been destroyed. "The man that killed Daisy is dead." Forbes hoped that would help.

Tears rolled down Noah's blood soaked face, "We got them."

"We sure did my friend, now you rest."

"The X-ray machine ..." Noah tried to raise his hand, but fainted with the pain.

The medics took Noah out on a stretcher. Forbes remained alone in the studio. He looked out over the magnificent view that is Hong Kong, but he saw nothing.

Minutes passed by before Forbes became aware of another presence in the studio. Mi Wai stood by the door, "Mr. Nahmad is in the building, he has requested that you join him. Right away, quick sharp now Mr. Forbes."

An incredible look passed over Forbes's face, "Why hasn't he been arrested?"

"On what charge?" Wai scooped an enormous finger between his shirt collar and his powerful neck.

Forbes was lost for words, but Wai continued, "We know

that Remmert van Braam was behind the theft in Paris. His man, his name was Thomas Woolner, by the ..."

"Really?" Forbes recognized the name from the brotherhood.

"Yes, he was the man that actually took the paintings."

"I guess he was." Forbes began to get skeptical.

"I think we can also guess he did the murders of Buscetti, Mosca, and miss Danese Kantargo..."

"Her name was Daisy ..."

"Yes I believe so, and of course he killed van Braam's assistant Xin, and Mr. Nahmad's security guard, Tien."

"So no connection to Mr. Nahmad," Forbes said sarcastically.

"Correct."

"What about the paintings? Nahmad had the paintings."

"The paintings are destroyed, there is no proof that they were ever here."

"Nahamd killed Charles Crombie, in Paris."

"Says who?"

"Says me, I saw the body."

"Where?"

"Doesn't matter, it's not there now, Nahmad's hidden it." Forbes shook his head in frustration.

"Really? Did you report this to the French police?" The finger traced down the inside of his collar again.

Forbes shook his head.

"Or did you leave Paris and come to Hong Kong?" The eyes narrowed.

Forbes argued, "Crombie had the paintings, he brought them to Paris and he gave them to Nahmad."

"You saw the paintings in Paris?"

Forbes shook his head. "But Coleman will verify that Nahmad asked him to forge the paintings."

"Mr. Coleman contacted Mr. Stonehouse, to reveal that van Braam had the paintings, and he was behind the Paris theft. When we got here, van Braam did have the paintings, but he destroyed them. There is no evidence that links Mr. Nahmad."

"Coleman was here on my instructions, he contacted the ALR to advise us that the stolen paintings were here, at Worldlife." He gestured around the room.

His eyes fell upon the Gilardoni Radiolite X-ray machine. At the bottom front corner, a small green light glowed.

"Agreed, van Braam had the paintings. If this went to trial, Mr. Coleman would tell the jury what exactly, that he has worked for Mr. Nahmad for many years, restoring and renovating old paintings."

"Forging paintings."

"He will not confess to that. The lawyers would have a field day."

Forbes wandered over to the X-ray machine, he recalled the words that Noah had said, just before he passed out. At the time Forbes had believed he was referring to the death of van Braam and Daisy's killer, *"We got them."* But suppose he meant something else.

Mi Wai was still speaking, "Nahmad wasn't even in the building today, at the time of the attack."

Forbes pressed the 'open' button. The drawer slid open, and there in front of William Forbes's eyes was *Le pigeon aux petits-pots.*

"The café!" He eased his fingers underneath it, his heart

beat louder as he realized there was something else, "It's the Léger." Forbes lifted the bundle from the drawer.

"What do you have there?"

"La Pastorale, by Henri Matisse, valued at seventy–five million euros."

"The stolen paintings?"

Yes, the Picasso is here, it wasn't destroyed, it's actually here; Noah must have sold them a dummy ..." he held them gently in his arms.

"What?" Wai asked.

"Noah hid the paintings." Big fat tears of joy rolled down his cheeks, "The Olive Tree by Braque, Woman with a fan, by Amedeo Modigliani; and Still-life with chandeliers, with fucking chandeliers my friend, a wonderful painting by Fernand Léger. They're all here. Noah saved them all."

Forbes rocked them in his arms, like a baby.

Wai's words were harsh, "Put the paintings down."

Forbes froze.

"Quick sharp now Mr. Forbes, put them on the table, and step away."

Forbes turned to look at him, his eyes were hard.

Wai cleared a space on the table, "I think Mr. Nahmad will have also handled them, if so, his fingerprints will be found," Wai smiled.

Forbes smiled back, relief spread through his body, "I think we have him." He placed the precious bundle on the table. "Look after them please, Mr. Wai, I'm going to see Mr. Nahmad right away."

"Give him my regards," Wai shouted over his shoulder.

Alone in the studio, Wai looked at the paintings, not really understanding what the fuss was all about.

A NERVOUS NAHMAD WAS WAITING BY THE ELEVATOR door. As Forbes emerged, he took him by the elbow, guiding him away from the small crowd of police.

"I am pleased you came to see me … before talking to the police, the Hong Kong constabulary can be so tiresome at times like these."

"Oh, you have no idea how pleased I am to see you Mr. Nahmad," Forbes could not hide the smile from his face.

Nahmad's eyes narrowed, "I did not think you would be in such a good mood, what with the destruction of the paintings …"

"There's more to life than art Mr. Nahmad …"

"Good, I wanted to see you before you spoke to the police, and the press. We need to make sure we fully understand what happened here today. I of course have been briefed on the course of events, but I would like to hear your views," Nahmad smiled expectedly.

Forbes looked back at him quizzically, "Strange, I gave instructions that no one should speak to you about the events of today. So who talked?"

They were now well away from the gaggle of police-officers, but still Nahmad lent close, so no one could overhear, "We have to get our stories straight, Forbes, our futures depend upon it."

"I'm not telling you anything, now answer my question, who talked about what happened here?"

Nahmad looked bemused at the question, when he spoke, it was as if the answer should have been obvious, "Agnes Monroe!"

"The woman you kidnapped." Forbes could not comprehend how she was involved.

"You have never considered that she came to Hong Kong of her own accord, have you? Or that she might have been abducted by Thomas Woolner, and is currently a captive at van Braam's residence?"

"No."

"Or that she wants to come back to me?" His smile was meant to irritate.

"Well I don't see her with you, you might have had a little fling in the past, but that relationship is well and truly finished. Abducted in Paris by Woolner, no, I know he went to London, following Coleman."

"Believe what you want."

"I will, but I don't see her at your side," Forbes glanced all around Nahmad, imitating a mime artist.

Nahmad ignored the provocation, "Let me tell you what happened, make sure we have our stories aligned."

"Oh I'm very clear about what's been going on."

"I'm sure I can clear up some grey areas. You would then be able to tell Miss Monroe, if you ever see her again."

"Another threat; you really are digging your own grave."

Nahmad pushed open the door and walked out onto the Heli-pad, the noise of the city drifted up to them. "Apparently a former employee of mine, Remmert van Braam, and a current employee, Noah Coleman, along with Charles Crombie, were responsible for the art theft in Paris. Buscetti, and Mosca, known art thieves carried out the theft. A professional hit-man, Thomas Woolner, was hired to kill them."

"Fascinating," remarked Forbes.

Nahmad nodded enthusiastically, then a deadly serious look came over his face. "The paintings were hidden at Sotheby's warehouse in London. Crombie, took them to Paris, where he passed them to Coleman for the purpose of copying them. Coleman brought the stolen paintings to my studio. One of my security staff, a former Shaolin monk, named Tien, raised the alarm."

"Forbes asked, "Was it a phone call to Leighton Stonehouse, by any chance?"

"Yes, I believe it was."

"Amazing."

"Tien, tried to apprehend them, unfortunately he was killed in the affray. Coleman was injured during the fight, he is currently in hospital, so will be easy to arrest. Woolner, and van Braam were both killed trying to escape."

"It's a good story, spoiled only by one small element."

"Spoiled by the fact that the stolen paintings were destroyed?"

"No," he shook his head, "I was thinking about your involvement." Forbes desperately wanted to see the look on Nahmad's face when he finally learnt that the paintings had been recovered.

"My involvement?"

Forbes laughed so loudly, that the group of police, in the Sky-lobby, looked at them.

Nahmad's face remained smiling, but his tone was menacing, "I have no connection to the Paris theft!"

"I agree, because you had nothing to do with it." Forbes

rubbed his face, thinking, *'You are going down, because your fingerprints will be all over the stolen paintings.'*

"The evidence implicating van Braam is compelling."

"I agree, because he did it." Forbes was enjoying toying with the little viper.

"The explosive used on the car, which also killed Buscetti." Forbes sobered up.

Nahmad continued, "It was the same explosive that he used today, to destroy the paintings. It was also a lime-bomb flare that he detonated when escaping from the police. That didn't go to well either, he ended up blinding himself that time."

Forbes's face dropped.

Nahamd pointed his finger at him, "Did you not make that connection?"

Forbes remained silent.

"I really don't know how you got this far? Still, follow my story and you have all the culprits. But you don't have the girl. To get her back, in one piece, I need to be kept out of this, so I think we can trade?"

Forbes desperately wanted to tell him that the paintings were safe and sound in the studio, but he kept his trump card well-hidden, "Go on, I'm listening."

"At last! So, you go back to Paris, you find Crombie's body, and I will ensure Miss Monroe is delivered to you."

"No deal Nahmad, I'm not going anywhere until I have Senga by my side."

"It gets cold out here of a night," Nahmad said sarcastically.

"Listen to me you little shit, let me tell you what happened. van Braam, pissed off that he'd lost his sight and his revenue stream, wanted to get even with Coleman. He got Woolner to steal the paintings, and intended to lure Coleman to Hong Kong, by offering a deal for Coleman to copy them. Mosca and Buscetti, the intended fall guys, did a double-cross, and Mosca came away with five stolen master-pieces that he couldn't sell, so he gave them to his Sotheby's contact, Crombie. Crombie wanting to enmesh himself in your mysterious future plans, approached you. Okay so far?"

"I believe that to be the truth."

"A concept you're not too familiar with I guess?"

"My version ties up all the loose ends."

"We can tweak it, but basically you leave Coleman out of the theft. I'm sure you could engineer a version, with Woolner killing Crombie?"

"Go on."

"Woolner brought the paintings to Hong Kong. Coleman raised the alarm, with a phone call to the ALR..."

"Can you get Coleman's buy-in to these events?" Nahmad asked.

"Yes."

"Splendid."

"But I want you to release Senga now. I won't move until I know she is safe."

"Very well ..."

"And I want you to return the real Madame X back to the Met."

"Very well ...Coleman's version is in every way as good as the original."

"And I want you to buy the Roman helmet from Senga."

"I already purchased it for her, she is relived of all debt to me."

Forbes began to worry, Nahamd was giving up everything,

in order to remain un-connected to the Paris theft. Had he missed something? Why was Nahmad so keen on being seen as innocent? It was all irrelevant anyway, he was going down for handling the stolen paintings.

But then his own words condemned him. "When you speak to Coleman, I must insist that you do not ask him to reveal any information about my plans for the future. I cannot allow you to know anything."

"Impossible, I cannot guarantee that he will not tell me some details, of his own free will." Forbes felt that whatever Nahmad was planning it must be something big. Shame that his finger-prints on the stolen paintings would wreck his dreams.

"I can assure you Mr. Coleman can be persuaded to keep my secrets to the grave. Shall we visit him in hospital? That would be a very fitting pace for you to become re-acquainted with Agnes."

"You haven't considered that Senga may actually want to press charges against you?"

"No, I have not."

"Then I only have one question."

"What?"

"Why do you call, Senga Munreaux, Agnes Monroe?"

"Because that is her real name, I think it is a beautiful name. But life is all about compromise, can we settle on, Senga Monroe?"

"I can live with that." Forbes climbed into the Bell Ranger, feeling life was good. Nahmad was keen that his involvement in Crombie's death was kept secret, for the sake of his future plans. He was sure this was not the first or last death that the Indian multi-billionaire would be involved with, but knowing that the paintings were safe, and that Senga would soon be released made everything worthwhile. He was confident that Noah would tell him everything he knew, after all, Nahmad was about to be arrested for handling stolen property.

The helicopter engine started up, the rotor began to spin like a roulette wheel, where it stopped, nobody knew. But, he did know that entering this game with Nahmad was a big gamble. A man as powerful as Nahmad, desperate to keep secrets would view a partner in crime like William Forbes as a very expendable partner. Noah, he needed, or thought he did, Senga he wanted, but he was nothing more than a disposable asset.

Hong Kong swept past beneath the helicopter, as it took Nahmad and Forbes to the hospital.

Forbes's mobile buzzed, "Hello, Forbes speaking."

Giancarlo Minardi's voice came across loud and clear, "Hello Bill, I have traced the owners of SANSOM."

"Okay, what do I need to know?"

"A couple of names are legitimate, seems the company operates as described, but there was one name which I thought you'd like to know about."

"Go on ..." Forbes felt the tension rise.

"Remmert van Braam."

The tension melted away, "Yeah, van Braam was behind the theft."

"Then we can arrest him?"

"It's Okay Gianni, van Braam is dead; I got him."

"Magnifico! Magnifico, then everything is okay?"

"It's going to be."

Chapter Twenty-eight

GEORGE BRAQUE (1882 - 1963)

Queen Mary Hospital, Hong Kong,
Monday, July 5.

QUEEN MARY HOSPITAL'S MAIN WARD TOWER, BLOCK K, is the tallest hospital building in Asia at 28 stories.

Noah became aware of the beep from his monitor. He smelt the antiseptic, and thought *'hospital'*. His eye lids flickered, and then opened. The plain white wall beyond him was broken only by the swirling pattern on his blanket. He turned to look at the monitor. The vital signs flashed, bright green Chinese characters, against the black background. Noah followed a clear plastic tube from an I.V. medical bag, to a needle, snuggly fitted among a swathe of bandages on his left hand, and forearm.

His hand! Suddenly the memory came back to him, he lifted his bandaged arm, but felt nothing. Slowly he rotated the arm, and felt relief flood through him, as he saw his fingers extending from it. They were swollen and bruised, but there were four of them.

With an effort he sent the signal for them to wiggle, nothing.

"Come on move!" he whispered lovingly, but stubbornly they would not.

The monitor beeped with an urgent deliberation.

A nurse entered the room, her crisp white uniform extenuating the darkness of her skin. She checked the monitor, and spoke to Noah. Although he could not understand a word she said, he understood that he should rest, and not wiggle his fingers.

At last he heard the word, "Doctor." He nodded in response, then closed his eyes.

In his own private darkness he waited for the doctor to arrive.

Whether it was moments or minutes later, Noah's next memory was of the door opening and the swish of the curtain being pulled back. The Doctor had arrived. Then he felt pressure over his nose and mouth. Noah's eyes flew open in terror, to reveal a man standing over him. Eyes blazing, intent on smothering him.

THE NURSE AT THE DESK DIRECTED WILLIAM FORBES to Noah Coleman's room, "Thank you, how's he doing?"

She smiled sweetly and replied, "Yes, very good." Her hand gestured toward the room. Forbes smiled in return, and set off.

He entered, and slowly walked over to the curtain which shielded the bed. Carefully he pulled it back, not wanting to disturb a sleeping Noah.

Robert Key, smiled back at Forbes, he had one hand tightly clamped over Noah's mouth, the other hand held a gun, which was quickly aimed at him.

"Nice of you to join us Mr. Forbes, I'll just take care of this cheating scumbag, then I'll attend to you."

Forbes was torn between answering Key's comment, and rushing over to help his friend, but he did neither, because he was tumbling to the floor from a blow to the back of his head.

As he tried to get up, a hefty kick was delivered to his ribs. He waited on all fours, room spinning, for the pain to stop.

"Please be patient Mr. Forbes, I told you your turn will come."

Forbes looked up from the floor, Robert Key was struggling to prepare a hypodermic syringe as Noah struggled under his other hand.

As he fought against Noah's struggles, he spoke, punctuating each word, as he wrestled with Noah's writhing body, "It's, just … a little … sedative … don't want you two causing a … disturbance now … do we?"

The man that had attacked Forbes, turned as the door opened, but relaxed, "Chairs are here, boss," he said in heavily accented English. Forbes thought the accent was Turkish. "Help me get him up," he said.

Instantly two pair of hands clamped down on Forbes body. They dragged him upright, and sat him back in a wheelchair.

Key called for assistance, "Help me keep him still, so I can get this damn needle in his arm,"

Forbes watched the new arrival walk past. "Where are you taking us?" he asked.

"Mr. Chellen want's a word," Key replied.

Forbes knew he had to do something quickly. Noah had undergone a horrific injury, but still managed to save the paintings. He couldn't let it all end like this. He readied his body. "Well, I don't want to see Chellen," he said petulantly.

Key, took a moment to let the words sink in. The other man had arrived at the bed, and began exerting pressure on Noah, forcing him to be still.

"Mr. Chellen always gets what he wants." Key proclaimed.

"Not this time," Springing from the wheelchair, Forbes shoulder barged the Turk, he continued the attack by snapping his fingers forward, catching the man under the nose. As he winced at the assault, Forbes raised his knee, connecting with the groin.

The man holding Noah turned just as Forbes smashed his elbow into the man's cheekbone.

As he went for his gun, Key stabbed the syringe into Noah's bag, the clear fluid became cloudy. He picked up the gun and rounded the bed, "Decision time Ducky, come after me or save Coleman's life?"

Forbes tracked Key. "Oh by the way, I lied about it being a sedative, its poison, Mr. Chellen didn't want him cheating anyone else."

"He's all heart, your boss." They looked at each other, a stalemate.

Key gestured to the saline drip, "Time to make your mind up." As Forbes glanced at the disclourouration sliding down the tube, Key opened the door and ran out, "Tell that little slut Monroe, we'll be back to take care of her ..."

Forbes leapt across to the bed, and hit the alarm button. He took hold of the tube, squeezing it to stop the poison from entering Noah's bloodstream.

The Turk was back on his feet, he quickly aimed a couple of body blows at Forbes, but he kept tight hold of the tube.

In a quick dart forward, Forbes pulled the gun from the Turk's waistband.

He pulled his fist back, to strike again, but Forbes was leveling the gun at him.

The Turk, backed out of the room.

Forbes squeezed the tube, but saw that the darker solution had got past the kink. Unstoppable, it continued to slide down the tube.

A nurse rushed into the room, Forbes shouted, "Get this out of his arm, it's poison!" and with that, he bolted for the door.

In the corridor, two more nurses and a doctor were heading for the room. A gaggle of visitors and cleaning staff were ambling along the brightly lit corridor.

Forbes raised his gun, high above his head, "Everyone down!"

As the people, understanding a ringing alarm, running nurses, and a man with a gun, hit the floor, no problem with translation there, Forbes saw the Turk disappearing around the corner.

Jumping over the nearest visitor, he set off in pursuit.

Forbes crashed through the door, and began winding down the staircase.

As he got to the last level he vaulted over the bannister, and observed a small crowd of people gathered around a man on the floor. As Forbes approached he saw that the man was a security guard. Forbes shouted, "Which way?"

An elderly lady stuck out an accusing finger. Forbes followed the direction.

The general alarms were sounding now. The directional

signs in the corridors meant nothing to him, and soon he became lost in a maze of turns and anonymous doors.

He stopped running. A scream behind him alerted him to the whereabouts of his targets. He backtracked up the corridor.

The sign on the door was white on green, depicting a man running, "Got to be the exit." He pushed the door open and found himself in another stairwell.

This was not so well lit, and only went down. Forbes charged down the stairs, careering off the walls.

Another snippet of raised voices came from below. As Forbes hit the floor running, and burst through the door, a loud piercing scream met him. Alone he tumbled into another soulless corridor. The voices, and rubber-souled shoes squeaked from his left. Forbes dug deep and set off again.

Just beyond another ninety-degree corner, he encountered two more nurses, running toward him. He held up two fingers, "Two men, running?" both nurses nodded and said something fast and unrecognizable, but Forbes followed their pointing fingers with ease.

As he ran, the nurses continued to shout at him, he turned back. One indicated that they had gone into the door on the right. Forbes waved the gun back at them, and they screamed encouragement.

Forbes lent his shoulder against the door, pressed the handle and rushed in. The stillness of the room was broken only by his ragged breathing.

The room was dark and empty. A silent M.R.I. scanner stood in the center of the room. Proceeding cautiously he checked behind, and then inside the machine.

Gasping for breath, Forbes stood in darkness by the scanner.

Suddenly the machine came to life, the mechanical whir began to hum. All around him harsh lights flickered, and then burst into life.

In the harsh light, Forbes could see that a control booth adjoined the scanner room, and even in its darkened state, Forbes could see human outlines standing in the booth.

Forbes stuffed the gun in his waist-band and picked up the mattress from the scanner bed, and in one fluid motion charged toward the windows, and then performed a swallow dive, as would a rugby player executing a try. The mattress, followed by Forbes smashed through the window, shattering the glass into a million tiny flakes.

The lights in the scanner room went off, plunging the room back into an inky black dream. Amidst the darkness and the broken glass Forbes lay, adjusting to his new battlefield, the gun felt good against the hollow of his back.

Key shouted, "Get him." He heard rather than saw the Turk attacking, his shoes crunched on the broken glass.

Forbes rolled and allowed the big man to come on to him, felt his hands reaching down for his collar, felt himself being lifted effortlessly. He waited for the exertion to end, but it didn't, the Turk's fingers moved inward, seeking the throat.

In the darkness the two men grappled. Forbes felt his training returning to him, remembered all those grueling sessions in Hereford, all the bar brawls in Sarajevo, all the life and death hand to hand fighting in Mogadishu.

Since leaving the SAS, life had been good for the boy with the Eton education, he was better than the doctors had diagnosed him. Back then he had nothing to fight for, now he had Senga.

He went for the Turk's eyes, and when the hands came up to protect, he went for the throat. Forbes felt the balance of power shifting.

In the darkness he saw her face smiling. The copper curls tumbling. His strength returned.

A sudden flare of light said that Key had left the booth, Forbes knew he had to get after him quickly. He slammed his elbow into the Turk's nose, then as he went to move a small box hit him on the temple, he dodged another three boxes of latex gloves, before finding the door handle, nothing the Turk could do was going to stop him. Forbes pulled open the door.

Then the hands smashed down on his shoulders, fingers raking for purchase. Forbes felt himself being pulled back into the booth.

He twisted, ducking his shoulder under the attack. When he came upright he fired out a straight front kick to the stomach, which resulted in the Turk clattering back into a rack full of metal objects. The noise, like a peel of bells was loud and uncompromising.

Forbes regained his composure, he hoped that the Turk was unconscious, but that thought was short-lived.

The swish was loud and close, and confirmed that whatever the Turk had crashed into, contained something more deadly than latex gloves.

Forbes embraced the darkness. The hideout beneath Rossini's monument, had been the scene of a success. It had become someone else's tomb, not his, he'd escaped with his life. The cellar in Goussainville-Vieux Pays, had proved lucky, he'd come away with the Luini. The catacombs of Belgrade seemed a distant memory, they still played with his mind, but at least he'd come away with hope.

The scalpel slashed close to his face. He lent back, twisted, and thrust out a vicious side kick. It struck ribs, and sounded final.

Forbes searched for the door. The handle was cool to his touch, he twisted it, and pulled. The light from the corridor spread over him.

He began running after Key, at each footfall, he remembered seeing Key in the underground station; he'd been hunting for Senga. He recalled the conversation in Helsinki. All the time Key had been mocking him, protecting Chellen.

He saw him again now, swiping his pass down the lock of an exit door. But the beep indicated the door was staying locked.

'Security have locked down the exits', he thought.

Key looked up from the door. He moved away, and readied himself for the attack.

It was then that the Turk came lumbering up behind him. Forbes lent back against the wall, glancing at both men. The Turk raised the scalpel, "Let's play."

At that moment a Doctor emerged from a door. He began speaking loudly, he gesticulated, and approached the Turk.

Forbes shouted "No!" but already, the big man had attacked the doctor, wrapping his stethoscope around the man's neck, holding the scalpel close to his face. "Back off Forbes, or Jackie Chan here gets his throat slit." The Turk dragged the struggling doctor past him. He backed him down the corridor closer to the curly-haired Robert Key.

Key waved a finger, "Listen to me Ducky, Mr. Chellen wants

his painting back, and Mr. Chellen always gets what he wants. Whatever it takes Forbes, get it for him, or I'll carve my initials in the Monroe girl with Mr. Obit's little knife."

The Turk gave a mirthless laugh, "I have her scent now." He sniffed the air. They began to back away. Forbes stepped forward. "Don't come any closer!"

Forbes continued to walk forward, he read aloud the name-tag on the doctor's coat, "Doctor Cheng. Don't worry I have this covered." He raised his gun. "They won't hurt you."

Doctor Cheng's eyes widened, he had good knowledge of English, and had understood the threat issued by the man choking him. So why, was the weirdly dressed man in a red waistcoat still walking toward them.

Obit, pulled the doctor in closer. "I mean it Forbes!"

"Kill him, then what?" Forbes moved to a better angle, all the time coming closer, "You won't kill me, you want me to steal the Luini for you, so what are you going to do?"

"Let you have this man's blood on your conscious," Obit, glanced at Key. In response, Key pulled out his own gun, "Are you intending to kill everyone, Forbes?" Obit thought he was going to shoot, but he turned and fired at the door lock.

As Obit's head was turned, Forbes fired, "No, only you," the single bullet ripped into Obit's face. Instantly he let go of the stethoscope, and dropped to the floor.

Dr. Cheng, crouched down on one knee, checking that the warm wet matter dripping from his head had all come from his attacker's face.

Forbes stepped over the doctor, and came face to face with Robert Key.

His hand clamped around his throat, the other chopped

down on Key's gun-hand, the gun clattered to the floor. "When are you going to realize you can't go around threatening innocent people?"

Key tried to respond, but the choking hand, and the pain emulating from his own wrist, stopped him from talking.

As with all bullies, when the tables are turned, their power diminishes.

Forbes smashed the butt of his gun into Key's forehead. The skin tore open. He dropped to the floor, both hands clutching the painful wound.

Forbes smashed a left fist into Key's nose, his involuntary cry confirmed it was broken. "Now go and tell LeCoyte Chellen, that if he ever comes near me, or any of my friends, or if he sends any cheap-shits like you, I will cut lumps off him, and send them to his children for Christmas." Forbes used the gun handle as a club, and battered it into Key's ear.

Key brought his hands up to protect his head. Forbes smashed it down on his fingers as an accompaniment to each word, "Do ...You ... Under ...stand?"

After a moment, Key replied feebly, "Yes."

As Forbes backed away, Dr. Cheng began to administer first-aid to Key.

Forbes watched in amazement, "Is there a doctor in the house?" he wondered why he was looking to help someone who moments before was threatening to kill him. "You can leave him to crawl away now doctor."

Cheng looked up, and asked, in broken English, "What kind of monster are you that can inflict such pain on another human being?"

Forbes shouted back at the little Chinese doctor, "These

monsters come directly from Hell. They are bought and paid for by a powerful evil that believes it can buy anything in life. To him, life is cheap, and death comes quickly to many innocent victims. What kind of monster am I? … I'm the kind that stops them." He began to walk away.

"Then I hope you can live with your nightmares."

"Don't worry about me Doctor, I have pills for that."

NOAH OPENED HIS EYES, "WELL THIS IS BETTER THAN last time." He scratched his chin with his good hand.

"I bet you never thought you'd see us two together? Senga put her arm around Mohini's shoulder. They stood at the foot of Noah's bed.

"Quite the contrary, laying here, I've been thinking about it quite a lot."

Senga blushed, and removed her arm. Mohini lent forward and kissed Noah on the cheek, "Are you feeling better?"

"Yes thank you; now what brings you two ladies to my bed? Besides the obvious."

Senga regained her composure, "Chandhok and Bill will be in shortly, and Chandhok says we need to be sure that our stories all tie up."

"Make sure we know what to say when the police interview us," Mohini smiled, "We might have to tell a few fibs."

"Do you have a problem with that?" Senga asked.

"Certainly not. So, how did Chandhok get you away from van Braam's place?"

Senga smiled a little awkwardly, "I'm sure everything will

be explained shortly, now in the meantime is there anything I can get for you?"

Noah began to answer, but Senga raised her hands and said, "Don't even think about it."

Mohini, had curled up on the bed, and was stroking Noah's hair. The door opened and Chandhok Nahmad entered the room.

Noah was not blind to the look that passed between him and Senga.

Forbes followed him in, looking bruised and battered.

"Bill are you okay? Senga asked.

"Are you alright Mr. Forbes? You look awful." Mohini asked.

"Hey, number one patient in ear-shot," Noah interrupted.

"I'm fine," Forbes sat heavily in the chair.

"Please," Nahmad raised his hands, "Can we talk about what we should say when interviewed; the police will be here soon." They all mumbled an agreement.

"Should the authorities discover the actual parts we have all played during the time since the five paintings were stolen from Paris; I think we might all have our future aspirations curtailed quite dramatically."

Senga thought about the Oleg. Noah thought about Madame X, the Olegs, and his intention to copy the five stolen paintings, "That's true."

Forbes coughed, and raised his hand, "I'll kick this off. I will submit a report that confirms that I believe that Remmert van Braam, masterminded the theft of the five paintings from the Museum of Modern Art, Paris; May the nineteenth. Interpol will support my findings."

"Let's hear it then," Noah encouraged.

"The actual theft was executed by an employee of van Braam, we believe his name was Thomas Woolner, although his real identity will probably never be known. He was assisted in the getaway by Tommaso Buscetti. It was van Braam's plan to have Woolner kill Buscetti after the theft, probably have some burned remnants of canvases, to make us believe the paintings had been destroyed. However, Buscetti had hired Giovanni Mosca, to kill Woolner and take the paintings for themselves. It didn't quite work out, but, Mosca did end up with the paintings. He gave them to Charles Crombie, someone that he had had dealings with in the past. Crombie, as head of Sotheby's then explored a number of avenues for disposal. As investigator for the theft, I interviewed a number of suspects, but I always thought it was LeCoyte Chellen."

"We all make mistakes," Nahmad looked at Senga.

"But I was so sure ..." Forbes shook his head.

"Bill, the summary, please," Noah reminded him.

"During my investigations, it appears Woolner was following me, in the hope of identifying his assailant, and recovering the paintings for van Braam. He identified Mosca, and killed him in Verona. That's where I found the link to Senga."

"You got that wrong too," Senga reminded him, her smile said it didn't matter.

"After I interviewed Miss Monroe..."

Senga winced at the simple pronunciation of her name, Chandhok smiled at her knowingly.

"Woolner followed her to St Tropez, having utilized van Braam's extensive criminal network to establish that Chellen was not going to see me in Helsinki."

Chandhok intervened, "Please to explain that Miss Monroe

was seeking advice in St Tropez, as to whether she should rekindle a relationship with a former lover."

"I'll be sure to mention that."

"The couple she confided in, work for me, and are therefore very relevant in your report." Nahmad winked at Noah.

"Thank you," Forbes brought the conversation back to the timeline of events, "Charles Crombie attempted to kill Miss Monroe, and myself, because we had stumbled upon the hiding place of the five stolen paintings."

Senga nodded her approval of his choice of words.

Forbes continued, "Crombie took the paintings to Paris, where Woolner killed him ..."

"Do we know who he was intending to meet in Paris?" Chandhok asked.

"No, there were just two fictitious names in his diary ..."

"Why was Woolner in Paris?" Noah asked.

"He'd followed you and Senga there, after killing Daisy."

"Thank you." Noah said quietly.

"Woolner brought the paintings to Hong Kong. van Braam wanted to make sure they were authentic, so he took them to Mr. Nahmad's art studio, to check them on the Gilardoni Radiolite X-ray machine."

"A place he knew well, and had 'no questions asked' access," Mohini added.

Nahmad interjected, "Where the brave Mr. Coleman, took, and hid the stolen paintings, substituting blank canvases in van Braam's case."

Forbes felt a little deflated at the revelation that Nahmad knew that the paintings were safe. "Mr. Coleman, also informed the ALR, that van Braam had the paintings. Along with government officials, I attempted to arrest van Braam, but he and Thomas Woolner tried to escape. They were killed whilst trying."

Nahmad stepped in again, "Mr. Coleman is still in my employ, acting as head tutor to a number of up and coming art students ...Naturally he is under contract not to disclose any of my future plans." He inclined his head, waiting for an affirmation.

"Absolutely. Secret to the grave, cross my heart," Noah mimed the action.

Nahmad bowed graciously, happy for the moment that at least his plans for Hastings and Sexton would remain a secret. Noah continued ... "I'm sure my remuneration package will reflect my status."

"Only to be expected, after all it's a job for life, Mr. Coleman ... only your discretion will determine how long you remain in the position for." The threat was thinly veiled.

Forbes felt frustrated at the thought of the veil of secrecy being drawn over the information. He desperately wanted to get Coleman on his own; however Nahmad seemed to have thought of everything. He watched Mohini, giggling at Noah's shoulder, and wondered how much she was being paid to keep an eye on him, and keep him quiet.

"And that just leaves Miss Monroe's involvement," Nahmad said, with a hint of 'do not ask Coleman anything' behind the words.

All eyes turned to Senga.

Forbes recited the words which he'd discussed with Nahmad in the helicopter. "Miss Monroe, purchased a very expensive artifact on behalf of Mr. Nahmad. Which has now been paid for."

"The full price?" Senga asked.

Nahmad nodded in answer.

"Miss Monroe, also procured a painting for the Hong Kong exhibition. This must be returned to the Met, in its original condition."

"Agreed." The smile seemed to hurt him, "It is the least I can do to repair the relationship. There have been many misunderstandings between myself and Miss Monroe, over the years." Nahmad's hand went to cover his heart.

Angrily, Senga spoke quickly, her words directed at Nahmad "Like at the gates of Lachaise cemetery, when you informed me that Bill had been killed by the assassin that tried to kill me …and that I needed to come to Hong Kong with you, to be safe!"

Noah broke the ensuing silence …"So it wasn't technically a kidnap then?"

Nahmad, waved both hands in a frantic denial, "And as soon as I learned that the information about Mr. Forbes was incorrect, I informed you immediately."

Senga's face had set, "Yesterday."

"And now you are free to make your choice."

"I already have," Senga moved to Forbes's side. The sarcastic smile in Nahmad's direction, was more final than a Decree Absolute.

Forbes pondered again on Nahmad's big plans for the future, he had accepted the lost opportunity to copy the stolen paintings without any real complaint. He knew that Noah was the key. But it was all superfluous, Nahmad was soon going to be arrested.

Noah asked, "Do you think that version of events will be accepted?"

"Miss Monroe and I are perfectly happy with the contents of my report," Forbes squeezed her hand.

Mohini made a little whooping sound, and snuggled in, squeezing Noah's shoulders, "That means you can stay with me."

Senga squeezed Forbes's arm, "And the name William Forbes will became as famous as Howard Carter, for discovering the lost Luini."

"And recovering the paintings," Noah added.

Nahmad broke the mood, "Yes, although he illegally entered the property, caused criminal damage; and stole a number of other artifacts from the site. I would worry that your fame may not be seen as fortuitous with LeCoyte Chellen, I think today's disturbance would bear witness to that." His eyebrows raised to emphasize the severity of the attempt on their lives.

"The Luini, and the Oleg," Noah said quietly, looking at Senga.

"It's such a shame that Mr. Chellen is not part of our conspiracy. I leave that part up to you to sort out," Nahmad bowed in Forbes's direction.

Forbes smiled, "I've sent a message to LeCoyte Chellen. He won't be bothering us again."

"That's comforting to know, not as comforting as my foresight not to leave my fingerprints on the paintings, but comforting none the less." Nahmad enjoyed seeing Forbes deflate.

Chapter Twenty-nine

JACKSON POLLOCK (1912 - 1956)

Hong Kong,
Tuesday, July 6.

IT HAD BEEN A LONG JOURNEY, FROM THE MUSEUM OF Modern Art, the day after the theft, through the discovery of Senga's existence in Verona, to their near death experiences in London and Paris, to the ultimate luxurious relaxation in the Jacuzzi, with champagne, in a fabulous hotel, in Hong Kong.

Senga carefully poured herself another chilled glass, as she pressed home her point, "Nahmad told me you were dead, that's why I ..."

"It doesn't matter, we're together now. We have the paintings..." he pressed the button, and Senga giggled as the bubbles assaulted her body.

"Shame you couldn't connect Chandhok to the paintings."

"Let's not talk, shop tonight," Forbes blew her a kiss.

"But I want to say sorry." She brought her knees up. The thick suds dripped off her.

"You can do that in other ways ..." His hand caressed her thigh.

Her hand clamped down on his, "Let's order more champagne."

"Good idea, we don't want to be disturbed later," he kissed her, her mouth opened, and they kissed.

He broke away and raised himself out of the bath. "Champagne, on its way."

"You look so much better out of your clothes." Senga brazenly admired his toned body.

"Thank you, I'm a bit battered and bruised, but I can still hold my own."

"Oh, I was hoping you'd let me do that," she giggled.

She watched him, standing unashamedly naked by the phone. He ordered the champagne, whilst looking at her.

"We better put robes on." He began to towel himself dry.

Senga stood slowly, allowing the water to slide from her sleek body. He was lost in her beauty, he held out the towel and cocooned her in it; they kissed again.

"Maybe you should get some new suits made while we're out here," she suggested, whilst taking the antique ivory Toucan-billed hair-grip from her copper curls, and allowing her hair to cascade over her shoulders.

"Why, what's wrong with my tweeds?"

"They're…green."

"Green's an earthy colour. Highland-green, it's Scottish, like you."

"I could see you in …black." She put the antique ivory Toucan-billed hair-grip in her mouth, as she wrestled with her hair.

Forbes lent forward and took it, "I think you should only ever wear this," he held up the hair-grip, "Or nothing at all."

"I look good in both." She tried to grab the hair-grip, but he snatched it away.

"And some nice crisp white shirts."

"For you or me?"

She lifted up the hem of the towel, "Both?"

The door-bell sounded. Forbes grabbed a robe, and put the hair-grip in the pocket, then went to the door.

Senga followed him, twisting her copper curls in her hands, "You'll look so sexy in black."

"It'll be like I'm going to a funeral."

"Hell no, I bet you'd like to see me in something black."

He turned, "Now there's an idea, do they do nylon out here?"

The waiter handed him the silver champagne ice-bucket. He turned, and Senga took it from him, "Give him a little something, it's a long way up here." She danced away with the champagne.

"He came up in the lift," said Forbes as he went to fetch his wallet. Senga took the bottle out of the ice bucket, and ripped off the foil.

"It's a 2004, is that a good year?"

"Definitely."

Her fingers gripped the neck, and she started to ease her thumbs behind the cork, "Ooh, I've always wanted to do this." The Hong Kong skyline looked resplendent behind her.

Forbes gave the waiter a tip, but he remained at the door. Senga watched them from beneath veiled eyes, her tongue thrust between tight lips in an effort to help remove the cork.

"Don't spill any," he shouted back over his shoulder, then turned his attention to the waiter, "Yes?"

The waiter pointed to the floor, "Have you seen this, sir?"

Forbes stepped out of the room, "What?" he asked following the pointed finger.

An ornate picture frame rested against the wall, the beige paper-back of the picture faced outward. A bright yellow Post-it note was attached to the center.

Written on the Post-it were the words "To Bill, and Senga, Return to Sender."

The waiter smiled, gave a traditional bow, and turned to leave.

Forbes stepped out of the suite, and picked up the picture, turning it over in his hands, "Portrait in Valencia," he whispered.

"It's coming," Senga shouted, as the cork started to slide up the neck.

Forbes stood in the corridor looking at the painting, he remembered that it was this painting that had caused such a ruckus at Sotheby's, "Senga?" he began, then he recalled that Noah had mentioned, *The Luini, and the Oleg"* in connection to Chellen's wrath.

"Come on," Senga shouted back, her thumbs applying pressure to the cork; and then with an effervescent pop it exploded from the bottle.

The explosion ripped through the peaceful hotel suite. The shockwave ballooned outward from the bottle. The force displaced every molecule it passed. The airwaves rippled through Senga's flesh and muscles so quickly that they detached at her joints. Her lungs collapsed. Her bones fractured instantly, expelling razor sharp splinters that tore through her skin.

The windows burst, unable to contain the force of the explosion. The window frames tore out of their concrete supports, dislodging the very fabric of the outer wall.

In addition to strength, explosive materials display a second characteristic, which is their shattering effect, or Brisance, (from the French word, *briser,* to break).

The characteristic is of primary importance in determining the effectiveness of an explosion. Basically the rapidity with which an explosive reaches its peak pressure, is the measure of its brisance.

The explosive that had been put in the bottle, was one that reached its maximum pressure so quickly, that a shock-wave was formed, shattering everything in its path.

The floor gave way. A tangle of shattered body parts, splintered materials, and carpet-fibers, tumbled down into the suite below.

From the epicenter of the chaos, the shock-wave broke-in on itself, and distorted again, sucking back the air it had displaced. Dust generated and billowed through the vacuum created by the rapid expulsion of air.

Instantly the dust consumed the space filled by the air, and produced a choking cloud that escaped through the torn windows, and wrecked floor.

William Forbes felt the force of the explosion, like an express train in the middle of his back. It lifted him, and propelled him down the corridor, away from the shattering. The force of the shock-wave drove him into the back of the waiter, whose body acted like a cushion when they crashed into the wall.

The explosion had slammed the suite-door back into its frame, forming a momentary bund. Then it shattered, ripping the interior wall with it, opening down the corridor like a zip.

The direction of the force had been through the bottom of the bottle, through Senga, and down into the floor, and out through the window behind her. Now, as the shock-wave turned in upon itself, the oxygen was pulled along the corridor, whipping and driving a dust cloud back into the epicenter of the room.

The fire-alarms sounded, and the sprinklers began to cascade a fine mist.

Forbes tasted blood in his mouth. He tried to wiggle his fingers, but nothing worked. The waiter beneath him was dead, crushed to a pulp.

In an instant, Forbes knew that Senga was dead too, the thought numbed him.

Someone rolled him over, and allowed the cold water to fall onto his blood stained face. "I think they're both dead," a voice declared from another world.

As the water trickled into his mouth, he pushed his hand deep into his pocket, and grasped the antique ivory Toucan-billed hair-grip, the movement proved he was still alive, but at least with the hair-grip in his hand, he knew he could die happy.

As other guests ran, screaming from their rooms, he lay, unable to move. Another voice from a distant land professed that, "He's dead, leave him."

As he lay he let his imagination put the pieces together; Chellen had been the buyer of Senga's fake Oleg. He, himself had stolen the Luini from under Chellen's nose, as a couple they had become prime targets for Chellen's revenge.

As Forbes's world closed down around him, and he balanced between life and death, he imagined that giving Robert Key a beating had done nothing but incense Chellen, *"I will cut lumps off him, and send them to his children for Christmas."* The threat had probably not helped. But this revenge, this was in another league, this was insane. The hand of God squeezed his heart, trying and failing to crush the sorrow. He'd lost everything. He had nothing left to give, only his life.

As he drifted into unconsciousness death held no fear. He satisfied his grief knowing that Senga was already there, waiting for him.

Chapter Thirty

Noah Coleman (1955 -)

Hotel, Auberge du Raisin.
Wednesday, August 4.

NOAH COLEMAN FLEXED HIS LEFT HAND, IT WAS THE first time he had driven since the operation, and it was still stiff.

He carried his battered old brown leather overnight bag from the car, and dropped it on the ground as he waited for the front door to be opened.

A jet screamed overhead.

After a few moments an elderly woman pulled the door open, she held a cat in her arms. Her dull weathered face gave the impression he was not welcome.

"C'est ferme," her crooked fingers stroked the cat's head.

"Madame Aspasie?" he noticed the pulls and holes in her cardigan sleeve.

"Oui," she replied suspiciously.

"The hotel was recommended, by a friend ..."

"We are closed," she had a whistle in her voice. The door started to close.

"But why? I would have expected the hotel to be full of art-lovers."

Her glazed expression did not change, "Why?"

"Is this not the hotel where the painting was found?"

"Tut, you know the story then?"

"Of course, doesn't everyone?"

"The painting that that man stole, it belonged to the owners of the hotel, and that is by law."

"You're so right. I'd like to discuss that fact with you. May I come in?"

She opened the door. The cat meowed.

Inside, the hotel smelled of cat and neglect.

"You were saying about the owners, and their rights to the painting?"

"The grand men from the museum came to talk with Sasha and Justine. They spoke about duty, and history. They were bullied into letting the museum keep the painting." Her voice whistled a lisp on the letter 'S'.

"The Luini will be appreciated by thousands. Surely the owners understand that?"

"No, they only understood the money." She put down the cat, which immediately rubbed itself against her legs.

"What money?"

"The museum gave them five hundred thousand euros."

"Half a million!" Noah exclaimed, "That's fantastic."

"Each."

"Even better, you must be proud?" Noah felt a little put out that he had only received one million for the Da Vinci sketch.

"No, I feel nothing for them, the girls left me alone. They have gone to sing their songs in America."

"The land of opportunity."

Madame Aspasie spat out her answer with venom and true hatred, "America is a decedent waste of resource, hooked on fossil fuels, like a kid on heroin." A jet flew over to support her claim.

"That's low," Noah glanced up, as if he would be able to see the plane.

"Every day, the same, they land and they take off." She grimaced, and performed the Gallic shrug. She moved behind the reception desk, "So you want a room, how long?"

"Two nights," Noah's smile was disarming.

Madame Aspasie, opened up the register. "What are you going to do here for two days?"

"Could you tell me, did the museum take anything else from the cellar?" Noah asked innocently, while all the while knowing the truth.

"Not everything, but I know now why you are here. I know why a friend recommended the hotel. You want to know about my pot du vin." Her old eyes twinkled.

"Jug of wine?" Noah asked. Madame Aspasie, rubbed her finger and thumb together, indicating money.

"Bribe?" Asked Noah

"Of course the bribe, Sasha and Justine allowed me to stay in the hotel, for the rest of my life, and allowed me to keep everything that remained in the trunks." The lisp was strong.

"I imagined that they would contain such beautiful things," she said slowly, the whistling lisp giving a sing-song lilt to her comments. "My great grandparents worked in the chateau." There was an undeniable pride to her voice now.

"A very generous accommodation, I'm sure."

"How long do you think I have left to live?" Her hand slapped the counter, a small cloud of dust rose into the air. "Five years tops. Bah, they took the sacks of silver, all that's left in the trunks are dresses, trinkets, and toiletries. They knew what they were doing when they made their deal."

"You still have them here?"

"Yes, someone is coming from Paris next week, to put a value on the trinkets, if I'm lucky, I'll get enough for the winter."

"May I see them?"

"As you wish." The old woman tilted her head back and cackled, the sound was a mixture of mirth and evil, her thin lips drew back in a gesture faintly resembling a smile; revealing she had already lost a number of teeth. "Maybe I should open up for business, if fools like you are wanting to see some old clothes."

Madame Aspasie, led Noah into the private lounge. The three trunks had been placed on the floor.

Noah looked at the jumble, "I don't believe it." The first trunk had its lid open, it was tilted back against a table.

She pointed to it with her crooked finger, "That is the trunk where they found the painting."

Noah approached the trunk slowly, and peered inside. "I don't believe it."

"It's empty now of course."

"Of course."

The second trunk was in the middle of the room, a bundle of clothing spilled over the top. The straps to the lid were broken, so it had been turned upside down and placed on the table.

Noah lovingly touched a cotton dress which lay on top of the bundle.

"There is no value in this," said Noah rummaged through the clothing.

"No more paintings, I have already looked," she cackled again.

Noah scooped out a ball-gown, and a night-dress, he placed them in the upturned lid. His fingers traced around the edges of the trunk, feeling where the straps had been cut.

"These were also inside the trunk," the old woman gestured to three bone-handled bedroom pieces.

Noah touched them lightly with his fingers. He noticed a long dark hair trapped in the hairbrush bristles.

"Brush, comb, and mirror. They're for sale, make me an offer."

Noah lifted the mirror and held it in front of his face. The edges were tarnished, where brown spots had seeped into the reflection. Noah looked into the mirror, it was too small to reflect the whole of his face; only his eyes looked back at him.

The eyes without a face, suddenly he thought of Daisy. "I would very much like to buy these from you-"

"One-thousand euros!" the old woman answered quickly.

"What? I'm sorry Madame Aspasie, but that is ten times the true value."

"No Monsieur, you seem to know what you are looking for; and you know the price you will ask on the fancy streets of Paris. In fact you know the price of everything, yet you know the value of nothing. These items are all rich in history, I will not sell for less than one-thousand."

"For one-thousand euros, I would want everything, including the trunks."

"So you did come to make me an offer." She wagged a finger at him.

Noah approached the third trunk, the lid was closed. Madame Aspasie, put her hand down on the lid. "The trinkets are in here, you can have a look for two-thousand euros."

"Why would I want to do that?"

"Because I have someone coming from Paris to value the contents, until then, I would be foolish to let anything go for less than the worth. You suggested one-thousand for everything, which means you have seen something for more. If you want to look, it will cost you two-thousand."

"Have you ever played poker?" Noah asked.

The old woman did not blink, "You came to make me an offer, go ahead."

"What will you take?"

"Five-thousand."

"Sight unseen?"

"Yes, are you a gambling man?"

Noah laughed with pure joy, "Yes I am."

"I know what is in this trunk," her eyes sparkled, "Five-thousand euros, and everything is yours. You must ask yourself, do you trust an old lady?"

As Noah ran his finger over the edge of the trunk, he asked, "The three trunks, and all the contents, and a bed for the night."

The old woman took out her fan, she opened it and fanned herself, "But no breakfast." A jet roared overhead.

"Not even coffee, and homemade bread from the bakery?"

"Will you be paying cash?" Her thin lips pursed.

Noah took out his wallet, she could see the notes folded neatly, "And marmalade?"

"You will have to take everything with you, in the morning."

"Of course," Noah put his wallet on the table and lifted the mirror and stared into the eyes without a face. He thought his own eyes looked very honest and trustworthy. Surely the old woman would have some idea of the value of the trinkets, and had set the five-thousand price tag accordingly. He looked at her. Her own sparkling eyes almost gave away her secret, almost.

Madame Aspasie, lifted her hand, "Deal?"

"Yes," Noah shook her hand, "but I want to open the last trunk and go through it alone."

"As you wish, but I would like the cash before we go any further."

Noah peeled off five-thousand euros.

"I will prepare your room for one night, and order the bread." She shuffled out of the room, pursued by the cat.

Alone, Noah carefully opened the lid. The trinkets were heaped on two blue and cream cushions which sat on top of the contents. Noah picked them out, and placed them on the table.

A Georgian double-heart pendant, set in silver, encrusted with Garnets and paste, probably Scottish circa 1750, value two-hundred euros.

Three belle époque long guard chains, one with a pretty silver pendant of moonstone and amethyst, fifty-euros no more. He allowed them to fall back on the cushions.

The next layer came into view. Expertly embroidered gay golden flowers bloomed upon the dark crimson background of a pair of drapes.

His heartbeat began to increase. Carefully he unfolded the curtains that had lain un-disturbed for 150 years.

Their full length unfolded before him, he laid them over the back of a chair.

Next was a small Appenzel lace tablecloth, as he un-folded it, a half-dozen lace handkerchiefs fell to the floor.

Noah dipped his hands back into the trunk. He began to un-load faster, not bothering to check the items, not caring about the value.

Two linen sheets were quickly unfolded, but nothing was hidden between them. He dug deeper into the trunk, emptying it as if he were bailing water from a sinking boat.

There was only one layer to go. Noah pulled out, what he thought to be a banquet linen tablecloth. It felt heavy, too heavy. He rested it on the table and carefully began to un-fold it. In the centre he discovered a round lace table cloth. "Well that's not going to buy an Aston. So what's left?"

Knowing the answer before he looked, Noah saw that the trunk was empty. He glanced around him at all the linen and cloth items spread over the table. The trinkets twinkled back at him from the cushions.

He allowed his fingers to fondle the Alencon point de gaze hand-made linen bedspread, as he totted up the values.

"Five-hundred euros the lot. Trinkets, about the same. So all in all, one thousand, and I paid five. Well, well, well, seems that Madame Aspasie, is a pretty shrewd gambler. Unfortunately for you Madame, I'm shrewder." He looked at the empty trunks.

He wiped his nose with the back of his hand, "Empty."

As if looking for inspiration, he delved deep into the closest trunk. Only the makers label looked back at him. He was glad he was alone because the tears had begun to flow freely now.

He looked up to heaven, and said, "Oh, Daisy, look at what I've got."

A jet roared overhead. He sniffed back more tears, then looked into all the empty trunks once more. At each one he quietly read the name on the maker's label, "Louis Vuitton."

"Oh Daisy, do you remember I told you that the Louis Vuitton label was founded by Monsieur Vuitton in 1854, in a small shop on the Rue des Capucines, in Paris?"

Noah checked the damage to the lid of the second trunk. "In 1858, Monsieur Vuitton introduced flat-bottom trunks, made out of Trianon canvas, making them lightweight and airtight. Before the introduction of Vuitton's trunks, rounded-tops were used to allow water to run off during travelling, but naturally they could not be stacked." He began placing the bundles of clothing back inside the trunks.

"It was Vuitton's grey Trianon canvas flat trunk that allowed the ability to stack for voyages that revolutionised the travel industry." Lovingly Noah closed the lids on all three trunks.

"Quickly he became successful and the brand very prestigious. Other luggage makers began to imitate Vuitton's style and design. It was the first example of brand forgery," Noah wiped his eyes.

"To protect against the duplication of his look, Vuitton changed the Trianon design to beige and brown in 1862. Examples of the grey trunks are rarer than Rocking-horse shit, and I have three of them."

Noah estimated that the three almost pristine examples standing before him would fetch a conservative one-million euros each.

"I don't believe it. I just love old suitcases."

411

Chapter Thirty-one

GIAN LORENZO BERNINI (1598 – 1680)

Suvarnabhumi Airport, Bangkok.
Monday August 9.

LOCATED IN THE BANG PHLI DISTRICT, ABOUT SIXTEEN miles east of Bangkok, Suvarnabhumi Airport, has the tallest control tower, and the third largest, single building airport terminal in the world, catering for all major international airlines.

It also has an exclusive runway catering for executive private jets, with a private reception terminal to allow the fastest processing for Asia's most important executives.

Lam Bok San, was everyone's idea of a fussy example of Thailand's younger generation. He flounced about the lounge, looking to please his clientele during the short time it took them to pass through immigration.

It seemed to everyone that his responsibility was that every person would receive a smile, and be treated like a king whilst in his domain.

He made everyone feel special.

He had worked in immigration for nearly four years. During that time his powers of observation had improved over one-thousand percent, his knowledge of how to read people was now as wide as his smile. Like a reflection in a mirror, whatever you projected, was reflected, in gratuities far and above the normal.

Now, as he watched the latest set of executives walking from the *Gulfstream IV*, he noticed that nine of the twelve passengers were men, they would receive his first attentions. Of the nine, four were wearing the same beige-linen suit, by Armani, only one of which was fake. He began to warm-up his smile for the three elegant dressers.

The leather that each carried in their hands, and the gold they wore upon their wrists would need closer scrutiny, before he could fully appreciate which were his ultimate priorities.

"Quick, quick." San, clapped his hands, and the four, beautifully made-up, ground attendants, dressed in traditional emerald-green Thai dresses, prepared the relaxing hot-towels, and trays of ice-cold champagne for their guests. After all, it had been an arduous one-hundred meter walk from the jet to the air-conditioned lounge, in the punishing midday heat.

"Hello, welcome," the pretty girls welcomed the passengers, some took the towels, most took the champagne.

Lam Bok San, made polite conversation to his primary guest, a forty thousand dollar Rolex, elevating the man to number one status. "How was the flight, do you have any special needs while here in Bangkok?" his voice was hypnotic, but all the time he watched from the corner of his dark eye for the single trailer of luggage, hauled over by two porters. He only had limited time to use his observational powers on his primaries.

Soon the internal glass doors would slide open, and more exotic ground attendants would escort the executives through

413

passport-control, assist in identifying their luggage, and finally see them through the customs hall. Once past there, the limousine drivers would take over, and whatever profession, career or intent they planned pursuing in Thailand would be lost to him.

The minutes passed by, certain guests looked around anxiously, wanting to put down their empty glasses. San realized something was wrong, they never usually took this long.

Lam Bok San, was forced away from his primary, he reluctantly took the empty glasses, asking if they would like refills. They did not. They wanted to get out of the airport. Quickly.

With an arthritic sigh, the glass doors slid open, San, breathed a happy sing-song, "Ladies and Gentlemen, would you please follow me."

But, instead of more pretty girls, bowing and smiling, it was two distressed looking porters, with two burly security officers, looking serious and focused. They approached two of the guests, sitting on a leather sofa.

"Senior, Juan del Marco Enrique Cassavanurnez?" one officer read from a passport.

A grey haired, dark skinned individual nodded. Lam Bok San, was immediately at their side, "Is there a problem?"

The officer looked cynically at the effeminate immigration receptionist, "Go play Mummy to the important passengers," he barked in Thai. Then turned back to the Spaniard.

Cassavanurnez, looked up, "Yes, what is the problem?"

The porter, spoke quietly, and politely, his voice full of apology, "I'm afraid your luggage has been damaged, please can you accompany me, to assess the damage, and fill out a claim form." His hand shot out, gesturing the direction.

Cassavanurnez got to his feet. He was about to go with

the porter when he turned to the man he'd been sitting with. Casually he offered him his business card, "Just in case this takes some time, here is my card, and please feel free to call me tonight, I would like to continue our conversation. Should you want company at dinner, of course?"

San thought that it would be a dinner he'd have loved to have attended, he tried to see the identity of the sitting man, but an Indian woman pushed her empty flute into his chest. He heard the man respond...

"That is very kind of you Senior Cassavanurnez, it would be my pleasure."

San, saw the fingers reach out and take the card, and place it in his shirt pocket. San looked to identify the passenger, but the bulky guard was in the way.

As San smiled and collected more towels and glasses, he saw that the second officer, and porter, remained in place, San strained to hear the seated man say, "I suppose my bag is damaged too? Who is responsible?" he sounded angry, as is often the case with aggressors, he was desperate to lay the blame at someone else's door. Lam Bok San deduced the accent was German, or maybe Dutch.

San collected more glasses as he watched all the men go through the doors. They sighed closed.

"More champagne, please be seated, we will not keep you a moment longer than necessary," San clapped his hands, and the girls appeared magically with more bubbling wine.

THE ROOM WAS STERILE WHITE, LIT BY A SINGLE high-wattage strip-light. The room contained just one piece of furniture, a plain wooden table, and two metal chairs bolted to the floor. Sitting upon the table was Cassavanurnez's, Valextra Avietta, wheeled carry-on bag. One of the Pirelli wheels, and the name tag were positioned next to it.

"The time is twelve-twenty. Can you identify this bag as your own?" the officer asked.

"Yes, of course." Cassavanurnez ran his finger down a deep gouge in the lacquered edge. "How did this happen?"

The officer, ignored the question, and asked, "May I ask that you open the bag, just to confirm none of the items are damaged."

"Of course," Cassavanurnez opened the bag.

The officer slipped on a pair of latex gloves, "I am so sorry, but I need to search."

"Be my guest, it's going to cost you a lot of money, so enjoy it." The luggage set retailed at seven-thousand US dollars.

The officer completed his search, and closed the bag. "Thank you sir, now we can fill out the claim form, and I can be your witness."

"How much time will this take, can we not complete the form at the hotel?"

"As you wish sir," the porter took the bag.

Cassvanurnez's mobile rang, "I'm with your driver; can you estimate how much longer those idiots will be keeping you?"

He recognised the Dutch voice as the man he'd sat with on the sofa, he must have used his business card to get his mobile number. "Tell him I'm on my way, thank you for your concern."

EYES WITHOUT A FACE

"Ah, luxury at last, I have just seen your limousine, a black S600. Mine is silver."

Cassavanurnez, looked through the glass panelled exit, "Mercedes?"

"Yes, finest car in the world." He entered the car via the rear door.

"I see you," Cassavanurnez, observed the door closing on his new friend. He watched the silver S600 Mercedes pull away from the curb. The shadowy hand of LeCoyte Chellen waved back at him.

From his own air-conditioned, double glazed luxury, Cassavanurnez watched the traffic ebb and flow on the Expressway. Four cars ahead, standing out clearly from the ubiquitous black and yellow taxis, the silver Mercedes glowed in the bright sunshine.

Three, small two-stroke motorbikes buzzed past the black S-class, weaving in and out of the traffic. Cassavanurnez watched the riders' shirts and football shorts billow in the wind. The youth of the city, a generation of eternal optimists, they never thought about crashing.

Cassavanurnez watched as they took up station, either side of the silver Mercedes. In the back of his mind he recognised something was wrong with the unfolding scene. Why would the riders be content with staying in their current formation?

He looked out of the side window, they passed four, five other suicide death-traps making their way to the busy capital. Each thin young male rider intent on defying the gods, none wore any protection. Colourful Tee-shirts and ink-black hair flapping in the wind, their eyes squeezed shut, their teeth set to prevent the high pitch scream of the engine from dislodging their filings …

"Helmets!" Cassvanurnez looked through the windscreen, the bikes still formed a guard around the silver S600. Each rider was wearing a shiny black full-face helmet.

In lurid slow motion, the riders, perfectly balanced, pulled out pistols from their baggy shirts. Cassavanurnez gripped the seat as he watched in horror, as they began firing into the car.

The silver Mercedes swerved away from the bike like a startled woman pursued by a wasp. The third motorcycle followed the S-class, as it strayed over the three lanes. The rider fired into the rear window, it cracked, broke, disintegrated before his eyes. Then they were upon them, the black Mercedes swept past the action. The side windows were both missing, the bodywork riddled with bullet holes.

"Wait, we must stop and help!" Cassavanurnez screamed at the chauffer.

Without taking his eyes from the busy road, the small driver eased out into the fast lane, put his foot down and quickly replied, "No sir, we must not stop."

Cassvanurnez took his mobile from his pocket, "What's the number for the police?" he turned to see the silver Mercedes zipping down the slip road, the three motorbikes in hot pursuit.

The driver pressed a button on the steering wheel, and began talking urgently into the car phone.

Cassavanurnez continued to look out of the rear window, but the slip road was fast disappearing, and the space was taken up with innocent traffic, eager to continue its journey. He looked at his watch, it was two-minutes past one; he knew the time would be important when he gave his statement to the police. It was probably the last time that he would ever see LeCoyte Chellen alive again.

THE ROOM WAS STERILE WHITE, LIT BY A SINGLE high-wattage strip-light. The room contained just one piece of furniture, a plain wooden table and two metal chairs bolted to the floor. Sitting upon the table were three, twenty eight inch Swaine Adeney Brigg, handmade red-leather Windsor suitcases.

"The time is twelve-twenty. Can you identify these bags as your own?" the officer asked.

LeCoyte Chellen examined the cases, "They're mine, but what's the damage?"

The officer, ignored the question, and asked, "May I ask that you open the bags, just to confirm none of the items are damaged."

"What's going on, you said my luggage had been damaged?"

The officer slipped on a pair of latex gloves, "I am so sorry, but I need to search."

"This is bullshit…"

The door opened, and Lam Bok San entered the room, his smile was not so wide, "I would ask you again Mr. Zuidof, please to open your suitcases."

"My name is LeCoyte Chellen." His skin was almost translucent under the harsh lighting. The walk from the jet had been torturous, his fair skin prickled.

"As you wish. Please take a seat." San sat in the chair, with his back to the door. Chellen walked around the table, and sat at the far side. The latex-gloved officer reclined against the wall.

"I think we should start again, is this the passport you presented for our customs department?" San opened the passport, and pushed it across the desk.

"That's not mine." Chellen's hands rested on the table.

"But it is your photograph," Lam Bok San turned the passport around to allow Chellen a better view.

Chellen brought his hands up in front of his pale face, as if he were using a cocktail shaker. "It is someone who looks like me, but I gave my passport to the flight attendant when I got on the plane, she must have given me this one by mistake."

"By mistake?"

"Yes, by mistake." His jowls wobbled.

"But no one else has been affected. Nobody else on the private jet is saying they received the wrong passport."

"What about the guy in the photo?"

"A man with a Dutch passport, who looks like you, talks with American accent. I'm sorry there was no one else on the flight that matches that description."

"Bullshit, I'm LeCoyte Chellen, chairman of the Chellen Corporation, and no lady-boy is going to tell me any different."

Lam Bok San ignored the insult, "Do you have any other identification?"

Chellen reached into his Armani jacket, and pulled out his Ettinger-sterling orange billfold wallet. He opened it and began to pull out his AmEx card. His mouth dropped open. "This is not my wallet!" He threw it on the table.

Lam Bok San picked up the wallet, and extracted the AmEx card, "Jan Zuidof. So, how do you explain this?"

Chellen jumped up, and ripped off the jacket, "This is not my jacket." The situation was spiralling out of control.

Lam Bok San spoke slowly, with more than a hint of sarcasm. "I suppose you were given it by mistake?"

Chellen recognised the tone, and took a step forward, the officer imitated the movement.

"That would be a big mistake Mr. Zuidof. Please sit down, you are in enough trouble as it is."

"Listen, the flight attendant obviously gave me the wrong jacket, which contained this wallet, and that passport."

"So why has no one been stopped trying to enter Thailand as LeCoyte Chellen?"

"He may not have noticed," Chellen said lamely. He ran his fingers through his fine white-blond hair. Soon this stupid man would recognise the error of his ways. Chellen knew he had to press home his advantage, and that was, that he was a multi-billionaire, and head of a massive international corporation. "I want to make a telephone call."

"You are not in Europe now Mr. Zuidoff."

Chellen smashed his fists down on the table. "I'm not Zuidof, give me a telephone, and I'll get someone to verify my identity. Look, this is simple; the flight attendant gave me the wrong jacket, other people were wearing the same damn suit."

San was aware of that fact. He had been given information that a large consignment of drugs was coming in on the Gulfstream. And that the culprit was wearing a beige Armani suit. Real. San had discounted the women, and the man wearing the fake, that just left three suspects. One, was the famous art-historian, Cassavanurnez, the other, had been his primary suspect at the beginning of the interrogation. Forty-thousand dollar Rolex's don't come cheap. But when the name on the computer matched a known drug dealer, the officers had come in, and separated the old Spaniard from their principle suspect.

"Wrong jacket, wrong passport, wrong identification. Are these your suitcases?"

"Yes." He took his key fob from his trousers pocket, tossing it on the table. "You open it."

San picked up the fob, reached forward and turned over the name tag on the first case. Silently Chellen read the name, 'Jan Zuidof', his world began to deflate. The moment San opened the case he knew his life would never be the same again.

AT TWO FORTY-FIVE, LAM BOK SAN EMERGED FROM the sterile room. His smile was wide again, it was as warm and infectious as ever.

Within the hour, he'd arrived at the Narcotics Suppression Bureau (NSB) on Vibhavadi Rangsit Road. Although the trafficking of drugs is a serious crime in Thailand the NSB HQ is still situated inside the Royal Thai Police Sports Club.

San presented himself at the office of Col Phornchai, the deputy commander of the NSB.

"Have you come to report a success, officer Lam Bok San?" he gestured for him to sit.

"Yes sir," he sat in the comfortable leather chair, "A man has just been arrested at the executive lounge. We found 2.6 kilograms of cocaine in his suitcase."

"Phew, that's a street value of about eight million baht. That's enough to get him on intent to distribute."

"Yes, sir." The smile was glowing.

"It was a good tip that you received today." Col Phornchai smoothed down his silky moustache.

"Yes, Interpol believe this man has trafficked cocaine into Bangkok on several occasions, we were advised to look for his name."

"Interpol? They are not looking to take credit for this are they?"

"No, they got the information from the Italian fraud department, apparently drugs are not his only crimes in Europe. They believe the drugs were to be used as payment for an assassination. The intended victim has recently been wrongly accused, and… well, they would prefer to keep this arrest quiet, so as to flush out others in his network."

"He used his own name?"

"If it is his own name, but yes it's the name he has used before, I have checked the flight records. He is very arrogant. He still protests his innocence. Saying this is mistaken identity."

"Can anyone, verify his claim?"

"He wanted to call a firm of solicitors in Geneva, but his mobile phone contained no such contact details."

"Family members?"

"The same, no numbers in his phone." San held out a business card, "Then he asked that we contact this man, they came in on the flight together."

"Could he be an accomplice?"

"No, he is a very famous Spanish painter, well respected in the world of art, his name is Juan del Marco Enrique Cassavanurnez. I recognised him in the lounge today, no doubt it was him."

"Who does this man Zuidof proclaim to be?"

San laughed, "LeCoyte Chellen."

"Of the Chellen Corporation?"

"Yes, it will be interesting to hear what Senior Cassavanurnez has to say."

⟜♪◯

SAN KEYED IN THE NUMBER AS HE WALKED ACROSS the basket-ball court. The sun was still merciless in its heat.

As the conversation intensified, San lost his smile.

His knock was urgent on Col Phornchai's door. "Sir, we have a problem."

"What is it?" Col Phornchai smoothed down his silky moustache.

"Senior Cassavanurnez claims that at one o'clock today, he saw LeCoyte Chellen's car attacked by gunmen on the Expressway. I have spoken to the *Royals* (Royal Thai Police) who confirm they attended, what they first believed to be a car-jacking on the Expressway at 1:10. The car, which was booked in the name of the Chellen Corporation, was found in the Barrak district, riddled with bullets. Mr. Chellen was not to be found."

"It is the assassination that Interpol mentioned!"

San nodded, "The drugs were to be the pay off."

"Shit! Well, Chellen can't have been on the Expressway, and in the airport with you. Get the Spaniard in, let's close this down quickly."

⟜♪◯

424

THE SUN HAD GONE DOWN, AND THE HEAT HAD BEGUN to drain from the city when Juan del Marco Enrique Cassavanurnez sat at a desk at the police station, in a comfortable room, which had a full size mirror on one of the walls.

Lam Bok San, placed a buff-coloured folder in front of him. "If you could go through the photographs, it would be most helpful."

Cassvanurnez, slowly turned the pages. Photographs of men stared back at him. Some front face, some side shots which reminded him of playing cards. At the end of the folder, he closed it, and pushed it back across the table.

San asked, "Do you recognise any of the men in the book?"

Slowly Cassavanurnez shook his head, "Was I supposed to? The men on the motorbikes were wearing helmets."

"But you did not recognise anyone in the book?"

"No, please can you tell me if there is any news about my colleague, LeCoyte Chellen?"

"I'm afraid not," San paused, "But I would like you to look at a suspect.

"I told you, they were wearing helmets!"

"Please, this man is sitting in the room next door, he would not be able to see you," San gestured toward the mirror.

"Of course, I will look, but I want to know what the police are doing to find Mr. Chellen."

San, spoke into his mobile. The mirror turned into a window. The old Spaniard walked over to the window and looked through.

LeCoyte Chellen, sat at a table. He wore regulation orange coveralls.

Cassavanurnez took a sharp intake of breath, "That is the man I was speaking to on the plane today."

"You know him?"

"Only from today, when we flew in."

"Do you know his name?" San asked, the tension began to rise.

"Of course, he is a Dutch national, name of Sodorph."

"Not, LeCoyte Chellen?"

"No! Of course not. I know LeCoyte Chellen, he is very famous. This man," he pointed through the window, "I just met today."

"Thank you, Senior Cassavanurnez," San picked up his pen, "Can you tell me his name again?"

"Sodorph; Jan, like Jan Smutts of South Africa." The old Spaniard raised a finger, "Zweedorf, pronounced Zuidorf, that's it; Jan Zuidorf. Does that help? How can he be a suspect, he only came to Bangkok today?"

"Thank you Senior, you have been most helpful."

"Please keep me informed as to the whereabouts of Mr. Chellen?"

"Of course, now someone will take you back to your hotel, thank you so much for your help. We will keep you updated as to our investigations."

CASSAVANURNEZ SAT IN SILENCE DURING THE JOURney back to his hotel. He spoke only to thank the officer that had chauffeured him home.

Once in the hotel, he went directly to his room. He closed,

and briefly rested against the door, then went directly to the bathroom.

Cassavanurnez began to take off his clothes, Tonight had been very stressful. Naked he stepped into the shower. The hot powerful jets of water washed the stress from his body.

Cassvanurnez scrubbed his face, thinking about the man in the orange coverall. Steam filled the bathroom.

Cassavanurnez switched off the shower, and Noah Coleman stepped out of the cubical.

Chapter Thirty-two

JUAN DEL MARCO ENRIQUE CASSAVANURNEZ (1942 -)

Bangkok, Thailand.
Tuesday, August 24.

THE PRISON, BANG KWANG, IS NICKNAMED *BIG TIGER* by the Thai's, because it prowls, and eats men alive. Everyone in the rest of the world calls it the *Bangkok Hilton*. It is an all-male establishment seven miles north of Bangkok.

Within the prison, a secure-unit holds foreign nationals and death-row prisoners.

All new inmates, whatever their crime, are required to wear leg-irons for the first three months of their sentences. Death-row inmates, have their leg-irons permanently welded on.

LeCoyte Chellen took his bowl of rice, moistened in a thin vegetable soup, from the unshaven Thai prisoner who lorded it over the *secure-unit* inmates from behind a protected wire-mesh screen. Favorites of the cell-boss got a large portion, any that had shown contempt were lucky to get anything.

All other food had to be purchased with *chits*, from the

prison canteen. The *chits* had to be earned by the prisoners as payment for the work they performed in the grounds.

As work was not allocated until after sentencing, those awaiting trial had no opportunity to purchase anything, and therefore had no food except for the pathetic diet of rice soup.

There was one other way a pre-sentence prisoner could obtain nutritious food; Chellen watched two young men openly flirting with the guards.

"Shit, I'm not that hungry," he said to himself, shuddering at the thought of what they had to do to earn the favours. He tried to lick his dry cracked lips.

Still, at tomorrow's trial the mix-up would be sorted out, so he looked upon the last fifteen days of gruel as an enforced diet. A number of kilos had already dropped off his bulky frame.

Chellen went to sit next to a young German. He had long greasy hair, a chipped tooth and a split lip. "Space free?"

"Sure," he answered. They ate their soup in silence. Chellen could feel the sun burning his sensitive skin, his fair hair provided no solace.

Chellen noticed the man had a piece of meat in his soup, he looked at the man in disgust, and was about to leave.

"It's okay," he laughed, when he understood what Chellen was looking so disgusted about. His lip split open, and he wiped the blood with his scabby hand. "Not what you think. We can receive chits from charities. If they ever ask if you want to see a Human Rights campaigner, a Priest, or a Rabbi, just say yes. I have someone coming into see me next week."

The German was from a poor upbringing, a class of person that Chellen would normally have avoided. But in these circumstances, he relished the conversation, and the information pertaining to the chits. He wished he'd spoken to him before.

THE TRIAL WENT BADLY. THE JUDGE DECLARED THE case was "Very simple."

The prosecution presented the facts, "The luggage, identified as belonging to the accused, contained 2.6 kilos of cocaine."

The thin faced judge looked over his glasses at Chellen. There was hatred in his eyes.

"A famous Spanish art-critic, Juan del Marco Enrique Cassavanurnez, identified the accused as Jan Zuidof."

Chellen felt the rage course through his body, why had the old Spaniard lied? They had spoken on the jet, and in the lounge, he'd even suggested having dinner to continue their conversation about Bernini's work in Rome after the accession of Pope Alexander. The old Spaniard had though it an extremely ambitious plan to transform Rome into a magnificent world capital by means of costly urban planning. Chellen banged his fists on the dock, why had he lied?

The prosecution continued, "Found in the accused's possession, was a passport, and credit-card, both bearing the name Jan Zuidof."

The judge paused only to verify the likeness of the passport photo. Again a look of utter disdain.

The defense barrister, a court appointed councilor, argued that this was a case of mistaken identity.

"We had confirmation that this man was carrying the drugs?" the judge asked.

"We did." The prosecutor stood up.

"So, mistaken identity." The judge asked, "Do we know the whereabouts of Mr. LeCoyte Chellen?"

"The prosecutor stood up again, "Sadly yes. The body of Mr. Chellen was discovered last week. He had been kidnapped from his car on the ninth of August. The day Mr. Zuidof flew into Bangkok."

"Is that relevant?"

"Interpol told us that the drugs were a pay-off for an assassination."

"But you have no proof?"

"The Royal Thai Police believe the kidnappers intended to ransom Mr. Chellen, but something went wrong, and he was killed. We cannot link the drugs to Mr. Chellen's death."

Chellen expected the judge to say "Shame." But he remained silent.

"The family have been informed, that the body was found."

LeCoyte Chellen felt that those words hurt more than the thirty year sentence given by the Judge.

&

PRISONERS SERVING UPWARDS OF THIRTY YEARS look forward to visits like addicts crave Heroin. Chellen realized that if his true identity, or wealth ever became known to his fellow prisoners whilst he was still inside, his life would become more of a living hell than he was currently experiencing, and yet the only way he was going to get out, was with contact to the outside world.

So, all through his first full sentenced day in the Bangkok Hilton he canvased other European prisoners, to understand how he could get a message to a trusted member of his corporation.

Quickly he discovered that the only chance of success lay with the need to have an organized visit.

During the trial he had come to accept that the passport containing his photograph, the forged credit cards, and the subsequent information from Interpol meant that his imprisonment was not a case of mistaken identity, this was a well thought out conspiracy. The aim of the action was to deprive him of his identity, his liberty, and confine him to a living hell which would kill him slower than any bullet, knife of bomb.

At the word bomb, he thought of Forbes and Monroe.

The apparent death of a man acknowledged by the world as himself was proof that this was an elaborate scheme, well-funded and supported.

LeCoyte Chellen knew he had been given a fate worse than death, a living nightmare of filth, pain, anger, and hopelessness.

He surmised that Chandhok Nahmad was behind the conspiracy, after all Forbes and Monroe were dead.

A wry smile passed over his face as he thought about the damage Key had reported the bomb had done in the hotel. He closed his eyes and thought about the complete obliteration of their bodies.

Forbes had cheated him out of the Luini, and the woman had had the nerve to sell him a forged painting.

"Serves them right," he whispered. He ground his sandal

down on two cockroaches that were exploring his foot. They crunched. His eyes travelled beyond the wall, they had a maniacal gleam within them, his revenge on Nahmad would be the stuff of legend; all he had to do was get the visit.

A visit then, from someone not related to the stinking hellhole was the only chance for his plan to work. It would be an escape of sorts, an escape of the mind numbing daily routine, and the ever present danger of violence.

Giving someone a cigarette, a book, a scrap of paper, or a little fresh food could really make the difference to the day. But, getting news from the outside world was like having the finest champagne, sweet and intoxicating.

On his third day after sentencing the news reached Chellen that a Human Rights campaigner was visiting the prison.

He'd come to see the German boy that he'd spoken to earlier in the week, but as he had only just survived a torturous beating, and was recovering in the hospital wing, Chellen bullied his way to the front of the cue.

He had already witnessed many atrocities committed by both prison guards, and his fellow inmates, but he told the guards that he was the ideal candidate to see the campaigner, because he was new to the prison, and still looked healthy.

"Other European prisoners that have been forced to eat rats," for the entertainment of the cell bosses, "don't look too good."

Chellen hinted that as it was only a matter of time before they wanted him to perform for them, this could be a good time for him to be put in front of the Human Rights person.

The guards and the cell bosses debated his request.

Chellen paced in his cell, stepping over his sleeping

companions. He'd argued that many long-term prisoners had turned to heroin, and looked like zombies, indeed the drug, so hated by the authorities seemed to be easily obtainable in the prison. Ironic, because drugs were the reason that so many were in the Big Tiger in the first place.

The alternative to rat eating was to provide sexual favours for the guards, and as Chellen's body reminded them of a plucked chicken, they decided that it may as well be him that faced the do-gooders.

The guard rattled his cane along the bars, all eyes turned to him. "It's you." He pointed at Chellen.

Chellen breathed a sigh of relief, not only for his objective to see the campaigner, but because those that refused to perform were either killed, or confined to solitary confinement, under terribly inhumane conditions.

Chellen had already witnessed the torture and execution of two stubborn Thai inmates. Their screams during the night had been as common as the insects and vermin trying to bite his body.

CHELLEN SAT ON A THIN WOODEN BENCH AS THE guards gave him a cloth and a bowl of water to tidy himself up. He shook with anticipation.

They removed his leg shackles. The guard shook his head, as he threw them into the corner. Chellen nodded, understanding it was best not to say anything about the leg-irons.

"Come with me," a guard said. Chellen put on his best smile. Quickly he sniffed his clothing, he smelt disgusting, he smelt of stale sweat and urine, but it was too late to do anything about it now. This was his time, this was his chance.

The door was opened. Chellen squeezed into a small room, it smelled of disinfectant, and it had a fan in the ceiling. Chellen almost salivated.

He composed himself, he must not come over as crazy or dangerous. He bowed his head, and lowered his eyes, *'Be sincere'*, he thought to himself. This could be his only chance at getting regular visits and communicating with the outside world. This might be his only opportunity of convincing the outside world that LeCoyte Chellen was still alive.

He heard the guards ushering the Human Rights campaigner into the adjoining room. He heard chairs sliding across the floor, and water being poured.

He looked through the small round window in the door, he could see two guards; they were clean-shaven with neatly pressed uniforms. It seemed everyone wanted to put on a good show for the Human Rights campaigner.

Each guard held a thin rattan cane, Chellen thought it ironic that with all the bullshit going on in the room they were still holding such cruel weapons in front of the Human Rights campaigner.

Chellen heard a guard speaking quietly to the man, "His name is Zuidof; he is a Dutchman. Sentence is thirty years. Drugs trafficking."

'Keep calm LeCoyte, they are only words, soon you will get your chance to convince this man that you are innocent of the charge, just get him to get a message to Robert Key, get him to visit. Then get out.'

"I've read about the case." The man sounded English, it was a wonderfully strong English accent.

"This man claims he's innocent."

'The English have such a fair justice system, he would be sympathetic.'

The guard laughed, he made it sound dirty. "They all claim innocence, and they still serve the same amount of time."

"But this man says his was a case of mistaken identity," it was an unmasked upper-class English accent, and he had heard of his case. Chellen's hands began to shake. It was going to be easier than he thought.

The door opened and a clean guard ushered him into the room.

Chellen presented himself, head bowed, full of remorse.

The English accented Human Rights campaigner asked, "I understand you like to be addressed as LeCoyte, is that correct, Mr. Chellen?"

Chellen's heart filled with hope, he raised his eyes and looked at a man dressed in a Highland-green, blue checked tweed suit. His heart stopped beating. His throat began to swell.

"Hello LeCoyte, long-time no see," said William Forbes.

Chellen fought down the bile that blocked his throat, his shaking finger pointed accusingly, "But you're dead!" his voice sounded hollow and thin.

"Hardly," replied Forbes. He raised his hand and waved, "No, I'm very much alive." Forbes asked the guard, "Does he think everyone is dead?"

Chellen began to convulse, he fell to his knees, crashing into a chair.

"You're dead!"

"Do you know, I always thought it was LeCoyte Chellen, but clearly I was wrong?"

The guards looked down at the pathetic writhing man, the noise coming from Chellen's throat wasn't human. Still pointing; he fell sideways, crashing to the floor, foaming from the mouth like a mad dog.

"I have some pills, if you think they'd help," Forbes offered.

❦

Wednesday, September 1.

HILLHOUSE, IS A CHURCH ON THE OUTSKIRTS OF Hamilton, Scotland.

It was a chilly start to September, with a cool breeze gently tugging at the stubborn leaves on the ancient oak. The tree stood close to the lychgate, the traditional covered gateway by which all funeral processions pass.

The leaves that had already been torn away softly swirled around the cemetery, leaping and hopping over the headstones, fluttering along the winding path.

William Forbes walked quietly along the church path, he was dressed in a crisp white shirt, and sober black suit.

The fresh flowers and clean headstone marked the grave as being new, he left the path.

Taking in the aroma of the freshly dug earth, he looked at the headstone.

The inscription was quietly poignant, and raised emotions which Forbes fought to keep hidden deep inside.

In loving memory of
Agnes Monroe
Beloved Daughter of Hugh and Caroline

Who can restrain a heart-felt tear?
And fail to weep for one so dear?
None but God, who gave us breath
And now compels us 'Submit to death'
Tis hard but patience must endure
And soothe the wound it cannot cure.

After paying his respects, William Forbes placed the antique ivory Toucan-billed hair-grip on the headstone, and left the cemetery, alone.

About the Author

PAUL TAYLOR IS A FORMER engineer and business manager whose novels have delighted fan fiction readers around the world. As the author of seven James Bond continuation novels, Taylor weaves plots of intrigue and cruelty with humor and empathy. He is a master of the multiple double-cross and final-page twist.